Whispers of the Wild.

by

GWEN COURTMAN

Whispers of the Wild

DEDICATION

The characters, settings, and themes have all been inspired by my time in Africa—the incredible people I've met, the unforgettable experiences, and my many safaris (though admittedly, none quite as thrilling as the ones in this book).

A huge thank you to everyone who contributed to the storyline, the title, and for putting up with my endless ideas for book covers until I finally settled on one. I'm sure they were ready to block my emails at some point.

Gillian, you've been the laugh in the storm, always managing to make me smile no matter what life throws our way. Brum Brum, my friend.

Beba, thanks for keeping better track of the cast than I ever could, I'm also grateful for your ability to listen to my weird ideas without laughing—and for not running away when I inevitably discarded them for no reason.

Helen, after twenty years apart, you were the first to read these books and keep me grounded. Thank you for your endless support.

And of course, a massive thank you to all my readers who continue to support me, send reviews, and reach out through social media. Your kind words and encouragement truly mean the world.

1 - PERI

Peri's rage threatened to overflow as she slammed the door, the sound of her boyfriend's angry shouts fading behind her. She glanced at the neighbors, their curious eyes peeking through the curtains. With a flip of her mousy brown hair, Peri managed a tiny nod, the weight of her overstuffed Lidl bag pulling on her arm. Tugging her flimsy jacket tighter around herself, she braced against the cold wind biting at her skin as it howled through the street.

After a few minutes, she reached the large blue door of her only close friend's house. Her knuckles drummed against the wood, and her fingers tapped nervously as she realised her friend wasn't home. She glanced at the wall separating the house from the neighbors, wishing for a moment of invisibility.

After knocking again and with a cautious glance over her shoulder, she leant forward and hauled her upper body over the gate. She landed on the other side with a soft thud, slid the latch open, and pulled the door wide, dragging her bag through like a treasure she was eager to hide.

Peri sank onto her friend's weathered garden bench, a sigh of relief escaping her lips. Within an hour, the cold crept in, and she reached for the soft blanket nestled in the basket beside the L-shaped sofa, cocooning herself in its warmth.

Her feet twitched as her hands trembled, rummaging through her bag. Her fingers grabbed at the items she'd stuffed haphazardly inside—more lacy bras than sweaters, a pair of heels wedged beside a crumpled shirt, and nothing particularly useful. Her heart raced, not just from the chaotic packing but from the strain of her long overdue decision.

With her phone battery at one percent, she sent one last message to Anton, her friend, and tossed the phone aside. She woke when Anton, alerted by the garden lights, popped her head around the gate and called out, "Peri?"

Peri opened her eyes, looked around, and grinned at her friend. "Thank God you're here. I was beginning to worry you were off on another tour already," she said, referring to Anton's job as an international tour guide.

"No, not yet. I leave on Tuesday. What the hell happened to you?" Anton asked.

"Didn't you see my messages?"

"I saw them come in; I just haven't read them yet," Anton explained as she plonked herself down beside Peri, wrapping some of the blanket around her legs.

"I finally did it," Peri said, her voice barely above a whisper, eyes damp with emotion. "I left Jake."

"About time," Anton said, grabbing Peri's hands. "My God, Peri, you're shivering. Let's get you inside."

Peri reached for her bag, dragging it behind her. She lifted it as she stepped through the sliding door into the warm kitchen. "Ah, warmth," she sighed.

"Here, take this jumper," Anton said, wrapping a fleecy sweater around Peri's shoulders and putting the kettle on.

"Can I stay here until I find somewhere else to live?" Peri asked, her voice muffled against her friend's shoulder, desperation creeping in.

"Of course," Anton replied, pulling back to look into Peri's eyes. "What will you do?"

"I don't know. I need to keep myself away from Jake. If I go near him, I'll fall for his manipulative tactics, and I can't let that happen," Peri said. "They say running away doesn't solve anything, but in this situation, it will. I need to get as far away from him as possible."

"I don't want to say 'I told you so,' but—" Anton began.

"I know. Moving in with him was a stupid thing to do. I mean, I already knew what kind of man he was, and I still did it."

"Well, it's too late to dwell on that now. Just focus on moving forward," Anton said softly.

"Thanks. You have no idea how much I appreciate this," Peri said.

"What about your job?" Anton asked.

"I guess I don't have one anymore. Jake said he never wanted to see me again, so I'm pretty sure that includes the office tomorrow," Peri said. "Sorry, are you making tea? I think this calls for something much stronger."

"No worries, honestly. Here, take this," Anton said, thrusting a large bottle of gin and a small tonic into Peri's shivering hands. "Right, come on. Tell me exactly what happened."

2 - PERI

"So, Jake didn't come home last night. He said he had a work thing," Peri explained as Anton poured the clear liquid into her tall glass.

Anton raised an eyebrow, shaking her head slightly. "You're his secretary. Surely you'd know that."

Peri nursed her drink, staring at it as she spoke. "You'd think, right? But I checked his online account, and last night he racked up a thousand pounds in hotel, dinner, and drinks at a hotel in London."

Stunned, Anton tucked her hair behind her ears and flopped onto the sofa. "Ah, so not good."

Peri's breathing softened as she tightened her grip on the glass, the liquid sloshing dangerously close to the rim. She took a quick sip, the sharp tang of gin burning her throat. "My God, is there any tonic in there?" she muttered, her lips twitching against the bitter taste. Peri rolled her eyes softly, the tension in her shoulders loosening as she clinked her glass against Anton's. The warmth of the gin spread through her as she said, "Wow, I can't feel my mouth."

Anton reclined in her chair, a cheeky sparkle in her eyes. "Drastic moves call for drastic portions of gin," she said, her laughter bubbling up like the fizz of freshly opened tonic water.

"Well, anyway, when I saw that hotel bill this morning, I lost the plot. I thought about everything I do for him. I'm the perfect homemaker; I'm amazing at my job. Where else is Jake going to find a secretary fluent in Italian, Spanish, and French, and who tolerates his narcissistic mood swings?" Peri asked.

Anton, intrigued, asked, "Wait, you speak all those languages?"

Peri nodded. "Yeah, and my Italian citizenship has kept him from tumbling through so many loopholes since Brexit. He'd have lost clients left and right if it weren't for me."

"You have Italian citizenship?" Anton asked.

"Yep, my dad's Italian," Peri shrugged, a casual gesture that said it wasn't relevant.

"How do I not know any of this?" Anton asked, eyebrows raised in surprise.

"I guess we only ever talk about work. And since you left that place, you're always off somewhere," Peri replied.

"I know. I'm sorry about that. Anyway, carry on," Anton urged.

Peri's gaze hardened. "I got so angry that I smashed his precious record collection and some of his trophies."

Anton raised an eyebrow, a lively smile creeping onto her face. "You don't do things by halves, do you?"

"What's the point in half-measures?" Peri shot back, her breath quickening with fury. "I've been teetering on the edge for a year, and then, bam. A fog lifted. I finally saw him—the lies, the deceit. It was like someone switched on the lights, and all the things I'd ignored came flooding in. He's just a pathological liar."

"And?" Anton prompted.

"And a cheater," Peri hissed.

"No, I mean, what happened after you stepped on his records?"

"He slapped me, and I kicked him, then went upstairs and started throwing things into a bag," she said, a fierce grin breaking through her anger.

"What did he say?" Anton asked.

"He just went on about his records and how those stupid trophies were his most prized possessions. They were just fishing trophies," Peri chuckled.

Anton blinked, incredulous. "He didn't even care that you were leaving him?"

"No. He was more concerned about his precious records than losing me. That's when I knew I'd made the right decision to walk away."

"And he just let you go?" Anton asked.

"Not really. He switched to work mode and told me he didn't need me or my mistakes. I reminded him that without my Italian passport, he would have never managed to work in Europe. He didn't want to hear it—slapped me and started rambling about how he didn't need my passport and that everything he ever said to me was to make me feel good, as if I were a waste of space."

"Honestly, you're so much better off without him," Anton said, her voice steady and supportive.

"I know. As he was screaming, I realised how selfish he was. It was clear that our relationship was one-sided and toxic. I felt free just by saying the words. Then he shoved me a few times, pushed me down the stairs, and, well, here I am."

"He pushed you? Oh my God. I hate that man. Are you okay?" Anton asked.

"I'll be fine. I'll be bruised, but fine. My body is so used to him pushing me around."

"Shit, Peri. Why didn't you ever tell me?" Anton asked.

Peri shrugged. "Who wants to admit to being a punching bag? Anyway, it's over. I'm out of that relationship."

Anton knew that behind the jokey smile and light-hearted chatter lay a sad and hurt young woman. She stroked Peri's arm and said, "He'll know you've come here. What if he turns up and bashes the door down to find you?"

Peri looked at Anton, shook her head, and muttered, "I'll deal with it. Don't worry."

"No way. I'm not leaving you here with him just around the corner. You're coming with me."

"With you, where?" Peri asked.

Anton chuckled and explained, "I'm off to Italy. I'm doing a north-to-south tour with a group of Americans. It's a lot of living out of suitcases, but it's fun. I'll tell the group you are a trainee guide."

Peri closed her eyes for a moment and blinked them open in surprise. "Can you do that? What will your bosses say?"

"I won't tell them if you won't," Anton said with a laugh.

3 - PERI

"Italy, wow," Peri said. "I haven't been since my father died. It's been a few years."

"Well, it's long overdue then, isn't it? Got a passport?" Anton asked.

"At home with Jake," Peri replied.

"Ah, we have a problem."

"Not really. Unless he changes the locks overnight, I'll wait for him to leave for work tomorrow and grab it—and the rest of my stuff."

"I can't fathom how you're so calm about this," Anton said, shaking her head.

Peri let out a laugh, surprising even herself. "Neither can I. But despite what he did—and said—I finally know I'll never go back. Ever."

"Good." Anton leant back, studying her. "So, you already know Italy? Maybe you can help me out—this is only my second north-to-south tour."

Peri didn't bother to hide her smile. "Sure, happy to help. A trip to Italy, a chance to reconnect with a country I love... It's a birthday surprise that's come at just the right time."

"Your birthday? How do I not know anything about you?" Anton mused.

"It was yesterday, which made it all the more painful to find out he was hooking up with someone while I was expecting a nice dinner. Maybe a bit of razzle-dazzle."

"Razzle-dazzle?" Anton chuckled. "Peri, you crack me up."

"Good—it's my superpower. Too bad it never worked on Jake. So, where are we going?"

Anton pulled out her tour notes and traced her finger along the map. "We'll start in Milan, head past the Italian lakes, then down to Florence, Rome, and Naples."

"This sounds incredible." Peri's voice brightened. "Who knows? I might even love it enough to find a new job."

"With all the languages you speak, my company could use someone like you."

"Maybe you should suggest I make it official. I don't want to get you in trouble, though."

Anton grinned. "I've always believed it's better to ask for forgiveness than permission."

Peri's jaw dropped before laughter bubbled out. "Alright, I'm with you. Italy sounds too good to miss. Let's do this."

The following morning, Peri stood at the door to the house she'd shared with Jake, her stomach churning as she fumbled with the key and shoved it in her jeans pocket. The house was silent, a stark contrast to the whirlwind inside her. Stepping inside, she was greeted by the familiar scent of Jake's cologne lingering in the air. Her eyes drifted over the shelves lined with framed memories—a holiday in Bali, a trip to Costa Rica, and a trip to Dubai. She clenched her jaw, fighting back the pull of nostalgia.

With a long breath, she turned away, forcing herself to focus. The sound of suitcases zipping filled the room as she began cramming them with her clothes. She hesitated for a moment when she reached the red dress she'd worn on their anniversary. Then, with a firm shake of her head, she tossed it in.

One by one, the pieces of her past life disappeared into the bags. With a deep breath, she shook her head; no amount of nostalgia could change her mind now Finally, with the last suitcase zipped, she straightened and glanced around the room. It looked the same—but felt entirely different. Taking a deep breath, she whispered a silent goodbye to the life she was leaving behind.

"Well done, you," Anton said as she flipped open the car bonnet and helped her throw everything in.

"Thanks for helping me. It was strange... knowing that I'll never go back there again."

"Don't think about it. Just focus on Italy and what's ahead." Anton's grin was infectious. "This is going to be amazing."

Peri smiled, the tightness in her chest beginning to ease. "You're right. Let's go."

4 - UNEZE

The piercing screams between his parents faded into an unsettling silence, and then the front door swung open with a creak that filled the stillness. Uneze's heart raced as he darted to his hiding place behind the kitchen sink, his small feet pattering across the cool tile floor.

Framed in the doorway, stood his father, a towering shadow that blocked the sunlight. His mother, dashing around in a fit of rage, dashed around, shoving his belongings into a bag and tossing them into a corner.

Uneze squinted, trying to make sense of his dad's restless shifting. The man moved, his feet bouncing in a frantic rhythm that sent a jolt of panic through Uneze's chest. Hot, salty tears streamed down his cheeks as he jumped up and launched himself toward his father, tugging at his trousers and begging, "Dad, no. Don't leave."

At just seven years old, Uneze grasped only bits of the chaos surrounding him, but one thing was clear: his father's departure felt like his world was splitting in two. His dad was his hero.

Suddenly, a firm grip pulled him back into the house, his mother's expression as cold as stone as he yanked at his arm. She stood in the doorway watching the man who had once filled their home with laughter and warmth. Her voice, devoid of any motherly emotion, cut through the air. "Leave him. Get back inside."

Uneze's heart sank as he turned back to the door, the sight of his father retreating into the blinding light making his chest ache. The realisation hit him like a wave, dragging him under—nothing would ever be the same again.

Tears blurred his vision as he choked out, "Mum, where did he go?"

His mother's laughter pierced through the air—sharp and unexpected, like the crack of a whip. "I don't care. We're better off without him," she retorted, her tone filled with bitterness, or was it relief? He wasn't quite sure what was going through her mind as, with rigid posture, she tossed her tangled, thick black hair back over her shoulder.

Uneze's voice quivered as he threw a pleading glare toward the peeling walls. "Who's going to fix things and bring us money?" He glared at the empty chair in the corner, the one that always welcomed his father's tired frame come nightfall.

"Money? He never brought home a dime," Quanda snapped, her voice slicing through Uneze's hope. "That's why I have two jobs." Her eyes darted away, avoiding eye contact as though looking at him might shatter her resolve.

"But I don't want to live here without him," Uneze whispered.

"Too bad," she replied, her voice softening just a fraction. "I do. I know he's your father, but he's gone. Just face it and move on."

"So, it's just us?" he asked, searching her face for reassurance.

"And your aunts and uncles," she added, her expression hardening again. "We're not alone, but you're now the head of the house." Her words carried a weighty obligation that meant little to her but everything to Uneze. "

"Me? I'm seven years old," Uneze called as he followed her around the dimly lit house.

"I already have three jobs. It's your turn to pitch in," his mother urged, her eyes darting around the cramped stone room for anything else that belonged to the man who had just left her house.

With a shaky breath, Uneze brushed the tears from his cheeks, a pathetic attempt to wipe away the ache in his chest. Memories of his father's laughter echoed in his mind, and he swallowed hard wondering how he could possibly step into his father's shoes.

"How can I replace him? I'm not enough." He stared at the mismatched furniture, shadows of his father lingering in every corner. "What did I do to make him leave?"

His mother's hand rested gently on his shoulder, a rare moment of warmth that felt almost foreign. "One day you'll understand that it wasn't about you," she said, her voice steady, though her eyes betrayed a storm of emotions that her son couldn't fathom. "Now, start thinking of ways to help me with dinner."

Uneze bit his lip, suppressing words bubbling up like soda in a shaken bottle. He read the annoyance etched on her face. "Dinner? Together?" The notion felt almost like a fairy tale, something reserved for Christmas and birthdays

"Yeah, tonight is special. But don't get used to it," she added, a hint of softness in her smile. "Go grab your dad's things. We need to pack them up and sell what we can."

His heart sank as he wandered through their tiny home, each item a reminder of laughter turned sour Rage built as he bagged each piece, his small hands trembling. A sudden bang at the front door jolted him. His heart raced with hope, but it was only his aunt. She rushed in, arms wide, engulfing his mother in a tight embrace. Uneze sat cross-legged on the floor, trying to blend into the shadows while straining to catch snippets of their conversation.

"So, it's done. He's gone?" his aunt asked, her voice a soft sigh that crashed like thunder in Uneze's chest.

"Yep," his mother replied, a tinge of relief lacing her words. "I told him to choose between me and that other woman."

Aunty offered and understanding hug, and then once she'd pulled back she asked, "What about Uneze?"

"The idiot never cared about the boy. Always doubted he was actually his son," she said.

Uneze sat still, the world buzzing around him. His aunt's concern and his mother's sharp words tore through him like a storm, leaving him adrift in the silence where laughter used to live.

5 - UNEZE

Uneze sat still, the world whizzing around him, a storm of silence where laughter used to be. He felt the sting of the truth in those words—sharp and cold—as he shuffled further into the shadows yet strained his ears for more information.

"What are you going to do now?" Aunty asked.

"I'll just get by somehow," she replied, a resoluteness settling over her like a heavy cloak. "I'm better off without him. It's a shame Uneze doesn't see that yet."

"Just give him time; it's only just happened," his aunt urged. "He doesn't know what's going on. You've hidden it well for so long."

"Speaking of Uneze, I need to get him some food," his mother said, her tone softening, if only for a moment.

"Okay, I'll see you later. And congratulations on getting rid of that waste of space," his aunt said, lifting her dress to leave, her voice triumphant.

"Uneze?" His aunt's voice cut through the air as she stepped into the sunlight, searching for Uneze in his favourite spot behind the door.

Uneze rushed to her side, squinting against the sunlight, his small arms wrapping tightly around her waist. "My dad left," he whispered.

Aunty glanced down at him, her face contorted with concern for her favourite nephew. "Yeah, I heard. Don't be upset; it's going to be okay. I promise you, everything will be fine." Her voice, calm and soothing, wrapped around him, but Uneze's wide, tear-filled eyes betrayed his sadness.

His voice trembled as he said, "I'm supposed to be the man of the house now. I don't know what to do."

Aunty chuckled softly, her smile a flicker of light in the shadows of his worry. "Well, it's a small house, and you're a small man. You'll be fine."

Yet, as Uneze looked up, his expression was anything but reassured. "Mum looks happy to me," he mumbled, tears streaming down his cheeks. "How can she be happy that Dad left?"

With a gentle tug at his sleeve, Aunty led him away from the house, her voice dropping to a whisper as they stepped into the cluster of neighbouring homes. "I understand that's how it seems to you. There's a lot your mother never told you. You should know that she wanted him to leave."

"Why? I don't understand it." His young mind raced, struggling to piece together the puzzle of adult emotions.

Aunty knelt to meet his confused face, her expression soft. "Uneze, your dad wasn't a good man. He was a man with no morals. Your mum and dad had a very tense relationship; he made her very unhappy."

"Oh." Tears continued to spill as he tried to wipe them away, but they flowed faster than his little hands could manage. "She was always screaming at him. It's her fault he left."

"Don't say bad things about my dad. He was good to me," Uneze stuttered.

"There are two sides to every story and two sides to every person," Aunty said softly. "One day you'll understand. But now, just support your mum. Tell her that you understand and help her out a little more."

"No. I want to live with my dad. I want to go and find him," Uneze pleaded.

"No. Don't do that. He doesn't want you. Just because you think your father is a good dad doesn't make it true. He brought out the worst in your mum. Give her some time, and she'll become the woman I knew before she met your dad. Go back inside; she'll be worried about you." Aunty brushed dirt off her colourful, belted dress and let go of Uneze's hand. With a soft voice, she added, "I'll see you in the morning. If you need anything, just come around."

"I can't go in there. I'm scared," Uneze muttered, turning to look at his home.

Aunty tussled his hair and looked him in the eyes. "Fear is just a feeling that's new to you. Once you get your head around this, you'll see it's for the best."

Uneze waited for her to leave and sat still with his head in his hands. He couldn't even imagine what would happen without his father around. His friend's dad had left, and now he and his mother lived on the streets, begging for food. Disorientated and confused, he felt unable to walk the few steps back to the house; he was crushed by the disappointment. After a few minutes, he heard his mother calling him. He took three long breaths, tried to embody his father as he walked back inside, and offered the biggest smile he could manage to his mother.

6 - UNEZE

Life in poverty-stricken Nigeria was a daily struggle for millions, and for Uneze, it was no different since his father had left. Each morning, he stepped into the relentless heat, his hands rough and calloused from days spent gathering fruit on his mother's small patch of land. Once his basket was full, he made his way through the bustling streets, offering the fruit to market sellers in exchange for a few coins.

The delight in his mother's smile, her arms encircling him in a hug that felt like triumph, made it all worthwhile. That smile, one he hadn't known until his father's departure, was a quiet promise of better days. Their home was modest—its bare walls told of hardship—but within them echoed laughter and moments that Uneze cherished above all else.

"This money puts food on our table. You're my little man," she would say, pride gleaming in her eyes. Uneze watched her cook as the fire's smoke curled around her and the stew bubbled in the pot.

"I'm happy with life—selling fruit is much better than school," Uneze remarked one day, his tone almost defiant.

His mother's gaze sharpened, her response both tender and resolute. "Work will make you strong and resourceful, but education is the only way forward. You could work in a bank, become a doctor, or even a lawyer."

"Me?" Uneze asked, disbelief etched on his face.

"Yes, you," she affirmed, her voice steady with conviction. "You'll be the exception. You're smart, young, and very handsome. You have what it takes to get us out of here and start a better life."

Reluctantly, Uneze returned to school after the summer break. As he entered the bustling schoolyard, a curious hush fell over the children. Clusters of them huddled together, their laughter fading as a tall figure strode through the gates.

Clad in a crisp shirt and tailored trousers, he stood out starkly against the earthy tones of their surroundings. His pale skin gleamed under the sun, his neatly trimmed brown hair catching the light. The children exchanged glances, their intrigue all over their faces as they stared at the unfamiliar man.

Uneze sat at his small wooden desk, fiddling with the frayed edges of his notebook as he observed the new teacher, Mr. Nolan. The man's words drifted through the room like a foreign melody, his accent alien yet captivating. Nervous giggles bubbled beneath the surface as the students tried to decipher his speech.

"Good morning, everyone," Mr. Nolan greeted, his smile warm and genuine. His presence radiated a disarming kindness, leaving the children simultaneously fascinated and intimidated.

"Did anyone understand what I just said?" he asked, his tone lively.

"You are Mr. Nolan," a brave voice piped up.

"Yes, that's right. It's written on the board, so you got an easy one," Mr. Nolan replied, adjusting his glasses with a grin. "Now, tell me your names."

"Chuma," one boy answered.

"No, I need you to reply in a full sentence: 'My name is...'" Mr. Nolan corrected gently.

Embarrassed, the boy repeated, "My name is Chuma."

"Perfect. Well done." Mr. Nolan praised, slowing his speech and gesturing to aid their understanding. He then held up a handful of colourful pens and pencils. "If you answer my questions correctly, you'll get one of these as a reward."

The promise of new stationery captured the students' attention. They sat up straighter, eager to participate. When they stumbled, Mr. Nolan patiently guided them, his encouragement fostering a newfound energy in the room. Classmates turned to one another, whispering explanations and sharing their growing understanding.

At the end of the lesson, Mr. Nolan handed out pens and pencils. "You all did wonderfully today. Take these with you and use them for your homework. I'll see you next time."

The children accepted the items with wide smiles, their gratitude shining through. Uneze slipped his share into his pocket, eager to show his mother.

When he arrived home, he burst through the door, excitement spilling over. "You won't believe it, Mama. We have a new English teacher—a white man."

His mother's brow furrowed. "Why would they send someone like that here? The last thing you need is someone looking down on you."

Uneze lined up the pencils on the table with pride. "He gave these to us. He must be rich. Do you think I could sell them?"

"Sell them?" His mother's voice was firm. "No. That man was generous enough to give you those. Respect the gift and use it for school."

"But some of my friends are selling theirs to the kids up the hill. They've got more money than us," Uneze countered.

"You're not like those other kids," she replied, her tone softening. "I've taught you respect, and you'll show it. Learn from him. If he came all this way, he must be smart."

Uneze paused, his fork hovering over his food. "Or maybe he's just stupid," he muttered. "If he's so smart, why would he come here?"

7 - UNEZE

As the bell rang to signal the start of class the following morning, Uneze carefully arranged his freshly sharpened pencils on the worn wooden surface of his school table. Their tips gleamed under the fluorescent lights, a small but personal triumph. He cast a sidelong glance at the other boys bursting through the door, their laughter punctuated by quiet, conspiratorial whispers.

"Why didn't you sell them?" one boy teased, a mischievous grin spreading across his face.

"My mum wouldn't let me."

"Why did you tell her? Whatever he gives you, hide it and sell it," another urged, his eyes sparkling with the thrill of rebellion.

Uneze chuckled softly, but a knot tightened in his stomach as he listened, torn between the unspoken pressure to conform and his desire to hold onto what was his.

As the class came to a close, Mr. Nolan's eyes swept the room before finally resting on Uneze. With a subtle flick of his hand, he beckoned Uneze forward. A chill ran down Uneze's spine as he inhaled sharply, the air suddenly feeling thick and heavy.

He lingered in the now-quiet classroom, watching as Mr. Nolan gestured toward an empty chair. Uneze sank into it, the wood creaking beneath his weight. His mind raced with thoughts of missteps and mistakes, each scenario more daunting than the last.

"Have I done something wrong?" Uneze asked hesitantly, his voice trembling, tinged with his upbringing.

"Not at all," Mr. Nolan replied, a warm smile breaking across his face and dissolving the tension in the air.

"I see you're the only person in class who still has the pencils I gave you."

Uneze straightened in his seat, a flicker of pride lighting up within him. "Yes, I like them. I like having nice things," he admitted shyly. Here's the continuation of the improved version with highlights:

"I'm happy to see that. Why didn't you sell them?" Mr. Nolan asked, his tone curious but kind.

"My mum said no. She told me I need to respect you and your gift," Uneze explained, his voice soft but resolute.

Mr. Nolan smiled warmly. "Your mum sounds like a wise woman. What's your name?"

"Uneze," he replied.

"Uneze, young man. Is there something you'd like?"

"What do you mean?" Uneze asked, tilting his head slightly in confusion.

"Something you want but can't have," Mr. Nolan clarified.

Uneze paused, his mind spinning. "A soda. I've never tasted one," he said finally.

"That's all you want? Any particular flavour?"

"I'd like a Coke... well, six of them—for my mum, aunt, uncle, and cousins."

Mr. Nolan chuckled softly. "I think I can manage that. But you can't tell anyone else; I can't be buying sodas for the whole school only to have them sold."

"I don't think they'd sell sodas. We see all those big ads around the city, but they're too expensive for us."

"Tomorrow, after the last lesson, hang back, and I'll give you a bag of sodas for your family."

"Thank you, Mr. Nolan," Uneze said, his smile widening with genuine gratitude.

"Thank you for respecting my gift. Oh, wait a second."

Uneze sat silently, his breathing quickening as Mr. Nolan reached into his bag.

"Here, take this," Mr. Nolan said, handing him a small, colourful book. Uneze ran his fingers over the flimsy pages, unable to suppress a smile.

"What is it?"

"It's a book in English. I was going to give one to everyone, but... well, you know what they'd do with it. It's got pictures to help you learn English, and here are some pens and pencils for notes. Leave these at home—don't bring them to school."

"Thank you. But I can read English okay. I just don't always understand you when you speak," Uneze admitted.

"Ah, I'm American. Maybe that's why."

"I don't know. The way we speak is different from you," Uneze explained.

"How do you think I can teach you better?"

"You should listen to how we say things and then tell us how to say them your way."

"Good idea, young man. I'll keep that in mind. Now, look after those things."

Uneze's feet splashed through the puddles, each step sending droplets flying as laughter bubbled up from his chest. The remnants of the afternoon storm clung to the air, but the sun peeked through the clouds, igniting a spark of joy within him that no amount of mud could extinguish.

Inside his home, shadows crept around the room as darkness enveloped it, but Uneze was unbothered. Patience was his ally; he understood the rhythm of waiting. Settling into the dimness, he sat in the faint shimmer of Gen City's twilight, clutching his treasures.

When his mother finally arrived, her tired form appeared like a beacon in the gloom.

"Look, Mum. Look what Mr. Nolan gave me," he gushed, his excitement spilling over as he brandished the small book and pencils. To him, they felt as magical as treasures from a far-off land.

Day by day, Uneze lingered after class, savouring fleeting moments that felt like sparks of light in an otherwise colourless world. The promise of another soda or a special lesson flowed through him like sweet nectar. Mr. Nolan's encouraging words gave him a sense of pride, making him feel seen and valued.

Two months passed before Uneze accepted another gift. The way it was offered told him it was special even before he clasped it in his hands.

"Open it," Mr. Nolan said.

Uneze carefully pulled out a sleek, glimmering iPod. The device seemed almost unreal, like something that had only existed in dreams.

"An iPod? For me?" he stammered, his mouth wide with disbelief.

"Yes, it's my old one. It's loaded with English conversational lessons," Mr. Nolan explained.

Uneze hesitated, his excitement dimming slightly. "I don't think I'll be able to use it much... We don't have electricity right now," he admitted, the thrill fading like the last light of day.

Mr. Nolan's face fell. "That's terrible. I can't imagine how tough it must be. What about the food in your fridge?"

"We don't have a fridge. They're expensive. We just eat rice, eggs, and beans most of the time. It was better before my dad left, but now we really struggle. My mum says we don't have two pennies to rub together."

Mr. Nolan froze, his jaw tightening. A fleeting doubt crept in—was Uneze playing on his sympathy? But as he looked into the boy's earnest eyes, the thought quickly evaporated.

"Uneze, it's charged. When the battery runs low, bring it back, and I'll charge it for you."

Uneze hesitated again before taking the device. "Mr. Nolan, why are you so nice to me?"

"Because you're my best student. I believe in helping people who want to better themselves. Even if I can change just one life, I'll die a happy man."

"Are you dying?" Uneze asked, alarmed.

Mr. Nolan chuckled. "No, of course not. Now, tell me—how can I help you and your mum pay for electricity?"

"My mum wouldn't accept money from anyone. She's proud. She won't even take help from my uncle unless it's to fix things around the house."

"I see. What if you told her you had a good weekend selling fruit, enough to charge the electricity metre? You have one of those prepaid metres, right?"

"Yeah."

Nolan pulled out a thin wad of notes. "Will forty dollars be enough, but not too suspicious?"

Uneze thought for a moment. "I could tell her I've been putting money away all week. That way, we could use twenty dollars for electricity and save twenty for food."

"Right. Take this, put it on the metre, and make sure you get some food too. Do you know how to top it up?"

"Yes. It was my job before we ran out of money. Thank you, Mr. Nolan. This is the best thing that's happened in a long time. I'll also get some fuel for the generator. We ran out so long ago I can't even remember."

Nolan swallowed hard, forcing back the emotions welling up inside. Forty dollars. It was what he spent on a single meal back home, yet it was transforming this boy's life.

"You could do that," he said softly. "Food is important."

"Thank you so much. I can't tell Mum you gave me the money, so I'm sorry she'll never be able to thank you."

"I don't need thanks, but I do want something from you," Mr. Nolan said.

Uneze looked up, curious. "I want to see the real Lagos. I see my apartment in Lekki and this school. I have a driver who takes me between the two. I want you to show me your Lagos."

Embarrassed, Uneze asked, "Why?"

"Because I can't expect to understand you and your friends if I know nothing about where you live or how you live."

"Can't you visit on your own?" Uneze asked, his voice interested, but mixed with caution.

"No way. I'm a white man in Lagos. If I visit the kind of area I think I'll be visiting, it wouldn't be safe. But if I'm with you, a local, I'll be safer— or at least I won't get lost."

"I'll have to ask my mother," Uneze said.

"I understand. And maybe, one day, I'll show you my side of Lagos."

Surprisingly, Quanda agreed, though reluctantly. The sudden return of electricity had lifted her spirits, but there was still an edge of suspicion in her eyes. "We'll have to get this place in order if he's coming here," she muttered as she surveyed the room, now bathed in a new light.

"So I can bring him?" Uneze asked, his voice barely containing his excitement.

"I don't see why he'd want to come here, but I see how much your studies make you smile. I want to thank him for that," Quanda said, her expression softening for a moment. But then, it darkened. "Does he treat everyone like he treats you?"

"In class, yes," Uneze answered honestly, "but after class, he makes me feel special."

Her eyes narrowed slightly, unease flickering across her face. "It's settled, then. I want to meet him. I'm not letting you wander the city with a man I don't know—even if he's rich and white. Just because he's white doesn't mean he's good."

Before she could change her mind, Uneze leapt forward and hugged her tightly. Something deep inside him told him that this moment might change his life forever.

8 - PERI

The clatter of pots and pans echoed softly in the kitchen as Peri chopped vegetables, lost in the task of preparing dinner. The warm scent of spices mingled with the curry sauce simmering on the hob, it was a smell that always made her feel calm.

Then, the serenity shattered. A pounding reverberated through the house. Peri's heart lurched as her eyes snapped to the door, a wave of dread pooling in her stomach. She knew who it was. Jake.

"Peri. Let me in. I know you're here," his voice pierced the quiet.

Each thud against the door matched the beat of her pulse, a reminder of the neighbours who were surely watching from behind their curtains, whispering about the storm brewing just beyond the door.

With a sharp breath, Peri set down her knife and wiped her hands on a dishtowel. She swung the door open with a deliberately polite gesture, masking her fury behind a mocking bow.

Jake stood in the doorway, his face flushed with rage, eyes burning with accusation. "So. Have you finished with your tantrum? Why the hell weren't you at work today?"

Peri's voice dripped with sarcasm, her frustration barely contained. Leaning against the doorframe, arms crossed, she shot back, "You said you never wanted to see me again, so I figured I was just following orders, Boss."

The tension crackled in the air, heavy and thick, as they faced off. Peri's breath hitched in her throat, the irony of their exchange hanging like an invisible weight between them.

"I didn't mean work. I expected you to show up at work," Jake snapped, his words slicing through the air like a knife.

"So you needed me at work? I thought I was useless, a waste of space," Peri retorted, each word a sharp jab.

Jake lunged forward, but Peri stepped back. "Not in this house. You don't get to lay a finger on me here. How dare you think you can intimidate me in my friend's home?"

Jake opened his mouth to argue, but stopped short when Anton appeared in the lounge. Her eyes flicked between them before settling on Jake.

"You need to get out. Leave my friend alone," Anton said firmly, her arms crossed in a stance that dared him to challenge her.

Jake took a step back, lowering his hands to his sides. "Fine. Consider yourself fired then."

Peri shook her head, her voice sharp. "Good. And you can consider yourself without a whole bunch of European clients who only deal with me. Let's see you find someone else who does what I do—and speaks as many languages as I do."

Jake rubbed his head, shoving his hands into his pockets. "You'll be back begging for a job soon. No one's going to want someone weak and needy like you."

Peri reached for the house and office keys, her fingers trembling slightly as she gripped them. It was a small, insignificant gesture, yet it felt immense. She had imagined this moment countless times—imagined the strength she would have when the day came to finally let go. But as the keys dangled from her hand, her heart twisted. A part of her still recoiled at the thought of truly walking away, of truly closing that door behind her. But there was no turning back now. She had fought too hard to let him keep control, even in this small way.

With a breath that almost felt like a surrender, she tossed the keys at him. They clinked in the air before landing in his outstretched palm. The finality of it hit her, sharp and cold.

"Here. Take them," she said, her voice steadier than she felt. "I don't need them. Never again will I set foot in your house or your office." The fire that had burned in her chest moments ago had cooled into something calmer, but there was a quiet strength in the act of releasing him, of refusing to let him take any more from her. She forced a smile, one that didn't quite reach her eyes, and continued, "Now, do Anton the honour of leaving her house without making any more of a scene."

Jake's words struck her like a slap, his voice laced with venom. "Oh, you think you're so bloody superior."

Her eyes didn't leave his as she responded, her smile fading into something far more bitter. "Thanks for the birthday present. My freedom is the best gift you could've given me."

The air felt lighter in the space between them, but Peri could still taste the bitterness on her tongue. She had let go of the past, but it would take more than a tossed key to erase the scars he'd left.

Anton stepped forward, her voice trembling with restrained fury. "Get out. Don't ever come near my friend again. I know what you've been doing to her—I've seen the bruises. Stay away from her and from this house, or I'll call the police."

Jake's eyes scanned the room, landing on a few items Peri had brought from their home. "You've been in there? You stole from my house?"

"Our house," Peri corrected, her voice steady. "And I only took what was mine."

"Looks like I'll be the one calling the police," Jake muttered, storming out, slamming the door behind him as he disappeared into the darkness of the night.

Peri extended her middle finger in his direction, then turned toward the bottle of gin on the counter.

"Peri, that was incredible. You were so strong," Anton said, her admiration clear.

Peri chuckled nervously, fumbling for words as she poured herself a drink. Once the ice settled in the glass, she placed it carefully on the table.

"Oh my God," Peri said, shaking her head. "That man has to have the last word. He couldn't just leave—he had to make sure he won the argument."

"How did you live with that for so many years?" Anton asked, incredulous.

"I have no idea," Peri admitted. "I spent the whole night wondering if he'd show up here, rehearsing a hundred things to say... but none of it came out."

"I'm still so impressed," Anton said, clinking her glass against Peri's.

Peri exhaled deeply, her posture softening. "I just saw that look in his eyes—the one where he thinks he can control me. I decided I wasn't going to take it anymore. I wasn't going down without a fight."

"Well, I never knew you had it in you. I'm impressed," Anton said, beaming.

"I feel so empowered. I thought I'd be picking up the pieces of my life if I ever left Jake... but no. I'm done being the person he said I was. I'm not pathetic, useless, or needy. I'm me. I'm Peri York."

"Yes, you are. The fabulous Peri York. And your new life starts here," Anton said, her excitement contagious.

Peri smoothed her hair with a sleek movement. "How are you with scissors? Peri York 2.0 has short hair. She's strong, independent, and doesn't need a man to make her happy. She sure as hell doesn't look like the unkempt woman standing here now."

Anton dashed to the bathroom, grabbed a pair of scissors, and called out, "Right, stick that head of yours under the tap. We're giving you a makeover."

9 - PERI

Peri's eyes widened with excitement as Anton began snipping away at her long, tangled hair. Each snip seemed to echo in the room, and with every falling lock, Peri felt her old self slipping away.

"So, I'm thinking short and spiky—or maybe a mohawk. What do you think?" Peri asked, her voice practically vibrating with excitement.

Anton raised an eyebrow playfully. "I'm thinking more Twiggy."

Peri giggled. "Which era? She's had so many hairstyles."

Anton grinned. "The one with the fringe. That's the look, trust me."

Peri's smile stretched wider. "Yeah, that sounds perfect. Short and sharp," she declared, as if it was already set in stone.

The final strands of hair fell to the floor, and Peri ran her fingers through her newly cropped locks, the coolness of the cut sending a thrill down her spine. She stepped closer to the mirror, the reflection that met her gaze was so different to the familiar face she'd known for years. The sharp angles of her cheekbones seemed to leap out, framed perfectly by the cropped hair.

A slow, triumphant smile spread across her lips. "I love it. I don't even look like me," she murmured, her voice barely above a whisper.

Anton stood nearby, slack-jawed with admiration. "You look stunning. I never knew you had such amazing cheekbones, and that skin—wow. You've been hiding behind that long hair for way too long."

Peri's heart swelled with a burst of newfound confidence. Anton's excitement was contagious.

"I know," Peri said, almost breathless. "Tomorrow, I'm going blonde. Then, my transformation will be complete."

"Go, girl," Anton cheered, raising her hands in a mock celebration. "I can't wait for you to showcase the new you. It's your time to shine, my fabulous friend."

The next morning, Peri swung her legs out of bed and stumbled across the soft carpet. She paused at the bathroom door, taking a deep breath before stepping inside. The mirror reflected an image that still surprised her: her freshly cropped hair gleamed in the light, the soft, edgy cut framing her face like it had always belonged there.

She approached the mirror, running her fingers through the soft strands, tugging them this way and that as surprise flickered in her eyes. A grin broke across her face, wide and unstoppable, as she recognised the fierce new version of herself staring back.

After getting ready, Peri left her packed bag and hand luggage by the door, following the sounds of movement into the kitchen.

Anton glanced at her over the rim of her coffee mug, her expression curious. "Do you still like it?"

"Love it," Peri said, plopping into a chair. "But I'm dying to go blonde. It feels like torture waiting."

"I get it," Anton said with a smirk. "You're so close. Your salon appointment at eleven, right?"

"Yep, and I'm walking down there. Will that give us enough time?"

"Plenty. I'll pick you up at the salon on the way to the airport."

"Perfect. I'll be the one with the bleached blonde short hair," Peri chuckled.

Anton smirked. "I was half-afraid you'd wake up regretting the haircut after all that gin."

"If vino veritas, then gin... well, gin gives courage-tas," Peri quipped, laughing at herself.

Anton raised an eyebrow, grinning. "Gin-telligence? Gincredible? Gin-sational?"

Peri tossed her fingers through her hair, tousling it upward, and pushed through the door into the chilly British morning.

10 - PERI

Two hours later, Peri burst through the doors of the hair salon, her heart dancing in rhythm with her hurried steps. Sunlight poured over her, catching the short strands that framed her face and making them sparkle like silver. With a playful twist, she spun the bag of hair products around her fingers, the crinkling sound of the packaging harmonising with her infectious laughter. Each step down the street felt lighter, as if the weight of the world had lifted away.

She caught a fleeting glance from a man nearby, and a thrill shot through her. His appreciative smile lingered in the air, igniting a spark of excitement that bubbled within her. She felt the transformation in every step she took, as if she'd just unlocked a new version of herself.

Peri almost jumped into Anton's car, her excitement bubbling over. "So, do you like the new look?"

Anton gave her an appraising look. "I almost didn't recognise you."

"Was I that bad before?" Peri asked, suddenly feeling a flicker of insecurity.

"No, you were just... hidden behind all that hair." Anton chuckled, eyes twinkling. "You're stunning now, and I think you're going to make a fabulous wingwoman."

"Wingwoman?" Peri raised an eyebrow, intrigued but confused.

Anton grinned, shifting the car into gear. "Yeah. There's one thing about the tours: it's the perfect place to meet men."

Peri's curiosity sparked. "Customers?"

"No, no. We steer clear of the customers. Just the men we meet along the way. You'll see."

A mischievous smile curled at the corner of Peri's mouth. "That sounds like fun."

Anton's tone shifted slightly as she got to the heart of the matter. "So, I have a mantourage."

Peri blinked. "A what?"

"A mantourage. It's like an entourage, but with men," Anton explained with a sly grin. "You'll meet tons of people on the tour, but you only stay for a day or two. Never get too attached, especially to the bus driver, or you'll be stuck with him for the whole tour."

Peri let out a soft laugh. "Okay, noted."

Anton leant back in her seat, her voice taking on a knowing tone. "Don't worry. I'll show you the ropes. The job's all about making sure the guests are happy, settled, healthy, safe, and in the right place at the right time. Once they're tucked in for the night, that's when we get to have our fun. I've done this tour before, so I've already got some dates lined up in Milan, Rome, Bologna. When we get to Amalfi, there's a guy who thinks I'm his girlfriend. Sweet guy, really. But his mum makes the best home-cooked meals."

Peri raised an eyebrow. "Do you sleep with all of them?"

Anton chuckled, shaking her head. "Oh, Peri, you look like a woman of the world, but I've got so much to teach you."

Peri leant forward, her eyes playful but with a hint of curiosity. "I'm here to learn."

Anton's grin widened. "No, I don't sleep with all of them. Most of the time, especially with the Italians, they're happy to take a beautiful woman out for dinner. They'll try their luck, but they'll respect it when you say you need to head back to the hotel. It's easier with two of us."

Peri shifted in her seat, her fingers nervously tapping the bag of hair products in her lap. "I've only had two boyfriends—my high school boyfriend, then Jake. I'm not sure about all this."

Anton looked over at her, her expression softening a little. "Hey, don't worry. You're not in this alone. You've got me. But, you know, there's a whole world out there. You're young. Live a little. You might surprise yourself."

Peri thought for a moment, feeling his words settle in her chest. She had always played it safe, stuck to what she knew. But a part of her, buried deep down, longed for something more. Something exciting. Her gaze shifted out the window, her mind pumping with thoughts of the new adventures that awaited.

11 - PERI

Peri sat quietly in the back of the bus, her pen flying across the pages of her notepad as Anton animatedly led the group. She watched her, her charisma effortlessly captivating everyone around her. Anton's voice carried easily over the bus, her laughter ringing out as she joked with the group.

Peri's eyes followed Anton, noting how natural and at ease she was. A flicker of envy stirred in her chest. Anton was everything Peri wasn't: confident, commanding, the centre of attention. Peri felt like a shadow in her wake, scribbling down notes but wishing she could take part more, speak out more. It had been easier to blend into the background, to stay quiet, to remain invisible. But here, surrounded by new faces, Peri felt silence press heavier against her chest.

As the bus rumbled out of Milan, the landscape outside unfolding in green, sun-drenched hills and vineyards, a strange shift occurred. The calm, steady beauty of the countryside sparked a flicker of something within her—a curiosity, something new that seemed to ignite with the passing scenery. It wasn't just the view; it was this new job, this new life. The thought of being part of this, of stepping out of the shadow of her own doubt, felt both thrilling and terrifying.

Anton's voice cut through her thoughts as she turned around to face Peri with a cheeky grin. She addressed the group, but her eyes locked with Peri's as she said, "Now, my colleague here, Peri, is going to tell you all about her life in an Italian family."

Peri's stomach dropped. Her heart beat a little too loudly in her chest as she blinked up at Anton, her face heating with a rush of embarrassment. The spotlight was on her now—*all eyes on her*. For a moment, all the air seemed to leave the bus, and she almost looked for an escape, an excuse.

"Really? Come on," she managed, laughing nervously, her voice cracking just a little.

Anton smiled wider, but there was an edge of something in her stare, a knowing look that made Peri's throat tighten. "We've got a twenty-kilometre traffic jam. I'm taking a break. Your turn."

The microphone felt like a foreign object as Peri hesitantly stood, her knees buckling slightly beneath her. Her fingers trembled around the mic, and the words seemed to evaporate in her mouth before she could even begin. But then, Anton's voice floated to her, almost as if on cue: "Just tell them the truth, Peri. It's easy. They're your people now." Her words were both a challenge and an encouragement, and the tension in Peri's chest loosened, just a little.

"Hi, everyone," Peri began, her voice small but steady. "So, I wasn't prepared for this." Her eyes darted to Anton, who raised an eyebrow in amusement. Peri's heartbeat quickened, but she powered through. "Does anyone have any questions that will set me off?"

A voice from the back piped up, "Why do people over here frown at us when we ask for cheese on our pasta?"

The question was silly, and it was enough to break through the last of Peri's nerves. She grinned, the tension in her shoulders easing as she let herself answer. "Ah, well, that depends on whether you are having fish pasta or meat pasta. Cheese suffocates the flavours of the fish, so if you're going to throw a whole bunch of parmesan on gnocchi with prawns, well, even I'd scowl at you."

Laughter erupted around the bus, and for the first time, Peri felt the warmth of the group, the buzz of connection. It was like stepping into the light, and she smiled at the sound of their laughter. It felt good to be seen, to be more than the quiet girl scribbling in the corner.

Another person raised their hand. "What about coffee? Last night, I asked for a cappuccino with my pizza, and the waiter refused."

"Well, firstly, I'd say he was arrogant. But, while we love our Italian arrogance, there are certain rules to abide by," Peri said, her confidence swelling with every word. "Cappuccino is a drink to have in the morning, before eleven. As are milky coffees. Anything else like that... well, a pizza should be accompanied by beer, maybe wine, but really, a beer."

The group chuckled again, but there was a moment where Peri felt a flicker of something—pride, maybe, or something more vulnerable—a realisation that maybe this was what she was meant to do.

"What other rules are there? I don't want to get kicked out of a restaurant," someone asked.

Peri's lips twisted into a playful grin. "Well, ice cream flavours. That's another one. You can't mix fruit with cream, so if you have a sorbet with strawberry cheesecake, you risk getting a good old kick in the butt." She turned to Anton with a mock frown. "Sorry, can I say that?"

Anton's smile was wide, almost proud. "Probably not, but carry on."

Peri's laughter mixed with the group's, her nerves melting away completely as she continued, her words flowing, her stories tumbling out. It was exhilarating—more than just talking, more than just answering questions. She was shaping the experience. She was taking charge of the moment. She was no longer just an observer.

By the time the coach pulled over for a quick refuel, Peri felt a shift in her chest—a space where hesitation used to be. She wasn't just tagging along; she was part of this. She was a storyteller.

Anton waited until the guests had joined the bathroom queue. She approached Peri, her smile a little more genuine than usual. "Peri, that was amazing. You were so funny."

Peri laughed, glancing down at her new fringe. "It's the hair. It's given me funny powers. I was never funny before that."

"Yeah, I know. Well, not that funny." Anton's voice was teasing, but there was something deeper in the way she said it, like she was seeing Peri for the first time. "But I think you actually have what it takes to do this job. You're a natural. Where'd you say you were from again?"

Peri paused, still catching her breath from the unexpected attention. "I spent my summer holidays around Rome, and the coast there. We went to Sorrento and Amalfi too. It was always a home from home for us. I guess Italy is in my blood."

Anton nodded thoughtfully. "Wow, I'm actually sort of jealous right now. I would have loved to have grown up like that. Alright, so I'll go through what you want to say for next time, but I'm giving you a shot down there. This group loves you more than me already."

Peri flicked her fringe with a mischievous smile. "It's the hair."

Anton chuckled, but there was something else in her eyes now. A certain pride that lingered as she watched Peri interact with the group.

"You're doing great. Just... don't forget who showed you the ropes, yeah?"

Peri grinned back. "Of course, Anton. Wouldn't dream of it."

12 - UNEZE

Uneze wiped his brow, hot and exhausted from the early-morning cleaning spree he had just finished. It was early Saturday morning, and Uneze had made sure his cousin would cover his fruit stand for him.

After meeting Mr. Nolan outside the school, Uneze felt a pang of insecurity as he walked alongside the white-skinned man. Everyone seemed to turn and stare at them. He was acutely aware of the whispers from passersby, wondering what this foreigner was doing in their neighbourhood. Uneze tried to keep his focus ahead, but he couldn't shake the feeling of being an outsider. As they walked, Uneze pointed out various landmarks and shared stories about his community, hoping to make Mr. Nolan feel more comfortable in unfamiliar surroundings.

"I think that when we're outside school, you should call me Nolan."

"Why? Don't you have a first name?" Uneze asked.

"Yes, but I hate it, so I've always been called Nolan. As long as in school you call me Mr. Nolan, I think that's cool."

By the time they reached the grubby narrow street that led to his house, the initial awkwardness had faded, replaced by a sense of connection between them. Though they came from entirely different worlds, both were driven by curiosity and a desire to understand one another.

Uneze nervously opened the door, still unsure of what to expect. He invited him inside, feeling a flicker of uncertainty rise again. As they sat down in his modest living room, Uneze braced himself for any judgment or pity that might come his way. Nolan looked around, his eyes briefly scanning the room before he turned his attention to Uneze.

Uneze pointed to the ancient, saggy armchair by the window, gesturing for Nolan to sit.

Nolan shifted uncomfortably in the armchair, the hard spring poking insistently into his back. He leant forward, glancing over his shoulder at the culprit, his brow furrowing in mild discomfort. "So, you still have electricity?" he asked, his curiosity evident.

"Yes, look," Uneze replied, a spark of pride lighting up his face as he flicked the switch on and off, the sudden flicker of light momentarily brightening the room.

"Let me know when you need more," Nolan replied, trying to ease the tension with a light-hearted tone. His satchel, which he had clung to all morning, now felt heavier in his hands. He unzipped it slowly and retrieved a bundle of carefully wrapped gifts. The colourful paper crinkled softly as he held them out. "Where should I put these? They're for your mum and aunty—put them somewhere they can see them."

Uneze pointed toward the table, his gaze fixed on the gifts. His eyes sparkled with excitement as he gestured to the small table by the wall.

Just then, Aunty swept into the room like a gust of wind, her presence commanding instant attention. The air thickened with a hush as she called out, "Uneze, I heard that you had your teacher here. I assume that's you?" she said, arching an eyebrow.

Nolan swatted a fly that buzzed annoyingly near his face. A smile broke across his features as he stood, grateful to escape the confines of the chair. "Yes, ma'am. I'm Nolan." The pleasantries flowed easily as they chatted about Uneze's progress at school, the conversation gradually lightening the atmosphere.

The door swung open again, revealing Mum, breathless from her hurried journey through the bustling streets. Her hair a little disheveled, and her cheeks flushed from the exertion. Despite the rushed appearance, she spoke calmly, brushing a stray lock of hair behind her ear. "Ah, you're here already. I'm sorry I wasn't here sooner, but I had to work."

"It's okay. We just got here," Nolan replied, his voice warm with sincerity. "Uneze's been an excellent tour guide."

"I'm Quanda," Uneze's mum said, her voice warm yet hesitant. She reached out, her hand extended, but there was a slight uncertainty in the gesture, as if she were offering a suspicious stroke rather than a handshake.

He stepped forward and placed the gifts gently into their open palms. The women's eyes widened in surprise as they looked down at the beautifully wrapped packages. A spark of joy ignited in the room as they exchanged glances. Their fingers danced over the paper, eager to tear it apart and uncover the thoughtful treasures hidden within.

"Nolan, thank you," Uneze's aunt replied, her voice filled with gratitude, even though she didn't know what the gift was.

Nolan simply smiled and shrugged. "I wanted to show my appreciation for the wonderful boy you send to my class every day. He's a very good student." They ignored his comment, instead admiring the gifts they had unwrapped. "It's French perfume," Nolan added, "I picked it up from a boutique near my apartment."

Quanda placed it down on the table, her disinterest obvious. "Sit," she ordered, gesturing for Nolan to take a seat in the armchair again. She waited for him to sit before continuing. "I thank you for the attention you're giving to my son. But I want to know why."

"Mum, stop it," Uneze pleaded, his voice strained.

Quanda crossed her arms, her brow furrowing as she fixed stared at Nolan. "Why, Uneze?" she pressed. "Out of all the kids in the school, you show him favour, send him home with gifts, and now you want to come to our house."

Nolan swallowed hard, a bead of sweat trickling down his temple. He nodded slowly, his face tense. "I know this seems strange," he began, his voice barely above a whisper. "In my country, America, this wouldn't be considered appropriate."

Quanda's expression softened slightly. Her hand found Uneze's shoulder, a gesture of quiet support. "Carry on," she urged, her voice more neutral now.

Nolan took a deep breath, his eyes darting between Uneze and his mum. "I came to this school to teach English, thinking it would be simple—just teach the kids, go home, and repeat for a year. But I'm learning so much from them." His gaze softened as he looked at Uneze. "Uneze has shown me what it means to find joy in simplicity. It's something I'd never considered until I met the kids. Can you imagine a room full of smiling faces, despite the trauma they face?"

Mum's lips tightened, her expression in defiance. "Do you think it's traumatic living here?" she asked sharply. "It's tough, but we're strong. We'll survive."

"No, I think 'traumatic' was the wrong word," he admitted, hesitating before continuing. "I should have said basic... simple." He shifted slightly in his chair, discomfort evident. "I like to think of myself as a mentor, and if I can help even one child change his life, then it's worth it."

"Still, you haven't explained why you chose Uneze to be your project."

Nolan hesitated, looking at Uneze, before offering a quiet confession. "I liked that Uneze didn't sell my gifts. I admire the others for making their situation work. If selling pens and pencils makes their lives a little easier, I'm happy for them. But Uneze's focus... it's on long-term education, not short-term gain."

Quanda's eyes narrowed, probing for more. "Why did you come here from America?"

Nolan's eyes dropped to the floor, his shoulders heavy. He took a deep, shaky breath. The words tumbled out before he could stop them, jagged and raw. "There's a terrible situation at my school. A student came in with a gun... and some kids were killed. I was shot, but I survived." He paused, his chest tight with the memory. "It felt like a sign. I needed to leave—to go somewhere I could actually help people, rather than teaching kids who couldn't see how lucky they were."

As Nolan spoke, the light in Quanda's eyes flickered briefly, but she quickly masked her concern. A warmth began to spread across her features, a softening that seemed to bridge the gap between their worlds. "Why here?" she asked, still suspicious, but with less bite in her words.

"It was where the school board sent me. I just followed instructions on the ticket they gave me," Nolan replied, his voice barely above a whisper.

Quanda tilted her head, studying him intently. "Uneze is glad you're here. He spends all his time studying now, instead of hanging out on the streets selling fruit."

"I'm sorry about that. I know he used to sell fruit to help the family."

Her smile faltered for a moment, the strain of their struggles evident. She exhaled softly, the reality of it all flickering in her eyes before she masked it again. "Yes, he does less of that now, but it's for his future. Somehow, he's selling more fruit before and after school."

"I wish there was something I could do to help. I feel guilty for taking Uneze away from his job. It can't be easy without the extra money," Nolan admitted.

Her expression shifted, hardening again. "We're fine. You may work for a charity, but we aren't a charity."

Nolan swallowed hard, discomfort pooling in his stomach. "I didn't mean to offend you. I just feel such joy when I see Uneze's smile after I give him good marks on his homework. You have to understand, I'm only here to help."

"That's all I want, too," Quanda replied softly, her voice softening as she moved to prepare tea. The small gesture felt monumental in the moment. "But why do you want to take my son to your area of the city? Why dangle riches in front of him? I can't see how that could ever help him."

Nolan cradled the steaming cup in his hands, the warmth radiating through his fingers. He set it gently on the table, the quiet thud of it breaking the tension in the room. "I don't see it that way," he said softly. "To me, it's about exploring life beyond these streets. Just crossing to the other side of the city can open your mind. There's a whole world out there—beyond this area, beyond Lagos, beyond Africa. I think Uneze deserves to see it."

13 - UNEZE

Quanda paused, her expression softening. "If we go on a Sunday, I can join too," she replied, a hint of a smile breaking through her usual stern composure.

"Really?" Nolan's eyebrows shot up in surprise.

"It can't hurt to breathe some fresh air and see something different," she added, her tone now laced with warmth.

With a plan in place, Nolan bowed his head slightly in gratitude before heading out, promising an exciting day on Sunday.

"I'll walk you to school; you'll never find it on your own," Uneze said, his tone teasing yet protective.

"Make sure you're back before it gets dark," Mum called after them in concern.

As they reached the school, Nolan's driver stood waiting, the car gleaming under the fading light. "Now, hurry home. I'll see you at school on Monday," he instructed, rummaging through his pockets. He thrust a handful of notes into Uneze's palm. "This is your fee for being my tour guide today."

Uneze's face froze as he stared at the neatly folded bills, quickly shoving them into the pockets of his worn trousers. "Thank you, Nolan," he stammered.

"Don't forget to study tomorrow. I'll be teaching you more verb tenses, so be sure to listen to that iPod of yours," Nolan said with a grin before disappearing into the car, leaving behind a swirl of excitement.

Uneze sprinted back home, and through the door, he shouted a breathless greeting, immediately drawing his mother's attention. "He paid me for being his guide today," Uneze said, laying the money onto the table.

His mother's hands flew to her mouth, eyes wide as she separated the coins from the notes. "Oh my God, this is fifty dollars."

Uneze's heart raced at the thought of possibilities. "What can we do with that?"

"Anything, everything. First, we'll get you some new clothes for school. Then the roof needs fixing, and if there's enough left, we can buy a fridge," she outlined, her voice bubbling with excitement.

"What about you, Mum? Don't you want some new clothes?" he asked, genuine concern lacing his words.

"Of course I do, but life is about priorities. My new clothes are at the bottom of the list," she replied, her voice steady but tinged with sacrifice. Her words hung in the air, weighty and profound. "Now, hide that money before anyone sees it through the window."

Uneze gathered the money, carefully placing it into the metal tin he had hidden in their usual spot.

14 - UNEZE

A week later, on Sunday, Uneze and his mother walked the short distance to school. Uneze, with his small hand clasped tightly in hers, beamed up at her. "You look very nice, Mum," he said, plopping down on the grass outside the school, his excitement bubbling over as he kicked his legs playfully.

"Thanks, love," she replied, forcing a smile. "I can't go on a trip in my work clothes—Nolan can't be embarrassed to show us around."

Before she could continue, the sharp honk of a car horn sliced through the air, and Nolan's friendly wave beckoned from the driver's seat. "Come on, jump in. I would have been happy to pick you up from your home," Nolan called out, his voice cheerful.

"No, it's better this way," Quanda insisted.

"So, I'm going to take you to an arts and culture centre, and then we'll take it from there," Nolan continued, oblivious to her discomfort.

"I thought you didn't know the city," Uneze pointed out, his brow furrowing.

"I don't, but my driver does. He's planned the day for us, and we'll end up at my complex for lunch. Then the driver will bring you home," Nolan explained.

As the car pulled away, the conversation fell into a hesitant rhythm, the trio grappling with the stress of impossible conversation. Uneze and his mother gazed wide-eyed at the unfamiliar cityscape flashing by, their breaths catching in their throats as tree-covered roads stretched out into the distance.

In just twenty minutes, Uneze found it hard to comprehend that such beauty lay so close to the cramped confines of his world. The opulence of sprawling mansions, the sleek luxury cars gliding effortlessly along the streets, and the gardens that looked like they belonged in a fairy tale made his heart race with disbelief.

Quanda sat silently, her fingers twisting nervously around the fabric of her dress. She tried to mask the pang of longing that twisted in her chest, a bittersweet ache for a life that glimmered just out of reach—so tantalisingly close yet painfully distant.

The affluent neighbourhood of Lekki buzzed with life. Expensive villas lined with lush gardens and sparkling pools stood proudly behind wrought-iron gates. Luxury cars glided silently along the smooth, paved roads, their polished exteriors reflecting the radiant shades of the evening sky. The sound of laughter and music drifted from stylish cafes and upscale restaurants. Boutiques beckoned with their exquisite window displays. This was a world where opulence met warmth, and affluence wove seamlessly into the fabric of everyday life.

After two cultural visits, Nolan told his driver to take them back to his area, where they settled around the pool of the ocean-view restaurant while he ordered chilled drinks for them all.

As they settled into the plush lounge chairs, Uneze found himself momentarily overwhelmed. The laughter of the group blended seamlessly with the soft lapping of the pool water, creating a symphony that felt both comforting and surreal. The contrast between this world and his own gnawed at him, vivid images of his mother scrubbing floors and dusting shelves for families who lived in places like this flashing through his mind.

Quanda leaned over, her voice pulling him out of his thoughts like a rope yanking him from a well. "Are you okay? You've been staring at that pool like it owes you money."

Uneze shook off the weight of his memories, smirking. "I'm fine. Just brainstorming a master plan to get us a place like this for good."

Quanda's eyebrow arched in suspicion. "Does this 'master plan' involve me cleaning houses like this for eternity?"

He leaned in, his grin contagious. "Actually, no. This place has inspired me. I'm going to work hard, make something of myself, and get us here legitimately. No brooms required."

Quanda rolled her eyes, but her lips betrayed a smile. "I'll believe it when I see it."

Before she could tease him further, Nolan returned. With the air of someone entirely at ease in such surroundings, he sat down and launched into tales of Boston's charm—the bustling streets, hidden spots and cherished memories with friends. Uneze tried to listen, but his stomach betrayed him, growling loudly as servers arrived with plates of freshly grilled fish.

Uneze and Quanda exchanged wide-eyed glances, their amazement growing as their gaze landed on the array of silverware glinting ominously on the table.

"Nolan," Uneze ventured, his voice low. "We've got a bit of a... problem."

Nolan paused, eyebrows raised. "What's wrong?"

Uneze gestured to the cutlery. "We don't know how to use all these things. Back home, we eat with our hands."

Nolan grinned, picking up a fork and knife. "It's not rocket science. Just copy me."

The pair hesitantly picked up their utensils, their movements stiff and uncoordinated. Metal clinked as Uneze managed to stab a rogue piece of fish that slid off his plate. Quanda muffled a laugh as Uneze muttered, "It's like trying to eat with construction tools."

Just as their frustration reached its peak, Nolan reached for a lobster claw, cracking it open with his hands and pulling out the succulent meat with ease. "Sometimes," he said, grinning, "you just have to forget the rules."

Relieved, Uneze and Quanda exchanged grins, ditching their utensils and diving in with their hands. The tension dissolved into laughter as they enjoyed the meal with unrestrained glee.

After the plates were cleared, they found themselves staring at an imposing bill that had been placed in the centre of the table. Quanda's face drained of colour as she nudged Uneze. "Look at that number. Is this real life?"

Uneze squinted at the amount, his voice barely above a whisper. "That's more than what you make in a year. Are we supposed to pay for this?"

Panic seeped into her voice. "I swear, if Nolan left us with this—"

Uneze gestured frantically toward Nolan, who was casually chatting on his phone nearby. "Relax. He's right there. He's probably calling his bank to approve the loan for this meal."

When Nolan returned, he plucked the bill from the table, sliding his card into the sleek black holder with a flourish. "Sorry about that. My dad called. Anyway, I've arranged for us to head to my complex. You can use the pool there. Do you know how to swim?"

Uneze shrugged. "Not really; well, actually, no."

Nolan's grin widened. "That's fine. The kiddy pool will be perfect for you. I'll make sure to bring floaties for him."

Nolan's offer to buy bathing suits and shorts sparked joy in Uneze. The idea of someone clothes just for swimming felt as fantastical as the scene around them. As they walked toward the boutique excitement flickered in Uneze's heart. Maybe, just maybe, he could turn this fleeting glimpse of luxury into a permanent reality.

15 - UNEZE

Once they arrived at Nolan's apartment complex, a modern oasis tucked away behind tall palm trees, Uneze splashed in the pool, marveling at the open blue sky. With a coy smile, he turned to his mother. Her smile was the widest he'd ever seen as she lay on the lounger sipping a drink while Nolan chatted with ease. A strange sense of calm washed over him as he rested his arm on the edge of the pool, watching the staff move around him. He crossed his arms and wondered how he could make this his reality.

Hours passed, and occasionally, he'd visit his mother and Nolan by the pool. Nolan seemed oblivious to the fact that Uneze's skin had turned a bright shade of red as he and his mother chatted.

"What time do we have to go home?" Uneze asked.

"Do you want to go home?" Nolan asked, clearly disappointed that Uneze wasn't enjoying himself.

"No, never. But Mum has to work at dawn."

Nolan let out a small smile and said, "Well, we were just talking about that. Why don't you both stay here with me tonight? I have plenty of room. Tomorrow morning, my driver can take your mum to work, then take you home and me to school."

"Stay here?" Uneze asked, a rush of excitement flooding through him. He turned to his mother, pleading, "Mum, can we?" He knew his mother well enough to expect she'd refuse, not wanting to be an inconvenience, so he added, "Please, that way Mr. Nolan can help me with my homework before school tomorrow."

As expected, Quanda replied, "No, I can't put you out like that."

"It's not putting me out. It gets lonely up here, and I love the company. As Uneze said, if we have to take you at dawn, that will give Uneze and me a couple of hours to prepare for the next English test." Nolan noticed the exchange of glances between mother and son, and Quanda's nod of agreement. He asked, "Have you ever tried pizza?"

Uneze shook his head. "I don't think so."

"Great. So we'll get a takeout pizza and eat it on the balcony. It's decided. I'll get the shop to send up toothbrushes and some T-shirts for you to sleep in."

Inside, the room was a treasure trove of curiosity. Uneze stopped, breath caught in his throat, as his eyes fell upon the laptop resting on the side table, its sleek body glinting under the soft light. The urge to reach out, to feel the cool metal beneath his fingertips, was overwhelming, but his mother's gentle tug brought him back to reality. She wandered around, her fingers tracing the bright paintings of African women that hung on the walls, each one alive with colour and culture.

"So, there are two single beds in that room. I hope you're okay sharing," Nolan said.

"You've seen where we live; you know we don't have a problem with sharing a room. This is the nicest bed I've ever slept in—no, the nicest house I've ever stepped into. What's that?" Uneze pointed, eyes frozen with wonder.

"It's a closet."

"Your clothes have a house?" Uneze asked. He burst into laughter, the sound filling the bright space. "It's bigger than my entire house."

"Now, settle in—have a shower or whatever you want. I'm going to get some things for you from the shop and order pizzas."

As evening fell, they made their way to the balcony. The sprawling city below was illuminated by the soft sparkle of streetlights. The tranquil sound of water cascading from the fountain by the pool mingled with the buzz of the city, creating a sound that seemed to welcome them into this new world. Nolan leant down, giving Uneze an affectionate squeeze on the cheek before retreating to his room for the night.

Uneze lay still, listening to the laughter that erupted from his mother. It was a melody he had almost forgotten—so rare and precious that he found himself lying wide-eyed, absorbing the moment.

16 - PERI

A month after the tour with Anton ended, Peri stepped through the polished glass doors of the hotel, her heart racing with nerves. The scent of fresh bagels wafted through the air, mingling with the faint sound of chatter and laughter from other attendees of the tour guide training course in London.

She shifted her bag over her shoulder, adjusting the strap as her palms began to sweat. Her steps echoed lightly on the marble floor, the soft clink of her shoes matching the rapid beat of her heart. She hurried down the hall, her footsteps quickening as she approached the door marked with a hastily scrawled sign reading "ExoTravel—Applicant Training."

Excitement surged through her, making her pulse flutter, but she forced herself to breathe slowly as she reached for the door. The moment she inched it open, a buzz of energy hit her—a undertone of eager voices, the energy crackling in the air. Rows of eager faces turned toward her, some with hopeful smiles, others with nervous glances. Their body language a mix of fidgeting, crossing arms, and shifting in their seats. She smiled back, a soft, nervous curve of her lips, as she slipped into a seat at the back of the room. Her eyes scanned the group, assessing the different personalities on display. Some were already deep in conversation, laughing, while others fidgeted with their pens or checked the papers in front of them. Whatever they were doing, they were all united by the same goal: to transform their passion for travel into a career.

By the time the instructor arrived, Peri had counted eighteen other people of all ages, each probably with their own unique language skills and qualities. She glanced around, feeling a flutter in her stomach as she wondered how she would fit in.

The instructor entered and immediately captured the room's attention. Dinah, a striking woman with shiny white hair that seemed to shine under the spotlight above her, stepped forward with an air of quiet authority. Despite her age, she radiated a youthful energy. Her attire—a crisp white blouse and black trousers—was elegant yet casual. She had a warm, welcoming smile, but there was a sharpness in her eyes that made Peri sit up straighter. The way she carried herself—confident, poised—made Peri feel that Dinah was someone who had seen it all and expected nothing less than perfection.

"Hello, everyone. I'm Dinah," she said, her voice calm but commanding. "I'm your trainer for this five-day course. It's going to be very full-on. We'll do role-plays, problem-solving situations, first aid, company procedure training, and we'll be going through some real-life situations that have happened to get your take on them and how you would have handled them. We'll also cover company decorum, uniform, presentation, and expectations. Does anyone have any questions so far?"

The room fell into a tense silence, everyone waiting for someone else to speak. Peri, still feeling nervous, kept her eyes focused on the table, her fingers absentmindedly tapping the edge of her notebook. She knew she had to stand out, but she wasn't sure how just yet.

"Good," Dinah said, breaking the silence. "So, sit back, relax, and watch this introduction about ExoTravel, our mission statement, and, for those of you who don't know what type of job you've actually applied for, some of our experienced guides talking about their lives, jobs, and experiences."

The lights dimmed, and the drop-down screen flickered to life, showing various shots of busy cities and colourful landscapes. As the video played, Peri found herself lost in the images. She leant forward slightly, her arms resting on her knees, absorbed in the possibilities. She glanced around at the others, wondering what drew them to this job. Did they have the same passion for travel? The same love for showing others the world?

Minutes blended into an hour, the video providing a fascinating backdrop to her thoughts. When the lights flipped back on, Dinah rose from her chair, breaking the reverie.

"Any questions?" she asked, her voice sharp, as though expecting one of them to speak up.

A few hands shot up with questions about travel logistics and accommodation. Peri stalled for a moment,, knowing she should speak up, but she decided to wait. She had seen this job in action through her best friend, but she needed to gauge the rest of the group first.

"You," Dinah said suddenly, pointing at Peri. "You must have a question?"

Peri's stomach lurched. All eyes turned to her, and she felt her face flush. "Not yet," she said, her voice a bit quieter than she intended. "My best friend works for ExoTravel, and I've been on a few tours with her, so I guess I know the basics."

Dinah's face changed in an instant. Her smile dropped, replaced by a sharp, critical look. "So you know it all already? Do you think you shouldn't be here?"

The room seemed to hold its breath. Peri swallowed hard, feeling a flush creep up her neck. She glanced around the room—eyes locked on hers, some curious, others judgmental—and quickly clarified, "Definitely not. Sorry, I mean, I definitely don't think I know it all. I'm flustered. I want to be here. After seeing my friend do the job, I know how much there is to learn. She's prepared for everything, and I want to be just like that."

Dinah's expression softened, and she nodded with approval. "Good save there," she said with a faint smile.

Peri exhaled slowly, her body relaxing as Dinah turned away. She gripped her pencil tighter, willing her heart rate to slow down. She felt a bead of sweat trickle down the side of her face but wiped it away quickly, trying to regain her composure.

After another hour of Dinah explaining the tourism industry and their place in it, she paused and looked up at the clock. "Now, it's time for coffee and the group introductions. This is something you'll do with every single group you deal with. It's your chance to get to know what your customers want you to know about them. If you're any good at your job, you'll find out the rest during the tour. You need to be mind readers. You need to know why they are on the tour and what they expect to get out of it. Start thinking of what you want to say, then we'll do these in the lounge area over coffee."

Peri nodded to herself, mentally preparing for her turn. She had practised her introduction countless times, but the nerves never quite went away.

Once everyone had taken a seat and either placed their drinks on the table or hugged their cups to their chests, Dinah stood up and pointed to one of the group. "So, you start. Tell me your name, where you're from, a little about yourself, and what you want to get out of the course. Then, follow up with a spiel that you think would be how you'd introduce yourself to a group of strangers on a coach."

"Ehh, I'm Joseph. I'm thirty, a non-smoker from Manchester. I'm single, and, well, I want to do this job so that I can travel the world."

Dinah's eyes narrowed, and she shook her head in disapproval. "This isn't a Tinder or online dating profile. You'll need to get better than that if you get through the course. Now, show me how you'd introduce yourself to a group of guests."

Joseph blinked, clearly thrown off, but he recovered quickly. "Uh, okay. So, hello everyone. I'm Joseph, your tour guide. This week we will be visiting, um, Turkey, and each day I'll give you an itinerary for the day."

He stopped, his shoulders tense, his hands shoved in his pockets, waiting for Dinah's response.

Dinah's face dropped, her expression one of disbelief. "What was that?" she asked, her tone flat.

Joseph shifted awkwardly, eyes darting between his fellow trainees. "I don't know. I guess I've still got to learn. How would you do it?"

Dinah paused for a beat, her gaze sweeping over the group. Then, she locked eyes with Peri. "Where is the girl whose friend does this?"

Peri, startled, raised her hand. "Here," she said softly.

Dinah nodded. "Right, you've seen it done, I assume." She turned her attention to Peri. "Go for it."

Peri's stomach flipped. She stood up slowly, smoothing down her dress as she tried to focus. She took a deep breath before speaking, feeling all eyes on her.

"Hello, everyone, welcome to Milan and this ExoTravel tour of Italy. My name is Peri, and I'm very excited to be able to show you the sights of Italy this week. Tomorrow morning at eight, we will be heading off to the stunning city of Verona, the city of romance, so make sure your bags are packed and outside your door before you go to breakfast at seven."

She glanced at Dinah, who gave her an encouraging nod. Peri continued, her voice gaining confidence as she went on, "Here is a printed itinerary of what to expect this week, although the order may change with the weather." She mimicked handing out papers, imagining the tourists in front of her. "We've got an incredible itinerary ahead: Verona,

Venice, Florence, Rome, and the Amalfi Coast. It's a stunning tour, and I'm confident you'll enjoy it as much as I will."

Dinah stepped forward, giving Peri a firm pat on the back. "That's enough. We don't want to scare the others. Now, that's how it's done. It's clear her friend the tour guide has taught her well."

The room, which had been tense, now seemed to relax, and a few people nodded in approval. Peri's shoulders loosened, her nerves fading. She had done it. She had shown them she belonged

The following days of training were grueling, pushing Peri and her fellow trainees to their limits. Dinah's methods were demanding, sometimes harsh, but Peri could feel herself growing with each task. Her confidence had increased, and she was beginning to grasp the intricacies of the job, like managing unruly tourists and adapting to the unpredictable nature of the job.

Lisa and Peri stuck together, quietly supporting one another, their bond growing stronger each day. They would often stay up late, talking through the day's lessons, and seeking advice from Anton via video chat. Peri would laugh at Anton's blunt but helpful remarks, her friend's experience guiding her through the more difficult parts of the training.

"You've got this," Anton had told her during one video chat. "But you've got to keep your wits about you. Don't let Dinah's antics get to you. It's all part of the test."

Each time Dinah would push the group to do something outside their comfort zones, Peri felt the pressure mounting. But there was also a strange sense of exhilaration that accompanied it. The days blurred together—practical exercises, assessments, and presentations. She felt like she was constantly on the edge, walking a fine line between anxiety and excitement.

By the end of the week, they had all faced their final assessments, a combination of role plays and practical exercises. The group was much smaller now, having shrunk significantly after the first few days, with only a few remaining who had the endurance and resilience to continue.

Lisa and Peri stood side by side, watching the last of the group finish their final tasks. When it was their turn, they stepped forward with a sense of calm that they hadn't had in the beginning. Peri could hear her heart beat in her ears, but her movements were smooth and deliberate.

Lisa, always a little more nervous, mirrored her, though she looked more relaxed than ever.

As they performed their role play with Dinah, Peri's mind was clear, her focus sharp. She felt the instructor's scrutiny, but she didn't let it rattle her. The conversation flowed naturally, and for the first time, she wasn't just following the script she had learned. She was adapting, listening, responding in real-time. Dinah's approval was palpable when it was over, though the trainer's expression remained neutral.

"Good," Dinah said, nodding. "You both handled that well. You're both ready."

Peri exhaled slowly, relief washing over her. She glanced at Lisa, who gave her a tired but proud smile.

"We did it," Lisa whispered, as if afraid to say it too loudly, lest it jinx them.

"Yeah," Peri whispered back. "We did."

The next morning, the final results were posted. Peri's name was at the top of the list. Her heart skipped a beat, and her hands trembled as she scanned the rest of the names. Lisa's name was there too, just a few spots below hers.

With a smile, Peri leant over to Lisa. "Looks like we're both in."

Lisa's eyes lit up with relief. "Thank God. I actually thought I might not make it."

"Well, now you've got your chance to travel," Peri said, grinning. "We both do."

Later that afternoon, they sat in a quiet corner of the hotel lobby, talking excitedly about the future. Where would they go first? What would the job be like when they finally hit the road? Would they be placed together, or would they have to work alone? The unknowns were thrilling.

"I can't believe we actually made it," Lisa said, running a hand through her hair. "I mean, after everything."

Peri smiled. "This was the best decision I've ever made."

They both laughed, the drama of the past few days falling away. The air was lighter now, the tension gone.

As the evening approached, they gathered their things and walked toward the lobby's exit. Peri felt a sense of triumph in her chest. She had survived. No longer just a tourist, she was about to become a guide, ready to lead others on adventures of their own.

She had no idea where the road would take her, but for the first time in a long time, it didn't matter. Whatever came next, she was ready for it.

17 - PERI

Each morning, the faces of the trainees appeared more lined with fatigue. They showed the same mixture of hope and exhaustion, their eyes a little duller but still shining with determination—or perhaps desperation. They gathered in tight circles, exchanging last-minute tips and whispering encouragement before each session. The walls, lined with pale, worn posters of exotic destinations, seemed to close in as the pressure mounted.

On the final morning, at the back of the room, a clock ticked steadily, its hands inching closer to the moment of truth for each of them. The room was charged, yet suffocating, the scent of stale coffee mixing with the sharp tang of nervous sweat. Everyone stood slightly hunched, their shoulders tense, eyes darting around as if they could catch a glimpse of what the future held. With each tick of the clock, the reality settled in: only half of them would succeed, and the thought loomed like a shadow over their weary minds.

"Alright, everyone," Dinah began, her voice cutting through the murmur. "So, I think it's best to be blunt. Not all of you have what it takes to work for this company. During lunch, I'll talk to each of you individually and give you your evaluation. Then, those who remain will spend this afternoon learning about ExoTours' policies and procedures." She paused, took a sip of water, and let the tension build before continuing, "So, in any order you like, please come and see me at my desk, and we'll see if today is a good day or a bad day for you."

The first to step up was Iain, a tall man with big blue eyes and a warm smile. He flashed a wide-mouthed grin, his posture casual as he stood and said, "Let's do it in order of where we sat during lessons. Back of the class first."

"Oh, thanks. So we have to go first?" Lisa asked, her voice tinged with mock annoyance, her arms crossed tightly in front of her chest.

"Why not? It's pretty obvious you two got jobs. You're her favourites," Iain teased, his lips curling into a half-smile.

Lisa rolled her eyes, her shoulders sagging in exasperation as she sighed deeply. Peri, her hands trembling slightly, swallowed nervously and said, "Okay, here goes nothing." She wiped her mouth with the back of her hand, placed her fork down, and pushed her chair back. The soft scrape of wood on tile echoed in the room as she stood, her legs slightly unsteady beneath her.

"Dinah," Peri muttered, offering a nervous smile as she approached.

"Ah, so you're the first to take the plunge," Dinah said with a laugh, leaning back in her chair, her fingers tapping lightly against the desk.

"We're going in order around the room. Back row first," Peri explained, her voice barely above a whisper as she glanced back at Lisa, who gave her an encouraging nod.

"Alright, at least I know which order to expect bad news in," Dinah joked, her lips curling into a wry smile.

"I hope I'm not the first one," Peri muttered, a distracted smile forming at the corner of her mouth.

"Peri, you've been great, and you work well with others. I think you'll be a fantastic addition to our overseas guiding team," Dinah said, her tone warm and reassuring.

Peri felt her fears melt away, her heart lifting as the relief poured in. "Really?" she asked, almost disbelieving.

"Of course. Next week, you'll be going on a tour of the Palladian villas in Italy, shadowing an experienced guide. Once that's sorted, we'll send you your placement details. Can you fill out this form with your information—your base location, nearest airport, and so on—and return it to me by the end of the day?"

Peri's fingers trembled as she clutched the paper, gripping the corner tightly to steady her excitement. A broad smile threatened to break free, but she forced herself to take a deep breath, pushing the elation deep inside as she stepped back toward the others. Her legs felt wobbly, but the excitement kept her steady as she clenched her fists at her sides.

"Well?" Lisa's eyes sparkled with worry as Peri slid into her seat, her legs bouncing nervously beneath the table, her foot tapping in rhythmic bursts.

"I'm in," Peri beamed, her voice barely containing the thrill surging through her. Her cheeks were flushed with disbelief and joy. The others leant in closer, eager to hear more. "I got the job, and I'm heading to Italy. Looks like once you're in, you get to fill out one of these forms." She waved the paper triumphantly. Her heart still raced, but the enormity of the moment was starting to sink in.

"But I have no clue what happens if you're not in."

"A kick up the ass," Iain said with a wide grin, his tone light but his eyes filled with a flicker of regret.

A few minutes later, Lisa walked out, waving her piece of paper and flashing a radiant smile. "I'm in too. I'm doing a Spain tour next week with a pro guide, and then I'm on my own. Oh my god, it's my first big girl job."

Peri pointed at the form, tapping her pen on the paper. "So, what do I put for my address?"

"Here, I'll fill that in for you," Lisa replied with a wink, listing her own address and clinking coffee cups with Peri. "Roomies."

"Roomies," Peri echoed with a grin, giving Lisa a fist bump.

Iain sauntered in next, his gait smooth, exuding an air of self-assurance that drew attention like a magnet. His posture was relaxed, but his eyes scanned the room with a calculated intensity. When he exited a moment later, his eyes swept across the room until it landed on Peri. In an instant, his expression darkened.

He marched towards the lift, his heavy footsteps resonating with indignation, his brows knitting into a fierce scowl. From the lobby, his voice cut through the chatter like a blade. "Heads up, everyone. Watch out for that smile of hers—one moment you're basking in its glow, and the next, you're flat on your back, no idea what just hit you. Seriously, it's time to rethink your life choices, folks. Five days wasted on that dull talk and waffle? I'll never get those days back." With that, he disappeared into the lift.

As the clock ticked away, the door swung open with a soft creak, and one by one, faces appeared—some bright with joy, their eyes wide with wonder, while others were shadowed by frustration, brows tense and shoulders hunched in defeat. In a corner of the bustling room; ten hopeful candidates huddled together, their chatter filled with plans and travel dates.

Dinah rubbed the back of her neck, tracing the tension that coiled there as she approached the group. "Well, here we are, or shall I say, here you are," Dinah said, her voice filled with pride. "Those who dared to dream big and are ready to make a name for themselves in the world we call tourism."

The group gave themselves a round of applause, their faces lighting up as they accepted the thick books handed to them. Peri skimmed the table of contents, her heart pounding with excitement.

"So, now we get down to the nitty-gritty: the what to do and what not to do while working for and representing the face of the company. You are the future of ExoTravel, and your new lives start here."

Lisa and Peri exchanged a subtle grin, their eyes sparkling with satisfaction as they leant closer to their notepads.

"Did anyone get the African safari tour?" Lisa asked.

"I wish. Anton said those tours are only for the really experienced guides."

"Nooo," one of the candidates said, her voice brimming with frustration. "That was the reason I did this. I wanted to do an African safari more than anything else. That's what I'm aiming for. They have this camping-across-Africa gig online, and it looks out of this world."

"I'm going to put that on my bucket list," Peri said excitedly, her face flushed. "I'm going to keep doing this until I get that tour."

18 - UNEZE

That was the first of many Sundays spent in the complex. Every time felt the same: living in a dreamlike state, in a world that bore no resemblance to his life during the rest of the week. Days at school were now something Uneze looked forward to, knowing that each day he'd receive a care package for his mum and something for himself from Nolan. Quanda would accept no money, only gifts; however, with Uneze's help, somehow the electricity metre always remained prepaid.

Nolan, a flicker of concern in his eyes, gently nudged the boy he now considered his friend. "Would you be okay if I took your mum out to dinner tomorrow?"

Uneze shrugged casually. "Why? We have food in the fridge."

Nolan, his face thoughtful, gestured with his hand. "I think it would be nice to treat her."

"It's not her birthday."

Nolan smiled. "I know, but she works so hard, and she deserves a special meal. I promise not to bring her home late. I'll even get an extra portion of everything for you, in a takeaway bag." He paused, realising Uneze's blank expression needed clarification. "A takeaway bag... for leftovers."

Uneze's face broke into a smile. "So, I get some food too? That's cool. Did Mum say she'd go?"

Nolan's confidence faltered. "I haven't asked her yet. I was thinking of having my driver pick her up from work and bring her to school so I can ask. I just wanted to make sure you'd be okay on your own."

Uneze waved him off nonchalantly. "It's fine. I'll eat with my aunt. She might say no though; she doesn't have the money for nice clothes to go anywhere fancy."

Nolan suddenly realised the social implications and quickly offered, "Ah, that's a good point. I'll get something for her. What would she like?"

"Anything long and colourful," Uneze grinned.

Quanda came home from the date, beaming with excitement as she threw the bag of food into the newly gifted fridge. "We went to a restaurant that was amazing."

"You look happy. I'm glad you had fun," Uneze said.

"I did, but I'm also happy because he offered me a job," Quanda said with a nervous grin.

"Another job?" Uneze asked, surprise evident.

"No, a real job. I'd be working in his apartment complex. They need someone to keep the lobby clean, restock the bathrooms with clean towels, and fill in at the reception desk sometimes."

Uneze's jaw dropped, though he managed to ask, "What about the other jobs?"

"This pays more than my other jobs put together," Quanda said, her words bubbling out like champagne. "I mean, it's amazing, but it's a long way to work."

Quanda nodded and sat down, grabbing Uneze's hands. "The place has staff housing. So, we could live up there."

"What about me? I don't work there; can I live there?"

"I need to sort out the details. I have an interview this weekend when we go up there. Nolan suggested that if I can't have you with me in staff housing, we move in with him. I told him I'd think about it."

Uneze let out a long sigh. He wanted to scream at his mum to take the job and move in with Nolan. This weekend, the life change they'd come to love could become a full-time dream, and he didn't want his mum's pride and need to provide for herself to get in the way. Instead of screaming, he just said, "Let's see what they say at the interview. I'd like to live with Nolan, or at least stay at the complex."

"Yes, let's see what happens."

19 - UNEZE

Two weeks later, Uneze and his mother moved into the staff accommodation at Nolan's complex. Uneze tossed and turned at night. The ceaseless noise of staff coming and going, the shared showers, the cramped spaces—each small annoyance felt like a weight, suffocating him. And yet, there was a burning need to survive it, a thrill for the life he'd imagined beyond these walls. The worn, faded walls of his tiny dorm room felt like a cage, and the prospect of leaving it behind was intoxicating.

Memories of his aunt's warm, friendly morning greetings echoed in his mind, reminding him of the family ties that linked him to the past. They reminded him that he didn't belong in the flashy, modern world in which he was playing make-believe.

Each morning, Uneze stepped out of the dorm and into the sun-drenched parking lot near Nolan's sleek car. Quanda shifted uncomfortably in the passenger seat, her fingers nervously playing with the hem of her shirt. The lavish surroundings of the condo felt stifling, a cage that hid the judgment lurking just outside. She could almost hear the staff talking about them: assumptions about her relationship with Nolan, the unspoken doubts that tainted their love with a dark cloud of skepticism. Each penetrating stare felt like an unwelcome spotlight, forcing her to confront the painful reality that, in the eyes of others, their love story was tainted by the colour of their skin.

One morning, while Nolan waited for his driver, Uneze turned to his mum. "I just don't get why we don't move in with Nolan. He wants us to, and it has to be better than the dorm."

Quanda, clearly annoyed, replied, "No. I don't want to be reliant on a man. What we have now could be taken away from us in the blink of an eye."

"How?" Uneze asked.

"With just one fight, he could kick us out. He could fall for another woman, he could get another job, or he could move back to America."

"He loves it here," Uneze said.

"I know, but his year is almost up, and if the charity moves him, we're back to slumming it. If we stay here in the dorm, even if Nolan goes, we still have my job and a place to stay."

"They won't send him away, will they?" Uneze asked.

"Who knows? I don't want you to get too comfortable here. Life can change in an instant, and we could be back home before we even know it. People like us have to be careful. Just one wrong move and we're back where we came from."

Uneze looked at Quanda, wide-eyed and scared. "I don't want to go back."

"So, keep up your obsession with watching American television and reading Nolan's books. You're at the top of your class, and that alone will get you, well, us, out of here on our own, without a man. You are my ticket out of here, boy."

Six months into their new living arrangement in the dorm, Nolan's stern face, usually brimming with warmth, held a look of fear. His focus flitted between Quanda and Uneze, his words heavy with unspoken emotions. "This is a happy day, but also a sad one," Nolan said, looking first at Quanda, then at Uneze.

"Why sad?" Uneze asked.

Nolan let out a huff and took a seat, gesturing for the others to do the same. "Because my year is up. I've decided to move to Cameroon. I've got a job there."

20 - UNEZE

Uneze's heart plummeted, and an unsettling flutter twisted in his stomach. His brows contorted as confusion clouded his wide eyes. "What? When?" he stammered, his voice barely above a whisper.

Nolan settled into a chair, his news hanging in the air like a storm cloud. "In three weeks, a new teacher will replace me," he said, his words steady but heavy. "I've got a permanent position at a private international school—better pay, you know? I can't turn it down."

Uneze inhaled sharply. "So that's it. You're leaving?" The words felt like a lead brick dropping into the pit of his stomach.

"Yes," Nolan said. "But I've read the fine print—my family can come with me."

Uneze blinked, glaring at Nolan. "You don't have a family."

"You are my family," Nolan replied, his voice tender. "Both of you. And I had an idea, though I'm not sure how you'll feel about it." He paused, the silence stretching like a taut string, making Uneze fidget with anticipation. "I was thinking we should get married."

"Married?" Quanda's voice boomed.

Nolan grabbed her hand. "Yes. We're in love, and I don't want to leave you behind. I would've proposed eventually."

"Yes," Uneze said, cutting through the tension, his eyes sparkling with excitement.

Nolan nodded, grinning. "Actually, it's your mother who needs to say yes, but I'm glad you're excited."

Quanda's brow distorted as she processed the idea. "So we'd leave here and move to Cameroon?"

"Yes, but we'd be a family. There, people won't look at you the way they do here. They won't judge you."

"It's okay," Quanda replied quietly, a flicker of understanding in her eyes. "I know how they look at me."

Nolan leant closer, his expression earnest. "It'd be a fresh start. Uneze would get the best education at that school, too."

Quanda met Uneze's gaze, the unspoken connection between them thrumming with uncontainable hope. Uneze's eyes sparkled like stars in the night sky; Quanda could feel his longing without a word.

"Okay, so yes. I accept," Quanda finally said, her voice steady, resolve blooming within her. "Let's get married."

"And move to Cameroon?" Nolan asked, his grin widening.

"Yes, of course," Quanda confirmed.

21 - UNEZE

The wedding was a modest affair, with white-covered chairs hastily arranged in the garden of the residence. Quanda's slim hands clutched a bouquet of wildflowers, her wide eyes darting between the smiling faces of close family and two of Nolan's colleagues, who stood awkwardly at the fringes, yet welcomed her with warm smiles.

Packing tape crisscrossed the cardboard, while maps of Cameroon sprawled across the coffee table, dotted with circles marking potential stops for their journey. The family piled into their sturdy SUV, the engine humming to life as they took one last look at their old home. With the horizon beckoning, they set off on their overland journey towards their new life.

Nolan, despite the demands of his job, carved out time to share in Uneze's schooling and studies. Their spacious living room filled with joy as they played games and told stories each day. Uneze thrived at the prestigious school, his confidence blossoming alongside his fluency in multiple languages, navigating growing up with classmates from diverse backgrounds.

Introduced as Nolan's wife, Quanda felt a transformation within her and a sense of acceptance from the community. No longer an outsider, she was invited to gatherings filled with laughter, music, and the rich flavours of local cuisine, forging bonds and friendships that warmed her heart.

One day, on a drive to a school event, Quanda's interest remained fixed outside, her brow tight as she watched the world unfold—mothers balancing baskets, the sun shimmering off their sweat-dampened brows.

"Why so sad?" Uneze asked.

"I'm not sad," she replied softly, her words barely rising above the bustling sounds. "It's just... strange. We've built this whole new life, and you have so many more opportunities ahead of you. But look at them." She gestured toward the crowd, her heart heavy with memories. "They're just like us back home in Lagos, struggling day by day. I don't want to forget what that felt like. Remembering keeps me grounded; it makes me appreciate what we have."

"I want to forget it all. This is so much better," Uneze shot back, his youthful impatience bubbling over.

"I know, and I'm glad to be Nolan's wife. I'm treated with respect here. Money talks; education is power in his world," she said, a hint of pride mingling with her sorrow.

Uneze leant forward, the firelight dancing in his eyes, igniting a spark of resolve. "It's our world now, not just his," he insisted, his voice steady despite the uncertainty that lingered in the air. "When I finish school, I'm going to do something big."

She raised an eyebrow, amused, and asked, "How big?"

He shrugged, a grin breaking through the seriousness. "I don't know yet."

"Do you at least know where?"

"America," he blurted, his excitement growing. "Nolan is taking us there for Christmas, and I'll figure out where I want to stay for the rest of my life."

Quanda chuckled, shaking her head. "You do know we're just going for two weeks, not forever, right?" His smile widened, a glimmer of defiance in his eyes.

"We'll see."

22 - UNEZE

Quanda and Uneze stood in their living room, surrounded by an array of zesty fabrics and carefully folded clothes. The air buzzed with excitement and anxiety as they zipped up their overstuffed suitcases, the sound echoing their racing hearts.

"You don't need all that stuff, guys," Nolan laughed. "We're going to America, not the end of the world. They have clothes there—different clothes for the cold weather. We can go shopping and get you everything you need. It's snowing right now."

"Snowing. Oh my gosh. I've never seen snow," Uneze said.

"You'll never have been so cold," Nolan laughed. "My sister is bringing us some coats to the airport. Now, are you ready for this? It's going to be amazing."

As the plane took off, they exchanged nervous glances, their breaths quick and shallow, each pulse of the fear of the unknown tightening the grip of their hands. The thought of soaring above the clouds, leaving behind the familiar landscapes of Cameroon for the vast unknown of America, sent shivers down their spines as the world below shrank away to be replaced by an expanse of sky.

Quanda and Uneze clasped hands tightly, their knuckles white as the plane ascended into the clouds, the patchwork of fields and concrete below shrinking into a distant memory. A grin spread across Uneze's face; this was it—his dream of America was within reach.

Eighteen hours stood between him and the land he envisioned making his own. As the plane touched down, Uneze's senses were bombarded by the enormity of it all. The shops towered like giants, their neon signs beckoning into buildings he didn't even know the names of. The air buzzed with a symphony of sounds—laughter, distant sirens, and the clanging of a nearby streetcar. Uneze brushed his fingers against the smooth glass of a towering skyscraper, marvelling at its height, then turned and watched excitedly as a street vendor served up steaming hot dogs and pretzels. His stomach rumbled in hunger.

He chuckled at the luxurious fur-lined boots and jacket Nolan had provided, their snug embrace a strange comfort in the unfamiliar brisk air.

Quanda walked with a stern face, her knuckles pale against the rough canvas of her bag, clutching it tightly as if it were a lifeline amid the chaotic melting pot of cultures. Each new scent and sound made her scowl, but she held it in, smiling as they ventured deeper into the heart of the city.

To Uneze, each new sight—a historic brick building, a mural, the scent of the local bakery—felt like an invitation into a world they had only ever seen in pictures. In that moment, they weren't just in Boston; Uneze felt he was in his new life.

Nolan's family greeted them with smiles and pleasantries that felt almost foreign, lacking the warmth and familiarity that enveloped them back home. On a morning walk with Uneze, while he grinned, almost skipping as he moved, Quanda felt relief not to have to pretend just to keep Nolan happy.

The bustling streets of Boston were a whirlwind of movement with people rushing in every direction with never a moment to spare. It was a wild contrast to the life she had known back in Africa where everyone had time for a morning greeting or a quick chat. She recalled the warmth of her tiny kitchen, the tasty spices flying in the air, and the joy of cooking together. Here, people barely glanced at the food they consumed, their faces buried in screens as they gobbled up bland, pre-packaged meals. Even the street vendors offered nothing more than cardboard-like snacks that left her yearning for the rich flavours of home. Disappointment settled heavily in her chest; in this fast-paced world, her love for cooking felt like a forgotten art, overshadowed by convenience and monotony.

The chill in the air nipped at Quanda's cheeks, turning them a rosy hue, while her layers of clothing felt like a suffocating embrace rather than a protective shield. "Do you really like it here?" she asked her son, her voice barely rising above the blend of honking cars and distant chatter.

Uneze, standing beside her, glanced up with uncertainty in his eyes. "Yeah, I mean, it's strange and cold, and everyone is in a hurry," he replied, gesturing broadly to the towering skyscrapers that seemed to scrape the grey sky. "But this is the new world. This is what everyone dreams of."

Quanda shook her head, scepticism heavy on her shoulders. "To live in this freezing cold city?" She wrapped her arms tighter around herself, as if trying to conjure warmth from the air.

Uneze shrugged, a hint of a smile playing on his lips. "No, Mum, to live in America. They have everything you could ever dream of."

Quanda lifted an eyebrow, her interest drifting to a nearby food stall where the pungent stench of Indian spices cut through the cold. "Apart from warm weather and tasty food," she replied dryly.

Uneze chuckled, the sound brightening the greyness around them. "Mum, just buy some spices and sprinkle it on your food."

Quanda let out a small laugh, but it faded quickly, replaced by a thoughtful frown. "And the warmth. Can you make it magically hot and sunny? All these clothes are suffocating me," she added, glancing down at the thick layers that felt more like a burden than a comfort.

"But they look good," Uneze offered, eyeing her outfit appreciatively. "What are we going to do when we get home? All of this is just a waste of money. The money we're spending here could feed a family for a year back home." Her voice grew strained, the tension in her shoulders evident as she stared into the crowd.

Uneze sighed, his youthful optimism clashing with her pragmatism. "Mum, just try and enjoy it. We've only got another couple of weeks, then we're going home."

Quanda shook her head again, her glare narrowing as she spotted Nolan in the distance, laughing heartily with a group of friends. "Even Nolan is different here."

Uneze's expression softened. "Of course he is. He hasn't seen his family in years; he's catching up. You can't expect him to be our tour guide all the time."

"No, it's not like that." Quanda's voice dropped, the vulnerability seeping through her words. "I feel like I did in the beginning, like everyone is looking down on us. They take one glance and think we're in it for the money."

"Mum, it's all in your head. There are loads of African people here," Uneze insisted, frustration creeping into his tone.

Quanda shook her head vehemently. "No, they are African Americans; we are Africans. We are out of place here." Her eyes held a mixture of determination and sadness. "We aren't fooling anyone, and you need to stop thinking you are like them."

23 - UNEZE

Once he grew tired of Boston, Uneze's heart yearned for the raw energy of New York, the city he believed held dreams dancing in its streets. That dream had helped him through restless nights and long days.

Nolan leant casually against the window, his eyes scanning the bustling streets below. "This place isn't like Boston," he muttered, shaking his head as he watched a group of tourists laugh and pose for selfies. "NYC is teeming with tourists, and every one of them is a target."

Uneze's curiosity flared. "What do you mean?"

Nolan gestured to a street vendor below, where a flashy backpack hung precariously from a passerby's shoulder. Just a few feet away, a pair of sharp eyes tracked the bag like a predator stalking prey. "Tourists come here with cameras, phones, cash—bags filled with expensive stuff. It's a thief's paradise. They'll do anything to get it. Trust me, they don't stop at snatching."

Uneze frowned, his expression tinged with disbelief. "But everyone here's rich. Why would they need to steal?"

Nolan gave a wry chuckle, shaking his head. "You've got a lot to learn, kid. This country's just like Lagos—only louder and without the power cuts. There's the rich, sure, but there's also the poor, struggling to get by. Some folks here are worse off than in Nigeria. And just like anywhere else, desperation can make people do crazy things."

Uneze's attention drifted longingly to the streets below. The gleaming skyscrapers stretched into the sky like ladders to a better life, and the thrumming crowds seemed to hum with possibilities. "Poor people. here?" he asked, his voice soft with a mix of awe and yearning.

"I know it looks bright and shiny out there, but you're not stepping a foot outside without me. Understood?" Nolan's voice was firm, his easy smile replaced with a seriousness that left no room for argument. "Tomorrow morning, I'll be tied up handling your citizenship papers. But I promise, we'll go out in the afternoon."

Uneze's shoulders sagged, the fire in his chest threatening to sputter out. "But it's New York. I didn't come all this way to stay inside."

Nolan's expression softened, but only slightly. "Look, I get it. You want to see everything, taste the city, feel its pulse. But it's not safe. Not yet. You can watch from the window for now. Besides," he added, glancing meaningfully at Uneze, "your mom's not feeling great. Do me a favour and promise you'll stay inside, alright?"

Uneze clenched his fists, his jaw tightening as he struggled to swallow the lump of frustration rising in his throat. His focus darted back to the window, where the city called to him with a siren's song. Staying inside felt like being caged, with freedom just out of reach.

"I promise," he said reluctantly, though his stare remained fixed on the streets below. In that moment, the skyscrapers didn't just look like ladders to a better life—they looked like prison bars keeping him from it.

24 - UNEZE

As dawn broke, Uneze tossed and turned, unable to escape the feeling of confinement. He grabbed some dollar bills from near the door and slipped out of their rented apartment, his bare feet brushing against the cool marble floor. He offered a cheerful smile to the doorman, who stood alert like a sentinel as Uneze slid on his socks and boots. "Young boy, do you need me to call a taxi for you?" the doorman asked.

"No, thanks. I'm just going for a walk," Uneze replied, injecting his voice with confidence, though his nerves churned.

"It's dark outside," the doorman noted, glancing at the streets stretching into the distance beyond the lobby doors.

"I'll be fine. I just want to take some photos of all the lights in Times Square. I'll be back soon," Uneze reassured him.

Stepping onto the sidewalk, Uneze's eyes widened at the sight before him. The honking of taxis and lively chatter of pedestrians were everywhere. He had traded the warm, earthen tones of his homeland for the energetic rhythm of New York City. A grin covered his entire face as he took in the world around him.

Within moments, the first light of dawn began to glow on the horizon. The lively square he had glimpsed from his window now felt farther than he had imagined. Turning left, then right, he soon found himself disorientated. With a neatly folded map and a nervous smile, he approached a group of tourists, their cameras bouncing gently against their chests like accessories of adventure.

"Excuse me, where is Times Square?" he asked.

They gestured animatedly, and Uneze began weaving his way through the streets. He marvelled at the towering billboards overhead, each one alive with vivid colours and advertisements that seemed to leap from a waking dream.

As the scent of freshly baked bread reached him, Uneze paused at a street vendor. He handed over a few dollars and ordered an everything bagel. With eager hands, he unwrapped the golden treat, its glossy surface making his mouth water. The first bite filled his mouth with a satisfying chew, the rich cream cheese spreading silkily into every bite. He savoured the last of it, licking a smear of cheese from his lips before tossing the wrapper into a nearby bin.

Continuing his exploration, Uneze wandered through Manhattan's iconic streets. He stopped to take in the entrance of the Empire State Building, its spire piercing the sky, before moving on to discover more of the city. Each turn revealed new sights—spotted the Brooklyn Bridge from a distance, admired the vibrancy of Soho, and eventually arrived at Washington Square Garden.

When he reached a hotdog stand, Uneze ordered one, lifting the warm bun to his mouth as the scent of grilled meat made his stomach growl. The tang of mustard and crisp onions exploded with each bite. For a moment, he stood still, soaking in the lively voices, and the antics of street performers. A smile stretched across his face as he finished his hotdog and continued walking, his steps leading him toward the tranquillity of Central Park.

There, he watched children laughing as they chased after pigeons, while couples wandered arm in arm beneath the canopy of trees. Each step felt heavier than the last, his shoes pinching tightly with every stride as he walked through the bustling crowds. The city's energy buzzed in his ears, but his attention was consumed by the sharp sting in his soles and the dull ache spreading through his legs. He paused at a corner, leaning heavily against a lamppost, his breath ragged as his eyes drifted upward to the skyscrapers towering above like sentinels. After a moment's reprieve, he pushed himself back into the throng, his jaw clenched as he heded in the direction the assumed to be his accommodation despite the throbbing pain urging him to stop.

Overwhelmed by the lack of energy, he collapsed onto the soft grass and let his heavy eyelids close. When he awoke, darkness covered the park, distorting the pathways he had crossed earlier into an unfamiliar labyrinth. Every faint rustle of leaves sent a shiver skittering down his spine. The laughter of children and the warm presence of couples had vanished, replaced by an eerie quiet. The occasional hoot of an owl echoed nearby, and Uneze flinched at every sound, his eyes darting toward the unseen. The landmarks he'd relied on earlier were now shrouded in black, swallowed by the encroaching night.

A growing unease churned in his stomach as his gaze swept the darkness, searching for any sign of life. Just as panic began to take root, the stillness was broken by a sudden flurry of footsteps behind him. Figures emerged from the shadows, their movements fluid and predatory.

Before he could react, a violent yank on his bag sent him sprawling to the ground. The impact jarred his senses, and as he tried to right himself, the first strike landed—a brutal blow that shot agony through his side. A crushing kick to his back left him breathless, the air forced from his lungs in a painful gasp. He stumbled forward, his hands scraping against the rough pavement, but the assault didn't stop. Each strike hit like a thunderclap, reverberating through his battered body as he curled inward, desperate for the torment to end.

The voices receded into the distance, their laughter dissipating into the cold night air. Silence fell, broken only by Uneze's laboured breathing. His body ached in ways he hadn't thought possible, the pain searing with each shallow breath. Staggering to his feet, his heart hammered in his chest, urging him to flee, but his vision blurred, and the world went black.

25 - UNEZE

The sharp, clinical scent of antiseptic drifted through the air as Uneze lay propped up in a sea of starched white sheets. The constant beeping of machines punctuated the stillness. Sunlight streamed through the window, illuminating the bruised skin on his arms—each mark a reminder of the ordeal he couldn't quite grasp. "Where am I?" Uneze whispered, his voice raspy and strained.

"In the hospital," his mother replied, her eyes shimmering with concern, her grip tightening around his hand.

"Why?"

"You were attacked and mugged in Central Park. Don't you remember?" Nolan explained.

Uneze shook his head slowly, the movement sending a jolt of pain through his chest. "No," he murmured as he winced at the throbbing ache.

"Well, you were," Nolan pressed on. "Some tourists found you and called 9-1-1." Uneze's eyes wandered to the window, where the world outside continued to spin as he tried to piece together tiny fragments of memory. "You'll be fine, but you'll be here for a couple of days, so get used to it," Nolan continued, attempting to infuse a sense of normality into the sterile environment.

"Here, in bed?" Uneze asked.

"I brought you a new phone so you can play your games and watch your YouTube videos. For now, this is your new home."

Uneze glanced at the phone resting on the bedside table, its screen flickering to life, and nodded thank you.

As he lay in the narrow bed, the walls began to feel like a cage, and with every visit from the nurses, Uneze's heart twisted further with despair. Images of Cameroon flooded his mind—the busy, dusty streets, the laughter of friends, the warmth of the sun on his skin—each memory a distant echo magnifying his hatred for the country that had turned so cruel in an instant.

In the waiting area, Nolan paced, the worry heavy on his shoulders. The furious anger he had felt over Uneze's disappearance had given way to a gnawing anxiety, his thoughts consumed by the sight of his stepson, damaged and silent in that hospital bed.

Nolan used the time alone to fumble through paperwork to process the citizenship request for Uneze and Quanda. "I'll handle the paperwork. Once it's done, we'll decide what to do next."

Uneze's eyes darted toward the window, where the world outside felt both inviting and terrifying. "Do I have to have American citizenship? I'm Nigerian," he whispered, his voice barely escaping the confines of his fear.

Nolan leant closer, his tone gentle yet firm. "You never have to set foot in America again," he reassured, "but you have no idea how far a US passport will take you. It's about the doors it'll open. If you want to stay in Africa forever, that's your choice, but that passport is the key to a new life."

Quanda's eyes flickered over her son's face, catching the slight quiver of his lip and the wide, uncertain eyes that mirrored her own turmoil. "We're going home."

"Yeah, we'll be back at the apartment in a few days when the boy is released."

"No," she cut him off, her resolve hardening. "Home to Cameroon, or even Nigeria. This place isn't for us."

Nolan's shoulders slumped, doubt creeping into his expression. "I know you are scared, but America is a great country."

Quanda's stare hardened as she leant closer, her voice low but fierce. "You stay here. We are going home. Please, book us a flight to Nigeria."

"Nigeria?" Uneze's eyes blinked rapidly, disbelief washing over him.

"Yes," Quanda pressed, her voice resolute. "We've been pretending to live this life. It's not ours. We are going back to Nigeria, to Lagos. My sister will look after us. Look what America has done to you. It's dangerous, and I don't want any associations with it."

"No. I won't allow it. We are a family," Nolan interjected defiantly.

Quanda shrugged, unyielding. "Okay. Don't allow it then. Somehow, I'll get us back home."

"Uneze?" Nolan asked.

"I'm with Mum on this one. I hate it here. I don't want to stay. I want to go back home and never leave Africa again."

.

26 - UNEZE

Quanda stared at the glowing screen, then glanced back at Nolan's card as Uneze tapped away, booking flights back home to Nigeria. The digital confirmation flashed before her eyes, a stark reminder of choices made in haste.

Uneze crossed his arms, frustration knitting his brows together. "What about our things? They're all in Cameroon."

"They are just things," Quanda replied, her tone clipped. "We don't need any of that in Nigeria. Nolan paid for it all; he can keep it."

"Mum, no. I like it in Cameroon. My friends, my school," Uneze said in despair. "I'm not going back to that local school."

Quanda's expression softened for a fleeting moment, but she remained firm. "We'll find a solution. Don't worry. Just be grateful that Nolan helped Aunty buy a bigger place. There's plenty of room for us."

The following day, the cab lurched forward, merging into the thrumming pulse of the city, honking horns weaving through bustling pedestrians and towering skyscrapers. Quanda sat stiffly beside Nolan, her eyes fixed on the blurred scenery outside, her fingers flicking her passport.

"Please, you don't have to do this," Nolan implored with pleading eyes. "Just fly to Cameroon and wait for me there. Once I finish your citizenship applications, I'll join you," he continued, his hope piercing through the tension like sunlight through clouds.

Quanda remained silent; her jaw clenched tight. "No," she snapped, her tone sharp as glass. "My mind is made up. We should have never left Nigeria. My family is there. In Cameroon, I'm just a glorified housekeeper, looking after you and being paraded around. Your friends are polite enough, but they don't accept us as a couple."

"Don't be ridiculous," Nolan shot back, disbelief etched across his face.

Quanda's eyes burned with fury, her words sharp and unyielding. "I didn't realise it until we came here," she said, her voice trembling with restrained anger. "The way your family spoke to us, treating us like we were nothing more than parasites clinging to you because of your nationality." Her voice rose, carrying the weight of her indignation. "Well, this ends now. I want nothing more to do with you or them."

The silence that followed was as heavy as a stone wall. Nolan's shoulders dropped as he exhaled deeply. "What about Uneze? He's my son. I adopted him."

Quanda's expression turned colder, her voice cutting through the air like broken glass. "While you're sorting out that paperwork, figure out how to unadopt him," she snapped, her tone leaving no room for compromise.

Uneze, holding his headphones tightly, slipped them on in an attempt to shut out the tension. Even so, the stress of the moment pressed down on him as the taxi finally pulled up to the airport.

At the terminal, Nolan crouched down, placing his hands gently on Uneze's shoulders. He kissed him on the forehead, his hands trembling as he pulled away. "Will we ever see him again?" Uneze asked quietly, his voice quivering.

"I doubt it," Quanda replied flatly, her words like a door slamming shut.

"But why? He's the closest thing I've ever had to a dad," Uneze pleaded, his voice breaking.

Quanda's face hardened, her frustration breaking through. "And where did that get us?" she snapped. "You were left lying in a park, beaten and alone."

"That wasn't his fault." Uneze argued, his voice rising. "I didn't listen to him. He told me to stay inside, and I didn't."

"It doesn't matter," Quanda said firmly, cutting him off. "We're going back to Nigeria. That's where we belong, and I'm not leaving again."

Uneze looked down, his voice barely audible. "But everyone we know dreams of leaving. Why are we going back when others would give anything to be anywhere but Nigeria? It doesn't make sense."

Quanda paused, her shoulders sagging under a weight Uneze couldn't see. "Dreams can break," she said, her voice low but resolute. "Mine did. I don't want to discuss this anymore. Get some rest. We'll be boarding soon."

Uneze didn't respond. He turned away, his headphones back over his ears, letting the quiet settle between them as he slumped into his seat.

27 - PERI

Three years had slipped by, and Peri found herself standing, week after week, in front of a crowd of tourists, her voice smooth and confident as she guided them through the ancient ruins of Athens, the streets of Rome, the waterways of Amterdam, and other places. Gone were the anxious whispers of Guy's criticisms; now, her days were filled with laughter, the thrill of discovery, travel, and the stress of living out of a suitcase.

She and Lisa operated like a well-oiled machine, navigating the flatmate situation with the precision of seasoned pros. Their shared home was filled with a patchwork of postcards from far-flung destinations. As they passed like ships in the night, they left behind colourful mementos; the worst fridge magnets imaginable clung to the fridge, and the tackiest, most tasteless souvenirs filled an empty bookshelf.

Peri sprawled on her sofa, the dim light glinting off the chilled glass of gin in her hand. She swirled the liquid, its coolness a fleeting comfort against the haze of jet lag that clung to her like a heavy blanket. The sound of keys rattling at the door jolted her upright. Her fingers wrapped around the knife hidden in the drawer by the sofa, the cold metal grounding her in the moment, ready for whatever intruder might emerge.

"Peri. It's me; I'm home." Lisa's voice sliced through the tension, and relief washed over Peri as she dropped the knife onto the cushion with a soft thud.

"You scared me," she said, laughter bubbling up despite the shock.

"Yeah, well, I was in Nepal, and we got evacuated due to a monsoon, so I'm back a week early." Lisa shrugged, a sheepish grin breaking across her face as she flung her bag onto the floor.

"Gin lag?" Peri quipped, her eyes sparkling. She hopped into the kitchen, her hands already reaching for the ingredients for Lisa's favourite cocktail.

"Of course. Let me just dump this stuff," Lisa called over her shoulder, her footsteps bounding up the stairs. Moments later, Lisa dashed back down, her hands cupped tightly around something, excitement dancing in her eyes.

"What did you get me? It can't be worse than that flashing gondola." Peri laughed.

"Actually, no, this time. I only had a chance to pick up something from the souvenir shop at the airport," Lisa said, a playful smirk on her lips.

"Yes," Peri cheered, executing a victorious fist bump. "That puts me on top of the lousy gift chart." She grabbed a pen and marked a tick on the makeshift scoreboard stuck to the front of the oven, an absurd trophy of their friendship.

As Lisa unveiled the gift, crinkled paper fell away to reveal a snow globe, its tiny mountain range capped with white, a miniature Everest trapped in glass. Peri chuckled, holding it up to the light. "Two points for this one; it's actually not a bad gift."

"And the fridge magnet," Lisa added, digging through a chaotic array of magnets on the refrigerator door, their collection spilling over the edges. "It's official; we need a bigger fridge."

"Or a new one, just for gin." Peri placed the snow globe on the shelf, nestled among their quirky assortment of souvenirs—the tackier, the better. This was their tradition: the most ridiculous gifts scored points, and at the year's end, the one with the highest tally treated the other to dinner, a whimsical celebration of their friendship.

"Update, please. Why are you so dressed up for a night on the sofa?" Lisa asked.

Peri shrugged and said, "Bad Tinder date. I know it's wrong to go on a date when my brain is in a different time zone, but god, he was boring. How's that guy? What's his name?"

"Bryce? Ah, the usual. It started off well. The whole 'I'm-going-away-for-a-month' thing kept him interested, then I got bored of the wait and started chatting to a guy in Nepal instead."

"Decent?"

"I don't know; he was a hiker from Denmark. We never met, though, you know, with all the monsoon mess going on. He was fun to chat with, though, but hey, we know it's a jungle out there in this dating world with our jobs."

"Fun though," Peri said.

"Way too much hard work. They always end up with one of us ghosting the other. I mean, I often wonder why we bother."

"Because we aren't nuns," Peri chuckled. "The day we let it bother us, it's time to hang up our Samsonites for good."

"Do you ever think about giving it up and settling down?" Lisa asked.

"No. Firstly, I wouldn't know where to settle, and secondly, with the tips we make, why would we go back to a normal job?" Peri asked.

"I hear ya. But I keep dreaming about Greece, or anywhere that means I'm not living out of a suitcase. I'm sort of heading towards making that my forever home," Lisa said.

"Greece or Greek men? It's definitely not for Greek wine or gin."

"Greek food," Lisa giggled.

"Are you serious about this?"

"I'm just thinking about it. But I didn't tell you this, not because it's a secret, but because I wasn't sure if I'd get it. I've applied for a job in the head office; it's just temporary. I told them I had family issues and needed to stay at home for a few months."

"Here, in the UK?" Peri asked, amazed.

"Yep, I've got a couple of tours left, and then I'm going to be on the emergency desk in head office. Dealing with all the guides that call in with problems," Lisa explained.

"Wow, that's news," Peri said as she raised her glass and clinked Lisa's glass.

"It's just temporary while I decide what to do next or how to move to Greece. Don't you ever get tired of the moving around?"

"Yep, but there are some tours I want to do first. There is no way I'm giving this up until I get to do either Costa Rica, the big African safari, or Route 66."

"Oh, so you're never giving up then? Those tours are only for the Dinahs of the world. They are the tours they give you when you threaten to resign, and they keep you at the company with the promise of those."

"I guess I'm not giving up yet. Where are you going next?" Peri asked.

"Not sure. I guess I'm waiting for the new schedule, which is due," Lisa said, looking at her phone to check the date. "Tomorrow, unless they've changed it."

"I've got a short Croatia, then back-to-back Asia," Peri said.

"Really? I thought they changed that," Lisa replied.

"Get you, in the know already. Now you're in the head office, you need to work your magic and get me on one of those tours I mentioned."

"Hold this," Lisa said. She handed over her drink and reached for her laptop.

Lisa let her fingers twitch nervously over the sleek surface of her laptop. The fluorescent light flickered softly above as she clicked open the email from head office. She skimmed the lines, her breath hitching as she caught sight of her name bolded in the text. A knot tightened in her stomach as she let her focus drift down the screen, landing abruptly on Peri's name, which seemed to leap out at her like a warning.

Peri's heart raced as she stared at the glowing screen, the urgent email from head office. "Okay, so what's the plan?" she asked, her voice trembling.

With a sigh that hinted at reluctance, Lisa leant back as her hand flew up to her lips. "I'm heading to head office the day after tomorrow. They need me to start immediately," she said, her tone flat, as if the very air had been sucked from the room.

"No way, so soon?" Peri blinked, confusion almost knitting her brows together. "And me...?"

Lisa's lips curved into a huge smile. "You're off on the Big African Safari."

"Wait, what? No way." Peri gasped, her fingers instinctively curling around the laptop as if it might slip away. "You're kidding me."

"Nope. Not quite sure how or why, but it's your dream tour." Lisa's eyes sparkled as she carried on reading. "In four days."

Peri felt a surge of electricity course through her, her heart leaping as the world around her began to fade into the background. "Why me? I've never even set foot in Africa."

"Well, rather you than me. Just remember—it's a camping tour."

"I know." Peri beamed.

"Seriously, sleeping in a tent? What's the appeal?" Lisa scoffed, rolling her eyes with a teasing grin.

"Think of the Big Five, Baobab trees, and Victoria Falls." Peri's voice rose with each word, her excitement bubbling over.

Lisa shrugged, a lively smirk on her face. "I guess it's your dream. I'd take tiny trattorias on the beach and Santorini sunsets any day."

"Can you just be happy for me?" Peri pleaded.

"Can I at least be worried about you?" Lisa chuckled, shaking her head as if trying to dispel the thought. "Come on, you're terrified of my sister's cat. How will you handle a lion?"

"I doubt they'll be vying for my lap like that cat does," Peri chuckled.

"Have you seen those YouTube videos where lions claw at tents while people sleep?"

Peri's felt herself bounce around on her seat; the thrill of possibility was too intoxicating to resist. "Stop it. I'm so excited. I can't believe I'm actually going on safari."

"You're working, not vacationing," Lisa reminded her, but the playful twinkle in her eye betrayed her own excitement.

"Yeah, that's what I meant. Oh crap, I need to start researching."

"And shopping—abandon the heels and short skirts," Lisa added, waving her hand as if shooing away the very thought.

"Okay, so, wanna come with me tomorrow?" Peri bounced in her seat, her energy infectious.

"Hells yes," Lisa agreed.

28 - PERI

The clock ticked insistently, its hands creeping toward four a.m. Peri's mind raced, a whirlwind of thoughts spinning like leaves caught in a gust of wind. With a sigh, she finally threw back the covers, feeling the chill of the floor beneath her feet. She pottered around the house until Lisa finally emerged.

Peri pulled out her laptop and reopened the travel website that had kept her up all night. A list of clothing items stared back at her, each line a reminder of the packed days ahead—and the challenge of finding everything.

She scribbled furiously, her pen scratching against the paper as she jotted down long sleeves for the evening chill, hiking boots for the gorillas.

When Lisa climbed into the car, still half-asleep, Peri thrust the crumpled list into her hands. "I've gone through everything. Long pants for evenings, shorts and bikinis for pool days, and oh God, the endless packing."

Lisa raised an eyebrow, her voice laced with playful sarcasm. "So, packing light is off the table? I remember my safari. I wasn't a guide yet—I was just on holiday with my sister. Every moment was like a scene from a horror movie—wild animals everywhere, and those men..."

Peri laughed. "Since when don't you like men?"

"It's not that," Lisa replied, rolling her eyes. "It's those men over there. They're charming, cute, and—let's be honest—sexy."

Peri smirked, teasing. "What's wrong with that?"

"Nothing, except they see us as a ticket out. Just a meal ticket for a better life."

Peri tipped her head, a frown creeping onto her face. "Isn't that a bit politically incorrect? A sweeping generalisation?"

"Maybe. But it's my truth. Some were subtle, making you feel like the queen of the world. Others? Not so much. They were bold—straightforward. They just came out and said it."

"They can't all be like that," Peri pointed out.

Lisa shook her head. "No, of course not. But back then—and it was probably ten years ago—they were fascinated by our white skin. And being two girls? We were like a magnet. They wouldn't leave us alone."

"I'll keep that in mind. Six weeks is a long time... who knows what could happen?" Laughter spilled from Peri's lips, mingling with the nervousness of her adventure. "And if anything terrible happens, you're in head office on the emergency desk," Peri joked.

"Just because I'm there, doesn't mean you can call me with your usual emergencies, like, 'What should I wear tonight for my date?'" Lisa laughed.

"I doubt I'll be dating in the African bush," Peri laughed. "It may be my most celibate tour ever."

Lisa smirked. "Now, seriously. Are you ready? Have you got everything on the list? Have you studied the trip notes?"

"Nope. I've never been less ready for anything in my life."

It was still dark, and Peri's fingers lingered over the last few items sprawled across her bed that wouldn't fit in her case, moving them back to her wardrobe. Slinging her hand luggage over her shoulder, she hoisted her two packed suitcases with a muffled grunt. The click of the lock echoed in the stillness of the empty house as Lisa slept.

Peri pressed her forehead against the cool window of her first-class seat, watching the clouds drift by like cotton candy. The vibrations of the plane faded into the background; she was kept awake by her thoughts bumping and jolting like the turbulence outside.

Her fingers played with the edges of her notes, crumpling the paper as she replayed the itinerary in her mind. She inhaled sharply, a flutter of doubt taking root. The thrill of guiding tourists across bustling cities was overshadowed by the creeping anxiety of entering a world she had never seen in person. She hadn't really had time to consider the reality. She was guiding a bunch of tourists over Africa, and she'd never even been there. She didn't know how to light a bonfire, or to put up a tent. She slouched back into her seat and muttered, "Oh God, they are going to hate me."

The excitement of the journey ahead clashed with the gnawing feeling that maybe—just maybe—she had taken on more than she could handle. She pressed her forehead against the cool window again, watching the earth shrink below her.

Several hours later, the landing jolted her back to reality, the plane thumping against the runway as if eager fly again.

29 - UNEZE

After several years of living in Nigeria, following his New York experience, Uneze counted down the days until he could leave and start his life far away from there. Quanda had been resolute, her voice firm as she reiterated their choice to stay put, to shun the modern world and remain with her family in Lagos.

On Uneze's eighteenth birthday, the mailman finally knocked on the door of their home, handing over a nondescript parcel cradled in his hands.

Uneze spotted the postmark, his heart racing with confusion. Who could it be from? He hurried inside, the breath of hope mingling with the warm air of their chaotic home. With trembling fingers, he tore open the package, revealing two passports nestled in plain brown wrapping—no note, no explanation—just the cold, official documentation staring back at him like ghosts of possibilities long buried.

He placed them on the tablecloth, the impact of the moment settling over him. His eyes darted between the passports and his mother, who stood rigid, arms crossed tightly over her chest, her silence loud in the room.

Uneze's voice broke through the quiet, laced with confusion and a rising disappointment. "Why didn't Nolan write a note? There isn't even a birthday card."

Quanda turned away, brushing a stray strand of hair from her face, her eyes flashing with anger. "He's done with us, as we are with him. He did us the honour of not divorcing me until these things came through. I bet he's already working on those papers right now." The sharpness of her words lingered in the air, bitter and raw.

"But, Mum..." Uneze began, his voice faltering. "I don't understand why you're so angry. You told him never to get in touch again."

Quanda's stare hardened, an impenetrable wall forming between them. "And look at us," she said, her voice tight, strained, but resolute. "We're okay on our own."

Uneze's shoulders slumped. "Only because he still pays for school and our bills."

"He owed us that," Quanda snapped. "And now that school's done, that's our last tie severed."

Uneze's heart ached, the fissures in their family dynamic deepening with each passing moment. "I miss him. I wish he was still in our lives. You never smile anymore; you are miserable."

"I'm at home. I'm good; I'm happy with my sister. This is my life and where I belong."

Two days later, Uneze stood at the head of the table, feeling the weight of his family's expectations pressing down on him. The room was still, the quiet almost suffocating, as he waited for everyone to join him.

Clearing his throat, he finally spoke, his voice unsteady. "I can't do this anymore."

His mother's eyes shot up, her brows knitting in concern, the sound of her spoon clattering against the porcelain revealing her unease. "What?"

"Pretend I've never seen more than this life," Uneze continued, his tone gaining strength. "I need to grow, to move on. I've graduated, and it's time for me to start my own life."

"Where?" The question hung in the air, his mother's shock visible.

"I don't know where I'll settle, but right now, I don't want to be here." The words spilled from his lips. "It feels like fate. The day the passport arrives is my eighteenth birthday."

"So, you're leaving me?" Quanda's voice barely registered, fear threading through her tone.

"No, I'm moving away for a while, to do what you've been pushing me to do since Dad died," Uneze said, his voice steadier now, though the impact of the words hung between them.

"Alright. I don't like it, but I accept it. Have you got a job lined up?" Quanda asked, the tension in her voice softening slightly.

"Do you remember Amani from school in Cameroon?" Uneze asked. "Well, he's in Tanzania now, and he said I should come up there and work with him."

"In Tanzania?" Quanda's jaw clenched, disbelief colouring her words. "That's the other side of Africa."

"I want to make a life change. It's time to do something new." Uneze's eyes swept the room over his family, a profound silence enveloping them, a shared understanding that life as they knew everything was about to change. "It's a risk," he continued, his voice firm. "But I'm not doing it without your blessing. I'm not disappearing off the face of the Earth. I'll be back."

30 - UNEZE

Uneze sank into the plane seat, gripping his well-worn bag as though it were a lifeline. He glanced at the creased flight ticket tucked inside his passport, the bold letters of 'Dar Es Salaam' standing out like a neon sign against the faded pages. This was it—the start of something new, uncharted.

When the plane landed, Uneze collected his luggage and slung his rucksack over his shoulder, the airport bustling with life around him. Stepping outside, he scanned the crowd, his heart leaping when he spotted a face he hadn't seen in years.

Nolan stood there, his tan deepened by the African sun, a wide grin spreading across his face. "Son!" Nolan called out, pulling him into a strong embrace. "I can't believe you're here."

Uneze chuckled nervously. "I wasn't sure if I'd come. But I missed you. When I got the ticket... I had to see what you were up to."

Nolan clapped him on the shoulder, his expression softening. "I missed you too, kid. You went quiet last year, and I was worried. I had to call the school to check on you."

Uneze laughed, the sound carrying a mix of guilt and amusement. "Mum found my fake profile, so that was the end of that. She was furious. Honestly, though, it's practically a rite of passage for Nigerians to have fake profiles. At least I wasn't claiming to be a prince."

Nolan burst out laughing, shaking his head. "Fair point. You've got to keep the family tradition alive somehow."

They made their way to Nolan's car, falling into an easy rhythm of conversation that felt both new and nostalgic.

"So," Uneze began, tossing his bag into the boot. "Why am I here? Not that I'm complaining."

Nolan's smile turned mischievous. "Well, you're eighteen now. You're free to travel, so I thought, why not? It was a gamble, but I had a hunch you'd say yes."

"Okay…" Uneze tilted his head. "But why here? What's the catch?"

Nolan let out a laugh as he started the engine. "No catch. Just a little career pivot. I've been miserable as a headmaster, so I quit. Decided to start something new here in Tanzania—a safari company."

Uneze blinked in surprise. "A safari company? That's… ambitious. Aren't there loads of those already?"

"Sure," Nolan replied, his enthusiasm undimmed. "But hear me out. Most of the tours around here are short—day trips, maybe a weekend if you're lucky. I want to create something bigger, something for high-end clients who want luxury but don't want to deal with the real Africa."

Uneze raised an eyebrow, the idea slowly sinking in. "You're serious about this?"

"Absolutely," Nolan said, his grin widening. "I can handle the American tourists, but I need someone I trust—someone who knows the culture, the languages, the ins and outs of the region. You're perfect. You speak English, French, and Swahili, right?"

"Yeah," Uneze said, scratching the back of his head. "But I'm not exactly a tour guide."

Nolan waved him off. "You don't need to be. I need your brains, kid. You've got a business studies diploma, and you're family. That's all I care about. Plus, we'll figure it out together. We'll be a team."

Uneze couldn't help but smile, the scepticism in his eyes giving way to curiosity. "Alright, but if we're doing this, we've got to make it stand out. What about making it eco-friendly?"

Nolan chuckled, the idea clearly amusing him. "Eco-friendly? With five-star hotels and private safaris? Doesn't exactly scream 'saving the planet.'"

Uneze let a sly grin form on his face. "That's the point. Americans love that kind of thing. They want to feel like they're saving the world while staying in luxury. We just need to spin it right."

Nolan laughed, shaking his head as he pulled out of the car park. "You're good at this already. Alright, eco-friendly safaris it is."

"No promises," Uneze said with a laugh. "But we're definitely getting you a khaki shirt and a big hat. You need to fit in with your kind."

Their laughter echoed in the car, the tension of their long separation melting away as they drove off into the Tanzanian evening, the beginnings of a new adventure ahead.

31 - UNEZE

It took about a year to get the first tour marketed and operational. As word spread about Nolan and Uneze's planet-friendly safari tours, more and more people began booking trips with 'Green Planet Safari.' The business grew rapidly, allowing Nolan to hire guides and open an office. They expanded their services to include educational programmes and community outreach initiatives as add-ons to the original tour. The affluent tourists, however, remained blissfully oblivious, snapping photos of wildlife and breathtaking landscapes from their air-conditioned bubble or luxury hotels.

Two years later, with the tours running every other week, Nolan was content with his position at home, organising sales. Despite thriving as the tour guide and manager, Uneze began to feel the itch to do something different.

To most of the tourists, Africa was a postcard—a curated paradise—but Uneze saw the gritty, buzzing reality that lay just beneath the surface. As he sat forward, the spark of an idea lit up his eyes. "Nolan, I don't know what you think of this, but I think we should set up a new branch of Green Planet Safaris. And I think I'm the right person for the job."

"Oh God," Nolan groaned, half-amused, "hit me with your idea before I finish this wine."

Uneze grabbed a tourist map from the nearby stand, unfolding it like a treasure trove of possibilities. His finger traced a route through regions he knew would offer more than the typical tourist experience—adventure and authenticity. Nolan watched him, seeing the same fire that had once motivated him to start his own tours. He raised an eyebrow. "Camping?"

"Actually, glamping," Uneze corrected with a grin.

"You know how many nice places are popping up all over the place? I've seen them on tour," Nolan remarked, leaning back as Uneze's enthusiasm was palpable. For a moment, the glamorous setting of the lounge faded. Uneze's passion was contagious.

"I'm talking about a real experience," Uneze continued. "Not just a 'stay in a luxury tent for a weekend' kind of thing, but something deeper. Something that connects people to the land, the people, the culture. What do you think?"

Nolan rubbed his chin, clearly considering it. "You know Africa. You've proved you know business. Alright, I'm in."

Uneze leant forward, excitement bubbling up. "But if it doesn't work out, can I have my old job back?"

Nolan's grin was sharp, but his eyes were warm. "Hell no. If you want to make it in the real world, you're on your own."

Uneze paused for a moment, uncertainty creeping in. "Really?"

"No, of course not. You're family. You'll always have a place here. But this? It's your show now." Nolan clapped him on the back, the playful tone of his voice belied by his firm words.

"Alright, I'll take that as a challenge. Let's see if I can get a tour up and running before Christmas."

"That's the spirit," Nolan said, grinning. "Don't let me down."

32 - UNEZE

Uneze poured everything into creating a truly authentic experience for his guests. He envisioned a camping tour where they would sleep under the stars, wake to the calls of exotic birds, and dine on traditional African cuisine prepared over an open fire. By the time he had found local guides, campsites, and excursions, it was time to start marketing the tour. He sat in the lobby of a campsite he hoped to use, the evening air buzzing with the distant sounds of birds settling for the night. Uneze could already picture his guests—wide-eyed and entranced—gathered around a crackling fire, sharing stories.

But tonight felt different. As he leant against the wooden post of the open-air clubhouse, the usual drone of tourists checking in faded into the background. A figure appeared in the dusty path behind him—a tall, pale-skinned man, his shirt clinging to his back with sweat. Panic was written all over his face as he scanned the room.

"Hey, do you work here?" The man's voice cracked with urgency.

Uneze raised an eyebrow, keeping his distance. "Nope," he said, his tone light but with a hint of amusement.

"Show me to someone who does," the man snapped, wiping his brow with a shaking hand. There was an entitlement to his words that made Uneze want to both laugh and cringe.

Uneze pointed toward the reception desk, where a calm receptionist was attending to a group of tourists. "Over there."

"Great," the man muttered, storming past Uneze. He found himself inexplicably drawn closer.

"Can I help you?" Uneze asked, stepping in his path.

"You work here?" the man asked, his frustration palpable.

"Still no," Uneze said, smirking. "But you look like you need help."

"I've got a group about two miles down the road. My truck's broken down, and my guide's passed out drunk. He can't even walk, let alone fix the damn thing."

Uneze couldn't help but grin. "Hey, I've got wheels."

"Really? Will it fit twelve people?" the man asked, his voice hopeful.

Uneze shrugged nonchalantly. "You know the whole 'gift horse' thing? I'm your gift horse. Let's roll." He slapped a hand on the man's back. "I'm Uneze, by the way."

"James. Nice to meet you." He gestured down the dusty road. "That way."

Uneze raised an eyebrow. "What's wrong with the truck?"

"Started smoking. Then BAM, it just died. We had the oil changed and topped off the water tanks, but now it's just... dead."

"Let me check it out," Uneze offered, already starting down the path.

"Play it cool when you get there," James warned. "The group's freaking out. The guide—who's also the driver—can't even sit up."

Uneze chuckled. "I've got your back. And I'm guessing that's your truck?" He nodded toward the vehicle, where a group of anxious tourists huddled together.

"Yeah, and that's the guide's passed out on the hubcap," James said.

"Keys?"Uneze asked.

"Probably in his pockets."

"Alright, you do the groping, I'll check the engine."

As James approached the truck, Uneze stood still, his eyes scanning the engine. "I figured it out," he said with a frown. "Your oil tank's full of water, and your water tank's full of oil."

"Shit, that's not good," James muttered.

"Yeah, it's beyond my repair skills here. There's a town about forty miles away. I'll take you there to see a mechanic."

"So, you're suggesting we sleep in the truck tonight?" James asked, disbelief in his voice.

"You made this mess," Uneze said. "I'm just trying to help. Ease up on the attitude."

"Sorry, dude. I didn't mean to snap."

Uneze softened. "Look, stay with the group. I'll ferry them back and forth to the campsite."

The rustling of leaves echoed, followed by a low growl that froze them both in place. Uneze's heart skipped a beat, but James's face went pale as the sound sent ripples of nervous tension through the group.

"Do these guys look like campers to you?" James asked, eyeing the nervous crowd.

"Well, they're either campers, or they'll be sleeping on the roadside in the Serengeti. Your choice."

Uneze's smirk was infectious, but James hesitated as the sun began to dip below the horizon. "Camping it is," James said, glancing at his group.

Uneze chuckled. "It's a campsite. They'll just add some extra tents for the budget crowd."

"Don't use the word 'budget,'" Uneze warned. "Call it 'authentic African experience.'"

"Call it whatever you want," James muttered. "I'll stick with 'safe.'" He turned back to the group. "Alright, I can take four at a time. Send them to me," Uneze called, already heading toward his car.

33 - UNEZE

By the time James arrived with the last of the group and dealt with the driver slumped in the back seat of Uneze's car, the clubhouse area of the campsite had descended into chaos. The group needed direction, and James seemed more than happy to let Uneze take the lead.

"My name's Uneze, and I'm your new local guide. I know this isn't quite the accommodation you were expecting tonight, but how does the word *safe* sound compared to 'roadside'?" A collective laugh rippled through the group as Uneze continued, grinning wide. "Safe, authentic, and a lifeline. Welcome to your oasis in the desert, your home behind the electric fence. Have I convinced you all yet?"

Another burst of laughter filled the room, and a woman chimed in, "We're fine. Just give us somewhere to sleep, and we're happy, right?"

Uneze's smile barely faltered as he took a beat, then replied, "Oh no, no. First, we have dinner by firelight. Then, a little stargazing before you close those tired eyes. Let's make an experience out of this adventure. Who wants some wine to go with your authentic African evening?"

Hands shot up eagerly, and murmurs of approval buzzed through the air. James, rubbing his cramping hands, entered, visibly stunned by the upbeat vibe.

"How's the driver?" someone asked.

"Stripped of his responsibilities. Demoted to backseat passenger until we can leave him at the next town," James quipped, his voice dry.

Uneze winked. "Don't worry, I'm with you now, and I won't hit the bottle until the end of the tour." He gestured toward the reception desk, where staff were busy directing guests. "Right, reception will show you to your tents. Yes, I said tents, but we'll meet back here for drinks around the fireplace. Who's in?"

"I think all of us," a lady said, her voice light with excitement.

"Go, campers. Do your thing. Your luggage will follow." Uneze threw his hands up in an exaggerated flourish, and the last of the group started to head out.

Once the last person had left, James turned to Uneze with a smirk. "Well, aren't you just an angel who fell from heaven?"

"I'm not gay. Hands off," Uneze chuckled.

"No, seriously. You were in the right place at the right time. You worked that group like putty in your hands," James said, still impressed.

"It's my job," Uneze said proudly, puffing out his chest.

"A putty moulder, huh?"

"No, I'm a local guide," Uneze shot back, laughing. "Well, my dad owns Green Planet Safari, and I used to run it for him."

"Wow, I've applied for jobs with GPS, but they never got back to me," James sighed, tapping his fingers on the truck's wooden dashboard.

"Ah, that would've been my fault. Sorry," Uneze replied, raising an eyebrow. "I do the staffing, but we just get too many CVs. We try to keep it local."

James nodded thoughtfully, a bit of disappointment in his eyes. "I get that. So, what's your deal here?"

Uneze's eyes sparkled as he leant forward, all energy now. "I'm setting up a new tour. This is the last campsite I need to contract. Just signed the deal, and I'm staying for the night."

"So, you're free for a few days?" James asked, a flicker of hope in his voice.

"Not quite. I already told your group I'm the new local guide," Uneze grinned mischievously.

James rolled his eyes. "Well, you don't lack confidence. You've got it in spades."

"Yeah, I sell it too. Want some?" Uneze laughed. He nudged James playfully. "Hey, tell me about the tour. What's the plan?"

"Just a ten-day tour. We're on day six, heading back to Dar es Salaam," James explained, his hands animated as he talked.

"Perfect, that's where I'm headed anyway. I'll just take the scenic route with you guys, follow in my hire car until I can drop it off." Uneze said casually.

"Thanks, man. You're a lifesaver," James beamed.

Uneze laughed, "I've got your back. Besides, it's fun to work with people who don't lose their cool."

Later, when they sat by the bonfire, the rich, oaky scent of wine enveloped them, easing the day's worries. As they poured glasses, Uneze spoke proudly about his new idea and the concept of glamping, and James felt the warmth of friendship as they discussed it.

One by one, the group gathered around the crackling fire, laughter and chatter filling the air. Glasses raised toward the star-filled sky, the evening took on an almost magical quality.

James, wide-eyed with wonder, murmured, "When you first said camping, I thought you were crazy, but now I see the charm."

"I think we can help each other out," Uneze said, smiling. "You're looking for a European guide, and I'm looking for a stable job. I work for Exo Travel, and I'm sent all over the world, but I want to stay here."

"How would that work?" James asked, intrigued.

"You contact Exo head office, and I'll be your guide on your tours."

"Well, if you promote this tour with Exo Travel, we've got a deal."

The pair clinked glasses as James said, "Sure. They're always looking for something new. This would be right up their alley."

"Yeah, all that hotel stuff can be a drag," Uneze replied, leaning back into the cushion, his voice filled with relief.

"Definitely never looked at the stars like this before. It's like fairy dust," James said, his voice filled with awe.

"Magical fairy dust that works wonders on the worst of groups," Uneze added, grinning as they both gazed up, lost in the magic of the evening.

James's hard work paid off spectacularly. Just two months later, their first tour set sail with excitement and expectancy, drawing in promoters, podcasters, influencers, and media alike. The internet exploded with stunning snapshots of their glamping success—a beautiful campsite dotted with enchanting tents that glimmered under a canopy of fairy lights.

Each tent became a cosy haven, inviting attendees to indulge in nature's wonders without giving up their creature comforts. Laughter echoed through the air, mingling with the crackle of campfires as people shared stories and created lasting memories.

On social media, the buzz was palpable; vivid images flooded feeds, capturing moments of joy, relaxation, and the thrill of adventure. Meanwhile, ticket sales soared, vanishing in a flurry of clicks as enthusiastic fans scrambled to secure their place in the next unforgettable experience.

Four years had flown by, and Uneze and James had become an unbreakable team. Now, uncertainty loomed heavy over Uneze. The rhythm of their partnership felt disrupted as James prepared for his new role as a father, leaving Uneze to face their first tour without his wingman by his side.

Uneze slumped into the passenger seat, the familiar scent of James's cologne enveloping him as the engine roared to life. The brisk morning air rustled through the open window, but it did little to ease the knot in his stomach.

"Are you ready to meet the new me?" James chirped, his eyes sparkling with mischief.

Uneze shook his head vigorously, his heart heavy. "Definitely not. This is our tour. I'm going to miss you, bro."

James's laughter bounced off the car's interior, a sound that always managed to lighten the mood, if only slightly. "Of course you'll miss me. But I've checked out my replacement online. She's definitely going to decorate your world. She's cute."

Uneze's expression shifted suddenly. He leant in closer, his voice dropping conspiratorially. "The new guide is a *she*?"

"Yes, drumroll please. A real, live woman. Can you cope?" James chuckled, his teasing tone unmistakable. "She's experienced. Peri has worked all over the world. She'll be fine."

Uneze rolled his eyes, the image of a nervous rookie flickering in his mind. "Fingers crossed she's not an African virgin. I don't need a guide who's never been to Africa before."

James smirked, nudging him lightly. "The odds are slim she'll be as amazing as me. I look forward to the gossip when you get back. You and that well-toned body of hers might just have some fun. Maybe you'll find a reason to share a tent."

"Not happening," Uneze shot back, his cheeks flushing at the thought. "I've learned to stay away from female guides; they get too clingy on safari. Do you remember the whole Anton mess?" Uneze chuckled.

"Look, it's the first time in four years you'll have a female wingman. Work your magic smile and charm."

Uneze tensed his brows. "Stop it. You know it's just a thing. I like vanilla. What's wrong with that?"

"Nothing, it's cool. Vanilla is your type; chocolate is mine," James laughed, his grin infectious. "So, with a face like that and abs like yours, it's your time to have some real fun on the tour."

"After last time?"

"Stop complaining and let this woman sprinkle some fairy dust on this tour. Or is having a cute woman too much of a drag for you?"

As they approached the airport, Uneze felt the tension in his shoulders ease slightly, but the thought of the upcoming tour still loomed large.

James pulled up to the curb and gestured for Uneze to get out. "Yes, but this Peri girl is yours for six weeks. You're not shackled with her for eternity, unless you want to. Now, drag that ass out of my car and get ready for six weeks of pure, idyllic, me-free time. Enjoy."

"Stop trying to help me; your advice sucks. It always has," Uneze shot back, opening the door reluctantly. But before he stepped out, he leant back through the window, his expression earnest. "Look, once the baby is born, can I call you to take over the tour if she's really bad?"

"No. That's the beauty of caller ID. I need some new daddy time with my boy. Just make the most of it. Now, go. Miss Vanilla is waiting."

34 - PERI

A knot twisted in Peri's stomach, tightening with every step she took through Cape Town International Airport. After an embarrassing blunder with her luggage—one she hoped no one would ever find out about— Peri stumbled through the bustling terminal, her movements sluggish. The undertone of voices blurred around her until she stepped outside, her eyes scanning the faces of the handmade signs and professionally printed names on clipboards. One sign caught her eye—a handwritten scrawl among a sea of banners. She quickened her pace and flashed a smile at the man holding the sign.

"That's me; I'm Peri," she said, her voice a soft blend of excitement and tiredness.

"Hi, I'm so glad to meet you. I'm Uneze. Let me take your bags," Uneze mumbled, eyeing the bags stacked on her trolley.

"It's okay, I've got them," Peri replied. "I've seen many people have their luggage stolen at the airport. Plus, I have a policy to only pack what I can carry."

"You're a cautious traveller; I like that," he said. "You have no idea how much people bring on this tour that they don't need, and they expect us to carry it around for them."

"Nope, these nails don't carry luggage," Peri said with amusement as she waved her fingers around.

"So, are you ready for this tour?" Uneze asked.

"Definitely not," she laughed. "So, Uneze, are you my driver for the tour?"

"I'm your guide. I'm just a driver in emergencies," Uneze explained.

Peri took in his appearance—a tall, good-looking man with the biggest brown eyes and a wide smile. The thing that struck her most was his confidence. His long and purposeful stride kept her moving quickly to keep up. Confused, she said, "I thought I was the guide."

"Yes, these safari gigs have two guides. You're the face of the company; you meet and greet at the airport, you check your guests in at hotels, arrange tours, payments, etc. You give out all the information, you know, the usual."

"Okay, so what's your role?" Peri asked.

"I'm on hand for help with cultural situations. As we're travelling mostly overland, I'm here to help with road border crossings, which isn't easy. We have a lot of breakdowns, and that's where a local is needed. I speak many African languages, so I'm also a translator. We have a few internal flights, but that's all prearranged, and you're in charge of getting people on the flights."

Peri nodded as she absorbed the information and replied, "Right."

"It's teamwork, and generally, it's fun. When we have optional excursions on one day, you do one, and I do the other. When we're on safari or other trips, we have local guides from the parks, and we either get time off or are spectators."

Peri wiped her brow in mock relief and said, "Oh, thank God. I was petrified I was going to have to wing it on my own. I've never been to Africa before."

"No way. You're an African virgin?" Uneze rolled his eyes, then muttered quietly, "It's a stupid move for a six-week tour."

Peri tried to smile. Despite his instant dislike, she felt the need for him to like her. "I don't know why they didn't move one of the regular safari guides from the shorter tours onto this and put me on a shorter one," she said.

Uneze's words sounded like curses; he spoke so quietly that Peri strained to hear him. "I have no idea. It would have made so much more sense."

"I'm sorry that you have me," Peri said, giving him a soft smile.

"It's not that I don't want you," Uneze said, his hands clenched into fists at his sides, betraying his frustration. "It's just that we need someone experienced. We'll split up quite a bit, and I need to know you can cope if disaster strikes."

Noting his fast pace, she tried to lighten the mood. "Could you have parked the car any further away?"

Uneze rolled his eyes again, reaching into his pocket for his phone, texting James, "Help me. She's a bimbo, first time in Africa. I need you." He turned his attention back to Peri and pointed to a car park. "It's just over there. I'm sorry to have inconvenienced you with the long walk."

"Do we get a lot of disasters and problems on safari?" Peri asked.

"This is Africa. Things are never easy, and it isn't like we're on a wine-tasting tour. It's a safari, with wild animals, dangerous land, unforgiving weather, and God knows what else."

Already sweating from the humidity, Peri wiped her brow and finally let Uneze take one of her bags. "Ah, okay. I guess that makes sense, and I hope I don't let you down. This is all so new. I've read the itinerary over and over again, and I've got my laptop filled with research. I'll have to do a bit of studying each day. I guess it sounds simple enough."

"A six-week camping safari isn't simple or fun. It's hard work, stressful, and it's like babysitting the group to make sure they don't do anything stupid. Do you think you can manage that?" Uneze asked, unable to hide his annoyance.

Peri trailed behind him, her fists clenched around the handle of her suitcase. The dazzling images of sunlit savannas and wildlife danced through her mind, but all Uneze saw was what Uneze saw—a girl who had never set foot on the dusty trails of Africa. Biting her lip, she resisted the urge to defend herself, choosing instead to let silence fill the space between them.

35 - PERI

Having arrived at the hotel in almost silence, Peri pushed open the door to her room with her shoulder, unclasped her case, unzipped it, and hung two outfits on the hooks. Once she'd showered and changed, she headed downstairs and found Uneze, chatting and laughing on the phone. She stood in front of him until he noticed her.

"Sorry, James, I've got to go. She's here," he muttered, placing the phone on the table.

Without asking, Peri pulled up a chair and sat opposite him. "I think we got off to a bad start. It's clear you don't like the blonde bimbo you've been matched with, but I'm not going anywhere, so you're just going to have to get used to me."

He sat back, crossed his arms, and asked, "Why are you here? I just don't get it."

"I'm not sure either. I asked to do this tour so many times that I just wore head office down."

"So, you want to be here; that's something," he mused.

"I am an excellent guide. I've worked for the agency for three years. I've travelled the world. I'm used to dealing with the unexpected. I was with a group in China when Covid hit, and if I can deal with that, I can deal with anything."

"Anything, huh? Alright, this should be interesting," Uneze chuckled. "Just tell me, did anything strange happen to you at the airport today?"

"Strange how?" Peri asked, raising an eyebrow.

"Did you leave your suitcase behind?" Uneze asked, a teasing smile forming on his lips.

Peri's face turned crimson, and she shot him a sharp look. "Erm, I was tired. How did you find out?"

"It's a big country, but small airport. I know the staff," Uneze replied with a knowing grin.

Peri rubbed the back of her neck, embarrassment spreading like wildfire. "Alright, fine, I had a blonde moment. I grabbed my bags from the belt, set them down to unlock them, and then saw the signs for security inspection."

Uneze raised an eyebrow. "And then?"

"Well, I thought I was clever, right? I joined the queue, breezed through, felt all smug. It wasn't until I got to arrivals that I realised... I never put the bags on the trolley."

"Wait—so you got through security... without any bags?" Uneze laughed, a loud, incredulous sound.

"Yup. And when I finally saw my empty trolley outside, I had to beg them to let me back in," Peri said, burying her face in her hands.

Uneze chuckled under his breath. "This is going to be fun. But hey, at least you're prepared for anything now, right?"

"Anything? I've had people dying on buses, four-day flight delays, people going missing in Vietnam... you name it," Peri said, trying to shake off her embarrassment.

"Right, well, knowing that you're in charge of this group is going to be a blast. Can't wait to see how this plays out," Uneze muttered, only half-laughing, before speeding up as the traffic light turned green.

"Oh, you're enjoying this, aren't you? Stop mocking me," Peri huffed, crossing her arms. "I've seen it all—people with broken limbs, stolen luggage, stolen passports, and flight delays. I'm ready for anything." Feeling frustrated at his smug grin, she continued, "Okay, today wasn't my best moment, but don't worry. Normally, I'm not this clueless," Peri said, forcing a smile. "Now, tell me what's happening today."

Uneze leant back, glancing at her with a nod. "So, it's a camping tour, but every now and then, we'll hit a hotel or self-catering apartment so everyone can recharge and do laundry."

"Yeah, I saw. A girl needs her power sockets," Peri laughed.

"For the first few tours, we didn't have a hotel stop, but it was a problem. People want their comforts. We use the city stops for things like phone chargers, computer repairs, you know the drill," Uneze explained.

"Right. Got it," Peri nodded. "I guess it's a lot to manage. I'm glad you're here."

"I'm glad you're here, too," Uneze said with a smirk. "At least you're going to keep me entertained." His words sounded insincere, but his smile softened. "The regular guide, James, is great. We're friends. He had a personal issue to deal with, though. I'm sure the agency wouldn't have sent you if you weren't up to it."

"Or they mixed up the names and thought I was someone else. Honestly, I'm still not sure why I'm here," Peri admitted with a small chuckle.

"I like your honesty." Uneze gave a half-shrug and handed her a bottle of water. "Alright, let's start again. Most of the group will have had a few days in Cape Town on their own before checking in here today."

"Yep, I know that much."

"We'll have a group welcome drink and dinner tonight. You'll hand out the itinerary. If you want, we've got a couple of hours. I can help you out this time, and tomorrow I'll take over the talking."

"That's alright. I've already memorised the itinerary. If you want to look over what I've got prepared, that'd be a big help," Peri said, passing him her notes with a grin.

Uneze glanced at the paper, waving it around as if conducting an orchestra. "This is so bland. Just a bunch of buzzwords. These people are paying serious money for a camping trip; you've got to make it exciting. They're dreaming of lions roaring, gorillas in Uganda, and the power of Victoria Falls. You need to paint a picture that sparks their imagination, makes them feel the adventure. Plans shift, sure, but make them want to get out there and live it."

"Right, yeah. I guess I was so excited about the experience that I forgot to make it more... enticing." Peri sighed, tapping her pen nervously. "I normally do that, but I guess it feels so different this time."

"Yep. But you haven't spent fifteen thousand dollars for a dull itinerary," Uneze said with a smirk. "Also, you'll need to mention the others who'll join the group later on. The shorter tours will join us along the way."

"A tour that keeps on giving," Peri grinned.

"Exactly. This company, Green Planet Holidays, is an agent for Exo Travel. They run safaris of varying lengths. Some are a week long, some two or three," Uneze continued. "The tours mix and match, so you'll have people coming and going throughout."

Peri nodded, processing the info. "Wow, okay."

"It keeps things interesting, for sure," Uneze said, his tone growing a little more serious. "But the road travel can be tough. Long hours on bumpy roads, unexpected delays. Locals take it in stride, but the tourists don't always react well."

Peri's face stiffened, and she shifted uncomfortably. Uneze noticed her change in mood and raised an eyebrow. "What's up? You scared?"

"No, not scared," Peri replied, straightening her back. "Just... curious."

Uneze let out a small huff. "I guess you've never had to deal with wild elephants blocking your path, or car breakdowns in the middle of nowhere."

"I can handle that. It just adds to the fun. Alright, so tell me about the people who do these tours?" Peri asked, eager to move past her moment of doubt.

"You'd be surprised. We get plenty of adventurous types, the ones who've done safaris before and are now looking for something longer. The first-timers? They have no clue what they're getting into," Uneze said, shaking his head.

"Like me?" Peri grinned.

"Yeah, but you've got a good sense of humour. That'll get you through six weeks on the floor," Uneze said, glancing at her with a wink.

"Why didn't you come a few days earlier to get a feel for the city? A couple of days would've helped," Uneze asked.

Peri wiped her brow, then took a gulp of water. "I wanted to, but I only found out four days ago that I was coming. I jumped on the flight they booked for me."

"So, you did a bit of Googling and just showed up thinking you were ready?" Uneze teased.

"What's life if not an adventure? That's why I love this job," Peri said, forcing a cheerful tone.

"Alright. Well, you'll find yourself surrounded by people from all walks of life. Some are escaping their pasts, like someone fresh off a breakup. Others are going through a divorce, spending their spouse's money while they still can. You'll meet bloggers, photographers... and then, of course, there are the ones who missed the 'camping' part of the description."

Peri burst out laughing. "But it's a camping tour."

"Exactly. And there's always one who thinks they know more than the guide," Uneze chuckled.

"In this case, that's definitely me. I know nothing," Peri laughed.

"That's why I'm here," Uneze said with a grin. "When people ask questions you don't know, don't try to make it up. I hate that. Just let them think you've done this before. You can say that we use different campsites, so you're never sure about the facilities."

Peri nodded, her smile widening. "Thanks, Uneze. That really helps."

"Oh, and one last thing," Uneze said, leaning in slightly. "When we meet a local guide or ranger, let them take over. Don't try to talk over them. They'll get pissed off, and you'll get some time off. James, the regular guy, uses that time to nap. After a while, safaris all feel the same."

"Well, this being my first time, I'm going on every tour," Peri said enthusiastically.

Uneze raised an eyebrow, chuckling softly. "We'll see. Give it a week, and you'll be begging for a break."

"We'll see," Peri repeated, grinning.

Uneze leant back in his chair, crossing his arms. "There's always some scandal in the group."

Peri's eyes lit up. "What kind of scandal?"

Uneze smirked. "I'm not going to spoil the fun. But just wait and see. And there's always a cougar or two hunting for a nice African man."

"Well, I'm safe then," Peri chuckled.

"Think again. There's always someone who thinks the guide is fair game," Uneze whispered with an amused twinkle in his eyes. "James always has fun with them."

Peri snickered. "Well, I'm not worried. Let's see what this group's got."

Uneze checked his watch and muttered, "Showtime."

36 - PERI

Peri and Uneze presented a united front as they greeted the group that had gathered around the area. They were clearly a mixed group, just as Uneze had predicted. A tall, striking woman glided in, her long legs accentuated by the daring outfit that clung to her curves, leaving little to the imagination. With each step, she moved with an effortless grace that drew eyes like moths to a flame. As she crossed her legs, the soft shine of her skin caught the light, and the collective intake of breath from the onlookers lingered as intrigue rippled through the group.

Uneze stood tall, the gentle clinking of his tall glass slicing through the buzz of chatter. A warm smile spread across his face as the group gradually hushed, their eager eyes turning toward him. Some of them seemed reassured by his presence, while others watched him with a hint of scepticism, sizing him up. With Peri by his side, he exuded a blend of authority and approachability, beckoning his audience closer.

"Alright everyone," he began, his voice smooth and inviting, "I hope you have your welcome drink in hand. If you need anything else, just wave over the servers and put it on your tab." As he surveyed the room, the excitement in the air crackled. "Welcome to the Oasi Green Apartment complex, the official starting point for our journey that begins tomorrow." He paused for a moment, allowing his words to settle before adding with an animated grin, "Before dinner, let's circle the group and share a little about ourselves. This is the original crew, affectionately dubbed the OGs. We'll be joined by others along our adventure, but with at least three weeks together, it's time to get acquainted." He turned to Peri, a silent cue for her to take the stage.

Peri stepped forward, her professional smile radiating confidence as she made eye contact with each member of the group. "My name is Peri," she declared, her voice steady and clear. "I'm the better half of your two tour guides for this safari camping tour," she added with a lively twist, "Think of us as Maverick and Goose."

Uneze chuckled, "I prefer Bonnie and Clyde," he quipped, his laughter mingling with the group's amusement.

Peri continued, her smile warm yet authoritative, "I'll handle everything related to the services you booked with the tour operator—arranging internal flights, managing pre-booked tours, and being at your service during breakfast every morning. You'll find me by your side throughout the day, so don't hesitate to reach out." Her eyes sparkled with enthusiasm, igniting a sense of excitement among the group, promising an unforgettable journey ahead.

"You'll be sick of her by tomorrow," Uneze laughed with a nudge. "I am."

"Okay, with that, over to you, Uneze," Peri said.

"Contrary to what Peri said, I'm the better half of the duo," Uneze declared, a playful grin stretching across his face as laughter bubbled up from the group around him. "I'm from Nigeria, but don't worry, I'm not a prince trying to con you out of your money with a spam email," he continued, his tone light yet confident. "I'm your on-the-ground guide, your local lifeline."

"I was looking for a prince," one of the girls chirped in, "Are you sure you can't be one? If I kiss you, maybe you'll turn into one."

"So, you're calling me a frog?" Uneze laughed along with the group. "Anyway, I'll be the one navigating the long, tedious border crossings and chatting with the local rangers who will join us on our safari adventures. And yes, I speak the lingos, so just come to me with anything you need."

Peri surveyed the group, noticing the puzzled expressions etched on several faces. Some people were nodding along, seemingly intrigued by the local lingo, while a few others exchanged wary glances, unsure of what to expect. She waited for a lull in Uneze's spirited introduction before stepping in. "You can approach either of us with anything that comes to mind—we'll sort it out together. Don't worry; we're both here to make this experience the best it can be."

"I hope you all read the safari notes you were emailed," Uneze continued, noticing some of the group's attention wane. "If so, you know that tomorrow we'll still be staying in this complex but will be heading to see the penguins in Simon's Bay and the Cape of Good Hope. You'll need sturdy footwear and probably a wind jacket."

The woman who'd captured the attention of the group when she'd arrived let out a long sigh, a tiny smile curving her lips as she raised an eyebrow. "What if we don't have any of those?" she asked with a stern expression. "I only have four-inch heels and miniskirts."

Uneze gave her a playful grin. "Well, find someone to huddle up to for warmth, or to carry you up the trails, as it's not exactly a stroll up there."

"Or you could go shopping and get something suitable," the woman sitting next to her said with a playful nudge, eliciting a few laughs from the group.

Uneze's focus landed on two girls lounging comfortably on the sofa, their chilled drinks glistening with condensation. "Now, it's your turn. Tell us about yourselves," he encouraged with infectious enthusiasm. "Who are you? Where are you from? Is this your first safari? What are you hoping to get out of it?" With a curious grin, he nodded toward them, eager to hear their stories and weave their narratives into how they fit into this group.

The woman with the four-inch heels sighed, clearly reluctant to be the first to speak. The woman next to her slapped her playfully on the wrist, urging her to stand.

She smiled at Uneze and Peri, ran her fingers over her fake lips and unnaturally high eyebrows, and said, "I'm Emily."

37 - EMILY

A few days before safari.

A wet, dull day greeted Emily as she stepped into the wedding car. Rain lashed against the windows, creating a relentless percussion that drowned out her thoughts, while the grey sky hung low, throwing a dark black cloud over what should have been the happiest day of her life. She had dreamt of sun-soaked vows beneath a vibrant blue sky, laughter ringing out like a melody. But now, the sombre drizzle painted a different picture—a blur of dampness and uncertainty.

She could barely hear her own thoughts as the rain hammered against the windows and sides of the vehicle as it pulled away from her family home. She had always imagined her wedding day filled with sunshine, laughter, and love. But instead, she faced a dreary sky, a heavy heart, and a feeling of dread that clung to her.

Her father's voice broke through her concentration. "You're about to marry the love of your life, surrounded by friends. No amount of rain can dampen the joy this day will bring."

Emily traced the rivulets racing down the glass with her fingertip. A bitter smile tugged at her lips. "Yeah, right."

Her father beamed at her, bleary-eyed. "I'm so proud of you. Guy's a great guy, and I think you'll be perfect together, even though it all happened so quickly."

"I just wish the sun would shine," Emily muttered, desperation creeping into her voice.

"Forget about the weather; just enjoy the moment."

Emily blushed, looking down and taking a series of long, deep breaths. As the car pulled up outside the church, they dashed into the shelter of the archway. Umbrellas bloomed around her, shielding her from the persistent rain. Emily took a moment to steady her frayed nerves.

"Ready to do this?" Michelle asked, her sister, the maid of honour, fluffing out her dress and giving her a kiss on the cheek.

"It's now or never," Emily replied. "Is he nervous?"

"Nope. Well... you'll see for yourself. He's really pulled out all the stops in the fashion department."

"That's okay," Emily said. "I mean, if he looks good, I'm cool with that."

"Good? Yes, let's go with good," Michelle laughed.

With a deep breath, Emily nodded at her father, then at her sister. She took one last look at herself in a stained glass window and watched Michelle take the first few steps down the aisle. A few seconds later, she grabbed her father's arm and prepared for the next chapter of her life to begin. With two large steps through the swinging wooden door, a cheerful noise emanated from the excited, smartly dressed guests.

Emily stopped at the end of the aisle, clutching her stomach, trying to focus on Guy, who stood at the altar in a luminous green jacket and matching trousers—an eye-watering contrast to the elegant tuxedo she'd imagined him wearing. Emily's stomach twisted in confusion as she tried to make sense of the situation. Her eyes darted to his five groomsmen, all dressed in the same garish shade of green. Michelle turned and beckoned her to move forward. Slowly, guided by her father's steady arm, she made it to the front. He kissed her on the cheek and stepped back to his seat, his pride as bright as ever.

Emily stood in shock as Guy flashed her a sheepish grin. Anger rose within her as she neared him, and she flashed him a look of disgust. "What are you, a walking string bean?" she blurted. "You look like you're in the veggie rack at the supermarket."

"I wanted to stand out," Guy replied, his voice defensive.

"At our wedding?" Emily shook her head in disbelief. "You have to be crazy. You look like someone vomited all over you."

Her joke was met by silence and a glare. She rubbed her thumb over the silver band of her huge diamond ring, glaring over her shoulder at her dad, who beamed with pride, oblivious to the storm brewing in his daughter's chest.

Emily's glare darted to her sister, seeking some validation, but Michelle only shrugged, amusement clouding her face.

A deep breath, a desperate attempt to regain control, and Emily launched into her tirade. "Guy, why can't you just wear a normal suit like everyone else?"

Guy's eyes softened momentarily, a flicker of hurt before he masked it with practised indifference. "I thought you loved me for who I am, not for what I wear," he murmured.

Guilt gnawed at Emily, the all to familiar rage rising within her like a tidal wave. "Oh shit," she muttered under her breath, her fingers digging into the fabric of her dress. Turning to Michelle, she whispered, "Come on. I need a moment."

The whispers of the church seemed to amplify, judging eyes following her as she fled towards the exit, her heart pounding a frantic rhythm. Emily burst out of the church, seeking relief in the doorway, the impact of her outburst settling over her like a leaden cloak.

"What just happened?" Michelle asked, concern lacing her voice.

"I can't do it," Emily choked out, a forced laugh escaping her lips. "Look at him. He looks like... Shrek."

Michelle raised an eyebrow. "Just use your imagination. Imagine him in a black suit instead. Pretend you're having one of your migraines, and instead of everything turning yellow, it's all turned green."

"Migraine, okay, that makes sense," Emily said, taking a shaky breath. "He's wearing a dark blue suit, and I'm just having a migraine washout. It doesn't matter what colour he's wearing. It's Guy, and I love him, right?"

"That's what you tell me," Michelle said.

Emily put her hands on her hips and paced in circles. The chatter from inside the church crowded her thoughts as she looked at her reflection once more. "It's okay. I can do this. I can go through with it."

"That's my girl. And remember the real reason you love him." Michelle smirked. "Because he's loaded and dotes on you."

Emily sighed deeply, her shoulders sagging as she muttered, "Loaded, yes, I love him, but I love his money, too."

"That's my girl. Now, go in there before he changes his mind. The clock is ticking."

"Alright. Do you need Dad to walk you down the aisle again?"

With a cool, easy swish of her dress, Emily turned toward the door and said, "No, you do it. Make sure I don't do another runner." She began muttering under her breath, giving herself a pep talk as she brushed down the layers of her dress.

"Let's do this," Michelle replied. She grabbed her sister's hand, and with a forced smile on her face, she pushed the door open. The two girls walked through it together.

Emily took a deep breath and tried to avoid eye contact with the rows of well-wishers murmuring about the scandal. Instead of focusing on the sea of green at the end of the aisle, she glared at her father. He no longer wore his pride like a badge; instead, determination covered him as he mouthed, "Come on, just keep walking."

Emily nodded, forcing a smile as she walked toward Guy. When she reached him, she clutched her stomach and said, "I'm sorry. I just had a panic attack. There were so many people watching me."

"It's okay. I knew you'd come back," Guy said softly, his hand gripping hers as his eyes welled up with joy. He gave her a moment to take in the scene.

She glanced at the flowers she had chosen, the people she'd invited, and the musicians rounding up their piece. The dull ache in her chest began to sink lower, settling uncomfortably in her stomach. She turned back to Guy, a cold reluctance in her eyes. She watched the colour drain from his face as he realised what was happening.

"I'm sorry. I can't do it."

He pulled her towards him, desperation in his grip. "What? Why not?"

"I just can't," Emily said. Her eyes locked on the faces of family and friends watching her, and she muttered, "I'm sorry, I'll pay you back."

38 - EMILY

A few days before safari.

With a wild gust of wind, Emily burst through the heavy doors, the world outside a blur of grey and silver. Raindrops hammered the pavement as she stumbled onto a nearby park bench, her clothes clinging to her skin, breath coming in ragged gasps as if she'd just run a marathon. The cold rain drummed a chaotic rhythm against the wood, soaking her through but somehow lifting the weight from her chest.

Michelle slid next to her on the bench and grabbed Emily's hand. Emily squeezed her eyes shut, letting the rain wash over her. With each droplet that kissed her cheeks, she felt lighter, like the shackles of expectation melted away, leaving only the exhilarating sense of freedom.

"Emily, what happened back there?" Michelle's voice was soft but insistent, slicing through the momentary bliss that kept Emily company.

Taking a deep, shaky breath, Emily finally confessed, "I couldn't go through with it. I couldn't marry him. I don't love him," she whispered, the words tasting bitter on her tongue. She let out a shaky breath, feeling a weight she didn't even know she was carrying begin to lift. The admission hung in the air, heavy yet liberating.

"Not even the fact that he's dripping in money squashed the fear?" Michelle prodded gently.

"Not even that. It was wrong. All wrong." Emily's eyes fluttered open, the storm's rhythm a soothing balm against her turbulent thoughts.

"Does it feel right now?" Michelle asked, glancing around at the drenched world, her voice filled with concern and curiosity.

Emily tilted her head back, allowing the rain to cascade over her face, each drop a whispered affirmation. "It feels amazing. I feel free, like doing it washed away all the stress of being with him."

"Maybe it's the rain that's doing that," Michelle countered.

Emily remained rooted, her focus drifting toward the sliver of sunlight breaking through the clouds. "I want to stay here," she murmured, her heart racing with something akin to joy. "This is where I belong."

"Emily, come on. You want to live on a bench?" Michelle's voice sharpened with worry. "You're soaking wet. Let's get you out of here."

"No, I can't move. My legs are like jelly," Emily said.

A distant shout from her father shattered the moment, and reality crashed back in. Panic sparked in Michelle's eyes. "He'll flip out if he sees you like this. We need to hide."

Emily shook her head, her spirit still dancing with the rain. "Even the weather thinks I did the right thing. This is my moment."

"I don't care what it thinks. That's Dad calling you. If he catches you—" Michelle's voice cracked with urgency.

The words sank in, and suddenly, Emily sprang to her feet searching for a plan. "We need a car. I need to get out of here," she said, fingers twisting nervously in her soaked hair. "Call me an Uber?"

"Alright, where to?" Michelle asked. Without overthinking it, she blurted out, "Rachel's house?"

"Rachel? She hates me," Emily shot back, her shoulders slumping. "Not exactly hate. She just thinks you're a spoilt, shallow, money-grubbing pain in the ass."

"Sounds like hate to me," Emily sighed, but her resolve was crumbling.

"Guy won't think to look at my best friend's house. He'll be calling your friends, not mine," Michelle said.

"Alright, do it. Get me out of here." Emily's voice surged with urgency. "Just one problem—we don't have a phone or money."

"Shit. Right, let's run for it. We'll find someone who can lend us a phone. Just look at me—I'll play the jilted bride card. It has to be worth something."

39 - EMILY

A few days before safari.

The ancient church gate protested as Emily heaved it open. She pushed through, her once-gleaming dress dragging through the mud, snagging on the peeling paint. Her muddy gown trailed in her wake as she surged toward the main road.

"Nobody's around. No one to call an Uber," Michelle said, her voice tinged with desperation.

Taking a deep breath, Emily stepped into the road, just as the jarring screech of brakes sent her sister spinning. She banged on the hood of a passing car, desperation fueling her frantic gestures at the driver. "Please. I've just been jilted at the altar—call me an Uber or give us a lift. I can't go back to that church."

"Actually, we need a lift; that's our dad coming for us," Michelle added, her eyes dancing with urgency.

With a bemused grin, the driver replied, "Alright, jump in." Michelle and Emily squeezed into the backseat, relaying Rachel's address. "Jilted at the altar? That sucks. How do you come back from that?" he asked, his voice casual as he sped away from the church.

Emily let out a long breath, relief washing over her as the distance from her past grew. Michelle coughed awkwardly and said, "Thank you so much for this. We're stranded here without phones or money."

"Sure, no problem. Happy to help," he replied, his eyes on the road. Minutes later, they arrived at Rachel's house, nestled in a quiet neighborhood.

"Thanks, and if anyone asks, you dropped us at the train station," Emily insisted.

"Sure, whatever works. Good luck, girls. Sorry for what happened," he said, a hint of sympathy in his voice.

"Thanks," Emily managed, her fingers nervously tracing the lace of her wedding dress, damp and heavy against her skin.

A distant smile almost surfaced at the thought of flirtation, but the weight of her loss anchored her down. She looked away, her spirit dimmed, as she banged on the door, hoping for sanctuary. When her knocks went unanswered, Michelle swiftly retrieved the spare key. "Shoes off," she commanded.

"What?" Emily asked, bewildered.

"Just do it. Drip in the kitchen. These carpets are new," Michelle explained.

"Oh, now I remember why I don't like Rachel," Emily muttered.

"Rachel," Michelle called out before turning to Emily and muttering, "She's your safe haven now, so be nice, be thankful, and don't be a bitch."

"Don't be a bitch, got it." Emily called from the kitchen. She pulled a dish cloth from a stack and wiped her face dry, the layers of make-up leaving traces of what should have been with every stroke.

"Rachel." Michelle called. "Is anyone home?"

Footsteps approached, and Rachel appeared, wrapped in a towel. She took in Michelle's damp appearance and asked, "What are you doing here? Is the wedding over already?"

"Not in the way you expected, but yes," Michelle replied, gesturing toward the kitchen.

Rachel's gasped as she took in Emily's muddy bridal shoes. "What happened?"

"Emily's here. She bolted. Twice," Michelle explained.

Rachel threw her head back in laughter. "She left him at the altar?"

"Yep. I had to bring her here so dad or Guy can't find her," Michelle said.

Rachel shook her head, still chuckling. "Wow. This is the first time I've ever respected your sister; it takes guts to do that."

"She's in the kitchen. I made her promise to be nice to you," Michelle said, her tone half-serious, half-teasing.

"Oh, she won't like that," Rachel replied, a smirk dancing on her lips as she headed toward the kitchen, ready to confront the storm that had just crashed into her home.

40 - EMILY

A few days before safari.

Emily paced the kitchen, her fingers tapping nervously against the cold beer can, the sound echoing in the tense silence. "I'm sorry, Rachel. I just needed something to take the edge off." The words tumbled out in a rush, a plea for understanding as she took a long swig, the liquid cooling her heated thoughts.

Rachel leant against the wall, arms crossed, her brow arched with curiosity. "What happened?"

"String bean," Emily muttered, the phrase escaping her lips like a chant, "He looked like a string bean..." The words were a mantra that spiralled into a dizzying loop until Michelle, perched on a stool, finally peeled the layers of chaos apart and painted the scene for Rachel.

Rachel's lips twisted into a mix of confusion, intrigue, and concern. "Okay, so this whole mess is beautiful and disturbing at the same time, but is that really a reason not to marry him?"

Emily's voice rose, laced with indignation. "Of course not. But I looked at him, and all I could think was, I can't live with someone who thinks it's okay to look like a string bean that's been vomited on by another string bean."

Rachel raised an eyebrow, scepticism dancing in her eyes. "What are you going to do now?"

"Get out of this wedding dress first, then I'll decide," Emily replied, her tone shifting from frustration to a hint of mischief as she tugged at the lace fabric that clung to her with every breath.

Michelle, still hovering near the dress, chuckled softly. "I can't believe we just spent an hour getting you into this thing, and you were joking about the fun you'd have when Guy ripped it off you later. You really are a strange one, sis." With a flick of her wrist, Michelle began unhooking the tiny buttons, each one releasing Emily from the confines of expectation.

"I wish I'd been there to see you running away," Rachel chimed in.

Emily laughed, shaking her head. "I wish you could have seen the idiot he looked like. I mean, bright green—not even a dark, almost grey colour. It was like mushy pea green."

"I hope there are some photos of it somewhere," Rachel mused, her voice light.

"Me too. Then if I ever see him again, I can hold it against him," Emily replied, her tone teasing as she swayed slightly, revelling in the freedom that was about to come.

"Okay, all the hooks are undone. Ready for the dress to drop?" Michelle asked.

"Do it," Emily commanded, a grin stretching across her face. She raised her arms as the dress pooled around her feet, and with a sigh of relief, she kicked it aside, reclaiming her breath.

The bottle of beer was back in her grasp, and she downed it in one go, the cold clarity washing over her.

"Take this," Rachel said, tossing Emily a floaty sundress that had been drying on the radiator.

But before Emily could respond, Rachel dashed out to answer a ringing phone, returning moments later and shoving it into Michelle's hands. "It's your dad." With a wave of her hand, Emily silenced the room, her finger pressed to her lips.

"Dad, you're on speaker with Emily," Michelle announced, her tone all business.

"What just happened?" he shouted, confusion lacing his voice. Silence hung heavy as Emily took a sip of her beer, gathering her thoughts. Michelle jumped in, "Ehm, she couldn't go through with it."

"That bit I got, but why not?"

Emily's reluctance was clear; there was a moment of hesitation before she muttered, "Did you see what he was wearing?"

Her dad paused, then chuckled, the sound bouncing off the walls. "You got me there. But come on, you don't do a runner for something as simple as that."

"Are you going to Photoshop him into a black suit? Because I'm not," Emily shot back, rolling her eyes at Rachel, who was barely containing a laugh.
"Well, what are you going to do now? Your mum is so humiliated she says you aren't coming home ever again," her dad continued, the concern rising in his voice.

"It's okay. I've got places to go. But Dad, I need one thing from you. I need to know where Guy is right now."

"He's at the church still. He's a wreck. The family is a mess; there is a major crisis unfolding here. Are you coming to talk to him or see him and explain?" Dad asked.

"Mmm... Okay, maybe. Just wait there." Emily said, "I'm soaked; I just need a few minutes to dry off and make myself decent again."

"Alright, hurry up." Dad said before ending the call.

41 - EMILY

A few days before safari.

Michelle glared at Emily in annoyance and asked, "What? You're going back to the church? I'm not putting that dress back on you again."

"No, but if they think I'm going there, then I can go home and get my things. I'll call Dad once we've finished."

"We?" Michelle asked.

"Yeah, it'll be quicker. Then we can dump it all at your place," Emily explained.

"Then what?" Rachel asked.

Emily, fidgeting nervously, replied, "One thing at a time. My stuff first."

The engine of Rachel's car roared to life as the three girls hopped in, forced laughter bubbling as they sped down the tree-lined street. Emily's stomach lurched with dread as they pulled up in front of her house. With a soft beep, she keyed in the code, the door clicking open like a secret waiting to be unlocked. Inside, the scent of home mingled with anxiety. She darted through the rooms, her hands a flurry of motion, stuffing clothes and keepsakes into four large suitcases.

She let the last of her belongings tumble into the bags with a resigned sigh. "I guess I'll have to fight him for furniture, but at least I've got my things. It's better than nothing, right?" Her half-smile barely hid the worry creeping in. "Right, let's get out of here," she declared, a nervous excitement replacing some of the anxiety.

Pulling up at Michelle's house, they hauled the bags into the garage and headed inside. "What next?" Michelle asked, curiosity creeping into her voice.

"Dad already found us at Rachel's. Where else can we go?" Emily asked.

"On holiday. Let's go to Ibiza or somewhere like that." Michelle said, her eyes sparkling with mischief.

"You could go on your honeymoon," Rachel mused, her voice tinged with sarcasm. "Or, you could lay low until the dust settles."

"Oh god, going on a honeymoon like this? That's a bit too Carrie Bradshaw for me. But maybe the drama will make a good story someday," Emily shot back, a hint of humor in her voice.

"Well, it's a good thing I work for him and can get the tickets from his office," Michelle replied, a note of pride lifting her spirits. Rachel burst into laughter, the sound bright and carefree. "Oh, shit, he's not going to like you anymore, is he?"

Michelle shook her head and replied, "I very much doubt it."

"Just come with me, then," Emily urged.

"Just like that? We go on your honeymoon?" Michelle asked.

"Why not? He's not going to want you around the office right now, and I need my sister," Emily retorted.

With a huff, Michelle crossed her arms and sank into a chair, the significance of the decision pressing down on her.

Rachel handed her a glass of wine, the rich red swirling like the chaos in their lives. "It could be a way out of this nightmare," she said, her voice softer now. "You never really liked that job anyway," Rachel continued, leaning closer. "You were only there because you didn't want to upset Guy by leaving. I think it's a win-win situation."

"So, I go on Emily's honeymoon and lose my job at the same time?" Michelle pondered.

"What the hell? As Dopey said, Why not?" Rachel teased, a playful sparkle in her eye.

"Who is Dopey?" Emily asked.

"Sorry, that's what I call you," Rachel replied, unabashed, as she raised her glass. "Do you want him to know where you are?"

"Of course not," Emily replied.

"Then you can't take the tickets from his office. He'll notice. Can you access his email?" Rachel asked Michelle.

"Of course."

"Well, do it that way. Get in there and print off whatever you find," Rachel suggested.

"Why do you call me Dopey?" Emily asked.

"Honestly, I don't know. It was years ago, when we were kids; you did something dumb, and the name just stuck. It's better than the other name I had for you recently."

"Which was?" Emily asked.

"Pokey. You know, because of all the Botox, you have a constant poker face."

Emily glared at her and said, "That's cruel."

"Well, so it is dumping a guy at the altar because he has a peculiar taste in clothes, twice, and sitting here laughing about it."

"I'm not laughing."

"Well, you certainly aren't sad about it, or maybe it's just that Botox face of yours that doesn't let any emotion through," Rachel said.

The two ladies, who had been arch rivals up until that moment, exchanged glances and burst into loud laughter. It was a moment of unexpected camaraderie, a shared understanding that transcended their previous animosity. As they laughed together, the tension between them melted away.

"Honestly, with Guy, you need a poker face just to not cringe at his terrible jokes and wild dress sense. When he turns up in purple paisley trousers for the first time he meets your parents, you have no idea," Emily said.

"So why are you so surprised about today?" Rachel asked.

"I guessed he'd realised that our wedding wasn't a joke," Emily explained.

"I wish I could have seen it." The two stared at each other for a moment before breaking into a loud roar of laughter. "You're not so bad after all."

"Thanks, right back at you. Look, I had doubts about the wedding. Doubts infect the mind and make people do strange things. I don't know what I should have done; I don't know if I did the right thing or not. I guess only time will tell," Emily said.

Michelle's heart raced as she leant closer to the door, ears straining to catch every whispered word from the other room. She scrambled around her friend's cluttered desk, pushing aside scattered notebooks until her fingers grazed the cool surface of a laptop.

The screen flickered to life as she typed, inserting passwords until she finally found the screen she needed.

"So, where are we going on honeymoon?" Emily asked.

"Shhh, I need to sort all of this out."

Finally, the printer whirred to life, releasing a flurry of papers that flickered in the air before settling into a neat stack.

With a confused grin, Michelle briskly crossed the room and pressed the documents into Emily's hands, her eyes sparkling with excitement. "We are going on a safari."

Emily's brow twisted in confusion, her voice barely above a whisper. "A safari? Where?"

"Africa. Where do you think you're going? The flights to South Africa are for tomorrow morning. This is going to be amazing. Can you believe it? A real safari." Her voice brimmed with delight, her eyes scanning the details on the colourful pages as if they were a treasure map.

Emily let out an exaggerated groan. "Safari? Seriously? I don't own anything even remotely practical for that."

Michelle grinned, seemingly unbothered by Emily's distress. "Oh, come on, Em, it's an adventure. You'll love it once we're out there, surrounded by elephants and sipping champagne under the stars." Michelle couldn't suppress a laugh, her excitement undimmed. "It means ditch the stilettos and pack a sense of humour. Look, we'll find you something to wear. There's bound to be a shop selling khaki somewhere nearby."

A flicker of doubt passed over Emily's face, quickly replaced by a growing smile as she imagined the adventure ahead. ""A bloody safari? I didn't expect that. But, wait—first-class tickets?" Emily's eyes went wide, her fingers almost trembling as she held the glossy papers.

Michelle's grin widened as she leant back, savoring the moment. "Well, that's a good start. At least he did something right. So, let's grab some takeaway food first, then it's time to pack and set the alarm for 5 a.m."

Emily clutched the papers, her mind racing with visions of luxury, glamour, and top-class hotels. "Alright. I'm doing this. Safari, glamour, and luxury hotels, here we come," she said, her excitement mirroring the beat of their adventure.

42 - EMILY

CAPE TOWN

Emily had planned to sit down after the introduction she'd just rehearsed, but for some inexplicable reason, she felt the need to carry on speaking. "So I made a split-second decision and ran. I left everything behind—the dress, the venue, the guests. The only thing I took was my sister, and here we are, on my honeymoon."

"Did you notice that she just called me a thing?" Michelle laughed.

"Sorry, Sis, I've called you much worse," Emily chuckled. "Anyway, my suitcase didn't arrive, so, get used to seeing me dressed like this until, well, who knows?"

"Maybe the string bean will come and find you here," a man said.

"No, he'll think I've gone to Ibiza or somewhere like that. I just hope all of this is the distraction I need," Emily said as she plonked herself down on her soft, cushioned chair and gestured for her sister to talk next.

A much prettier girl with a more youthful, natural 'girl-next-door' look stood up. She swept her shaggy blonde hair back from her neck and spoke confidently. "So, I'm Michelle, Emily's sister. She didn't say, but we are from Scotland, Glasgow to be precise. I'm on this safari because it was already paid for by Emily's almost-husband. So, as a single woman who never wants to get married, I'm somehow on a honeymoon. Win-win, I guess."

She turned to sit down when Uneze flashed his widest grin. "But tell us something about you."

"Oh, umm, well, I guess I'm grateful for this unexpected adventure. I'm a dental nurse and really needed to get away. Seeing as my boss is actually the guy my sister stood up, it wasn't hard to get time off. I don't think he wants to see me either right now." Michelle stopped talking while a group of rowdy new arrivals looked around the space. Once they'd left, she let a smile cross her face and said, "This is my first real travelling holiday, and I've never camped a day in my life. So, despite already feeling a sense of freedom that I've never felt before, and never being as hot and sweaty as I am now," she paused, raised her glass, and said, "I'm excited. Here goes nothing."

"Thank you, Emily and Michelle. Who's next?" Peri said, offering a smile at the lady sitting next to them.

The group turned their attention to her; she felt the weight of their eyes pressing down, but she kept her voice low, almost a whisper. "I'm Melanie." The words fell from her lips like a soft sigh, barely audible against the backdrop of laughter and conversation. She could feel the tension in her chest, a knot of defiance and resolve hidden beneath her timid exterior. The corners of her mouth threatened to lift into a smile, but she quelled it; her plan hinged on this fragile act of vulnerability, the perfect disguise for the plan.

"Welcome aboard, Melanie," Peri said.

"Thanks, I'm here with my husband, Dave."

43 - MELANIE

Two months before Safari

Melanie sat on the edge of the bed, staring blankly at the crumpled sheets, her fingers tracing the patterns absentmindedly. She glanced at the wedding photo on the nightstand—her and Dave laughing, their eyes alive with hope and joy. A faint smile flickered across her lips, but it quickly vanished, replaced by a tightness in her chest that brought no relief.

Melanie shuffled through the kitchen, the clattering of dishes echoing in the silence. As she poured a cup of coffee, she caught a glimpse of herself in the window—a shadow of the dazzling woman she used to be, her reflection dull and weary. The dreams that once filled her days had slipped through her fingers like sand, each grain a reminder of the joy that had long since dried up.

She glanced at the empty chair where Andrew, her son, used to sit, his phone always in hand, eyes glued to the screen, oblivious to everything— except the digital world that kept him from noticing the one around him. Now, the silence was a welcome reprieve. No more late-night texts demanding rides or ungrateful pleas for money without a word of thanks. As she wiped her hands on a dish towel, she felt an unexpected lightness in her chest. She poured herself a glass of wine, a soft laugh escaping her lips—a laugh that had been buried beneath frustration for years. This wasn't just an empty nest; it was her chance to rediscover who she was outside of the role of caretaker. Now, she just needed to work out what came next. The only thing she knew for sure was that her husband wouldn't be part of it.

Melanie stood by the window, her gaze drifting beyond the glass panes to the colourful garden next door, where Ivan and Denise's laughter floated through the air, a gentle, comforting presence. Their faces radiant with a joy that both comforted and reminded her of the happiness that felt just out of reach. They would often invite her over for tea, their cozy kitchen filled with the scent of freshly baked pies. At times, Melanie would sit on their porch, soaking in their words of wisdom that lifted her spirits in ways she never thought possible. She lived for their stories of their exciting travels to faraway places, places she doubted she'd ever go.

The idea of travelling with Dave flashed through her mind, and the prospect of being alone with him twisted her stomach into knots. She let her mind wander, weaving darker fantasies—scenarios where fate dealt him a cruel hand. Perhaps he'd tumble down the stairs, laughing with that awful, carefree grin plastered on his face, or maybe his heart would falter during one of his late-night escapades with his latest fling. The thought of his absence brought a strange satisfaction, a twisted comfort in the possibility of freedom wrapped in sweet silence.

After a long walk around the local park, Melanie tugged at her jacket to open it and paused at the entrance of her quiet home, the key resting in her hand as she took a deep breath. Each step she took during her endless morning walks felt like a rebellion against the confines of her life, buried under all of its responsibilities. She caught glimpses of her reflection in shop windows; the woman staring back at her was slimmer, lighter, almost foreign. Yet, back at home, she buried this new shape beneath baggy sweatshirts and oversized trousers, every fabric an armour against unwanted attention from her husband.

Later that afternoon, as she joined Denise and Ivan, Melanie's smile brightened the room, a burst of warmth breaking through the lingering clouds. "Welcome back. I've missed you guys," she beamed, her eyes sparkling with genuine warmth.

Denise, with an enthusiasm that bubbled over, leant closer, her eyes gleaming with excitement. "Thanks. We missed you too. We have so many fun stories to tell you. What are your plans later?"

Melanie shrugged lightly, her smile faltering for a brief moment. "Mine? Nothing as always," she replied, her voice carrying a hint of resignation. "Dave is off with his latest bimbo, with the excuse of a work trip."

"I'm sorry," Denise said gently, the concern in her voice palpable.

Melanie waved her hand dismissively, a bitter laugh escaping her lips. "Don't be. The more time he spends with her, the less time he's at home," she said, her voice laced with a surprising sense of relief.

"Have you ever thought of just getting a divorce?" Denise probed, her eyebrows raised in hope.

Melanie's smile faded, replaced by a look of longing. "Every second of every day," she admitted, her voice a whisper. "But I know he'd fight me on it. I've never worked a day in my life. I wouldn't be able to afford this life."

Denise leant in, excitement sparking in her eyes. "We met a great lawyer a few months ago in Spain. He's a newly divorced divorce lawyer. We told him about you, and he wants to meet you."

Melanie's laughter rang out, but it lacked joy. "No, it's okay for Dave to cheat, but I can't."

"No, not as a new love interest—as a divorce lawyer. Although he is extremely good-looking, and you may like him," Denise teased, nudging her arm softly, trying to coax a smile back into Melanie's eyes. "Ready to see the holiday photos?" Denise asked.

"Always."

Denise waited for the computer to turn on and moved closer to the glowing screen, her eyes sparkling with excitement as dazzling images of the African savanna danced before her. "Look at that sunset," she said, her voice dripping with enthusiasm.

Ivan nodded, a grin plastered on his face, recounting tales of their encounters with majestic elephants and playful monkeys. As each photo flickered by, Melanie's smile slowly morphed into something darker. She could almost hear the rustle of the grass and the distant roar of a lion, each sound echoing in her mind like a sinister whisper. Melanie envisioned herself standing in the shadow of a towering baobab tree, the warm breeze tousling her hair, while Dave lingered at the edge of danger, oblivious.

A wicked plan began to take shape, wrapping around her thoughts like a vine—she would lure him into this wild paradise and ensure he never returned. The thrill of the thought sent a shiver down her spine, and she couldn't help but smile as she continued to flip through the memories of what now felt like a world full of possibilities.

Melanie sunk back in her chair, her fingers tapping nervously on the last image, lost in thought. "You have no idea how much I want to go on a safari like this," she sighed, her eyes brightening at the imagined sights of roaring lions and sweeping savannahs.

Ivan raised an eyebrow, a cheeky smirk tugging at the corners of his lips. "You could ask Dave," he suggested, leaning forward with a conspiratorial gleam in his eyes.

Melanie shook her head vigorously, a laugh escaping her lips that was laced with frustration. "No. If I suggest it, he'd say no. It has to be his idea."

Ivan scratched his chin, glancing at the photo album resting nearby, its pages filled with snapshots of their last adventure. "What if we invite him over for dinner? We could pull out the photos again," he proposed.

Melanie chuckled, shaking her head again. "Yes, and the more I insist that I'd hate a safari, the more he'll want to go," she said, a hint of sarcasm colouring her voice as she rolled her eyes. "You have to make him realise how dangerous it is over there. He loves to boast about danger."

Denise, who had been silent until now, leant in, her expression serious. "Honestly, I don't see why you don't just leave him," she said, a determined gleam in her eye. "I'm going to do two dinners: one to convince Dave to go on safari and another with Julius, the divorce lawyer. So you can meet him. I've decided it's time to get you out of this life. You deserve so much better than that idiot."

44 - DAVE

Cape Town

Melanie finished her introduction, sat down, and let her husband do the talking. Something about his stance screamed arrogance as he glanced around the room like he owned the place. His strong Liverpool accent, combined with the slurring of his words between sips of his drink, made it hard for everyone to understand him. "I'm Dave. We are here on this African safari to do something a bit different from our usual beach holidays. I'm very laid back, unphased by anything, so this should be fun. The bigger the animals, the better."

"Welcome to both of you," Peri said, trying her best to keep her poker face in place despite her immediate dislike for this man, Dave.

Dave shot a quick glare at Peri, his brow twisting as her words interrupted his flow. Then he glanced around him, searching for any signs of movement around the doorway. With an exasperated sigh, he pivoted back to the other men, a confident smirk tugging at his lips. "I lead a hectic life back home," he boasted, his chest puffed slightly. "I'm the top salesman in the UK for my plastics company. Everyone else looks up to me, trying to outdo my success. Spoiler alert: they can't. I'm best." He leant back, arms crossed, as if waiting for accolades to rain down on him. The silence stretched uncomfortably, the other men exchanging glances, unsure of how to fill the void. Dave lifted his glass, the ice clinking softly against the rim as he took a slow sip, his eyes gleaming with enthusiasm.

Finally, he broke the stillness, his voice taking on an adventurous tone. "This is the first real break I've had in years. I craved something thrilling and different. An African safari? That's the ticket."

Dave gestured, his words flowing effortlessly, while Melanie sat quietly, a silent backdrop to his charisma. When he wrapped up his story, his eyes sparkled as he turned to the man beside her, leaving Melanie in the shadows of his spotlight, her smile wavering as she remained unnoticed. Uneze took his moment to interject and speak to Melanie, "So, Melanie. Are you excited about this?"

Melanie inhaled deeply, her breath barely making a sound as she shifted her attention to the two sisters at the table. With her hands trembling slightly, she lifted the menu, using it to fan her heated cheeks, which betrayed her nervousness. Her voice emerged as a whisper, barely rising above the ambient chatter. "Ehm, well, a safari wasn't my choice of holiday, but Dave is happy, so that's all that matters." The way she spoke, her words almost losing their way, revealed her discomfort, as though she were trying to shrink into her seat, the bright colours of the restaurant only amplifying her shyness.

With a swift motion, Dave snatched the menu from her grip, sending it skidding across the table. His piercing stare locked onto hers, a storm brewing behind his eyes. "Melanie doesn't know what she does or doesn't want," he spat, his voice dripping with disdain. "She'd be perfectly content lounging on that sofa all day. Just look at her. Honestly, if we stumble upon a hippo, good luck telling the difference," he added, delivering a cheeky slap on the shoulder of the man next to him.

He scratched the back of his neck, the awkwardness hanging thick in the air. Meanwhile, on the other side of the table, the girls exchanged wide-eyed glances, their jaws nearly hitting the floor as they turned to Peri, disbelief written all over their faces.

45 - Dave

Two months before Safari

Dave watched as his wife's heavy figure thudded through the house. He barely offered a mumbled goodbye before slamming the door behind him. The sound echoed in his chest as he absorbed it into the silence. He was sick of having to make excuses to his wife, so just leaving had become the only way to spend time with his girlfriend of almost two years.

Twenty minutes later, he stood before Lauren's door. As he stepped inside, he was greeted not by the warm embrace he craved but by an icy silence. Lauren stood with her arms crossed, her brow twisted, her glare piercing. He slumped onto his usual spot on the sofa, the familiar cushions feeling less inviting than before.

"Dave. I've had enough of this. It's ridiculous," she said, her voice firm, slicing through the silence like a knife. The intensity in her eyes was a storm brewing, ready to unleash. "You promised me you'd leave her, and yet you're still there."

Dave attempted to deflect her glare, but the frustration in her stance pinned him down. "I will leave her. I just need the timing to be right," he stammered, his voice shaky.

"Right? You said you'd leave when your little brat went to college, but here you are, still tiptoeing around it. You said you needed to make sure he settled in. Yesterday you said after Christmas." Her words spit out like bullets, each one hitting harder than the last.

"Babe, don't be angry about this. It's just a matter of time; I will leave her," he said, trying to soothe the mood between them.

"No, you'll leave here now. I'm sick of it. It's her or me." Her resolve was unshakeable as she glared at him.

"You know I don't love her, or even go near her." He stood with his arms crossed, fingers gripping his biceps tightly, as if trying to shield himself from her piercing stare.

"Prove it. Do something about it," Lauren screamed.

The intensity of her stare felt like a spotlight, illuminating Dave's internal battle, the choice looming like a dense fog that crept into his chest, squeezing his heart. "I just need to sort out the financial side of things first," he murmured, glancing down to avoid her scrutinizing eyes. "You know she gets half of everything in the divorce."

Her posture was resolute, arms crossed, lips pursed, sending a clear message that she had drawn a line in the sand. "Well, sort it out, and quickly." Lauren stepped back, her fiery red curls bouncing defiantly with each movement. "Do what you need to do, but I'm not hanging around waiting for a poor man with no money."

"I pay for your bills here in this house already. What more do you want?" The desperation seeped into his voice, his brows twisting together as he searched her face for any signs of compassion.

Lauren took a deep breath, her chest rising and falling dramatically, as if the air she inhaled was heavy with all the unspoken frustrations. "Big wow. You pay for my electricity and water," she said, her fingers tracing the curves of her hourglass figure with exaggerated disdain. "Look at me, look at this." She gestured to herself, the confidence radiating from her stance, illuminating the stark contrast between them. "I could have so much more than you and your measly bill money. Sort it out. I'll give you one month."

"You are giving me an ultimatum?" Dave asked.

The finality of her words echoed in the silence that followed, the atmosphere thick with tension. "Don't come here; don't call me. I'll wait for one month, then I'm officially on the market again. I'll be snapped up in a second with someone who'll treat me the way you used to treat me."

Dave's first stop was to his colleague in accounts at his workplace. He stormed into the office, his breath ragged. He barely glanced at Howard before plopping down in front of him. "Ever heard of making an appointment?" Howard quipped, arching an eyebrow, his attention shifting between his watch and Dave's agitated demeanor.

"This is too urgent. I need your help," Dave shot back, his voice barely above a whisper as he hovered, the intensity of his stare demanding attention.

Howard sighed, glancing at the clock on the wall. "I've got a meeting in ten minutes. Make it quick."

"Alright... I need to divorce my wife, but I need to hide my money first."

With a chuckle, Howard sank back, crossing his arms. "It's about time. I don't know how you've stayed with her so long."

"Lauren's given me an ultimatum, so I have to move the money. You helped me... acquire it, so I need your help to get rid of it, make it disappear until I need it."

"Never mention how you got the money again," Howard said, his expression shifting to one of caution. "Look, I want to help you, but since that near miss with the internal audit, I have to keep my nose clean— bright and shiny clean."

"So, you can't help me?" Dave's voice edged on desperation, his face taut with tension.

"No, but..." Howard reached for a notepad, scribbling down a number with a quick motion. "This man here is the one to see. Arnie can make money disappear—quickly, too. He did it when I left my missus."

Dave's eyes followed the paper as Howard passed it over. He folded it carefully, slipping it into his pocket with a determined nod. "Thanks. How much does he charge?"

"He isn't cheap; he takes a percentage of the money he moves. But it was worth it. I kept my hands clean and seventy percent of my money. The missus got nothing more than an allowance and a small flat."

"What about your houses?" Howard smirked, a gleam of mischief in his eyes.

"This guy made it look like I'd taken a second mortgage out on both the summer house and our main house. She couldn't touch those," Howard said.

"Seventy percent, you said. So, this dude takes thirty percent of everything?"

"Exactly. But he's good and worth every penny. Now look, I have to go. We never had this conversation, right?" Howard said as he rose from his seat and grabbed his briefcase.

With a playful zip of his fingers across his lips, Dave slipped out of the office. His fingers drummed nervously against the edge of the crisp, white business card. He glanced at his watch and finally dialled the number, his heart racing as the phone rang and he made an appointment.

When he stepped into Arnie's office later that day, the first thing that hit him was the open space— the walls stretched high and bare, letting in beams of sunlight through floor-to-ceiling windows. A striking secretary, dressed in a form-fitting outfit, flashed a bright smile that felt more out of place than welcoming.

Dave's eyes scanned the room, the sleek, minimalist office throwing him off guard. This was not the image he'd conjured of a man capable of erasing a life.

Arnie's initial greeting shattered any preconceived ideas. Instead of the sleazy figure Dave had imagined, Arnie exuded an air of authority and sincerity, his demeanor calm and professional.

"Dave, it's nice to meet you." Arnie extended a hand, his grip firm and reassuring.

"Thanks, and thanks for seeing me so soon," Dave replied, desperation lacing his voice.

Arnie settled into his chair, a notepad poised and ready. "What can I do for you?"

With each word, Dave unravelled the tangled mess of his life, the burden of his marriage spilling out alongside his frustrations.

Arnie's pen danced across the paper, capturing every detail with a swift precision that made Dave feel both exposed and hopeful. As he finished, he sank back in his seat, the long sigh escaping him like a deflating balloon.

Arnie's tone was matter-of-fact as he threw his pen down onto the pad and said, "It's a pretty standard situation and easy enough to handle. When do you need it done?"

"As soon as possible. I need to show Lauren that I've started divorce proceedings."

"I can get this done in a few weeks. I take thirty percent of everything," Arnie said.

"So, I have to give you thirty percent of everything just to ensure my wife doesn't get fifty percent? That doesn't make much sense," Dave said.

"Yes, but this way, your wife will get nothing at all, apart from a small allowance. I'll even make sure you keep your house." Arnie said with a smirk dancing on his lips.

As the steam from the coffee the secretary delivered curled into the air, Dave stared at Arnie, the tension pooling in the pit of his stomach. "Let me think about it," he finally said, his voice low.

"Think quickly. If you come back with more questions and don't hire me on the spot, the percentage goes up to forty," Arnie warned, a hint of playfulness in his tone.

"Are there any other solutions? I mean, thirty percent is a bit steep."

"Apart from killing the poor woman? No. It's this way, or no way." Arnie chuckled.

46 - Dave

A month before Safari

Dave trudged out of the office, his shoulders slumped like a wilted flower, as he walked to his own office to finish his day at work. The fluorescent lights flickered overhead as he passed his coworkers, but he couldn't muster the energy to return their cheerful greetings. He pottered at his desk until it was time to return home.

Once inside the house, he dropped his bag by the door and shot a look at Melanie, who stood in the kitchen, animatedly stirring a pot. "Hey, we're going out for dinner with Denise and Ivan tonight," she announced, her voice oddly excited.

His brow tensed, and he let out a heavy sigh that seemed to echo through the silence of the room. "Really, do we have to? I can't face them," he muttered, his eyes dropping to the floor as if the tiles held the answer to his despair.

Melanie's shoulders squared with determination. "They just got back from holiday. I haven't seen them in weeks. They want to show us their holiday photos."

"Not again," he grumbled, his voice laced with exhaustion.

"Come on. It'll be fun. They did a six-week camping safari in Africa. It sounds really dangerous. They've got stories about lions, elephants, snakes, and God knows what else," she encouraged, her eyes sparkling with enthusiasm.

Dave rolled his eyes, but a hint of a smirk tugged at the corner of his mouth. "At least it's not pictures of Roman ruins like last time," he mumbled under his breath.

Melanie stepped closer, placing a gentle hand on his arm. "Please, for me. It's the closest to danger I will ever be, and all we have to do is look at photos, and they always have great food."

He pondered for a moment, glancing at the clock on the wall as if it might offer an escape. "Alright. Just don't be annoyed if I make an excuse after half an hour and come home."

"Whatever, just please, for me, stay a while," Melanie said.

Dave propped himself up against his neighbors' kitchen counter, arms crossed tightly over his chest. He raised an eyebrow, while Melanie, perched on the edge of her seat, toyed with her hair, tucking it behind her ear. With a sigh, Dave accepted the bottle of beer that Ivan thrust toward him, his lips curling into a forced smile that barely concealed his disdain.

"Dave. It's been a while," Ivan greeted, extending a hand.

"Work, you know. Keeps me busy and away from home," Dave replied, his voice laced with a hint of irritation as he forced a chuckle.

"More time for us with your delightful wife," Ivan continued, an earnestness in his voice that made Dave's smile falter momentarily.

"If you like her so much, you can keep her. I don't mind," he shot back, masking a flicker of annoyance with a jovial tone, though the gleam in his eye hinted at deeper feelings beneath the surface.

"Come on in, get settled. We wanted to show you the photos of our safari." Ivan's excitement was infectious as he beckoned them forward. Dave's curiosity battled against his reluctance. "Don't worry, we remembered about your nut allergy, the meal is nut-free."

As the images of electric landscapes and wild animals flashed across the screen, Ivan animatedly recounted their adventures, his voice rising with enthusiasm. "We slept under the African skies, listening to the wild calls in the distance. We climbed sand dunes and rafted down rapids. We have never had a holiday like it."

"Camping? Why? Surely you can afford hotels," Dave mused, an eyebrow raised.

"It's not about the money. It's about the experience," Ivan insisted, the thrill of their escapades lighting up his features. "And the danger. We came face to face with elephants, hippos, and lions. You can't imagine how scary and thrilling that is."

"Yeah, but is it really dangerous, or do they just make you feel like it is?" Dave challenged, leaning in slightly, intrigued despite himself.

"Both," Denise chimed in, her eyes sparkling with mischief. "It was, beyond a shadow of a doubt, the scariest yet thrilling holiday we've ever been on. You could easily slip on a rock or down a cliff face during your free time."

As the stories filled the room, Dave, arms still crossed, was caught in a whirlwind of curiosity, wondering if perhaps his neighbors weren't as dull as he'd thought after all.

Ivan took over the narrating and said, "These were our two guides. Uneze and James. They were like glorified babysitters, keeping us safe. There was another tour that we crossed paths with, and they'd had a nightmare. A lion had entered their camp at night and pawed and ripped the tent. They barely escaped."

"Oh my god, what happened?" Melanie asked.

"From what we heard, the camp security got there just in time and somehow got rid of the lions. The couple was terrified. It was a hard lesson on how fleeting life is out there in the African bush. From what I heard, they left soon after. No one could shake that nightmare. Then on our tour, there was a woman on her own who woke up to find her tent full of snakes. She ended up in the hospital, and she's still there. They aren't sure if she'll make it or not."

"Oh my god. I will never go on a safari in my life," Melanie said.

Dave leant back, a mischievous grin creeping across his face. "I think it sounds fun. I could do with a bit of danger in my life." His words hung in the air, a daring challenge to the fears that wrapped around his wife.

Ivan shot Denise a quick nod, his eyes glinting with mischief as he leant in slightly, the corners of his mouth twitching upward. He lowered his voice conspiratorially, leaning closer. "You know, knowing what I know now, I probably wouldn't have booked this trip. Sure, it's a thrill for the tough guys, but honestly, an African safari feels a bit too perilous for some folks."

Denise crossed her arms, eyebrows knitting together as she shot him a disapproving look. "Come on, Ivan. That's not nice," he chuckled, shaking his head slightly.

"But let's be real. Remember those moments when you looked like you'd seen a ghost? You wanted to bolt back home a couple of times."

Denise's lips pursed in reluctant acknowledgment, her eyes darting sideways. "I guess."

Melanie chimed in, with a shake of her head and said, "I would hate it."

Dave chuckled and said, "So, tell me, what company did you use? Because I think we've just discovered our next holiday destination."

Melanie let her draw job as she said, "Don't I get a say in this holiday decision-making process?"

Across the table, Dave took another swig of his drink, the amber liquid swirling in the glass as it caught the soft sparkle of the overhead lights. A carefree grin tugged at his lips, a stark contrast to the tension that crackled in the air. "I think it will be amazing," he said, his words slurring slightly, each syllable dripping with a casual indifference.

Dave savored the idea of a dangerous safari—an escape not just from the mundane, but from Melanie herself. As the days rolled by and he secured the safari booking, his excitement of taking his wife on a safari from which she wouldn't return alive morphed into a nagging unease.

The sprawling sand dunes and roaring rapids transformed in his mind from an exhilarating escape into a daunting maze of challenges, mainly security systems and video surveillance that the campsites boasted of having. It dawned on him that orchestrating his grand plan would require more than just bravado; it would need careful plotting and assistance. He wasn't exactly sure who, but as the thoughts of paying someone to move his money faded into the past, they were exchanged with paying someone to help him kill his wife on safari. Now his only question was who

47 - Dave

A month before Safari

Alistair glanced over his shoulder, his son's stern stare pressing down on him like a heavy cape. As soon as AJ turned the corner, Alistair fled the small, f confines of his home. He stumbled through the dimly lit streets, navigating his way to the bar that had become his refuge. The worn sign swung gently above him, flickering in the evening light as he pushed through the door, the scent of spilt beer and old wood wrapping around him like a well-worn blanket.

"Alistair, what the hell happened to you?" Annalisa's voice cut through the haze as he dropped onto a stool with a thud, his shoulders slumping under an invisible weight.

"The usual," he chuckled, the sound hollow. "This is what happens when I come face to face with someone twice my size." He gestured toward the beer pump, a nervous laugh escaping his lips.

"You tell me you aren't here for trouble," she replied, her brow arched sceptically as she huffed at his dishevelled appearance—his shirt askew and a bruise blooming on his cheek.

"I promise. I've had enough trouble for the week. I just want a beer and a smile from the pretty barmaid." He tried to flash her a charming grin, but it faltered under her expression of scrutiny.

Annalisa chuckled, arms crossed, her eyes sparkling with a concern. "I'll give you the beer, but I'll save the smile for when you walk out of here without throwing a single punch or even a single glance at anyone." She paused, eyeing him more seriously. "Anyway, what happened this time?"

"Let's just say my argumentative nature wasn't appreciated by my last employer," he confessed, the words spilling out like secrets. "So, I've moved on. I'm a paid bully now, you know, debt retrieval and making threats."

"Oh, you must be so proud," her tone dripped with sarcasm, but her eyes softened with sympathy. "Where are all your old friends? I haven't seen any of them around here recently."

"They're not friends anymore. They all dumped me when I got kicked off the force."

"Oh, can't you just change jobs? Clean yourself up a bit, dry out, and make a fresh start." The pleading tone in her voice betrayed her concern, eyes searching his for a flicker of hope.

"It's just a matter of time, and I'll find something," he said, but the confidence in his voice wavered. He hated how weak he sounded.

"No, it's just a matter of time until you get yourself into real trouble," Annalisa replied, her eyes narrowing. She had seen this before.

A few minutes later, a middle-aged man walked in and plonked himself down at the bar. "Double whisky, neat," he said to Annalisa.

"Yes," she answered with a smile. "Had a difficult day?"

"You have no idea," he replied.

Alistair turned to Annalisa with a cheeky grin and asked, "Now, honey, why don't I get that same smile? Is it too much to ask?"

"You get that smile when you prove to me that you're not up to any tricks, like beating up any of our patrons tonight."

The man who sat beside Alistair turned, interested in this conversation, and said, "Tricks and beatings; intriguing."

"She's exaggerating. Just because I'm a bit wild and will do anything for some money in my bank, it doesn't mean I'm a bad person," Alistair said.

"Just a desperate one," Annalisa added, leaning in, her smile softening but filled so many things she wanted to say. "And a very annoying drunk."

"It's not my fault people want to pay me to do their dirty work." Alistair shrugged his shoulders. "It's staggering what people will do for money."

This conversation had suddenly grabbed the man's full attention. He stretched his hand out towards Alistair and said, "Well, your work sounds more interesting than mine. I'm Dave."

"Alistair," he said, clinking his glass against Dave's.

"So, tell me more about your work," Dave said, leaning in with genuine curiosity.

"I've already said too much."

"Come on, I have a boring job, a dumbass, useless wife that I can't seem to get away from, and I need some excitement."

"Excitement isn't my thing, although I could probably help you with that wife situation," Alistair teased.

"What do you have in mind?" Dave asked, his eyes narrowing slightly, intrigued.

"Nothing. I'm just drunk. Ignore me. Ask Annalisa here; it's best to ignore anything I say, right?"

"No doubt about that," Annalisa said with a grin.

Alistair turned back to his drink, finished it, ordered another one, and turned away from the talkative stranger.

48 - Dave

Three weeks before Safari

A few days later, Alistair sat at the counter, the clink of glasses and muffled conversations fading into the background as he nursed his drink, lost in thought. A figure emerged from the haze, and as the man approached, a flicker of recognition crossed Dave's face, like a switch being flipped in a dark room.

"Hey, you look a bit more respectable without all the bruises," he said, a hint of a smirk playing on his lips.

Alistair squinted, his brow furrowing as he searched the depths of his memory. "Ah, the guy from last week," he finally replied, waving a dismissive hand. The man's outfit was jarring: a baggy hoodie that swallowed his frame, paired with oversized sunglasses that screamed of paranoia. "You look like the stereotypical Unabomber," Alistair teased, a laugh escaping him.

"I don't want people to recognise me," the man replied, his voice dropping as if sharing a secret.

"Didn't think I'd see you back here. This place doesn't exactly scream 'your vibe.'" Alistair gestured around, taking in the dingy surroundings with a smirk.

"Normally I wouldn't, but I was hoping to bump into you again. You don't come here much," he said, his eyes darting nervously around the room, as if expecting someone to eavesdrop.

"Look, Annalisa, I have my own private stalker," Alistair joked.

"No, I'm not a stalker," Dave protested, leaning closer, his voice barely above a whisper. "I just need some help, and I thought you may like to earn some money."

Alistair raised an eyebrow, intrigued. "I never say no to money. What do you need?"

Dave glanced around the bar as if the walls could hear him. "I don't think we can discuss this here. Is there somewhere we can go?"

"Let's go outside for a smoke," Alistair suggested, leading the way through the bar's heavy door. Once in the cool night air, Dave propped himself up against a brick wall, fidgeting. "I need you to help me lose my wife."

"Lose her?" Alistair asked, a wry smile tugging at his lips.

"Yes, I've booked us on a camping safari, and the more I think about it, the more I'm going to need help."

"I'm sorry, but you need me to accompany you on safari so that you can send your wife into the wilderness and never come back?" Alistair asked, incredulous.

"Something like that, yes," Dave confirmed.

"I'm not your man, sorry. I beat up scumbags who don't pay their bills. I threaten people who haven't paid their rent. I'm a bodyguard for thugs. I don't kill people, especially innocent women."

"Innocent? She ruined my life. She murdered my life," Dave said, his voice strained with barely controlled anger.

"That's a bit of a flimsy argument," Alistair replied, crossing his arms and leaning back against the brick wall.

"She made me sign a prenup, and if I divorce her, I lose half of everything."

"How long have you been married?" Alistair asked, curiosity sparked despite himself.

"Eighteen very long years," Dave replied, voice flat.

"Well, maybe she deserves half of everything. You don't seem like a likeable fella to me," Alistair said with an almost wicked laugh.

"I'm in love with another woman, and I want to be with her. However, she won't be interested in me if I don't have any money," Dave explained.

"Sure, that sounds like true love to me." Alistair chuckled, shaking his head. "One more chance to convince me."

"I'll pay you fifty thousand pounds to do it."

Alistair halted abruptly and directed his scrutiny toward Dave, his expression shifting. "Give me your driving license, then I'll decide what to do with you and this obscene request of yours." Alistair extended his hand, waiting patiently for Dave to fumble in his wallet. Eventually, Dave slid out his license and placed it in Alistair's hand.

"What are you going to do with it?" Dave asked, frowning.

"A background check on you."

Dave's heart raced, pounding against his ribcage like a drum. A cold sweat trickled down his back, and his palms grew clammy as the gravity of his words sank in. "What? Are you a cop? What are you going to do? Arrest me?"

"No. I just need to know who I'm talking to right now. And weigh my options," Alistair said, his voice calm but firm.

"What then?"

"Nothing; we go inside, we finish our drinks, and you never come here again." Alistair stubbed his cigarette out on the pavement and turned towards the bar. "If I decide to do this, don't worry. I'll find you. You've already told me where you work, and your address is on here."

As it dawned on Dave what a stupid decision he'd just made, he seemed disorientated and confused. He followed Alistair in silence as he grabbed his drink and moved back to the bar. "Say something," Dave insisted.

Alistair shot a quick glance from the corner of his eye, his jaw tightening. "See you around," he muttered before turning sharply on his heel, leaving a heavy silence in his wake.

As soon as the door clicked shut behind him, Dave's face twisted into a grimace. His lips moved soundlessly as he shot a frustrated glance at Annalisa.

She met his glance with a raised eyebrow, her hands moving deftly. With a sharp bang, she set another glass down in front of him, the crystal ringing out like a warning bell. "He's trouble. If I were you, I'd stay a long way from him."

49 - Dave

Three weeks before Safari

Alistair had spent a few days mulling over his options. The background check he had his friend run came up clean. He yawned as he read about Dave's dull, uneventful past, and followed him to study his routine. To Alistair, Dave was the epitome of predictability—a textbook character with no plot twists. He was utterly unremarkable except for his desire to be rid of his wife.

Once he'd sussed out Dave, Alistair turned his attention to Dave's wife. He had hoped there'd be something in her history that would justify his involvement. Yet, nothing stood out. As she shuffled down the street, her oversized cardigan hung loosely, the fabric worn at the edges. She kept her eyes downward, avoiding connecting with her surroundings or people in it, her lips pressed into a thin line of disinterest.

Alistair could see why Dave wasn't interested in her and even had another woman. But nothing about Melanie screamed bitterness or malice. She certainly didn't seem like someone who needed to be murdered.

Despite this, Alistair couldn't shake the thoughts of what he could do with the money—trips he could take, debts he could pay off. He mentally tallied up how much it would take to get back on track. His fingers rifled through the crumpled bills in his wallet, offering little reassurance. The echo of laughter and clinking glasses from a nearby poker table lingered in his mind—an agonizing reminder of the night that had left him empty. He clenched his jaw and pulled out his phone, dialing the number that could change everything

At the next meeting, in the dim light of a secluded grove, tension crackled between Alistair and Dave. Alistair leant against the rough bark of an ancient tree, his posture rigid, eyes scanning the shadowy surroundings.

"I'll take half upfront, half upon completion of your wife's disappearance, plus the cost of the safari and flights."

Dave's voice remained steady, though a bead of sweat trickled down his temple. Alistair observed, noting his nerves. He nodded slowly, eyes narrowing.

"Alright," Alistair replied, his tone sharp. "You'll need to be quick. I'll book you on the three-week safari so you can get the job done and go."

"Cash only," Alistair insisted.

"What?" Dave blinked, taken aback.

"Cash or nothing. You don't want this traced through a bank, and neither do I," Alistair added.

"I don't have that much cash," Dave stammered with desperation in his voice.

"Find it, or the deal's off. Same time, same place in a week," Alistair said, turning and walking away, leaving Dave standing alone, uncertainty in his eyes.

A week later, the city lights filtered softly through the sprawling branches of an oak tree in the park. Dave shifted nervously, glancing around before pulling a bulging bag from his coat. He handed it to Alistair, who accepted it with steady hands.

"That's it—all of it. The tickets for the flight to Cape Town are in there, along with the safari voucher," Dave murmured, anxiety creasing his forehead. "How will I know you'll do it?" His voice was barely above a whisper, as if speaking too loudly might shatter the fragile agreement.

Alistair's lips curled into a brief smirk, his eyes locking with Dave's. "You don't," he replied coolly, his words final and chilling.

"I'll see you on safari, then?" Dave asked, his voice quivering.

Alistair shoved the money deep into his coat pocket, the fabric rustling like leaves. "Maybe," he said, turning on his heel and walking away, his footsteps crunching on the gravel.

50 - Melanie

A month before safari.

With the safari booked, Melanie knew better than to search online and leave a trace. Instead, she sat hunched over a weathered wooden table in the dimly lit library, the musty scent of old books filling the air. Her pencil scratched rapidly on paper as she jotted down frantic notes.

Each turn of the page brought vivid images of the vast African bush, filled with menacing yet thrilling sights lurking behind tall grasses. Harsh sunlight cast an unforgiving glare on rocky cliffs. Her thoughts spiraled deeper as she read about toxic plants thriving in the unforgiving wilderness. She thumbed through chapters on dangerous creatures—the lions, hyenas, and leopards that roamed the savanna.

A shiver ran down her spine as she sketched a crude diagram of the tour route, noting incidents where tourists had met tragic ends— waterfalls leading to deceptive pools, rafting excursions where lives had been lost. Melanie's lips curled into a grim smile as she snapped her notebook shut. The library buzzed with the whispers of countless stories, but for Melanie, her own plot was coming together—a dark tale with a purpose far removed from the innocent adventure Dave had imagined.

Melanie walked into the bustling café, her heart fluttering as she spotted Julius sitting at a corner table. His dark hair was effortlessly tousled, and a confident smile played on his lips. She felt a blush creep up her neck, the warmth spreading to her cheeks. The crisp lines of his tailored suit contrasted sharply with her oversized sweater and baggy jeans, an outfit chosen more for comfort than charm. Looking at her own reflection, a pang of regret hit her. If she had known this meeting would bring her face to face with someone so striking, perhaps she would have dressed differently.

Nervously, Melanie shifted in her seat and fiddled with the strap of her bag, offering a tentative smile. "Hi, I'm Melanie. Thanks for meeting me."

Julius uncrossed his arms, a hint of curiosity in his eyes. "You're welcome. Denise and Ivan told me a lot about you. You're in a bit of a pickle, aren't you?" His casual tone didn't match the knot tightening in her stomach.

Melanie's fingers drummed on the table. Her eyes dropped to the polished wood. "No, I'm in a loveless marriage with a manipulative psycho." The words slipped out, heavy with the burden of her reality.

Julius raised an eyebrow, a smirk tugging at the corners of his mouth. "That's not the best type of marriage, or the best person to divorce."

Melanie sighed, deflating like a balloon. "That's why I'm still in it. I know I've got a prenup; I've read it over and over. I can't get out of this without walking away penniless. If he leaves me, then I get half of everything." Her voice cracked under the weight of her desperation.

Julius leant forward, determination flickering in his eyes. "Let me be the judge of that. Do you have it with you?" Melanie hesitated, heart pounding, before pulling a manila envelope from her bag.

She placed it on the table, palm resting on the edge as if afraid to sever the connection. "It's okay," Julius said gently, brushing his fingers across the envelope. "I'll look and see what we can do with it."

Melanie's mind raced, she stared at him. He was striking—his features could belong to a movie star. She wondered what flaws lay beneath that handsome exterior. Before she could stop herself, a question slipped out, raw and unfiltered. "So, how was your divorce, and why on earth would she want to divorce you?"

Julius leant back in his chair, a wry smile creeping across his face as he rubbed his chin thoughtfully. "We were fantastic together, you know? Fireworks, laughter. But somewhere along the line, that excitement fizzled out. By the end, it felt like we were plotting each other's demise instead of sharing a life." He paused, staring out the window where the sun cast a warm sparkle. "Twenty years... and then just like that, we drifted apart." A bitter chuckle escaped him.

"I'm sorry," Melanie whispered.

"The divorce was surprisingly civil. I was cordial, but then I found out she had someone else waiting in the wings. Maybe I should've been tougher on her." He shook his head, amusement flickering in his eyes as he leant forward, elbows on the table.

Melanie, embarrassed, hoped her cheeks weren't as flushed as she felt. "Seriously, though. Why do we still cling to the idea of marriage? Look at the younger generations—they just live together, no strings attached. When it's over, they pack up and move out. It's like they've cracked the code, while we're still dragging our old-fashioned baggage around."

They chatted for two hours before making plans to meet again. Their afternoon meetings shifted from tense discussions of divorce to a space where laughter echoed, and vulnerabilities were shared.

Each time Melanie left, the heavy weight of her long coat stayed in the car—a symbolic shedding of her past and the constraints of her marriage, allowing her to breathe in the freedom of newfound femininity.

Each outing together felt like a mini-adventure, whether it was gliding effortlessly on the gentle waves of the south coast or trudging through the lush trails of Cheshire, or even wandering through the charming Cotswolds with Julius's dogs.

As the weeks passed, Melanie's heart raced at the thought of their first kiss, a moment that could change everything. But the fear of losing everything she held dear loomed over her like a storm cloud.

One crisp morning, as they strolled through the dew-kissed grass, the air thick with foreboding,They spoke in unison, their eyes locking in a moment of shared understanding. "I need to talk to you."

The spontaneity of their words hung in the air, sparking a flicker of curiosity between them, quickly followed by a burst of nervous laughter.

"You first," Julius urged, his brow knitted, concern pooling in his eyes.

Carrying the weight of her confession like a lead balloon, Melanie exhaled sharply, her voice laced with frustration. "Dave is so obsessed with this safari idea that he wants us to start skydiving again. He's convinced it'll... reignite something in us."

Julius's eyes widened, the words slicing through him. "You skydive? Since when?"

"We used to. For years," Melanie admitted, her tone softening as the memories floated to the surface—adrenaline, weightlessness, freedom. "Until life got in the way, like it always does. Now, he wants to do a jump

Julius's jaw tightened, his mind catching on the word safari. He forced his voice to remain neutral. "Wait... are you saying you're going on a safari with him?"

Melanie blinked, her lips parting in slight surprise, as if she hadn't meant to let that slip. "Oh. Yeah, I guess I am. It's just... part of the trip, you know? It wasn't really my idea."

His stomach sank, but he kept his expression carefully composed. "Sounds... exciting," he managed, though the words tasted bitter. "A safari in Africa with your husband. That's... a big deal."

She gave a noncommittal shrug, her fingers fidgeting with her sleeve. "It's not like we're doing it to reconnect or anything. Trust me, Julius, I'm not going because I want to. I just—" She paused, her eyes flicking away. "It's complicated."

Julius nodded, his chest tightening. But the thought of her sharing something as awe-inspiring as the African savannah with someone else—especially Dave—made his pulse quicken with sadness.

"Well," he said finally, his voice quieter, "I hope it's worth it. You deserve something amazing, Melanie."

She glanced up, her smile softening. "Thanks. But honestly, I'd rather just skydive and skip the safari altogether. Flying is the only part of this trip I'm looking forward to."

Her words sent a small ripple of relief through him, though he hated himself for it. He wanted to say more, to tell her that she didn't need to go at all, that she could leave Dave behind and do something for herself. But it wasn't his place. Not yet.

Instead, he tilted forward, keeping his tone light. "So, you're doing this for you, then? Not for him?"

"Exactly," she said, her voice firm but laced with weariness. "Flying was when I felt most alive. Once I'm divorced, I won't be able to afford it anymore. So, I might as well make the most of it now."

The word *divorced* sent an thrill through Julius's chest, but it was the mention of Dave—the idea of her standing beside him on an adventure—that twisted the knife. "I just hate that you're doing this with him," he said, his tone thick with barely masked pain. "I'm jealous, okay? I know I shouldn't be, but I am."

Melanie raised an eyebrow, her lips curving into a small, almost mischievous smile. "Jealous, huh? Is it wrong that I kind of like hearing that?" She let the moment linger before quickly redirecting the conversation. "But enough about that. What did you want to talk about?"

Julius shifted in his seat, his expression clouded. He looked down for a moment, as though weighing his next words carefully, before meeting her gaze head-on. "I can't be your lawyer anymore."

Her smile faded, confusion knitting her brow. "What? Why? Did something happen?"

"I found you someone great—better than me," he began, his voice trembling slightly. "I'll cover her fees, Melanie. She's incredible, and I promise—"

"I don't want someone else." Her voice sharpened, cutting through his. "I want you. Why are you doing this?"

Julius inhaled deeply, the vulnerability in his eyes stripping away any pretense. "Because a lawyer can't represent someone they're in love with."

Melanie froze, her breath hitching as the weight of his words hit her square in the chest. "What? Julius... we're just friends. You *can* be my lawyer."

He shook his head, the raw honesty of his confession hanging between them. "Melanie, I'm in love with you. I have been for a while. And if I represent you, I can't be objective. I can't... separate what I feel."

Her laughter was nervous, disbelieving, but the rapid pounding of her heart betrayed her. "Surely, if you're in love with me, then you'd fight even harder for me."

Julius chuckled softly, but the strain was evident in his expression. "Maybe. But right now, all I want is to be with you. I can't focus on anything else."

The world around them blurred, shrinking until it was just the two of them in the moment. The air crackled with something unspoken but undeniable.

"Me too," Melanie whispered, her voice trembling as she stepped closer, her fingers brushing against his. She leaned into his warmth, and when their lips met, it was like the final click of a lock—fragile yet unstoppable, as if the universe itself had conspired to bring them to this moment.

51 - Melanie

A month before safari.

A few days after her first refresher skydive, a process needed to be able to solo fly internationally, Melanie sat in a sleek, modern office. Her heart raced, not from the thrill of free-falling but from the thought of the conversation ahead.

Julius sat beside her, his presence like a steady anchor in the chaos of her mind. The lawyer, a sharp-eyed woman with a no-nonsense demeanor, spoke in a calm, reassuring tone, outlining the possibilities in front of them. Melanie's fingers fumbled with the hem of her blouse as she processed the implications.

"Julius tells me that although you get half of everything if he leaves you, you said that he's moved all the money offshore."

"Yes, I checked all of our accounts, and there is nothing in them. He's probably taken a second mortgage on the house, so it will look like we have nothing," Melanie said.

The lawyer scribbled notes and said, "So, we are going to need forensic accountants involved; that's costly. The best outcome hinges on catching him—cheating, stealing, breaking the law, or in a scandal."

"He'd never let me catch him. He's too careful for that." Melanie explained. "He cheats all the time; I could try and get some proof."

Melanie glanced at Julius, his reassuring nod igniting a flicker of hope within her.

"What about your son?" the lawyer asked, her focus sharp and probing.

Melanie sighed, the corners of her mouth drooping. "He's grown up, in college, and as far as I'm concerned, he hates both of us. Probably wouldn't come home if we paid him." Her voice was laced with resignation, yet a hint of bitter humor danced in her eyes.

The lawyer offered a knowing smile. "Oh, you wish. They always come back. Once they've realised how tough life is out there, then they come running."

"Okay, in that case, Dave gets him. He's like a mini version of his father, and I'm happy to be rid of him until he gives me grandkids to raise." Laughter bubbled from Melanie, lightening the mood, even if just for a moment.

"How soon do you want to get this started?" the lawyer asked, her pen poised over a notepad.

Melanie looked at Julius and grabbed his hand before replying, "Soon. But we are going on safari next week, and I don't want to be stuck in a tent with him in the middle of a divorce."

"You could just do it before and get out of the safari," Julius suggested.

Melanie shook her head vehemently. "No. He wouldn't go either as he wants to watch me suffer. I'd be stuck here with him, missing out on the adventure of a lifetime."

"You'd stay with him for a safari?" The lawyer raised an eyebrow, skepticism clear in her voice.

"It's the best trip I will have ever taken. He isn't interested in me; in fact, he's probably got a plan to get rid of me while we're over there," Melanie quipped, a wry grin dancing in her eyes, her voice laced with dark humor.

Julius leant closer, his expression serious. "Melanie. You can't go if you seriously think that."

"Julius, I was only joking. It's fine. I bet he'll have his bimbo in the next tent anyway. I know it seems strange, but this is something I have to do. I'd rather be with you instead, but Dave owes me this," Melanie explained.

"I don't like the thought of him touching you." Concern creased Julius's brow, a protective instinct surfacing.

"He hasn't touched me in years. Don't worry; I can defend myself if he should even bother—though I know he won't. I'm twenty years too old for his taste in women." Melanie's laugh rang out, light and defiant. "I have to go to Africa. There is something I need to do before I divorce him and end up living on the streets."

"Be careful," the lawyer said.

"I'll see you when I get back from safari. We'll get started then. Just let me know what you need from me, and I'll make sure it's ready before I leave," Melanie said.

52 - DENNIS

Cape Town

Dave wrapped up his enthusiastic monologue, his eyes gleaming with excitement. "So, that's why we're here. The holiday of a lifetime. I can't wait to get started. I've been here two days, and I've got my own private elephant right here," he said, gesturing towards his wife, "but now it's time to see the real thing."

Peri dismissed Dave's comment with a tight smile, her glare cold and focused on him as she forced herself to say, "Welcome, Melanie and Dave." The slight emphasis on Melanie's name felt like a small victory, a moment to reclaim her space in the room. Dave didn't seem to listen, his eyes moving constantly towards the door, as if watching for someone— or something. Whatever it was, it clearly made Dave uneasy.

Just the sight of him made Peri's irritation bubble up. Six weeks with him? The thought made her stomach twist. "Alright, I guess it's your time to introduce yourself," she gestured to the man sitting beside Dave.

The man set his beer down with a soft thud, cleared his throat, and nervously raked a hand through his mousey brown hair, almost as if trying to tame his own anxiety. He glanced around the group, his eyes flickering from one face to another before cracking a cheeky grin.

"I'm Dennis, from Sydney, Australia, and I'm stoked to be here with you. I own a bar and practically live there, tinny in hand from sunrise to sundown. But, well, I'm here because my wife just dumped me. This African safari is my chance to prove I'm not the dud she thinks I am. I'll flood her social media with all my adventures and show her that I'm strong and adventurous."

He paused, taking a long sip from his beer, the gravity of his words settling in. His expression shifted, seriousness replacing the bravado.

Peri, assuming he had finished, said, "Dennis, welcome to South Africa. I hope it's everything you expect it to be."

"Thanks," Dennis replied before launching into the second part of his monologue. "Maybe if she sees me in this new light, she'll take me back. I'll face any wild beast just to get the best selfies. I refuse to let her see me as a dag anymore."

"Maybe if you talked less, she'd be more interested," Dave teased.

"I've just been alone for three days in this city and needed to get all of that off my chest," Dennis added. "Anyway, Eve, my ex, has another man already, and I plan to win her back. This is how I'll do it."

53 - DENNIS

Two months before safari

Dennis stood frozen, the words hanging in the air like fog in a deserted alley. His heart thudded in his chest, a wild drumbeat that drowned out the chatter of the bar.

He pulled Eve closer, their bodies almost touching, but the space between them felt like an abyss. He stared at her, searching her eyes for some hint of a joke, a glimmer of hope, but all he found was resolve etched into her features.

Eve's lips pressed into a thin line as she repeated her news, her voice steady but laced with a cold finality. Each word was a shard of glass, cutting through the fog of disbelief that clouded Dennis's mind. His hands clenched into fists at his sides, fighting against the impulse to shake some sense into her.

Dennis moved forward instinctively, as if he could pull her back into his world of familiarity and warmth. "Why?" he blurted out, the question tumbling from his lips with desperation.

"It's just the way it is," Eve shot back, her tone sharp and unyielding, like a door slamming shut.

Dennis's breath quickened, each inhale a reminder of the chasm that had opened between them. "So that's it?" he asked, his voice barely above a whisper, as though he feared the answer. "You just don't want me anymore and you get to decide that it's over?"

"Of course not," she snapped, a flash of anger igniting her eyes. "It's about you. You don't see how other people see you. They see you as a loser, an idiot."

He felt his cheeks burn with shame, the sting of her words embedding themselves like nails in his chest. "What do you mean?" he demanded, rage boiling beneath the surface.

"You spend all your time here," she gestured dismissively around the bar, "you have no ambition, no drive." Her smile cut through him like a knife, a sharp reminder of the void that had grown between them. "You really want to know?" she taunted, her voice dripping with derision. "You think you're a man, but you're just... pathetic."

He leant back as if struck, the air rushing from his lungs, each breath becoming a laborious effort. "I can change," he protested, desperation creeping into his voice.

But Eve was unmoved, her stare hard as steel. "You should know what I want. But you don't. You haven't even realised how far you've fallen."

Dennis felt the tears prick at the corners of his eyes. "I thought you were happy," he said, the words coming out as a choked whisper.

Her expression softened for the briefest moment, a flicker of something that might have been regret. But it vanished as quickly as it appeared. "Not here. Not with you. Not anymore."

As she turned to leave, Dennis saw the finality in her movements, the way she reached for her keys with a sense of purpose. "Goodbye, Dennis," she said, her voice echoing like a distant thunderclap, each syllable resonating with loss.

He reached out, a whisper of a plea escaping his lips, "See you at home?" But Eve didn't look back; she simply walked away, leaving him alone in the bar, clutching the remnants of a life he no longer recognised.

Her breath quickened as she tossed her hair over her shoulder, her keys jingling like a countdown to a final goodbye. "Goodbye, Dennis. My lawyer will be in touch," she declared, her voice steady but filled with an undercurrent of hurt.

The air thickened, and Dennis's heart raced as he scanned her face, searching for a hint of the warmth that once softened her features. "Please, come home and we can talk," he pleaded, his voice cracking like the glass that held his untouched drink.

"No, I've moved out. Good luck with, well, everything," she shot back, her eyes dropped, refusing to meet his desperate eyes. Each word was a stake driven deeper into his chest, twisting painfully.

"Together, we can open that flower shop you've always dreamed of," he blurted out, the words tumbling from his mouth in a desperate attempt to cling to the remnants of their life together.

Eve shook her head, a bitter smile ghosting her lips. "This isn't about a flower shop, Dennis. It's about you. You're so afraid of the world outside, you refuse to step beyond your own shadow."

Each accusation felt like a punch, and Dennis fought to keep his composure. "That's not true," he insisted, though the tremor in his voice betrayed him. A moment of silence hung between them, heavy and suffocating.

Eve reached into her handbag, and Dennis instinctively leant in, his heart pounding as he wondered if she would pull out something to bridge the gap. But instead, with a sudden shout, she pierced the air, "Boo."

Dennis jumped, instinctively clutching his chest, his heart racing for an entirely different reason now. "What was that?" he gasped.

"See? You're scared of me," she said, her voice laced with both anger and sadness.

"Accept yourself, own your issues, or keep pretending. I just don't want to be around you anymore."

Her words cut through him, and he felt as though he were being hollowed out. Desperation clawed at his throat as he made another attempt, "We can go on holiday. Let's travel somewhere," he suggested, his jaw slack as he waited for a reply.

"Why? It would just be the same you in a different place," she replied, her tone dismissive, as if his dreams were nothing but a child's fairy tale.

"Okay, I admit it. I've never left the country, but I'll do it. We can go somewhere fun," he stammered, clinging to the fraying edges of their relationship.

"Fun? You think of Disney World while I dream of Africa, of facing lions and climbing Kilimanjaro. You're lost in your own small world, Dennis," she snapped, her frustration boiling over.

"I'll sell my baseball cards. I'll make it work." The desperation in his voice echoed through the bar as he fought back tears.

Eve stood firm, shaking her head in disbelief. "You're drowning in debt, and you want to sell your childhood collection for a trip? It doesn't matter. I don't want to go anywhere with you. I hope you understand that."

With those final words, she turned sharply on her heels, her footsteps echoing like the tolling of a bell. Dennis watched her walk away, a wave of despair washing over him as he sank to the floor, the bar around him fading into a blur, leaving him alone in the painful realisation of his world crumbling.

54 - DENNIS

Two months before safari

For three endless days, Dennis drifted through his life like a ghost haunting a familiar but hollow house. The world outside felt muted, colours dulled, and each movement came with the burden of a thousand thoughts—a slow-motion reel playing on repeat as he shuffled from the worn-out couch to the fridge, his only companions a cold beer and the rhythmic sound of his own breath.

As he sank deeper into the cushions, he couldn't escape the ghost of Eve, her touch lingering in every corner like an uninvited guest. The soft cushions she had chosen sat perfectly aligned, while the kitchen glittered with a brightness that felt foreign to him now. He scanned the room, a twinge of panic rising in his chest. Where were his old belongings? Did they blend into the backdrop of her meticulously curated life?

The image of her, carefree and radiant, was a sharp contrast to the muted existence he now faced. How had he let it slip away? The realisation struck him like a cold wave—he had been blind to the slow unravelling of himself, his identity fading into the wallpaper.

As the anger that had bubbled beneath the surface began to fade, a dull ache of realisation took its place. This life, once filled with vibrance and laughter, had turned into a monotonous routine, each day blending into the next without meaning.

He rubbed his temples, the pressure of despair tightening its grip. He could no longer linger in this stasis. It was time to reclaim his life, to rediscover the man he had allowed to be overshadowed. Eve had seen it all too clearly; he had lost himself in her world, and now it was time to find his way back. His first stop was to his accountant to find out the real state of his affairs

The accountant's fingers drummed nervously against the polished mahogany desk as he lowered his head, squinting at the columns of numbers flickering on the screen. The room hung heavy with an air of unspoken tension, illuminated only by the flickering of the monitor.

"So, to summarise, I have to change my whole life?" Dave finally murmured, his voice barely above a whisper, frustration threading through each syllable.

A sigh escaped his friend, who leant back in his chair, arms crossed tightly over his chest. "Well, not quite," he replied, his tone steady yet sharp, "but if you don't want to file for bankruptcy, then you've got to make some changes."

Dennis rubbed his temples, the awkwardness of the situation gnawing at him. "What do you suggest?"

"Rent out your bar," he stated plainly, locking eyes with him. "It's not a good time to sell, and honestly, it's in a great location. With the right manager and crowd, it could turn around."

"So, someone else can do better than me?" The words tasted bitter on his tongue, a stinging realization that cut deeper than he wanted to admit.

His friend's expression softened, but his honesty remained blunt. "I hate to be so harsh, but yes. You've let the place go to ruin. It isn't inviting— hell, I wouldn't even go there, and we're friends."

"Rent it out, huh?" Dennis echoed.

"Yep. That'll generate some income. In a few months, you could be debt-free," his friend continued, a hint of encouragement creeping into his voice.

"And what about me?" Dennis asked, sinking deeper into his chair, the leather creaking beneath him.

"Anything you want. Pick up a hobby, find a new job, study—it's your call. Get a new place to live that's cheaper to maintain."

The thought of his grandfather's house loomed large in his mind as he shook his head and said, "I've got the house, and I'm not moving."

"Then rent it out. That place is huge. Do you really need such a big house?"

"No, but my grandfather left it to me, and it's where I lived with Eve," he replied, nostalgia anchoring him in place.

"I know, but it could bring in good money. If selling isn't an option, renting is a smart move. Get a smaller place nearby. You could easily rent it out for five thousand dollars a month and find a cosy spot for two thousand. You'd be living off the income."

Slowly, Dennis leant back in his chair, fingers lacing behind his head, the battle inside him shifting. He had come prepared to defend his choices, but instead, he felt a spark of excitement igniting within him. In just a month, he had rented out both properties and secured a smaller apartment. Now, with the horizon open before him, he felt a reckless thrill at the thought of proving to Eve—and to himself—that he could embrace adventure.

He scoured the internet for safari options, a wave of exhilaration surged through him, washing away the tension of the past. This was his moment to reclaim his identity. He immersed himself in the idea of the wild—booking the longest camping safari available—determined to face both the challenges and the unknown by living in a tent. With each click, he edged closer to transformation; the countdown to his safari had begun.

55 – DENNIS

CAPE TOWN.

Uneze scanned the room, his sharp gaze taking in the energy and excitement radiating from the group. He tilted forward slightly, the corners of his mouth curling into a lively grin. "Well, Dennis," he began, his tone teasing but laced with curiosity, "I hope you don't do anything reckless in your quest for manhood. Is this your first safari?"

Dennis hesitated, his easy smile faltering for a fraction of a second. Uneze's words landed with more weight than he'd expected, stirring a familiar ache of inadequacy. He swallowed hard, masking his unease with a shrug. "Yeah," he muttered, his voice softer now. "It's also my first time leaving Australia. I've spent time in the bush, sure, but I guess kangaroos and lions are a bit… different."

Uneze chuckled, a knowing flash in his eye. "Well, get ready for quite the ride."

The tension in Dennis's posture eased slightly. He shuffled on his seat, his voice dropping to a conspiratorial whisper, as though sharing a personal secret. "I'm looking forward to getting some tips from the ladies here. You know, advice on how to make a woman love you."

Before Uneze could respond, Michelle burst out laughing, her sparkling energy filling the room like sunlight breaking through clouds. The laughter was infectious, pulling everyone's attention toward her. She flicked her hair back dramatically, her grin wickedly playful. "I'm sorry, Dennis, but you can't. You can't make a woman do anything she doesn't want to do," she declared with a confident edge. Her eyes sparkled with mischief as she added, "But I've learned one thing—if you're less available, you might just pique her interest."

Dennis raised an eyebrow, her words igniting a flicker of arrogance in his expression. The self-deprecating insecurity from earlier seemed to fade, replaced by a spark of playful bravado.

"Well," he said with a smirk, his voice lifting with mock confidence, "I guess I'm off to a good start, then. I mean, I'm already on the other side of the world."

Michelle rolled her eyes, but her smile lingered. The exchange drew a ripple of amused chuckles from the group, easing the tension that had hovered moments before.

Uneze shuffled back in his chair, his grin widening. "Careful, Dennis," he said, his voice light but edged with meaning. "Africa has a way of surprising you—and not always in the ways you expect."

56 - ANYA & JOHAN

CAPE TOWN

Anya and Johan stood before the group, the sinking sun projecting a warm shimmer on their already sun-kissed skin. With a shared glance, a silent agreement passed between them; it was Johan's turn to break the silence.

He shifted slightly, his hands fidgeting at his sides as he cleared his throat, the initial tremor in his voice reminiscent of a shy child. But as Peri's encouraging smile met his, a spark of confidence ignited within him. "Hey there," he began, his tone brightening, his smile melting away like ice in the sun. "I'm Johan, and this is my best friend, Anya. We're from Holland. Last year, we did a short safari in Kenya, and it was so good that we decided to go for this camping safari this year."

Anya's eyes sparkled as she watched him, pride swelling in her chest. She gently tugged at his arm, her laughter mingling with the gentle breeze as her grin radiated joy to everyone around them. Johan stood tall, his floppy brown hair catching the light, framing his wide, inviting eyes that seemed to invite trust from strangers.

"And how long have you been friends?" Peri asked.

"Since we were kids—so, about twenty-five years," Anya replied, her voice rich with nostalgia.

"That's so nice. Do you work together?" Peri continued, eager to learn more.

"No, I'm an engineer, and Johan is an artist," she said, glancing at Johan, who shrugged nonchalantly.

"Talk about role reversal." Dave scoffed, his tone dripping with sarcasm.
Anya, unfazed by his jibe, continued with a mischievous smile, "But we do share a house. We're like a platonic married couple."

"What's the point in that? Surely the only benefit of marriage is to have sex on hand, even if it's lousy," Dave retorted, rubbing his middle-aged paunch as if it were a magic lamp.

Johan's brows shifted, tension creeping into his shoulders, but he kept his smile steady. He gently squeezed Anya's arm, tucking a rebellious strand of her long, blonde hair behind her ear—a small gesture filled with warmth. "I think it takes all kinds of people to keep the world spinning, and we're just two of them," he replied, his voice steady now, a soft strength emerging in his words. "We're very happy to meet you all and look forward to this amazing adventure together."

"Thank you, Johan and Anya, that was very kind," Peri said, nodding appreciatively.

Emily's full attention was fixed on Johan, a dreamy smile playing on her lips. She licked her lips slowly, the corners of her mouth twitching with excitement. Her wide, sparkling eyes followed every little movement he made, and she tossed her hair back with a soft flick, her body subtly swaying as if drawn to his magnetic presence.

Peri's focus shifted to the last man, a smile dancing on her lips as she encouraged, "Last, but not least, it's your turn."

57 - ALEX

CAPE TOWN

Alex stood at the edge of the room, his sharp eyes scanning the group with barely-contained judgment. He wasn't here for small talk, but something about the forced pleasantries irritated him more than usual.

He stood, glanced at everyone and said, "I'm Alex." Without another word, he grabbed his phone and left—another invisible crack in the fragile facade of his calm.

Moments later, a server glided in, clearing away empty glasses, while the remaining group sat in stunned disbelief, their conversations abruptly halted like a record scratched mid-song.

Peri, sensing the shift in energy, broke the silence with a smile, attempting to restore some levity.

"Well, as Anya and Johan said, it takes a lot of different things to make the world go round, and some people don't like public speaking. That's it for now unless you have any questions."

An awkward chuckle rippled through the group, easing the tension ever so slightly.

"Okay, so I'm going to ask something well, very dumb," Emily said, her voice laced with a hint of embarrassment.

"Well, all that Botox may have gone to your brain," Michelle quipped, a teasing smile dancing across her lips.

"You keep mentioning camping. Do you mean camping in the traditional sense, like in tents?"

"What did you think camping meant?" Dave shot back, amusement brightening his tone.

"I didn't know it was a camping safari. Guy, I mean the string bean, booked it all. I've just found another reason why I left him at the altar. Did he really think that I, and by I, I mean all of this," Emily gestured dramatically to her slim, toned body, "would be suitable for camping?"

"You'll be fine. Those heels you are wearing will be great when you are trekking through the desert and climbing on and off boats," Dave laughed, his eyes gleaming with mischief.

"No, these heels will be a great weapon against creeps like you," she shot back, her tone lively yet fierce.

"Let's get freshened up and see you for dinner in an hour," Peri interjected, her voice pulling everyone back to the moment, the room buzzing once more with conversation as they readied themselves for the evening ahead.

58 - PERI

CAPE TOWN

The air hung thick with the unknown as Uneze's clipped voice rattled off the itinerary, safety regulations, and finally, a sharp nod, releasing the campers to the welcoming smell of curried chicken and the clinking of wine glasses. Peri and Uneze took a back seat, enjoying their position as simple observers, allowing the group to talk amongst themselves.

After the main course, Uneze stood and spoke, saying, "See you in the morning at eight. Leave your luggage here and just bring a day bag."

Uneze and Peri smiled politely until everyone had scattered and ambled out of the room. "Drinks in my apartment?" Uneze asked.

"Wow, you move quickly." Peri chuckled.

"No, I want your take on the group before we leave tomorrow. All the balconies look onto this courtyard, and this place has ears everywhere."

"Ok, I'll grab some wine, and let's go," Peri said.

The door to Uneze's kitchen swung open with a grunt from Peri, who collapsed onto a soft armchair. "Sorry," she breathed. "Dennis cornered me. He wanted to join our 'post-dinner debrief.' I faked a report deadline."

Uneze took the bag from Peri's hands. "Good call."

Uneze uncorked a bottle of wine, the scent filling the room. "Okay," he said, swirling the wine in his glass, "natural habitat observation complete. Verdict?"

"Oh my god," Peri whispered. "Safari guests... are they always this... much?"

Uneze chuckled, taking a sip of wine. "Not usually this bad. But... eccentric? Absolutely. I mean, people are paying a fortune to sleep in glorified pop-up tents. Dennis—the 'know-it-all'—has never even been to

Africa, but he talks like he wrote all the documentaries out there. He'll be the first one ignoring our warnings about animals."

Peri nodded grimly. "Gender war, I'm calling it. I love Johan and Anya; they are adorable. But Dennis and Dave? Arrogant clones. And Emily? Poor thing. She's clueless."

Uneze clinked Peri's glass. "She'll be tromping through the bush in heels, covered in mosquito bites, and the second she sees a town, it's mani-pedis and sushi. She'll be on the lookout for someone to replace her string bean." Uneze continued, a soft, amused look on his face. "Tent life is different. Everyone hears everything. We need nicknames so they can't tell we're gossiping."

"Emily's definitely a 'Cougar,'" Peri giggled.

Uneze smirked. "Calling her 'Cougar' on safari? People might panic."

"Point taken."

Uneze leant back, a thoughtful expression crossing his face. "Did you see that look in Alex's eyes? Pure evil. He's hiding something. I know that look."

Peri tapped a finger against her glass. "Or maybe... he's an undercover traveler reporting back to HQ?"

"I doubt it. He'd be more subtle. Whatever. We have weeks to figure him out." Uneze sighed.

59 - PERI

The following morning, with rucksacks and satchels packed over their shoulders, the group waited in the apartment car park for their departure.

"Did you hear the ruckus at 2 am?"

Peri tensed her brow in curiosity. "No, who was it?"

Uneze leant closer, lowering his voice conspiratorially. "I think it was Melanie and Dave. You'd never guess it, but Melanie looks like a timid little mouse. If it was her, though—wow, she's got some fight in her, and an attitude, too."

"What were they saying?" Peri asked.

Uneze shrugged, a grin tugging at his lips. "I couldn't catch it all, but Dave blurted something about her making the most of this holiday because it was her last one. And she snapped back, warning him to watch out because she had tricks up her sleeve."

"I guess it's just the usual husband-wife stuff. I always keep out of that," Peri said.

"Me, too," Uneze said. "There's going to be way too much other stuff going on to worry about couples and their trivial, day-to-day stuff."

Peri hastily tossed her bags into the truck, her cheeks flushed with excitement as she gulped down the last of her juice. She turned, her smile infectious as she waved the group to board the vehicle.

Peri clutched the microphone tightly, her fingers dancing over its cool surface as she turned to face her group. "We'll weave through the colourful neighborhoods, each one buzzing with life and stories of its own, until the sparkling shores of Muizenberg beach greet us with open arms." She glanced at the group, her eyes sparkling with excitement, painting vivid pictures of colourful beach huts and rolling waves, pulling everyone into her vision of the day ahead.

The minibus rolled to a halt, the sound of waves crashing against the shore filtering through the open windows. As the engine quieted, the scent of salty air drifted in. Uneze caught Peri's curious glance, uncertainty dancing in her eyes. With an encouraging smile, Uneze stepped out, gesturing towards the sun-kissed sands. "Alright, everyone. Just a quick stop here at the beach for some photos," he called out, his voice buoyant and inviting. "Then we'll grab a coffee at the bar across the street, a quick toilet break, and we'll be back on board in no time."

"Can we go for a swim?" Dennis asked, his voice eager, eyes sparkling with the promise of turquoise waves and sun-soaked fun.

Uneze let out a light chuckle, shaking his head as he gestured toward the horizon where the ocean met the sky. "It's an area known for sharks, so I'd say not."

"But I can see people swimming," Dennis huffed.

"Well, they aren't my responsibility; you are." His tone shifted, firm yet laced with warmth. "We'll have plenty of time to swim later on, so for now, just take some photos, enjoy the sand between your toes, and a good coffee. Don't even think about getting in there and holding us all up. The bus waits for no one." The half-scowl on his face spoke volumes, a blend of authority and affection as he turned, leading the way toward the beach.

As Uneze walked ahead, the others exchanged glances, their spirits lifting like the tides. Laughter and excited chatter hung in the air as the group snapped photos against the backdrop of Muizenberg's pastel-coloured houses.

With a spirited grin, Dennis wandered to the spot where the soft sand kissed the rolling waves of the Indian Ocean. He paused, feeling the cool water tickle his ankles, a teasing invitation to dive in. For a fleeting moment, he considered surrendering to the waves, but a glance back at his companions, their joyous shouts echoing in the salty breeze, pulled him away. With a quick turn, he sprinted back to join them and walked next to Emily, who strolled with her black high heels in her fingers until they reached the bus.

Dennis propped himself against the bus as he dried his feet on the leg of his trousers. "Are you okay, you know, with the string bean situation?" he asked, his voice low and cautious.

Emily tucked a loose strand of hair behind her ear, her eyes sparkling with mischief. "I'm better than ever, but thanks," she replied, her laughter ringing out like chimes in the gentle breeze. "I doubt I'll last the whole six-week safari, but at least, for now, I'm far enough from home to dodge family drama. I've even plotted all the airports along our route, just in case I need a quick escape back to civilization." She flashed him a grin that held a hint of rebellious glee.

Dennis shook his head, a teasing smile creeping onto his lips. "That's a shame," he said, leaning in closer as if to share a secret.

"Yeah, well, you're here trying to prove yourself," Emily said, her laughter bubbling up again, bright and carefree. "I have nothing to prove. I just need some Mum-and-Dad-free time."

With a knowing look, Dennis raised an eyebrow. "I've seen you stealing glances at Johan, that cute little smile creeping onto your face. Why not just have some fun while you're here?"

Emily rolled her eyes playfully, a reluctant smile forming on her lips. "I plan on doing exactly that, just not for a whole six weeks.

60 - DENNIS

An hour later, the salty breeze tousled their hair as they hopped out of the bus, chatter echoing in the crisp air. They stretched, peeling off their jackets, reveling in the warmth of the sun that kissed their skin. After grabbing their tickets from Uneze, they ambled down the wooden boardwalk, anticipation bubbling with each step. As they turned the corner, a sight of waddling tuxedoed bodies greeted them, the penguins playfully darting in and out of the surf, their cheerful squawks harmonizing with the sound of the sea.

As cameras clicked and videos rolled, Emily's high-pitched scream sliced through the jovial atmosphere, drawing every gaze toward her. Panic surged in her eyes as her heel wedged tightly between the wooden slats, the railing offering little comfort while her stylish black leather hat danced away on the wind, soaring off her tousled blonde hair and landing with a soft thud on the sand below.

A flock of waddling penguins ambled past it, treating the designer cap as just another curious object in their world.

"Sis, it's just a hat—and honestly, it looked ridiculous on you," Michelle shouted, barely containing her laughter.

Emily's voice wavered with indignation. "It's an eight-hundred-pound designer hat. I refuse to let those penguins turn it into a nest."

"You really know nothing about penguins, do you?" Michelle teased, her laughter mingling with the roar of the ocean.

As the chaos unfolded, Dennis surveyed the scene. With a sudden burst of daring, he vaulted over the wooden railing, landing with a soft thud on the beach. Ignoring the gusts of wind whipping around him, he lunged for the hat, the penguins flanking him as if welcoming him to their colony.

"Dennis. What the hell are you doing?" Peri shouted, pointing at the clear signs that warned against venturing onto the beach.

"Emily needed me," he replied, his voice barely heard over the wind, triumph radiating from his face as he clutched the hat between his fingers and scanned the beach for a way back up.

"Over there. Climb up the boulders," Uneze called, her voice rising above the laughs and cheers of the onlookers. With a comedic flourish, Dennis scrambled back up, the crowd erupting into applause as he rejoined the group, bowing dramatically. He presented the hat to Emily with a bow, a grin plastered on his face as the chaos of the moment transformed into a strange bonding experience.

61 - DAVE

As the group strolled through Simon's Town, admiring the charming arcades, their footsteps a rhythmic dance on the cobblestones. They paused at zebra crossings, amused at the whimsical penguin designs painted across the pavement, each stride a reminder of the local wildlife they'd just seen. The scent of fried fish wafted through the air as they entered a cozy fish and chip shop, its walls lined with nautical knick-knacks and windows framing a bustling fishing harbor.

Just as they settled into their seats, a sudden commotion erupted. The door flew open with a crash, and in stormed a chaotic troupe of baboons, their raucous screams filling the air as they bounded across the polished floor. Silverware clattered to the ground, and startled patrons leapt from their seats, jaws tense with disbelief. Emily, heart racing, scrambled onto a chair, her pulse pounding in her ears. With a quick flick, she kicked off a shoe, sending it flying toward the nearest baboon, who paused mid-stride, its beady eyes narrowing in challenge. Meanwhile, the restaurant owner, panic etched on his face, fumbled beneath the counter, emerging with a peculiar-looking gun that shot out colourful balls. With an experienced squeeze of the trigger, he unleashed a barrage of bright projectiles, each one bursting with a pop. The baboons, momentarily stunned by the sudden explosion of colours, dithered before retreating in a flurry of fur and chaos, leaving the patrons gasping in relief.

"You wanted wildlife, Dennis? I think you got it," Johan said, a wry smile curling at the corners of his lips.

Dennis's eyes darted around the room, searching for the elusive evidence of their wild encounter. "Did anyone get any photos of it?" he asked, his voice filled with urgency.

"Who had time?" Johan shrugged, a cheeky twinkle in his eyes.

"I did," Alex chimed in, flashing his phone with a flourish, the screen illuminating his blank expression. "I was already filming when they came in."

Dave raised an eyebrow, disbelief etched across his face. "What were you filming? Us?"

"Just what's happening. Just so I don't forget when I get back. I need to write all about it," he said, a hint of determination lacing his words.

"So, you're a writer?" Peri probed, a curious tilt to her head.

"No," Alex replied, a hint of uncertainty flickering in his eyes as he tucked his phone back into his pocket.

Dave sat back, glaring at Melanie, who, still panicked from the encounter with the baboons, shook with fear as she struggled to speak. She rubbed her hands up and down her crossed arms, letting the situation unfold around her rather than participating.

"Snap out of it. You're going to see way worse than that," he muttered to his wife as he pulled out his phone.

His fingers drummed impatiently against the screen, sending yet another text to Alistair, the words laced with irritation. The message flashed back at him, unanswered, like an unyielding wall. He fumbled for his cigarettes, his hands shaking slightly as he pulled one out. With a flick of the lighter, he watched the flame dance before him, but his focus remained fixed on the phone, a silent plea for a response that never came.

62 - PERI

Peri and Uneze huddled together, their voices low but animated as they weighed their options at a sudden change of plan. With a nod, they decided to carry on as planned. Peri waved her arm, summoning everyone back onto the bus with an air of authority.

As the bus rolled into Cape Point, Uneze maneuvered slowly through the winding roads of the national park. The overcast sky cast a muted tone over the normally vibrant landscape, with the rich greens of the shrubbery and rolling hills appearing almost gray. Suddenly, a troop of baboons erupted outside the window, their lively antics drawing laughter from the passengers as they leapt and tumbled, completely unfazed by the bus whizzing past.

At one of the viewpoint stops, Melanie settled onto a weathered bench, her gaze distant as she absorbed the breathtaking scenery. The world's colours seemed to fade into the background, overshadowed by the vivid memories of Julius's warm embrace. A sigh escaped her lips, and she wrestled with Dave's arrogance. She felt trapped in a cage of her own making as she decided that she would leave the tour as soon as she could. She pulled out her phone, her heart fluttering as she scrolled through Julius's messages, a smile breaking through her uncertainty. The words danced before her, but she stalled for a moment,, unsure how to bridge the distance between her longing and the reality of her current situation.

"Who are you talking to?" Dave's voice cut through her thoughts, sharp and probing.

Melanie's heart raced as she quickly flipped her phone onto her lap, masking her guilty surprise with a feigned nonchalance. "Ehm, no one. Just reading a group chat from the village. They're all buzzing about the bake sale at the church this weekend," she replied.

"Well, stop it. You're here in Africa; enjoy it," Dave ordered.

63 - PERI

The salty breeze whipped through their hair as they approached the iconic landmark of the Cape of Good Hope, the wind howling like a restless spirit. After a series of sun-kissed beaches, the relentless gusts felt like nature's way of reminding them of the raw power of the ocean. They hopped aboard the Flying Dutchman train, its slow chugging a contrast to the turbulent winds, and after one last hike, soon found themselves at the mountain's peak.

Alex, a picture of vitality, burst forth from the group, his athletic frame surging ahead as he made his way to the lighthouse. He perched on the weathered stone wall, leaning forward, his body tense like a coiled spring ready to launch. The expansive horizon stretched before him, waves crashing violently against the rocks far below.

Anya ventured closer, her voice barely carrying over the howling wind. "Are you alright?"

His eyes remained fixed on the distant waves, a faint smile playing at the corners of his lips. "Yes, of course. Just admiring the view," he replied nonchalantly, swinging his legs over the edge, the void below beckoning like a dark secret.

A chill crept up Anya's spine. "You're making me nervous; please, get down from there."

Alex offered no immediate response, lost in the moment, a fortress of solitude amidst the clamor of the world. "I just need a minute with my thoughts," he said, the finality in his tone making it clear he wished to retreat into his own mind.

Anya stepped back, her heart racing as she watched him, the thrill of the precipice contrasting starkly with her concern. Soon, the rest of their group arrived, panting and disheveled from the climb, Peri trailing behind, urging Melanie to keep pace and not let the steps beat her.

Emily's grip tightened around Johan's arm as she wobbled on the uneven steps, her heels clicking erratically against the pavement. The breeze whipped through her sundress, sending it fluttering like a flag, revealing her petite figure in a animated dance with the wind. A lighthearted giggle escaped her lips as Johan, a teasing smile playing on his face, suggested, "I could carry you on my back, you know."

She shook her head, her cheeks blushing with a hint of embarrassment. "No, I need a bit of dignity. I'm fine."

Johan raised an eyebrow, a grin spreading across his face. "Why don't you just buy some shoes? There are plenty of shops near the apartment. I can take you to the Cape Quarter mall; I spotted a couple of sports shops."

Emily shrugged, a playful pout forming as her foot slipped slightly. "Maybe, I guess. I thought it would be easier than this," she admitted, her playful demeanor slightly dimmed.

Johan chuckled, his eyes sparkling with mischief. "So, you actually thought this through?"

"Not very well, clearly. Maybe I'll just skip all of the walking bits from now on," she replied, her tone light but laced with a hint of frustration.

Johan raised an eyebrow, teasingly quizzical. "So, you'll be on the bus for six weeks?"

Emily paused, a thoughtful smile creeping onto her face as they finally reached the top, the world sprawling out before them. "Hmm. I'll need a better plan," she mused, the joyful spark in her eyes returning as they reached the top.

Dave, after catching his breath at the stop of the steps, sauntered over to the edge, shaking his head in disbelief as he spotted Alex perched perilously on the edge. "Dude, it's called the Cape of Good Hope, not the cape of jump off and kill yourself," he quipped, hands on his hips, string with a look of amusement.

"What do you care?" Alex shot back.

"Honestly, do whatever you like, you weird creep," Dave said, a half smirk on his lips as he stomped away.

64 - PERI

"That's enough," Uneze interrupted. "Dave, go and help your wife. Alex, please, get on this side of the wall." He waited while both followed his instructions. Ten minutes ticked by, and as he ied them down the steps, the air felt heavy with unspoken tension.

When they reached the fork in the path, Uneze's eyes fell on Emily, who clung to Johan as though he were a lifeline. Her knuckles were white, and her eyes darted, betraying her unease.

"Emily," Uneze said gently, "if you want to, you can take the train back down to the car park and wait for us."

Relief washed over her face momentarily, but it was quickly overshadowed by uncertainty. "Um, alright," she stammered, her voice a fragile whisper. "Johan, please come with me. I don't want to go on my own."

Johan hesitated, glancing down the picturesque route that unfolded before him, the beauty of the route only seemed to emphasize the anxiety radiating from Emily. She nibbled her lip, a nervous habit that only made her look smaller and more fragile.

"Well, I wanted to walk the route. It looks stunning," he said, his voice barely masking his reluctance.

Emily shot him a glare that could've melted steel, but her sister's voice interjected with a teasing lilt. "Ems, come on. You can navigate the underground in London alone, but a tiny two-minute train ride is too much for you? Give the poor man a break."

"Does anyone else... want to come with me?"

Melanie perked up, her eyes brightening. "I will, happily. Those steps are murder on my ankles," she declared, a grin spreading across her face.

The rest of the group descended the winding path from Cape Hope lighthouse, their footsteps thumping against the rocky terrain. At the cliff's edge, the breathtaking expanse of blue bays stretched out before them, the sun glinting off the water like scattered diamonds.

Michelle lingered a moment longer, her concentration distant, as the salty breeze tousled her hair. "I'm sorry about my sister," she finally said, her voice almost lost in the sound of crashing waves. "She lives on planet Emily—a world where she can't do anything alone. If she's not the centre of attention, she feels lost. She won't even buy shoes—because that means she won't be able to ask for help. It's just... what she does."

Johan chuckled softly, shaking his head. "Sisterly love, huh?"

Michelle's lips twisted in a half-smile, but her eyes remained hard. "I love her, but I can see right through her act. I'm used to it, but I thought I should warn you all."

"So, she's going to be like this for the entire six weeks?" Dave asked.

Michelle shrugged her shoulders and said, "Who knows? I'm not going to be looking after her, and I suggest you all just leave her to get on with it, too. She'll do anything to get out of being alone."

"I think a woman should look after a man, not the other way around," Dave said in an arrogant tone. His words left a trail of silence as they reached the end of the trail and shuffled back onto the bus.

The group arrived back at the apartments, and Emily, still frustrated at being humiliated and turned down by Johan, decided that shopping would help her. Having convinced Michelle to join her, the two girls walked to the nearest shopping centre and eyed some sensible, safari-suitable shoes.

"Come on, you can do it, Ems," Michelle teased.

"You expect me to buy those things? Why would I ever want to dress like a man?" Emily asked.

"Of course. Why dress like a man when you can fall over and break your neck in true glitzy style?" Michelle said.

"Oh, I don't know why I invited you here on my safari. You are ruining it for me," Emily huffed.

"Really? Me? I'm going to enjoy it no matter what. Are you buying them or not?" Michelle asked.

"No. I'm going to try and find a compromise. Nice but also a bit more outdoor appropriate."

"Alright, it's a step. Where are we going then?"

"It's okay. I'll go on my own. You'll only criticise my choice in shoes. I'd rather hear your insults once I've already paid for them."

"So, I'm hearing right? You want to do this on your own? Will you get back okay?"

"It's two hundred metres. Up the escalator, turn left, then up the hill. It's easy."

"Alright then. I'll see you at home with something better on your feet."

"See ya, sis. I can do this," Emily replied.

65 - MICHELLE

Michelle stepped onto the rooftop, waving at the others who lay on sunbeds. She let her fingers dance across the water's surface as she tested the temperature. With an animated flick, she kicked off her flip-flops, relishing the cool sensation as her feet sank into the refreshing depths and watched the clouds sinking on top of Table Mountain like a tablecloth. "Well, I've left Emily, all alone, to get some shoes. She didn't want me there, so pass me the wine, please," she said, a hint of mischief in her voice.

A while later, Peri and Uneze peeked around the windbreaker, their grins infectious. "Alright, I need your drink orders. We're hitting the road for the camping, and some places won't have bars. Jot down what you want—beer, gin, wine—and I'll do my best to keep us stocked for the tour," Uneze announced. "Sign-up sheets are here, and we'll settle up once a week," he added.

"Alright, everyone, have a lovely dinner—it'll be served in an hour. See you tomorrow at eight am, bags packed. The bus waits for no one," Peri chimed in, her tone brisk but friendly.

Just then, a figure burst into the scene, a whirlwind of energy that sliced through the rooftop's calm. The man's eyes flitted around the group, landing on Dave for a fleeting moment before locking onto the woman with the short blonde hair.

"Alistair?" Peri's voice was steady, but the tension in the air was palpable.

"Sorry," Alistair mumbled, his collar askew, a hint of dishevelment clinging to him. "I missed my connecting flight and had to spend the night in Istanbul."

"No problem. Welcome aboard," Uneze replied, his tone warm, as if to ease the sudden shift in atmosphere. "You're just in time for dinner; if you want drinks, just call the waiter."

"Thanks," Alistair replied, his voice barely above a whisper.

Across the table, Dave's expression hardened, his jaw tightening as he fixated on the new arrival. He shifted in his chair, desperation to speak to Alistair pulsing through him. When he looked up, his glare met Alistair's for just a heartbeat before he quickly turned away, the tension between them thick enough to cut.

Once Alistair had a drink and settled into a seat, Uneze asked him to share his story with them. "Yes, even if it's quick."

"Okay, so, I'm Alistair. And I work in private security. I was involved in an incident at work and am currently on leave. I'm here to have some real fun. I am seeking a sense of danger, excitement, and, of course, the company of women." He pulled up his wide-armed shirt and revealed a fading tattoo that curled around his arm.

"I'm on this safari to take a break from social media, and to experience a masculine version of the 'Eat, Pray, Love' experience my wife had a few years ago. She came home from Italy with a man twenty years younger than her, so I guess I'm planning on doing the same thing on this little tour."

Michelle's face tightened in disgust, and she didn't even bother to fake a smile as she muttered, exasperated, "Soul searching and looking for hookers are very different things."

"You don't know what you're missing out on," Alistair said with a wink.

"You disgusting prick," Alex shouted at the top of his voice as he stood, downed his drink, and stormed out of the space.

66 - ALISTAIR

Once the drama had quietened down, Dave pushed himself up from the circle, a cigarette dangling from his fingertips like a reluctant thought. He took slow strides toward the edge of the terrace, where the city lights blinked like distant stars. As he settled into the darkness the cool evening breeze tousled his hair. Alistair shuffled up beside him, his fingers deftly retrieving a lighter from his pocket, the flicker of the flame illuminating their faces for a brief moment. They both took deep drags, exhaling clouds of smoke that spiraled into the night, their attention fixed on Table Mountain, its silhouette outlined against the twilight sky.

"You could have given me a heads-up about your arrival. I've been contemplating how to handle this mess myself. At one point, I nearly pushed her off the Cape of Good Hope, but there were too many eyes around," Dave said, a smirk tugging at the corners of his mouth.

"That wouldn't have been the brightest move, now, would it?" Alistair replied, his voice low and steady. "Discretion is key. You want to be the ghost in the room, the man who goes unnoticed. That's how you slip through the cracks."

"Not exactly how people see you, though. They've already got you labeled as a creep," Dave shot back, his laughter mingling with the crisp air.

"It's all a façade, my friend. Like your 'devoted family man' act that I hope you're pulling off," Alistair countered, a sly grin breaking across his face.

"Ah, well, I might have just blown my cover," Dave chuckled, shaking his head. "So, what's the next move?"

"You let me take the reins. Just keep up appearances, and it'll all be over before you know it," Alistair replied, his tone reassuring, as the shadows deepened around them.

After dinner, Peri and Uneze retreated to his apartment, settling in to watch the second half of *Mamma Mia* on Netflix, after missing the second half the night before, with a glass of wine.

After just a few minutes, Peri pressed pause, unable to hold down her thoughts, and said, "Alistair spent dinner practically glued to Michelle. Creepy. Do we play protectors, or is it every woman for herself?"

"We'll keep an eye on Alistair," Uneze said. "He'll try with the group, then find other 'entertainment.' Though I hope not. Telling the difference between lion mating calls and... other noises... is nearly impossible, and in the tents, we can hear everything."

Peri slapped his arm, laughing. "At least you're here to help me with the differentiating."

"We'll find Alistair a few female friends and he'll be fine," Uneze said, chuckling. "But Alex? I've never seen anything like it. Your thoughts?"

"He's probably disgusted by the others," Peri said. "Same as me. At least he doesn't even try to hide it. I admire that in him."

"I think there are a lot more layers to that man, we just have to peel them back," Uneze said as he unpaused the film and pulled a bag of salted popcorn to his chest

67 - EMILY

Emily loved the vibrancy of Cape Town—the bright colours, the buzzing markets, the delicious smells wafting from street vendors. It was all so alive, so full of promise. That morning, the sun was high, the streets were busy with people, and the air carried a warm, familiar energy. The winding alleys of Bo-Kaap, with their iconic pastel houses, felt like a painter's palette come to life. Despite already being lost and too far from her apartment for comfort, she wandered off the main streets, eager to get lost in the charm of Bo-Kaap's narrow lanes. Her phone was in her hand, snapping pictures of the colourful buildings, the quiet streets, and the occasional curious face peeking from behind an ornate door. She was enjoying the moment, feeling like an explorer, when she noticed the small group of boys ahead.

They couldn't have been older than twelve, maybe thirteen at most. Their clothes were too big for them, their faces too serious, and their eyes—sharp, calculating. She thought nothing of it at first. In any city, there are kids playing, hanging out, and sometimes, causing a bit of mischief. She gave them a quick nod and smiled, but they didn't smile back.

One of them, the tallest of the group, stepped forward as the others flanked her. He had a mischievous shimmer in his eye, and before Emily could fully process what was happening, he grabbed her phone from her hands.

"Give me your bag." Emily froze for a moment, not quite understanding the request. "I said, give me your bag," the boy repeated.

The words hit her like a slap. Her mind scrambled for a way out, but the other boys had already moved closer, their hands reaching for her silk bag, their eyes glinting with a quiet, terrifying confidence. The boy who spoke wasn't alone in his demand—he was merely the leader, and the rest followed with an unsettling synchronization, as though they had practised this many times before.

In an instant, the bag she had carefully slung over her shoulder was snatched away. Emily felt a pang of panic rise in her chest.

Without a word, the boys turned and dashed away, their footsteps quick and assured, as though this was just another part of their day. Emily stood there for a long moment, her mind still trying to catch up to the reality of the situation. She glanced at the street around her—people were walking, chatting, completely unaware. No one had seen what had just happened. The moment felt like a cruel joke, a nightmare that she couldn't wake from.

Her hands were shaking as she fumbled to find her breath. She couldn't let them get away. Not with everything. But they were already disappearing into the maze of streets. Fear surged, mingled with frustration. What if she couldn't get it back? What if she couldn't even report it?

With a deep breath, she tossed her heels into her bag, threw on the new dark brown espadrilles she'd begrudgingly purchased, and sprinted toward the nearest shopping centre, her heart racing with each hurried step. Her footsteps echoed off the narrow streets, the rhythm of her breath matching the frantic pulse in her chest.

The nearest shopping centre wasn't far—she'd passed it on her way in, just around the corner. It felt like a mile away now. Her lungs burned with the effort as she entered the building and nearly collided with a security guard who gave her a startled look.

"They took everything," Emily gasped, pointing over her shoulder. "Some kids stole my phone and my purse." She took a few shaky breaths, trying to calm her racing heart. People bustled around her, going about their business, and for a moment, she felt disorientated. She was back in civilization, back in the hustle and bustle of normal life. A part of her still felt like the outside world—the real world—was a much more dangerous place than she'd ever imagined.

The security stared for a moment, unsure what to do with this woman in front of him. "Sorry?"

"Didn't you hear me? I need help," Emily said, her voice hoarse. "I've been robbed... they took my phone and my purse."

"Come with me," he replied.

Emily shuffled into the dimly lit office, her hands still trembling as shadows danced across the walls. The security guard's eyes flickered over her, an initial glimmer of concern quickly fading into indifference as he realised the mugging hadn't happened in his workplace. He handed her a plastic cup filled with lukewarm water. She took a tentative sip, her throat dry, and recounted the harrowing details of the mugging.

With a dismissive wave, he pointed toward the exit, directing her to the nearest police station like an afterthought.

The police station loomed ahead, its sterile exterior contrasting sharply with the chaos in her mind. Uniformed officers bustled about, but their faces wore a disheartening absence of warmth. The cramped waiting area felt like an eternity; the clock ticked loudly, each second stretching into the next until she was finally ushered into an office. The officer slid a stack of forms across the table, the sound of paper scraping against wood echoing in the silence as Emily's heart sank. She stared at the blank lines, knowing she had to recount every item taken, every moment lost, but her pen felt heavy. Three hours stretched, and when she finally emerged, the sun had dipped beyond the horizon, leaving her with nothing but a crumpled map and a sense of displacement and only darkness to guide her back to the apartment.

68 - PERI

Peri stood at the entrance of the bus, her clipboard gripped tightly in her hand, eyes sparkling as she counted her group with a quick flick of her wrist. Last night's late study session replayed in her mind. Images and maps that sat hidden under her passenger list gave her an inkling of self-assurance that she knew what to say. "One, two, three...six, almost all aboard."

Her cheerful tone sliced through the morning air like a song, but the bright energy was abruptly dimmed when Emily's voice cut in, sharp and brittle. "I was mugged last night. I need to stop and buy a new phone," she declared, arms crossed tightly.

Peri's brows knitted together as she looked at Emily, concern flaring in her eyes. "You were mugged? How? Where?"

Emily thrust a crumpled police report toward her, lips pressed into a thin line. "It's all here. I went to the police, and I had to walk home in the dark. You should have been there."

"If you had called me, I would have been," Peri said, her voice softening, but Emily's glare remained icy.

"They took my phone," Emily replied, a tremor of frustration escaping her lips.

"What else?" Peri probed, her instinct to help kicking in. "Just my makeup. My credit card and wallet were in the bag with these ugly shoes I'd just bought, so I've still got those. Even muggers could see that these shoes weren't worth stealing." Emily scoffed, her voice laced with bitter humor.

"Passport?" Peri ventured, searching for a glimmer of hope in the chaos.

"In the safe," Emily replied, the fight in her voice faltering slightly.

"Alright, so you got off lightly considering what could have happened." Peri attempted a reassuring smile, but it felt more like an apology.

"I lost my phone. How is that getting off lightly?" Emily shot back, disbelief etched on her face.

"It could have been much worse. Consider yourself lucky," Michelle chimed in as she approached, brushing past the tension like it was nothing.

"Lucky, huh," Emily muttered, resentment brewing beneath her skin.

"You can use my phone, and at least Guy can't get hold of you. We'll get you a phone at the next town, right, Peri?" Michelle smiled, trying to lift the mood.

"Of course," Peri confirmed, but Emily's fury simmered just below the surface, her cheeks flushed with humiliation as she climbed onto the minibus and repeated her story yet again.

"Come on," Alex said, his back turned, dismissing her with a wave of his hand. "Isn't listening to Dennis's endless droning enough? Now we have to endure you too?" The sting of his words settled over her like a heavy blanket.

Emily's shoulders slumped, and she sank deeper into her seat, pulling an eye mask down over her face as if it could shield her from the world around her. Across the minibus, Michelle stifled a laugh, her face scrunching up in a playful effort to contain her amusement.

With a quick, conspiratorial glance, she mouthed a silent "Thank you" to Alex, who, for the first time, responded with a genuine smile that lit up his features, breaking the tension that hung in the air.

As the bus traveled smoothly, the scenery transformed from bustling streets to sprawling vineyards. When they arrived at Spier winery, the air was fragrant with the earthy scent of the land.

Uneze, with a twinkle in his eye, unveiled an array of colourful, fresh delicacies—crusty bread, ripe cheeses, and sliced fruits—each one a local delicacy from the store that lay by the garden. Peri busied herself, carefully spreading out the blankets in the dappled shade of a sturdy oak tree. She laid out wine glasses and bottles in ice buckets on a nearby picnic table and gave the signal it was time to dig in.

Peri sprawled on the soft grass, sunlight dancing on her skin, a glass of deep crimson wine cradled in her hand. She squinted towards the sprawling vineyard, the rows of grapevines stretching endlessly under a brilliant blue sky.

A lazy breeze rustled the leaves, and the scent of ripe fruit hung sweetly in the air. Uneze, sitting cross-legged nearby, raised an eyebrow, a smirk tugging at the corners of his mouth. "What's that smug smile?"

Peri shrugged, her grin widening. "Look where we are. A vineyard, good wine, a picnic in the sun. What's the fuss? This whole safari thing is just a doddle." She swirled her wine, the sunlight catching the glass and leaving a rosy hue on her cheeks.

Uneze chuckled, his laughter bubbling up like a spring after a long dry spell. "You do know the safari hasn't started yet, don't you?" His eyes twinkled with mischief as he leant back, reveling in the moment. "Sure, but come on, what's not to love?" Peri replied, her carefree tone brushing off reality like dust on a mantelpiece.

Uneze burst into a hearty laugh, the sound hearty and genuine, before taking a deep breath to regain composure. "Nice? That's your word for this tour? There's so much more to come."

Peri rolled her eyes, her smile still in place but filled with playful defiance. "Why are you always so negative?"

"Realistic, not negative," he replied, feigning a serious expression that was quickly broken by a wink.

"Realistic, huh? Well, I'm sure this is going to be great. Safaris happen every day. What could possibly go wrong?" Peri teased, raising her glass as if to toast the universe's sense of humor.

69 - PERI

With a quick glance at her watch, she grabbed her phone and struck a pose, the morning light throwing a golden haze around her as she snapped a selfie, a cheeky smile plastered on her face. *"Ready for the adventure,"* she typed, sending it off to her bosses and Lisa.

They boarded the Frankenshoek Wine Tram; the clatter of wheels on metal tracks echoed through the valley. Vibrant green hills rolled gently in the distance, framed by rows of grapevines heavy with ripe fruit, each cluster promising the rich flavours of the wines yet to come.

As the tram glided smoothly along its scenic route, passengers leant out to capture the breathtaking views—grape-laden vines stretching as far as the eye could see, quaint wineries dotted along the hillside, and the majestic mountains standing sentinel in the background.

With each stop, the tram became a bustling hub of activity. Glasses clinked and laughter erupted as friends shared their favourite vintages, while knowledgeable guides passionately recounted the history of the region and the intricate art of winemaking.

"Have you seen Michelle? She's hammered," Uneze remarked, squinting as he took in the sight of Michelle teetering off the bus, her gait resembling a wobbly toddler on ice skates.

Peri erupted into laughter, the sound bright and carefree. "It was supposed to be wine tasting, not wine guzzling. At this rate, she'll be rolling her way to her tent."

Uneze chuckled, a cheeky twinkle in his eyes. "What if she rolls out of it and down a hill or something?"

By the time the bus pulled into the boutique-style campsite, night had draped itself over the landscape. Peri's jaw dropped at the glamping paradise before her: the moonlight danced on the shimmering pool, while the scent of grilled meats wafted from cozy BBQ areas nearby, and steam curled invitingly from the hot showers.

"Don't get too comfortable. Once we cross into Namibia, it's all mud and mosquitoes," he warned playfully.

"Well, at least tonight, everyone came prepared with their own sleeping bags and pillows," Peri laughed.

"Looks like they read the important items email. Kudos," he grinned. "But if you want, you can sleep under the stars here. It's safe."

"Not too sure about that. Maybe just drinks under the stars? Care to join?" Peri suggested.

"Absolutely. After dinner, I'll swing by your tent," he replied, his smile lingering as the night wrapped its arms around them, the promise of adventure shimmering in the starlit sky.

After checking the campers in and savouring a dinner of grilled delights, Peri and Uneze drifted towards a dry patch of ground beside their tents, a hush settling around them.

Turning to Uneze, her grin was infectious, illuminating her face as if she were lit from within. "This is the life."

"So far, so good," he replied, laughter sparkling in his eyes like stars against the darkening sky. "Long may it last."

"Our tents will be next to each other for convenience, but just far enough to give the flock a bit of privacy. But when we're in the wild, we'll stick closer together."

"Sounds good," Peri replied, feeling her heart skip at the warmth of his touch. "Is it actually dangerous out there, or is it all for show?"

"Just wait and see. I don't want to scare you away," Uneze quirked an eyebrow, a joyful smirk tugging at his lips. "No matter what happens, I'll set up your tent for a glass of wine each evening."

"Deal. As long as there's wine wherever we go," she shot back, her eyes glinting with mischief, a spark igniting the air between them.

"Don't worry, I've got a stash ready in the truck," he assured her, a conspiratorial grin spreading across his face.

"I think I'm going to love this tour even more than I thought," she admitted, giggles bubbling up inside her like champagne fizz.

Just then, Emily stormed past, her face twisted in a scowl as she shot Peri a quick glance. Peri smiled brightly at Uneze, but Emily's demeanour darkened the moment. With a sharp turn, she gestured for Uneze to follow her with a flick of her head.

"Well, she hates me," Peri said, the scowl lingering in the air.

"No, she's just as hammered as her sister. She probably came here to look for me and try it on," Uneze replied, shrugging off the suggestion, yet still staring at Emily as she disappeared into the trees.

"Oh, well, Mr. I-love-myself-way-too-much, go and see what she wants," Peri teased, refusing to let the mood dampen.

"No thanks. I'd rather not," he replied, gathering the empty glasses, rinsing them out with water as he placed them back in the cool box. "See you in the morning, sleep well," he said, a soft finality in his voice.

Peri pushed herself up, surprised at how quickly he had wrapped up the evening. She turned towards her tent, the fabric of her sleeping bag promising warmth for her first night beneath the stars.

70 - PERI

The following morning, Peri took paracetamol, her favourite hangover cure, and looked around her. She tapped her phone to see the time, and as quickly as she could, she jumped up and rushed across the gardens to the breakfast room.

"Did you sleep well?" Uneze asked. "I thought you needed a lie-in."

"I was out like a light until the group got back; they were steaming and made so much noise. Didn't you hear them partying into the small hours?"

"Yeah, that'll stop after a night or two when they all get sick of camping life," Uneze explained. He loaded the bags onto the waiting bus, urging the sleepy travellers to gather their belongings and hurry along.

"So, how was your night with Emily?" Peri asked, a teasing flicker in her eyes.

Uneze shot a quick glance, his smile faltering. "What? No, I didn't. I just followed her to check that nothing was wrong. When I saw she was going to her tent, I went for a shower and came back."

"Alright, I just thought—" Peri began, but Uneze cut her off.

"You thought wrong. Right, let's go," he replied, his tone shifting to one of urgency. The bus's engine rumbled in response, ready for the day's journey. "It's a long drive today, and we pick up the new transport at the campsite tonight."

Peri squinted at the crumpled map in her hands, confusion distorting her brow. "I can't work out exactly where we're staying. I looked at the map, and it looks like it's in the middle of nowhere."

Uneze chuckled, glancing around at the sparse landscape dotted with tents and distant trees. "It is. It's literally a campsite for people like us, travelling overland from here to Windhoek."

As the bus rumbled down the highway, the result of a restless and booze-filled night hung heavily in the air, causing the silence that wrapped around the group. Bloodshot eyes stared blankly at the passing landscape, while the faint sound of a playlist droned on in the background. Peri leant forward, animating her hands as she spoke, her enthusiasm clashing sharply with the lethargy that surrounded her.

Alex, propped up in the front seat, occasionally glanced her way, but his gaze drifted off toward the horizon, lost in a haze.

Frustrated, Peri finally let out a soft sigh, lowering the microphone and sliding into the seat beside Uneze.

Uneze swerved the van off the main road, the shimmer of neon lights beckoning them from the distance as he made an unscheduled stop at a Windhoek shopping centre. He rushed Emily into the sleek shopping mall, the air buzzing with the chatter of excited shoppers.

Within minutes, Emily emerged from a trendy electronics store, her face alight with glee. She held up her new iPhone, the sleek device shining under the bright overhead lights. "Look what I got." she said, her eyes sparkling with pride.

Emily's fingers flew over the screen, her brow scrunched in frustration. A string of colourful expletives escaped her lips as the phone slid from her grasp, landing with a dull thud against her thigh. "Why is it so hard to do this?" she muttered, shaking her head in disbelief.

"What?" Michelle asked.

"This whole phone thing. iPhone to iPhone—it should be a breeze. But no, it keeps stalling on the software update," Emily huffed, her voice brimming with annoyance.

Alex leant in, his tone gentle as he extended his hand. "Give it here. Just tell me your passcode and iTunes login, and I'll handle it."

A flicker of surprise lit Emily's eyes, her heart skipping a beat as she passed the phone to him, their fingers brushing together briefly, igniting an electric connection.

Alex's eyes met hers, steady and serious. "I'll fix your phone, but I'm not interested in any of those flirtatious moves. Save them for Johan."

The warmth in Emily's cheeks deepened as she looked away, the silence stretching between them as he focused on the device. Finally, he handed it back, an amused smile playing at the corners of his lips. "Thanks."

"My pleasure. Just don't lose this one," he teased.

"I didn't lose it; I was—"

"Mugged, yes, we know," he cut in, standing up. He raised his glass slightly to the group, the gesture casual yet dismissive, before turning to leave.

The bus's engine rumbled to a halt, and the door swung open with a hiss. One by one, the group spilled out, their legs unsteady from hours of sitting. They staggered under the weight of their backpacks, faces drawn and eyes heavy with fatigue. As they trudged toward the flickering lights of the campsite, the evening air was thick with the scent of pine and smoke. Once at their tents, they dropped their bags with a dull thud. Around the campfire, shadows and shapes flashed on their tired faces as they sat, plates in hand, the flicker of flames the only source of light. The only sounds were the soft crackling of the fire and the muted clanging of utensils against metal. Few words were exchanged; each person focused on the simple act of eating, their minds lingering on the long journey behind them.

71 - PERI

Uneze, his face flushed from the heat, carefully placed two chilled glasses and a bottle of wine beside a rug spread on the sand by their tent.

"They were quiet," Peri said.

"And that is why we never join in the after-dinner festivities with the group. We have to be on the ball, not a mess like them."

Peri, gazing skyward, let out a breath of awe. "Look," she whispered, pointing. "They're almost close enough to touch." The clinking of glass against glass was a quiet counterpoint to her words. "Another tour, another sunset," she sighed, her attention drifting to the horizon. "Sometimes I think about giving it all up, but then moments like this remind me how lucky I am. I get paid to travel the world in exchange for being polite, friendly, and on the ball."

Uneze poured the wine, the amber liquid shimmering in the fading light. "What else would you do?"

"I have no idea at all. I have money saved, but I don't know what for. I guess I'll find my path when the time is right. I'd love to move to Italy. There's a little town there called Rocca Pinta that I adore. I can't imagine going to the UK." Peri finally asked, her eyes intense. "What would you do if you weren't doing this?"

Uneze's hand tightened around his glass. "A mechanic, maybe. I don't know. I can't imagine doing anything other than this. It's my life." He started talking about his childhood, his voice a rich baritone weaving stories of his native Nigeria, his fingers moving rhythmically as he spoke.

Peri felt a flicker of something deep in her chest, a connection more intense than just a shared experience. "Africa is in you," she breathed, eyes   captivated.
He took another sip, a wry grin spreading across his face. "Deep down, man, the dirt, the animals, the heat..." He shook his head. "I went to

America once. Hated it. It was soulless. I was stunned that after all those years dreaming about it, I hated it."

Peri, mischievous now, raised an eyebrow. "And is there a certain someone who keeps a piece of your heart here?" She took a sip of her wine, the liquid cool and crisp on her tongue.

Uneze's smile deepened. "The million-dollar question. Not yet. But I'm hoping to find her someday. It's tough on the road, though."

A warmth, unexpected and sudden, spread through Peri's chest. She returned his smile. "Elusive, aren't they? Those special someones? I prefer the 'different man in every country' approach for now. Though..." She paused, tilting her head. "Maybe it's time for a hiatus. This nomadic life is exhausting..."

They both lay back against the sand, their hands brushing. A soft breeze stirred the air, cool against her skin. Sleep overtook Peri in moments. He carefully scooped her up, tucking her gently into her tent. He paused, placed a feather-light kiss on her forehead, then quietly withdrew. Peri, nestled deep in her sleeping bag, felt the thump-thump of her heart against her ribs. She traced the outline of the kiss, and a smile played gently on her lips as she drifted to sleep.

Uneze halted just a few metres from Peri's tent, his breath catching in his throat. There, partially obscured by the gnarled trunk of an ancient tree, stood Alistair. His eyes darted nervously, fixed on the forest floor, while he extended a small, trembling box away from his body. The way he held it—arms stretched out as if it were a live creature ready to bite— told Uneze everything he needed to know. He had to stay alert, awake, and keep watch over his flock. After zipping up his tent from the outside, he looked around yet Alistair was gone.

72 - MELANIE

After wishing the others good night, Melanie followed Dave to their tent and brushed the sand from her feet outside before entering. She looked around her and admired the desert stretched out beneath a cold, unfeeling moon, a wash of pale light spilling over the vast Namibian landscape."I'm going for a shower, back in a bit," Dave said as he grabbed his shower bag and headed off into the darkness.

Inside the tent, Melanie shifted restlessly on her sleeping bag. Her eyes flicked to the flashlight beside her, the only source of light in the otherwise dark space. Now, only the cool breath of night moved through the tent, and she was trying to force her mind to settle, to drift into sleep. But then, she heard something—a sudden skittering noise, soft but unmistakable, coming from the dark corner of the tent.

Melanie's heart skipped. She froze, straining to hear over the pounding of her pulse. The noise wasn't the wind, nor the rattling of a misplaced utensil. No. It was alive. Something was moving inside the tent. She swore under her breath, sitting up, her mind already spinning through possibilities. A rat? A bat, maybe?

The sound stopped and Melanie's eyes darted around the tent, trying to search through the thin walls. She reached for the flashlight, a deep unease knotting in her stomach. Slowly, she clicked on the flashlight, the beam slicing through the darkness.

The light settled on the far corner of the tent, where a single shadow lay curled and still. At first, Melanie thought it was a trick of the light—some disfigured scrap of equipment or an item fallen from a bag, but then it moved. A faint, slow wriggle. Then another. A shape that slowly uncoiled, like a nightmare unfurling before her eyes: A scorpion.

Not just any scorpion, though. Melanie had seen a few in her research before coming. But this one—this one was different. Its body was pale, almost ghostly. Its pincers were wide and poised, as if ready to snap. Its tail arched high, the venomous stinger curved like a sinister scythe. There was no time to dwell on that now. Her mind raced.

The scorpion was inching closer, its movements deliberate. Melanie held her breath, trying not to make a sound, the beam of light following its every shift. Melanie knew she couldn't just let it continue to move freely. The thing could strike at any moment, its venom already waiting in the deadly barb at the end of its tail.

Without thinking, Melanie grabbed the nearest object—a heavy walking book that had been left on the ground—and swung it toward the scorpion.
The scorpion darted back, surprisingly fast, its pincers snapping in warning. She swung again, this time landing the edge of the shoe directly on the creature's back. It scuttled away with a screech of chitin scraping against the fabric of the tent.

For a moment, it seemed like the danger had passed. Melanie's breath was ragged, her body trembling as the scorpion launched itself with terrifying speed.

The sting came out of nowhere. The pain was instant. White-hot, blinding agony that shot up her arm and into her chest. Melanie gasped, her body jerking as if struck by an electric shock. Her heart raced, her breathing coming in sharp, shallow gasps as she managed to let out a pain-filled scream. "God, no..." Melanie barely managed the words, her vision beginning to blur.

She looked down at her ankle. The scorpion was already retracting its tail, its venom seeping into her skin. Her whole arm was going numb, and a strange, tingling sensation was creeping through her fingertips.

"Melanie," Uneze called. "What's wrong?" Hearing nothing but a scream, he announced, "I'm coming in."

"Scorpion," Melanie muttered through the pain as she pointed to her ankle.

A cold sweat broke out across Uneze's brow. He forced himself to think—he had to act fast. "Medic. Medic," he called as loud as he could as lights turned on in the tents around him. "Security."

Melanie's world started to spin as the venom took hold and her vision darkened.

"Everyone, stay together. Zip up your tents, check for scorpions and sleep fully dressed tonight," Uneze called out as he left the group. "And someone wake Peri up to stay with you."

73 - MELANIE

The guards carried Melanie to the medic station on the campsite. Her face was now pale and drawn, though her lips were pressed tight in an attempt to stay calm. The venom was spreading fast, darkening her skin like ink blotting out the light of day.

"Hold on, Melanie, just hold on," Uneze muttered under his breath, his grip tightening around her hands. His voice trembled, barely audible over the chaotic rush of adrenaline pounding in his ears.

"Get her in here. Now." A medic shouted as Uneze pushed past the entrance flap of the tent, nearly knocking it off its hinges.

Melanie was laid down onto the nearest cot, her head falling back into the pillow with a soft thud. Her breathing was shallow, and beads of sweat lined her forehead, her body temperature spiking in reaction to the venom coursing through her veins.

Uneze clenched his fists, struggling to keep himself composed. "She'll make it, right? She'll be okay?"

The doctor looked up, her face taut with concern. "The venom of a Deathstalker is a powerful neurotoxin. It can paralyze, shut down the respiratory system... but if we can slow it down, she has a chance. Just keep her awake, don't let her fall unconscious. Talk to her if you have to, keep her focused."

Uneze nodded, though his throat was tight with emotion. "Melanie? Melanie, listen to me. Stay with me, okay?"

The doctor quickly unzipped her medical bag and began to sort through vials of various medicines. She worked with quick, practised motions, her face a mask of concentration as she injected the antivenom. "We need time for the antivenom to work. If the swelling in her throat doesn't recede soon, we may need to intubate her..."

"You've got this, Mel. Just stay with me." Uneze whispered into her ear.

"What else can we do?" Uneze asked, his voice urgent as he watched

Melanie's body tremble with the force of the venom's attack. "Just wait," The doctor replied without looking up.

Melanie's eyelids fluttered open again, and this time, she managed a little more than a smile—a weak but determined one. "Uneze... what happened to the... to the scorpion?" Her voice was so faint, he barely heard her.

He forced a smile, doing his best to appear calm, even though his heart was hammering in his chest. "The scorpion? Don't worry about it. You just focus on getting better, okay?"

Her eyes struggled to stay open, but she managed a faint nod. "Okay... Uneze... I don't want to die."

Uneze's breath caught in his throat, and the world seemed to tilt dangerously. "You're not going to die, Melanie. I won't let that happen." His voice broke as the weight of those words settled in his chest like a stone. All Uneze could do was stand there, watch, and hope.

The doctor smiled, let out a sigh, and said, "She's lucid and talking. That means we got there in time."

"So, she's going to be alright?"

"Yes, we'll keep her here tonight, but you need to tell your group to sleep fully covered and with the tents zipped tonight.

74 - PERI

The campsite lay draped in a comforting stillness when Uneze left the medical centre. Drawn by the inviting scent of freshly brewed coffee, he meandered toward the clubhouse, where he found Peri cradling a warm cup between her hands, steam curling upward like a soft whisper. She passed the cup to him.

She looked up, her brow knitted with curiosity. "What was that about?"

Uneze ran a hand through his tousled hair, his expression sombre. "There was a scorpion in Melanie's tent. It got her, but she's okay now."

Peri's grip tightened around another cup from the stand. "A scorpion? You didn't mention those. That's not like you to skip a million warnings."

Uneze shrugged. "I've never seen a scorpion around here. This campsite isn't in a scorpion hot spot."

Peri drummed her fingers on the table, her mind racing. "So, how did it get here?"

Uneze leant closer, lowering his voice as if sharing a secret. "That's the thing. I have a feeling Alistair put it there... in her tent."

Peri's brow knitted together, suspicion creeping in. "Alistair? Why?"

Uneze paused, recalling the image of Alistair, a shadowy figure clutching a box just moments before chaos erupted. "I spotted him before it happened, and he was holding a box of something. I don't know. Maybe it's just my imagination."

"Where was Dave when all of this was happening?" Peri pressed, her tone sharp.

"I don't know, but I would love to find out," Uneze replied, a determined flicker in his eye.

As the night wore on, the soft cushions of the clubhouse sofas cradled Peri into a deep slumber, the sounds of conversation and laughter a distant lullaby. A gentle shake on her arm pulled her from dreams, and she blinked awake to find Uneze smiling down at her, the warmth of morning sunlight filtering through the windows.

"I just gave the flock a wake-up call," he said, casting a glance over his shoulder as if sharing a delightful secret. "You've got time—enjoy your breakfast, handle your PR, and I'll tackle the tents."

The scent of sizzling bacon and toasted bread wafted in, and Peri sighed, letting the comfort of the moment envelop her. After a whirlwind of activity, they picked up Melanie from the clinic, her face pale but determined as she climbed into the truck with their help. Uneze turned to the other campers, his voice booming with playful urgency. "Come on, campers. It's a long drive. If you're not on the truck in five minutes, you're staying here." Laughter mingled with shouts as the last few stragglers hurried into their seats, and Uneze glanced at his watch, a triumphant grin spreading across his face. "Alright, only two minutes late."

The truck roared to life, its engine rumbling like a restless beast, and as they pulled away from the campsite, the scenery shifted dramatically. Lush greenery gave way to rugged terrain, the promise of adventure crackling in the air as they approached the Namibia border crossing. In the back of the truck, Melanie leant her head against her jumper, eyes fluttering shut, while Dave chatted animatedly with Alistair, the night's events seemingly forgotten, the scorpion a mere shadow in the rearview mirror of their journey.

"What the hell happened?" Dave asked under his breath.

Alistair shook his head and said, "I don't know. Uneze acted too quickly. No one was supposed to find her until it was too late."

"Well, do something else, and this time, make sure it works," Dave ordered as he turned his attention to the rest of the group.

Dennis droned on about the lack of animals, adventure, and selfie moments for the entire duration, until finally, Michelle snapped. "What the hell, man. Come on, grow a set. She dumped you, move on already. Look where you are—you're in Africa."

"Eve would love it here," Dennis said.

"She isn't here; we are. Give our ears a rest and stop whining about her," Dave said.

"Well said," Alistair agreed, the two exchanging looks that spoke volumes, yet nothing at all. "You should be glad you're away from her; she sounds like a pain in the butt. At least she left you and saved you from wondering how to get away from her like most of us have to."

"You don't know her," Dennis said as he put his headphones on and sank into his chair.

A collective sigh of relief erupted, mingling with the laughter that echoed through the cramped vehicle as it hit potholes and swerved around bends, jolting them with each sharp break.

Their new transport was an already dusty overlander, offering a nice bounce to the potholes as they drove towards the Fish River Canyon, their home for the evening. Peri handed out sign-up sheets for the following day: hiking trails through the canyon, canyoning, rock climbing, and boat trips.

As they stopped for a glance over the canyon's edge, a collective hush fell over the group. Breathless, they stood shoulder to shoulder, their mouths slightly agape as they glared at the sheer drop before them. The sun threw warm shades across the rock formations, highlighting the deep crevices, rugged cliffs, and rust-coloured river that seemed to stretch endlessly. A hawk, a dark silhouette against the blinding sky, circled lazily above the rim.

The campsite for the evening sprawled wide and far beneath a blanket of twinkling stars. The air was rich with the reek of smoked wood, lingering after their early dinner—a feast of grilled meats and fresh vegetables that had left their bellies content and their spirits lifted. As the group gathered close, laughter and chatter filled the night, but Peri and Uneze slipped away, cradling their glasses of deep red wine.

They sat on a weathered log, feeling the hot breeze rustling through the trees. Uneze tilted his head, a smile teasing his lips. "Can you hear that? The distant wildlife calls? It takes a trained ear to hear from a distance," he mused, his voice almost blending into the serenade of nature.

Peri chuckled softly, rolling her eyes. "All I can hear is Dennis squawking about his ex and his grand plans for a selfie with a lion," she replied, gesturing toward the raucous group huddled near the fire. "Do you reckon he'll do something stupid?"

"Very probably," Uneze replied as he slid down from the rock onto the floor, letting his focus return to the stars.

75 - PERI

The following morning at breakfast, Peri beamed as she sorted through the sign-up sheets, her fingers dancing over the descriptions of the tours, figuring out which one would have spave left for her, too.

With some of the group finally settled onto the small river canoe, Peri felt Uneze's eyes upon her. He flashed a grin as he studied the faces of the group, now embarking on their first real adventure. The local river guide spoke in broken English and pointed out the fauna and flora in the distance.

The guide navigated through the calm waters, surrounded by towering red rock walls and lush greenery. As they navigated the twists and turns of the river, they marvelled at the natural beauty surrounding them. Peri shared their excitement and wonder reflected in their faces and realised why people, including herself, longed to do such a tour.

Alex seemed lost in thought, his focus and attention fixed on some distant point ahead. Uneze wondered what he was thinking about, what memories or dreams were playing out behind his stoic expression, and why he'd chosen to come on this safari alone with no intention of connecting with anyone.

Emily pulled her knees to her chest, her pink, silky top stood out awkwardly in the wild surroundings, the fabric clinging uncomfortably in the humid air. She swatted at imaginary flies buzzing around her and let out long, rapid huffs. Each time she muttered, "Why? Why am I here?"

The Fish River Canyon stretched out before them, a vast, jagged expanse that seemed to swallow the horizon. Dennis stood at the railing of the riverboat, his sunglasses perched on his nose, arms crossed as he searched for wildlife lurking in the water. The riverboat, cutting lazily through the Fish River Canyon's base, seemed tame by comparison. As the boat glided along the still water, its gentle sways and the occasional splash of a fish breaking the surface did little to satisfy Dennis's thirst for real risk.

"I'm going to touch it," he declared with a mischevious grin.

Johan's eyes narrowed, half-exasperated, half-amused. "You're going to put your hand in the water? In the Fish River?"

Dennis gave him a sideways glance. "What's the worst that could happen?"

Before he could respond, Dennis leant farther forward, his hand now fully outstretched above the river, a dangerous twinkle in his eyes.

Uneze turned his attention to the group; his smile faded as he spotted Dennis swirling his fingers and hands in the calm waters. "Dennis," Uneze called out. "Keep your arms in the boat. You don't want to get eaten by hippos, do you?"

Dennis ignored Uneze's instructions as he swirled his fingers and wrists in the water. "Dennis. I'm being serious. This isn't the River Thames; these waters are infested with a whole range of swimmer killers," he said with a laugh. "Do you want to finish the tour alive or in a body bag?" Uneze called out over the noise of the crowd.

Dennis replied with a scowl, pulled his fingers back inside the boat, and turned to his fellow travellers to complain about the strict rules. "The tour promised excitement, and so far, it's been wine and potholes in the roads. I'm going to have my excitement one way or another."

"You will have a lot of excitement; it's my job to make sure it's safe excitement," Uneze said.

Amidst the crowd, Alex sat a little taller, the corners of his mouth twitching upward for the first time in what felt like ages. His admiration flicked between the powerful hippos, their massive bodies bobbing lazily, and the sleek predator basking on the shore.

Peri noticed something. It was just a second, but there was a nod and a look between Dave and Alistair. It was so quick she almost didn't notice it, but no matter how fleeting it was, there was something in that unspoken gesture that said more than any words. She'd heard them whispering and sneaking off into the night, past her tent, and returning twenty minutes later. It appeared strange to her that they'd formed this bond so quickly.

She had only known them for two days, but they'd introduced themselves as complete strangers. Peri noticed subtle touches and shared glances that hinted at a closeness beyond what was typical for two people who had just met.

As the boat glided further down the river, the current spiralled with an unsettling strength, drawing Dave closer to the edge. "Come on, just a little closer," he shouted, his voice drowning out the river guide's urgent pleas to sit down.

Peri's heart raced as Uneze's earlier warning echoed in her mind—trust the guide, stay calm, and keep quiet. From her spot at the back of the boat, she caught sight of Melanie, her movements slow and calculated, like a predator stalking its prey.

Melanie's fingers hovered near her husband's back, tense and poised, as if contemplating a nudge that might send him tumbling into the churning, dangerous waters below. With a furtive glance around, she smiled at the others and her hand slipped back down, retreating into a casual position, but the tension in the air crackled like static, leaving Peri acutely aware that all was not as it seemed on the Melanie and Dave front.

As the river cruise came to a close, the group disembarked, laughter surrounding them. Emily stumbled off last, her heels teetering precariously on the dock.

Ignoring her theatrics, the others stepped away, leaving Emily to flounder in her high-heeled struggle. "Ems, you bought those other shoes, why don't you wear them?" Michelle called over her shoulder, a smirk playing on her lips.

"Have you seen my legs? I need heels to look half decent." Emily shot back.

"Who is it you are trying to impress here? Have you looked around? Just try it, come on. Try and walk a little closer to the ground; it's nice down here." Michelle teased.

"And dress like a common camper?" Emily scoffed, eyeing the ragtag group assembled nearby, a kaleidoscope of mismatched attire and carefree spirits.

"You are a common camper; we all are. Come on, Emily. Just let loose a little," Michelle urged, her tone light but insistent. "We have six weeks with these people. Try being friendly for once," Michelle replied, her eyes narrowing playfully. "Blonde extensions, fake nails, and six-inch heels won't save you here. You might even discover something new about yourself. You were nice once; try it again."

"I'm already nice," Emily hissed, her annoyance palpable.

"Yeah, well, you've buried that version of yourself pretty deep," Michelle said, her voice softening with sincerity.

"Really? Isn't that version of me a bit boring?" Emily asked.

"Let's find out together. Put away the pouting, try smiling, and ask about others. It's called making friends," Michelle encouraged, her grin widening.

"Ugh, must I?" Emily groaned.

"Yes. Otherwise, it's going to be a very long six weeks for you," Michelle insisted, crossing her arms as if standing guard.

"We could just leave and go home," Emily suggested, a hint of mischief in her eyes.

"If you want to, go ahead. But I'm staying. This is going to be fun—with or without you," Michelle replied as she turned to join the rest of the group, leaving Emily to ponder her next move.

Emily let her eyes drop to the floor, her shoulders slumping as she unfastened the buckle of her heels. The moment they hit the ground, she exhaled, a soft, defeated sound that echoed her relief. With a flick of her wrist, she fished into her bag, fingers brushing against the texture of her brown espadrilles. "Goodbye elegance and style; hello, eugh," she muttered under her breath as she slipped them on.

76 - PERI

After dinner, Uneze took Peri to the outskirts of the camp and set down a blanket under a clearing in the twisted tree branches. "Just look at this," Uneze said. "There is no light pollution around here; it's one of the best places to stargaze."

"Look, a shooting star," Peri said as she stared into the sky. "Make a wish." She looked up at the night sky, feeling a sense of wonder and awe at the fleeting moment of beauty that had just passed. The shooting star had streaked across the darkness, leaving a trail of light in its wake. Peri turned to him and said, "Wow, I've seen them before, but never as clear as this. That was so beautiful."

They exchanged a glance that sent Peri's pulse racing into a spiral. She wasn't sure what it was about Uneze; maybe it was his sense of humour, or the fact that they had been thrown into the same boiling pot together, or maybe it was just the simplicity and beauty of what lay around them.

"That's Africa for you. It just keeps giving," Uneze said softly. "You have to love it."

"I don't feel like stargazing tonight. I need to tell you something," Peri said.

"What? Don't tell me that you've fallen for me already," Uneze said in jest.

"Be serious for a moment. I noticed something today; I wanted to tell you about it. For one, Alistair might be sitting there with his headphones on, but he's not listening to anything."

"How do you know?" Uneze asked.

"Well, first of all, his facial expressions changed when you were giving Dennis a telling off."

"Well, I was shouting, so maybe he just heard that," Uneze pointed out.

"Right, I know, but at one point, when he stood up, I noticed that his headphone wire wasn't connected to his phone. It's as if he's pretending to not be interested in what's going on, but sneakily, he's sussing us all out."

"Paranoid much?" Uneze said with a wide smile.

Peri's tone turned urgent as she said, "No, I'm not paranoid. I spotted a glance between him and Dave. It was when you were waffling on about crocodiles that Dave turned to Alistair, and they did this nodding thing. It was weird."

Uneze listened quietly, stared at her with an amused glance, paused for a moment, and asked, "Weird how?"

"I think they know each other and aren't letting on," Peri said.

"So, you think they are secret lovers?" Uneze asked, his tone breathy from laughter.

Peri shot him a glance filled with relief and said, "I didn't think of that. I hope that's all it is; I had so many murder scenarios on my mind."

Uneze, with his signature wide grin, let his hand graze her arm and said, "Well, only time will tell."

"Well, I don't trust him." Trying to lighten the mood, Peri turned the conversation back to the day. "If Dennis keeps that up, he'll have us running towards the lions to get away from his droning on about his ex."

"Maybe this is what he needs, then. An adventure," Uneze said.

"No, he needs a bucket full of common sense or maybe a good holiday romance. Emily has definitely got the hots for you. She's always looking at you with googly eyes," Peri said.

"I noticed, but a fake Barbie isn't my thing. There's one of them on every single tour," Uneze laughed.

"Tempted?" Peri asked, curiously.

"Nope, I made that mistake once. I'll keep it in my pants. I learnt to keep it professional with the groups," Uneze replied with a chuckle.

Peri beamed at him with a cheeky flicker in her eye and said, "Yeah, my idea exactly; it's a long tour. What about Melanie and Dave? I haven't sussed them out yet."

"Me neither, but there is something not right," Uneze said.

"Why do you say that?" Peri asked.

"I don't know; I've just got a feeling, and my gut feelings aren't usually wrong."

Peri thought for a moment and then said, "Today on the boat I noticed something strange. When Dave was sitting on the edge, Melanie had her hand on his back, and I'm sure she wanted to push him. It was so weird, then suddenly, she whipped the hand away, and it was like nothing happened."

"I'm sure you're either overthinking it, or you're paranoid. Just enjoy the moment and feel Africa take over you," Uneze explained.

Uneze gently guided Peri back down onto the blanket, his fingers brushing against hers as if testing the waters. A warm thrill coursed through her, but in an instant, a sharp jolt of caution ignited within her. With a quick, instinctive motion, she drew her fingers away, resting them on her belly, as if to create a protective barrier.

77 - MELANIE

Unable to sleep, Peri meandered through the bustling camp, the lively chatter and crackling of campfires surrounding her. Suddenly, the sharp clatter of boots against the ground cut through the air, accompanied by raised voices carrying tension and frustration.

Peri's heart quickened, her fingers grazing the rough fabric of the nearest tent as she instinctively took a step back. Fearfully, she retreated to the safety of Uneze's tent, stopping just outside.

"Uneze?" Peri whispered urgently into the dark tent.

"What's happened?"

"Come with me," Peri whispered urgently.

Uneze unzipped his tent and stepped out. Peri grabbed his arm, ignoring his questions as she followed the sounds of raised voices until she reached the spot where she'd seen the two figures. Peri and Uneze stood under the shadow of the tree, trying to make out the voices in this deep and frantic conversation.

"Shhhh," Uneze ordered. "It's Dave and Melanie."

Peri crouched low, her heart racing as she peered through the veil of darkness. The tension in the air felt electric, and she could almost taste the anxiety crackling between Dave and Melanie. His wild hand movements sliced through the silence like a knife, while Melanie's face paled under the faint moonlight.

"Is he threatening her?" Peri whispered, her eyes frozen with disbelief.

Uneze scoffed softly. "Wow, you have sonic hearing."

"Yeah, it's my superpower," she shot back, pressing her fingers to her lips and urging him to quiet down.

Uneze tugged at her arm, panic lighting up his eyes as they navigated the underbrush. Each crack of a branch beneath their feet sounded like a shout in the stillness. Finally, they found refuge in a dilapidated bamboo hut, the slats providing a narrow glimpse into the unfolding drama. They huddled together, holding their breaths as they strained to catch every word.

Dave's voice cut through the night, rough and jagged. "You stupid bitch. You wanted to come on safari, and now all you do is complain."

Melanie recoiled, her expression one of fear. "I didn't want to come. I'm not complaining. Just spend time with the others. I'm fine here with my books and podcasts."

"Fine." His voice turned venomous. "I'm sick of you moping around. Do you know how much I spent on this trip? I wanted you to be more adventurous."

Peri's breath hitched as she watched Melanie take a step back and stumble. Dave seemed to be dragging Melanie to the edge and encouraged her to peer down. Melanie, clearly uneasy, instinctively wrapped her arms around herself and took a cautious step back, her eyes darting to the dark abyss below.

"Come on, babe. Take a closer look," Dave urged, his voice heavy with impatience.

"I don't want to. Have you seen how steep that cliff is?" Melanie replied nervously.

Undeterred, Dave firmly grasped her upper arm and pulled her closer. "Look, it's breathtaking."

"It's dark; I can't see a thing apart from a void. I'm not comfortable with this, Dave. I don't like heights," she insisted.

Dave sighed, frustration evident in his voice. "But we came all this way to see the view. You can't miss out on this once-in-a-lifetime experience."

Uneze, still too far away to help in person, lurched forward, unsure how to react. "Dave, stop," he urged. The plea fell silent as Dave's rage manifested, each movement echoing like thunder against the quiet night as Melanie stumbled, unbalanced, and hit the ground.

As Uneze continued his way toward the commotion, Peri felt the burden of helplessness crashing down on her. Melanie curled into a tight ball, desperation etched across her face. With a primal roar, Dave yanked her to her feet, dragging her toward the abyss of darkness.

"Stop it. You're going to kill me." Melanie's hands clawed at the ground, grasping for anything to support and hold her as she teetered on the brink.

The edge of the cliff loomed, and Peri's heart sank further with each frantic plea. "Let go," Melanie cried, her voice a raw whisper of fear as she looked into the eyes of the man she once trusted, now a stranger with a heart of stone.

Another figure appeared from the side and grabbed Melanie, but with a surge of will, she fought back, muscles straining as she broke free. Time seemed to slow as she fell, the world around her blurring into chaos.

Uneze burst through the trees, urgency in his voice as he screamed as loud as he could. "Dave, what's going on here?"

Dave stopped suddenly and placed his hands behind his back. "Nothing; leave us alone."

"That's not going to happen. Step away from your wife. Now," Uneze ordered, his tall, bulky figure looming over Dave's much shorter frame.

Melanie turned and looked up, struggling to make out the figure of the person who'd saved her as Uneze leant down. "Melanie, it's Uneze. You're safe. Go with Peri back to camp."

The dark, unidentified figure scooted backwards, tripping on the ground as Uneze ran forward and grabbed him by the arm. "Alistair?" Uneze asked. "What are you doing here?"

"Ehm, I was out for a walk when I heard the argument. I wasn't sure what was going on, but I saw how close they were to the edge, so I tried to pull them back to safety."

"Why did you run off?" Uneze pressed.

"I didn't want them to think I was spying," Alistair replied.

"Alright, well, get back to camp and stay away from the edge," Uneze ordered, turning back to Dave, who leant, slumped against a tree.

"Dave, what the hell?" Uneze's voice pierced the night, sharp and cutting through the heavy silence of the campsite.

Dave turned, his face a twisted mask of frustration, the muscles in his jaw flexing angrily. "Leave me alone," he growled, a derisive snort escaping his lips.

"Are you stupid? Have you seen the ravine down there? You could've gotten your wife killed," Uneze shot back, his voice low and urgent.

Dave's silence was a heavy cloak as he stepped away, retreating into the depths of the darkness, his footsteps echoing the stubbornness in his heart.

At a nearby wooden bench, Peri and Melanie sat, shrouded in the glow of the clubhouse lights. Peri's looked at Melanie, who dabbed at her tear-streaked cheeks, her breath hitching in a desperate rhythm.

"Are you okay?" Peri whispered, her voice barely above a murmur.

"Yeah, I'm fine. Dave has a temper when he drinks," Melanie replied, her voice trembling like a fragile leaf caught in the wind.

Peri studied Melanie's pallid complexion, her skin ghostly under the harsh light, a stark reminder of the fear etched across her features. She gently squeezed Melanie's shoulder, a silent offer of support. "I've noticed. You can't stay with him tonight. He's lost his mind."

Melanie's hands shook as she spoke, betraying her resolve. "I have to. Where else can I sleep?"

Peri's smile was soft yet insistent, her voice a gentle anchor amidst the storm. "You can stay in my tent. We're up the hill, away from yours. You'll be safe."

Melanie's uncertainty wavered on her lips, a fragile smile flickering. "He won't like that. Or maybe he will; I get the impression he wants me out of the way, anyway."

"I'm responsible for your safety. So, you are staying with me, and that's the end of the discussion," Peri stated firmly, the resolve in her voice brokering no argument.

Melanie's tension seemed to loosen, her lips quivering as she considered the offer. "Look, I don't want to put you out. I'll sleep outside your tent," she countered, a half-hearted attempt at independence.

"No way. That's not happening," Peri replied, a protective fire igniting in her eyes. "I'll stay with Uneze; our tents are bigger than yours, so we can both fit in his. You'll be right next to us, and we'll hear if Dave comes near."

Melanie managed a fragile smile, a flicker of gratitude breaking through her fear. "Oh, he won't. He'll ignore me for the next two days. It happens all the time."

"Okay, let's grab your stuff while he's gone, and I'll ask camp security to keep an eye out for him and my tent tonight," Peri suggested, rising from the bench.

"Thanks, Peri," Melanie murmured as they moved quietly through the darkness.

Peri slipped into Uneze's tent and waited for him to arrive. Seeing Peri, he smiled and studied her face for a moment. "Are you okay?"

"I'm fine, but I put Melanie in my tent, so you're stuck with me."

"Cool with me," Uneze said. The flirting had disappeared, replaced with frustration as he said, "That was wild."

"What the hell happened out there?" Peri asked.

"I have no idea, but I guess we'll find out tomorrow," Uneze replied.

They nestled onto the mattress, the fabric yielding softly beneath their weight as they pressed together, the warmth of their bodies creating a snug cocoon.

Peri's laughter danced in the air, light and infectious. "This is cosy," she whispered, her breath brushing against Uneze's ear like a playful breeze.

"Shhh," he replied, glancing toward the darkness outside as if they could hear. "Dave can't know Melanie is alone."

"Sorry," she murmured, her voice barely above a whisper. "So, the plot thickens," she mused.

Uneze sighed and replied, "So, do you think that was all about getting his tent to himself for a rendezvous with Alistair?"

"Who knows? I don't get why Alistair was there in the woods. I mean, if it was just the two of them, why take Melanie there if he was going for a romantic moment by the cliff?" Peri asked.

Uneze shifted, trying to find a comfortable position, and replied, "No idea at all. I guess the truth will surface soon enough. I told you, there's always a massive scandal on each tour."

Peri's eyes widened, the flicker of the dim light catching her worry. "Do you think Dave realised how close they were to the edge?"

For a moment, Uneze hesitated, his attention slipping away as he considered the darkness outside. He exhaled, a heavy sigh slipping from his lips. "I don't know. It was dark. I guess we have to give him the benefit of the doubt."

Peri shook her head, frustration etching lines on her forehead. "Maybe, but did you see the way he was tugging her? He definitely wanted to seriously hurt her. I feel so bad; she's alone in the world . She hasn't bonded with the girls of the group and now she has to deal with this."

"Yeah, we're going to have to keep a very close eye on them. How long are they with us?" Uneze asked.

Peri pictured the list of participants and replied, "The whole six weeks."

He rolled his eyes, sarcasm lacing his tone. "Oh, lucky us. We'll add bodyguard to our list of duties for the next few weeks." He cast a glance toward the opening of the tent, a shadow of worry creeping into his voice. "Let's hope she's still there in the morning."

"It's nice though. I was dreading having a female guide, but I have to say it's great to have a woman; you've got that soft touch and compassion that James definitely doesn't have."

Their faces were so near, Peri felt she was breathing him in. With her eyes lowered, she cuddled up and bid good night. In the silence she felt his hand move from his chest, down his body until his fingers stopped and skimmed hers. With a sigh, Peri turned onto her side, pushing his hand away from her.

78 - PERI

As the first sounds of the staff preparing breakfast, Peri stirred awake, blinking against the golden light.

She caught Uneze's eye, a flicker of guilt shadowing his playful grin. "Sorry if I gave you a scare last night," he said, his tone light but his eyes earnest. "I didn't mean to come off all lovey-dovey. I just got lost in the moment."

Peri glanced down, fiddling with the edge of his sleeping bag. "So, would you ever consider holding James's hand?" She asked, half-joking, yet searching for something deeper.

Uneze's laughter rang out, bright and clear. "No way, not a chance."

Peri's smile dimmed slightly, but she pressed on, "Well, how about this? Treat me like James. I enjoyed our time in the tent, really, but under these circumstances, holding hands just feels... wrong." She pondered for a moment, then added, "The thought of working together for another six weeks feels daunting. I just don't want to complicate things."

A light breeze fluttered through the tent, ruffling their hair, and Uneze's expression softened. "I get it. I'm sorry," he said, a cheeky smile returning.

"I've went out a couple of hours ago to check on things; it was all quiet. Melanie was sleeping, well, snoring actually. Dave's tent was open, and he was in there, also fast asleep," Uneze said.

"Right, let's go and keep the peace. You stick by Dave; I'll stick by Melanie," Peri said.

"Sure," Uneze said, before adding, "See you later, James."

Peri's footsteps crunched softly against the gravel as she scanned the camp, her eyes darting from tent to tent. "Melanie?" she called, her voice echoing in the stillness.

Feeling panicked, Peri threw her shower bag on a table. As she wandered further, a chill gripped her spine when she spotted Melanie's figure—a solitary silhouette crouched near the spot where the confrontation had taken place.

The ground was still scarred from the nighttime chaos, and Peri felt unease swell in her chest. "Melanie. What are you doing here?" she asked.

Melanie turned, her expression distant as if lost in a memory. "I couldn't sleep. I wanted to check out where the fight happened." Her voice was barely above a whisper, carrying the awkwardness unease.

"Ah, back to the scene of the crime," Peri chuckled, trying to lighten the mood, but the smile faded when she saw the shadow of fear flicker in Melanie's eyes.

"It's just weird. I'm convinced he wanted to push me over the edge," Melanie murmured as she stared at the ground, tracing patterns in the dirt.

"Why would he want to do that?" Peri questioned, her heart pounding as she caught the tremor in Melanie's voice.

"I don't know. He's got a million faults, but it was so out of character." A shiver ran through Melanie as she recalled the confrontation, her hands fidgeting with the hem of her jacket.

"If you're sure he meant what you said, then we can ask him to be removed from the tour." Peri's protective instincts flared, but Melanie shook her head.

"No, that's not necessary. He just had a bit too much to drink." Melanie's voice wavered, and Peri noticed her discomfort, the way her shoulders pulled in like a shield.

"Are you ready to see him at breakfast?" Peri pressed, hoping to gauge the situation.

"Well, I guess I have to face the music and head up there."

"I can bring your breakfast here, or to my tent if you like," Peri offered, sensing the tension radiating off Melanie.

"No, I need to show my face. Let him know he hasn't beaten my spirit with his outburst last night." Melanie's chin lifted defiantly, but Peri could see the uncertainty lurking beneath the surface.

"What happened? Did you have a fight?" Peri asked.

"It was all so strange." Melanie's voice steadied as she recounted the events. "He convinced me to go for a walk with him, and then he picked a fight over nothing. The even weirder thing was that just before you turned up, I spotted Alistair heading towards us. I'm sure he grabbed me. He definitely wasn't coming to help. It was the strangest feeling, then he just bolted when he heard your voices."

The morning sunlight around them felt dimmer, dull shadows and shapes creeping into her Peri's expression. "Are you going to be okay? We can always set up an extra tent or find you a room—whatever you need," she offered, her voice barely above a whisper, as if afraid to disturb the fragile peace.

Melanie's lips curled slightly; the flicker of courage that danced there was quickly doused by her unspoken fears. "Thanks, but I'll be fine." She straightened, her chin lifting just a notch. "He just wants me out of the way when he's like this, so I'll keep my distance. I've got a good book I wanted to finish."

Peri's expression softened, and a hint of desperation crept into her tone. "You could talk to the other girls; they're all really nice," she suggested, hoping to pull Melanie from her solitude.

Melanie shook her head, a shadow crossing her face. "No, I don't want to have to explain any of this. It's better if I just keep to myself." The determination in her voice was a fragile thread, fraying at the edges but refusing to snap.

"Alright," Peri conceded, a reluctant sigh escaping her lips. "But make sure you aren't alone with him on any more cliffs."

79 - EMILY

At breakfast, Peri gestured for Melanie to dine with her, Anya, and Johan. "Look, these guys are going to an indigenous cultures centre. Why don't you join them? You don't have to explain anything; you're just being friendly."

With a nod, they walked to the table where the girls sat, Melanie gestured to an empty seat and asked, "May I?"

"Of course, we'd love to have you," Anya replied.

"Thanks so much, and thanks, Peri. I need a bit of company today." Melanie said. She looked around her and said, "Dave's not here. Do you think he's left?" Melanie asked in whispers.

"Who knows? Maybe he's just avoiding you."

"No, if he had to choose between food and an awkward situation, he'd choose food," Melanie said. Suddenly a look of pure hatred filled her face as a silhouetted figure appeared, looming in the early morning sun. He simply moved past her, an unspoken distance stretching between them.

"Morning, guys," Dave said in a general greeting to everyone. He cast a glance in Melanie's direction, shaking his head. "Oh, Ems, I like the new look," he said, looking Emily up and down.

"It's Emily, Not Ems, but thank you. My sister insisted that I wear this, this, what can I call it? Costume,"

"No, I'd call those girly clothes a costume. Now, you just look like us," Dave said.

"Oh, great. I look like an idiot then," Emily retorted.

Dave shook his head and walked off as Michelle neared her sister and whispered, "Nice, remember. Smile and be nice. He was saying you looked good."

"Nice. Got it. I'll try, but it's actually harder than it looks," Emily said.

"You just tried once. I'm sure you'll get the hang of it," Michelle said. She turned to Alex and said, "Emily is feeling insecure about her new look. What do you think?"

"Er, well. You look like you belong on safari now," Alex said with a teasing tone. "Now you just need to try and look like you're enjoying it."

"Look who's talking," Emily retorted as she turned away and scowled.

"Emily," Michelle scolded. "Nice, God, why is it so hard?"

Melanie sat at the corner of the bustling clubhouse, staring the spread of food before her. Each colourful dish seemed to pulse with life, yet her thoughts remained distant, a tight knot of tension forming in her chest as she watched him join Alistair and laugh loudly as if the evening before hadn't even happened. "I can't even look at him," Melanie muttered, her voice barely above a whisper, the words laced with disdain.

"Then don't. Focus on your plate," came the casual reply from Peri, but the suggestion fell flat in the charged atmosphere.

Dennis, ever the chatterbox in awkward moments, seized the lull with a monologue about his Eve's latest social media antics. "So, what does that mean?" he implored, glancing hopefully at the women, seeking validation.

"Dennis, enough," Michelle interjected, her tone sharp like a knife cutting through the chatter. "Stop moping over someone who clearly doesn't want you. Do you really think posting pictures of tall grass and hinting at some imaginary beast will win her back?"

"What else am I supposed to do? No lions or elephants around here," he grumbled, the frustration evident in eyes.

Michelle pulled her hair back into a tight ponytail, adjustments to her sunglasses lending her an air of determination. "You need to make her jealous. That's your ticket if she still has any feelings left."

"How?" he asked, scepticism lacing his words.

"Come here," she chuckled, conspiratorial. She draped her arm around him, lifting her lips to brush against his cheek, a playful grin spreading across her face.

"Cheese," Dennis said.

"Now, post that," she commanded with mock seriousness. "If she's the slightest bit interested, it'll send her heart racing. If not, it's time to move on."

"You think this is more effective than a lion or a hippo?" he questioned, still half-joking.

"Trust me, this is the only play that works with women. Now, just wait and see," she replied, her confidence infectious.

Before Dennis could respond, Uneze crashed his little drum, a thump that summoned the group's attention. He announced the plans and departure times for each tour, and the group buzzed back to life.

80 - MELANIE

The group prepared to separate for their tours with local guides as Peri and Uneze handed out water, snacks and introduced them to their guides.

"Where are you headed?" Dave's voice sliced through the chatter as he caught up to Melanie, who was already striding away.

"Why? So, you can try to push me off a cliff again? Keep your distance," she shot back, glancing over her shoulder with a glare that betrayed a hint of fear.

"Hmm," he mused, a smirk tugging at the corners of his mouth as he closed the gap between them.

"Uneze," Melanie called out with urgency in her voice as she tapped Dave on the shoulder, her eyes sparkling with mischief. "Can you remind my husband that he needs to keep his distance?"

"You don't need a bodyguard. Honestly, you're not cut out for these tours and this heat. By the end of the morning, you might just find yourself in a ditch, thanks to your own bad health," Dave replied, turning away with a laugh, following Alistair's lead down the trail.

"What's with those two?" Melanie asked Uneze.

"I'm not sure I like this. We should keep an eye on them—make sure neither of them is ever alone with you on a day tour," Uneze insisted, his tone serious.

"That seems a bit over the top," Melanie replied, shaking her head. "Last night might have looked weird to you, but Dave's just got a temper. " Her voice softened, revealing an underlying trust.

Anya and Johan were a whirlwind of laughter and playful jabs, their chemistry lighting up the rugged trail as they visited a cultural centre at the end of a long, rocky trail. Melanie limped behind them, her feet protesting with every step, counting down the miles until they finally stumbled back into the embrace of their camp. The fatigue tugged at her muscles, yet the warmth of the new friendship wrapped around her like a warm sunny morning.

As the group joined for tasty treats as the sky darkened, Melanie's heart swelled with gratitude for the new friendship and company that she longed so much. It seemed to shield her from the chilling indifference of Dave, who passed by silently, his glare heavy with unspoken words.

In the midst of the joyful noise, Melanie nestled into her chair, a soft smile breaking across her face as Emily and Michelle chatted about the spent day by the pool.

"I needed a bit of tan topping," Emily retorted, her grin widening.

"And, of course, Emily does nothing alone, so I got stuck babysitting her," Michelle added with an amused roll of her eyes.

"Did we miss anything here?" Anya asked.

"Nothing much, just Emily trying to strut her stuff around the pool and taking a spectacular dive, only to be heroically rescued by a cute pool boy," Michelle chimed, laughter dancing in her voice. "

"It took me ages to get him to the right spot at the right time, but it worked. We're meeting for drinks later," Emily beamed, a triumphant sparkle in her eyes as she pulled out a tiny mirror and ran her fingers through her hair and over her lips.

"Meet my sister, the devastated, heartbroken woman who ran from the altar a week ago," Michelle teased.

81 - MELANIE

After promising Peri she'd be fine sharing with Dave, Melanie huddled deep in her sleeping bag, her back pressed against the cold tent fabric. A hot breeze whispered through the thin walls as Dave stumbled inside and threw himself onto his mattress, letting out a loud "ouch" as he landed. His voice sent a cold jolt of fear down her spine. The silence wrapped around them like a thick fog, each minute ticking by with a heavy tension that made her breath feel shallow until she finally drifted off.

Melanie emerged into the bustling camp to find Anya and Johan already gathered, their faces flushed after an early morning walk. She forced a smile, hiding the lingering chill from the night before, and joined them. An hour later, with bags packed, they all climbed onto the transport and headed off in the direction of the Sossusvlei sand dunes of the Namib desert.

Emily stepped onto the bus, her heart racing slightly as Michelle leant over the seat, a cheeky smirk on her face. "Mingle, try it," she teased, wagging her finger.

"What do I say?" Emily grimaced, glancing around at the unfamiliar faces. "I don't do girl talk unless it's about cocktails or Louis Vuitton, and there are none of those here."

"Em, just do it. Talk to Anya; she's the nicest one here," Michelle urged, her eyes sparkling with encouragement.

Taking a deep breath, Emily slid into the seat beside Anya, plastering on her brightest smile. "Hi, I'm Emily," she chirped, her voice a little too high-pitched.

"Eh, yes. I know. We've been together for a few days," Anya replied, with a hint of sarcasm.

"Yeah, sorry. I've been a bit distracted," Emily admitted, her cheeks warming under Anya's scrutiny.

"You look good out of the heels and skirts," Anya remarked, her tone light and friendly. "You'll find it a lot easier to get around dressed like you're ready for a safari."

Emily chuckled, a hint of sarcasm lacing her words. "I'd like to blame it on the missing suitcase, but honestly, there's nothing in there that would help me out. Just a suitcase full of shiny dresses, heels, and makeup."

"Your makeup looks nice," Anya complimented, tilting her head in curiosity. "How do you do it without a bedroom mirror?"

"I can do it without a mirror; fifteen years of practice," Emily confessed with a shy smile. "I don't think anyone has seen my real face since I was around fifteen."

"Wow. I think I only wear it on special occasions. I don't have any in my suitcase at all," Anya said, her tone casual, but Emily could see a flicker of understanding in her eyes.

"Yes, well, this is hand luggage supplies. I think by tomorrow I'll be forced to go au naturel, which isn't my best look," Emily replied, a hint of dread in her voice.

Michelle suddenly popped her head over the seat, her voice bubbling with excitement. "Emily, look at us. Can you see any mascara around these faces? This is a chance to be one with nature and all that stuff. You have a beautiful face—or at least, you have a wonderful structure. I'd love to see your face without all that stuff on it."

"Really?" Emily asked.

"Yeah. Come on, you've ditched the heels and skirts. Don't you feel better?" Anya chimed in.

"No," Emily said, her brows furrowing as she fiddled with her clothes, feeling utterly out of place. "I don't like myself like this," Emily admitted, her fingers brushing over her simple outfit. "But I do think it's going to make my life easier."

"You look better," Anya insisted, leaning closer. "Now, you look like someone I'd like to get to know. Until yesterday, I really didn't want to waste time on you."

"Really?" Emily repeated.

"Yeah, you just looked, well, like someone who wasn't happy with herself. Now, you're looking more like a person who likes herself," Anya said, her voice gentle but firm.

"There you go. Baby steps," Michelle said, her enthusiasm infectious. "We'll have those hair extensions out in no time at all."

As laughter filled the space between them, Emily felt something shift within her—a flicker of possibility, a hint of acceptance among other women, a concept entirely novel to her.

82 - MELANIE

Just before they arrived at the campsite, Peri stood at the edge of the towering dunes, her breath caught in her throat as she took in the undulating waves of golden sand, their ripples glistening under the sun like strands of silk. Each grain twinkled like a tiny star, swirling gently in the breeze, creating a mesmerising dance that captivated her attention. In the distance, she heard the soft laughter of her clients, the sound a gentle hum against the expansive silence of Deadvei.

When they finally reached their destination, the lively chatter faded into an uneasy hush. One by one, they slipped into their tents, the soft rustle of fabric the only sound breaking the quiet.

The cooking lesson, offered by the campsite as an alternative to those who needed time away from the heat, was the perfect way to step away from the sweltering sun and into a world of culinary discovery.

Melanie adjusted her apron, her fingers slightly trembling with dread as she stood in the warm, fragrant kitchen of the campsite's cooking school. The class was a quaint, bustling affair held in a shady courtyard, with woven baskets of colourful local produce and earthen pots neatly arranged on wooden counters. Melanie was joined by Emily and Anya, who chatted until the teacher, Aisha, shushed them.

"Today, we make four dishes," Aisha announced, her voice commanding yet comforting, as if the very spirit of the dish resided in her tone. "You must learn to balance the flavors. The herbs are key. Without them, it's just... bland." She let out a hearty laugh, and the women chuckled politely.

As they chopped and mixed vegetables, they chatted between themselves.

"This is so much nicer than hiking," Emily said with a scowl. "I can't believe Guy expected me to do this outdoorsy stuff on our honeymoon."

"Maybe it would have been different with him, more romantic," Melanie suggested.

"Nope, it would have been awful. Stuck in a tent with him. I don't hike or cook, but at least cooking is in the shade and doesn't require hiking boots."

Emily turned to her, a genuine smile breaking through her frustration. "It's nice to see you smile. I think that's the first time I've heard you laugh."

Melanie's expression shifted slightly, her laughter fading into a soft sigh. "I don't laugh much around Dave. It's just not worth it. If I even smile, he's right there, ready to wipe it off my face. I've perfected this miserable look."

"Well, we need to change that," Anya said, her voice brightening. "I like the smiley Melanie."

"Thanks. Luckily, he's usually off with one of his bimbos, so I don't have to deal with him too often. I can't believe he chose this safari for me instead of one of them."

"Didn't you want to come?" Michelle chimed in.

"Yes, I genuinely did. But I had to play it cool. My neighbours came on this tour a couple of months ago, and when they showed off their photos, I told them I'd hate a safari, just to annoy Dave. And, of course, he booked it to spite me. So here I am."

"Well played," Emily said, shaking her head in disbelief. "Why do men always do things like that?"

Melanie shrugged. "He's a caveman—he likes having things his way. But I've learned how to dance to his tune when I need to."

Just then, the cooking teacher returned, cradling a bowl overflowing with ingredients. As the scents wafted through the air, Melanie felt a rush of warmth, not just from the spices but from a burgeoning excitement deep within her. Thoughts of Julius and the future they could share danced in her mind, urging her to act. In this moment, surrounded by the dazzling flavours of Namibia, she knew it was time to craft a plan—one that would ensure Dave didn't hold her back from the life she truly wanted.

83 - MELANIE

Melanie grasped the tiny vacuum-sealed bag of mixed nuts, her fingers trembling. It was a secret weapon she had prepared. She read the label: *South African Ginger Powder.* The memory of her sneaky swap from their first day in Cape Town flashed in her mind. She picked up the ginger powder and carefully measured it into the mortar—a generous helping, far more than she hoped she'd need.

The soapy water bubbled as she rinsed the empty bag before tossing it into her pocket. She placed her hand on her belly, unable to flee from the unease knotting in her stomach.

By the time the hikers returned, the meal was ready; Melanie's stomach churned with tension and dread all mixed together.

A few hours later, the sun dipped low, and a campfire flickered nearby, throwing dull shadows across the campsite. Melanie's pulse quickened as the server approached, each dish a new wave of anxiety crashing over her.

Laughter erupted like the crackle of flames, each chuckle mingling with the night as plates filled with colourful culinary creations.

Nods of approval and delighted smiles illuminated their faces in the firelight, a shared moment that ignited more laughter.

"This is amazing; well done, guys," Dennis said, his voice ringing with genuine admiration. "Now, I wish I'd stayed here and cooked rather than almost crippling myself out there."

Melanie's cheeks flushed as she glanced down, her voice barely above a whisper. "We didn't do it alone; we just did the stirring and chopping."

"Don't downplay your role," Michelle chimed in, grinning. "Choosing the spices was no small feat, and Melanie did that."

"Oh, Melanie made a choice all on her own. Kudos," Dave teased, an unamused twinkle in his eyes. "Her cooking at home? Let's just say it leaves something to be desired. I'd stay away from anything she touches in the kitchen. Just saying."

"Shut it, Dave. Just enjoy the food," Emily ordered, a desire to slap him bubbling beneath her words.

The steam wafted from the serving platter as the spicy meatballs made their grand entrance, their deep colours glistening under the dim lights of the dining table. Melanie's eyes darted between the plate and Dave, who was chuckling like a young boy as he and Alistair made inappropriate comments about the young female server.

Melanie sat back, her eyes sharp and expectant, as though she were a spectator at a boxing match, eagerly awaiting the first punch. Time seemed to stretch, a thick tension hanging in the air until Dave gleefully dipped each meatball into the rich tomato sauce, oblivious to the brewing storm. Melanie waited, barely able to contain her excitement, envisioning the moment when Dave's nut allergy would strike—a chaotic crescendo to their evening.

With a sigh, Dave dipped his fork into the food and took a large mouthful. He chewed, swallowed, and paused. His face reddened slightly, and he coughed. "Bloody hell, Melanie. Did you dump a spice rack in this?"

"Too much for you?" she asked innocently.

Dave waved her off, his bravado kicking in. "I can handle it. Just... unexpected." He took another bite, then another, until the bowl was nearly empty. Melanie watched, a strange expression of fascination and disappointment on her face.

It was only fifteen minutes later, as Dave's face turned pale and he clutched his stomach, that her plan seemed to bear fruit.

"Mel, what the... what was in that soup?" he groaned, doubling over.

"Just local spices," she replied, her voice calm but her hands trembling. "Why?"

"I need the toilet," he shouted, bolting from the room.

"What's wrong with him?" Michelle asked.

Melanie shrugged, nibbling on her food, wishing Dave's dramatic collapse had been discreet enough to spare the group from trauma. Moments later, Dave returned, his hand pressed against his stomach, a dark cloud of displeasure shadowing his features.

"See? You can tell Melanie cooked this; it's given me a dodgy stomach." His whiny tone sliced through the air, prompting an eye roll from Michelle.

Melanie leant against the counter, arms crossed, an eyebrow arched in amusement. "No, it wouldn't happen in five minutes. If I wanted to give you a dodgy stomach, I'd use three-day-old cooking cream." Her voice was smooth, almost teasing, as she flicked her glare towards Dave.

"See, you're all my witnesses. She wants me to get sick." Dave's voice boomed, each word dripping with venom as he pointed an accusatory finger at Melanie, his body stiff as if ready to pounce. His dramatic flair had the others exchanging glances, eyebrows raised, and intrigue dancing on their faces.

"Dave, shut up. You are humiliating yourself," Michelle shot back, her words slicing through the tension like a knife. She stood rigid, arms folded tightly across her chest, her lips pressed into a thin line as she glared at him.

The room pulsed with the intensity of their standoff. "Who do you think you are, telling me to shut up? Leave me alone." Dave's voice was a crescendo, defiance radiating from him as he faced Michelle.

Her smirk was sharp, her tone low yet laced with sardonic sweetness. "If I were Melanie, I would've put nuts in your food years ago and let you die a quick but painful death."

Suddenly, panic flickered in Dave's eyes, wide and frantic. "Nuts? Oh my god, Melanie, you put nuts in my food, you stupid bitch."

"No, if I'd put nuts in your food, you'd be over there gasping for breath right now," Melanie shot back, the corners of her mouth twitching upward.

"You'd like that, wouldn't you?" Dave hissed, the air thickening with tension.

As Melanie waited, the only sound that followed was Dave's frequent, panicked dashes to the bathroom. Each time he returned, he hurled another accusation into the charged atmosphere, his face a mask of indignation.

"Hang on, so you're telling me you have the runs, and now you think I poisoned you? You're saying that nuts don't actually set off an allergic reaction that'll kill you? All they do is send you running to the bathroom?"

Melanie's voice dripped with incredulity, her eyes searching his face for a trace of reason.

All eyes fixed on Dave, who hesitated, their stares amplifying his discomfort. "It's still a reaction. Getting chronic diarrhea is still a reaction to nuts," he insisted, fists clenching at his sides.

"Hell no," Melanie retorted, her tone firm. "Eighteen years of making sure there were no nuts in the house, at restaurants—calling ahead to warn everyone about your allergies—and all for a bit of a bellyache."

"I wouldn't call it a bellyache. It's an allergic reaction." Dave shot back, his voice rising again as he squared his shoulders defiantly. "So, I'm guessing you did put nuts in my food then?"

Emily chimed in, her voice steady. "No, we were all very careful. We even cleaned the utensils before we started cooking to make sure they hadn't touched them."

"That's right," Michelle added, her tone accusative. "We can say 100% that there were no nuts in the food we prepared. Maybe you just drank some water from the tap."

"No, she tried to poison me. Keep her away from me. She's the devil." Dave declared, his voice rising once more as he bolted from his chair, the wooden legs scraping against the floor in protest as he rushed toward the bathroom.

The tension in the room was about to boil over, their laughter stifled by the absurdity of the unfolding drama. Whatever Melanie had hoped to achieve, it hadn't freed her from the toxic relationship. If anything, it had only added another layer of mess.

84 – DAVE

Dave hadn't emerged from the bathroom for what felt like ages, leaving an amused tension hanging over the messy table.

"I didn't do it, although I wish I had," Melanie said. "You have no idea how hard it is to avoid nuts, and how much work I put into avoiding them."

"Well, at least we can put nuts back on the menu now," Peri said.

"And can we do it three times a day, please, so he'll spend the entire holiday on the loo?" Alex said.

Everyone looked at Alex. His habit of adding the odd comment and then shutting up had become a thing, yet everyone stopped whatever they were doing to listen. "I'm sorry. I shouldn't say anything like that, but he really is an idiot. Now, can we find some way of keeping Alistair away from us too?" Alex said.

"Maybe a simple laxative will work with him," Johan said as the group returned to a hushed quiet as Alistair neared.

"Did I hear my name?" he asked.

"Nope, we were just wondering if you'd gotten sick seeing as you were away so long," Alex said. "Actually, we were just hoping you'd gotten sick, too."

"Ah, the mystery man speaks again," Alistair said as he reached in and grabbed Dave's beer, gulping it down. Feeling everyone glare at him, he added, "Well, Dave's not going to be drinking it, is he? No point wasting a good beer."

Uneze glanced at the door, worry creasing his brow as he turned to Peri and asked, "Do you think he's okay?"

Peri let out a light chuckle, her eyes sparkling with mischief. "I'm not going to check on him—that's a man's job."

Uneze, leaning back on his hands, wore a teasing grin. "Nope. I might catch what he's got," he joked, a chuckle escaping as he flicked a twig into the flames. "Alright, I'll go," he said reluctantly, rising from his seat and trudging toward the bathroom.

"Hold your nose, bro," Dennis called behind him.

When Uneze returned, the corners of his mouth turned upward despite his words. "He prefers to stay near a toilet."

Laughter erupted from the group, a burst of sound that clashed with the unspoken tension in Melanie's chest. The realization cut through her like a jagged edge—she had been a puppet in Dave's game, strings pulled at his whim throughout their marriage. Eventually, she stood and drifted toward her tent, hoping to find some peace and quiet.

Peri intercepted her, catching her just before she crossed the threshold. "Do you want to stay in my tent?" Peri asked, her voice low, concern threading through her tone.

Melanie hesitated, her heart racing. "I don't know. I was thinking of asking you for a new tent on my own. I'll pay extra for it. I don't think it's a good idea for me to be near him tonight. He thinks I tried to poison him." The words tumbled out, laced with vulnerability.

"Don't worry. We know you didn't," Peri reassured her, the warmth of friendship growing between them. "Do you know how many people get sick in Africa, especially on safari? They just have to eat what they're given."

"I guess."

"Stay in my tent, and tomorrow we'll get you sorted out," Peri smiled, squeezing her shoulder gently, grounding her in a moment that felt far too heavy.

85 - PERI

Peri tilted her head, gesturing for Uneze to join her at the back of the camp. He hesitated for a moment, as if weighing the invitation, then slid his hands into his pockets and strolled over, his presence commanding yet unassuming.

"What's happened now?" he asked, his tone light but filled with curiosity.

"Nothing," Peri replied, a flirty shimmer in her eyes. "But it's your lucky night. I'm in with you again. Melanie decided my tent was more appealing."

Uneze chuckled softly, the sound warm and rich, like a melody that made Peri's nerves settle. "I guess I should be flattered, then. You keep ending up with me."

They exchanged knowing smiles before falling into a comfortable rhythm of conversation. The evening's oddities—the allergy situation, Alex's sudden animosity towards Dave and Alistair—provided easy fodder for laughter and speculation. Yet beneath their banter, something unspoken hung in the air, like the quiet note of a song waiting to resolve.

After a while, the conversation ebbed, giving way to a silence that was neither awkward nor forced. Uneze tilted his head towards the open expanse of desert and sky, his voice dropping to a low murmur.

"Lie next to me," he said. "Just for a moment. Listen to the sounds out here—it makes everything else feel so... small."

Peri hesitated, her eyes lifting to the night sky. The stars were a symphony of light, scattered across a canvas of endless black. The desert, vast and untouched, seemed to breathe with its own quiet life—the rustling of the dunes, the occasional sigh of the wind. It was the kind of beauty that could make a person feel insignificant in an instant.

"It is beautiful," she admitted, finally lowering herself beside him.

"It's more than that," Uneze said, his voice soft but sure. "It's grounding. Out here, under this sky, everything else—problems, worries—just fades away."

His words settled over her, sinking deep, brushing against the parts of herself she rarely shared. For a moment, she let herself relax, her guard lowering in the stillness of the night.

When Uneze's hand brushed hers, the touch was almost imperceptible, but it sent a jolt through her, igniting a warmth that spread from her fingertips to her cheeks. She turned to him, her heart pounding as she searched his face for something—permission, explanation, or maybe just confirmation that he felt it too.

"What's that?" Peri asked softly, her voice barely above a whisper. Her hand remained where it was, the warmth of his touch anchoring her in the moment.

Uneze smiled, his expression both amused and tender. "My hand," he said, his tone playful. "Again. Sorry, it seems to have a mind of its own."

"Maybe it has Tourette's," she quipped, her laughter soft but genuine, breaking the tension just enough to keep it bearable.

"Or maybe it just likes you," he replied, the humour in his voice giving way to something deeper. His gaze held hers, steady and unflinching, as if daring her to look away.

Peri felt her breath catch, her mind scrambling for the safety of a wall to put between them. "Uneze," she began, her tone measured but not cold. "Remember, I'm James. We have to work together, and this... this isn't a good idea."

He pulled back slightly, withdrawing his hand with a laugh that was as much for himself as it was for her. "You really know how to kill a moment, don't you?"

She smiled, though it didn't seem sincere in her eyes. "It's a gift."

They sat in silence for a beat longer, the tension now laced with something bittersweet. "Goodnight, Uneze," Peri said finally, turning away and pulling her jacket tighter around her.

"Goodnight, Peri," he replied, his voice softer now, almost wistful.

But even as Peri lay there, her eyes closed against the vastness of the night, she couldn't shake the feeling that something had shifted between them. The warmth of his hand lingered on hers, a phantom touch that made her pulse quicken despite herself.

And as the stars twinkled above them, indifferent yet eternal, both Peri and Uneze knew they had crossed an invisible line. Whether they would retreat or take a step forward, only time—and the desert—would tell.

86 - PERI

Peri jolted awake, the murmurs and scattered laughter of the campsite seeping through the fabric of the tent. For a moment, she tried to pull herself back into sleep, but the noise persisted, gnawing at her thoughts. She propped herself up on her elbows, scanning the dimly lit tent for Uneze. He was still deep in slumber, his breathing steady and calm. Quietly, she slid from under the covers and slipped outside.

The voices came from a distance, near the camp's toilet area. She crept closer, careful not to make a sound. As she neared, she saw two figures silhouetted against the pale light of the moon. Alistair and Dave were seated on a moss-covered log, their voices low and conspiratorial, their laughter sharp and unsettling.

Peri paused just out of sight, watching them closely. For a few minutes, she remained still, letting the sounds wash over her. But something about their conversation felt off—there was a tension in the air that made her uneasy. She stepped back, about to retreat towards Uneze's tent when her foot brushed against a dry twig. It snapped loudly in the silence, and both men immediately fell silent, their attention sharpening in her direction. Peri froze for a moment, her heart racing in her chest. Then, instinct took over, and she darted away, slipping silently into the shadows, her breath catching in her throat as she moved.

Behind her, Dave and Alistair waited in the stillness. They let the moment stretch out before resuming their conversation.

"She did it," Dave's voice was low, laced with a venomous edge. "I know she tried to poison me. I've been watching her, waiting. She's been slipping things into my food, and I've had enough of it."

Alistair's laughter cut through the night air like a knife. "You think she's trying to poison you? That's a bit dramatic, don't you think? This is Melanie, she's a softie."

"No." Dave's voice was thick with rage. "She's been poisoning me. I can feel it. And I had hoped by now you'd have done something about it, well, her. I can't take much more of this."

Alistair exhaled a breath, his tone almost lazy. "I'm working on it, alright? You can't rush this stuff. I can't just bash her head in or throw her out in front of everyone. It's got to be more subtle than that. If you don't start behaving, though, I don't know how the hell I'm supposed to get her alone."

Dave clenched his fists, the thought of Melanie so close yet so far from him driving him to a boiling point. "What do you want me to do? I just want her gone. I can't stand her any longer."

"I get that, but you've got to stop acting like a maniac. If you keep this up, it's going to blow up in both our faces. You need to blend in more. Start acting like a normal husband, at least in front of people."

"Acting normal... like you? That's asking a lot." Dave's voice was overflowing with bitter sarcasm, though a chuckle escaped him as he ran a hand through his hair.

Alistair's eyes narrowed, the smile never leaving his lips. "I'm doing this carefully, Dave. Patience is the key here. You're going to screw it up if you don't calm down. You need to think long-term."

Dave's anger flared again, but this time it was mixed with a gnawing desperation, a suffocating need for escape. "Patience? What the hell do you mean patience?" He glanced at Alistair, his fists tightening around the beer bottle in his hand. "What exactly are you waiting for? I'm sick of waiting."

Alistair's eyes gleamed, unfazed by the sudden rise in Dave's temper. He shifted back on the log, stretching his arms out lazily. "It's all about timing, mate. You're jumping the gun. You're not seeing the bigger picture. The skydiving trip you two have planned is when I'll make my move."

Dave froze, his expression hardening. "Skydiving? That's in a week."

"Exactly. We've got time," Alistair said, the calmness in his voice unsettling in its certainty. "But you've got to play it cool. Don't let anyone know what's brewing beneath the surface. If you start acting like a desperate fool, it'll all blow up in your face."

Dave swallowed hard, his focus flickering toward the firelight in the distance, the figures of the others dancing in the shadows. "And what do you expect me to do in the meantime? Pretend everything's fine? Smile at her while she plans my death?"

"You're going to fake it," Alistair said sharply, his voice growing more intense. "You're going to act like the sad, desperate husband, the one who's been wronged. Because that's the story you need to sell. You can't pull this off if you keep showing your true colours. It'll be too obvious."

Dave exhaled a bitter laugh, the sound hollow and dark. "This is impossible. Pretend to be the husband she deserves? You're asking the impossible."

Alistair's eyes flashed with impatience. "It's not impossible. You've got to think. Skydiving's the key. And when the time is right, you won't even have to lift a finger. I'll take care of the rest."

Dave's thoughts spiraled, the pressure in his chest growing heavier with each passing second. "And what if something goes wrong?" he whispered, a chill creeping into his voice. "What if it doesn't go as planned?"

Alistair's smile never faltered, but there was a coldness to it now, a knowing edge. "It will go as planned. Trust me. I'm good at this. But you... you have to behave like a man who's in love with his wife. That's the story you need to sell."

"Yeah, well... I'll try my best," Dave said through gritted teeth, his hand trembling slightly as he passed the beer bottle back to Alistair.

87 - PERI

The evening was fading, and the soft sparkle of the campfire cast long shadows across the clearing. The group had settled into a comfortable quiet, the occasional crackling of the fire accompanying the hushed conversations. Emily, thought back to Uneze. She found herself drawn to him more than usual tonight. There was something about the way he laughed with the others, so at ease, so natural—yet Emily couldn't shake the feeling of wanting to be closer to him.

She slipped away from the group, her steps deliberate. She slipped open the tent and slid inside. She positioned herself just a little closer, close enough that the heat from his body made her skin tingle, close enough that their shoulders brushed; for a brief moment, she felt the familiar flutter in her chest as she let her finger stroke his sleeping face.

Peri approached Uneze's tent; however, a single voice broke the silence, melodic and enticing, weaving through the fabric of the night. Moving closer, she recognised Emily's soft murmur, laced with flirtation and enticing tones.

Her breath hitched when Uneze's voice cut through the night, laced with irritation he bolted upright and pushed emily's arm away. "What's wrong? What are you doing here?"

"Nothing," Emily replied, the sound of the zipper rustling behind her punctuating the tension.

"If there is nothing wrong, then please, get out." Uneze's voice was firm, but Peri sensed the hesitation beneath.

"I'm scared out there," Emily countered, a hint of vulnerability creeping into her tone.

"Scared of sand dunes? I'm not security; I'm the guide. You're fine in your tent with your sister.

Emilie's voice dripped with a coyness that made Peri's stomach twist. "Can't I just stay here with you? My sister is driving me mad. She's forcing me to be nice to people, and I just can't do it. I can't relate to women; I much prefer to spend time with men."

Uneze laughed and asked, "Why on earth do you have to try to be nice? The girls here are all great, and no, you can't stay here. You need to go back to your tent."

Ignoring him, Emily leant in closer, her hand finding its way to his chest. "Emily, stop it," Uneze warned.

Peri's pulse raced as she pushed aside the tent flap, the zipper whispering in the quiet. The dim light revealed Emilie's lithe figure inching toward Uneze, a slow-motion tableau that made Peri's skin crawl.

In a moment of instinct, she flicked on her torch, the beam slicing through the dark and landing squarely on Uneze's face. "Uneze, honey, what's going on?" she asked.

Emily turned to see Peri at the entrance and pulled her hand back.

"Emily and I were just having a quick chat about tomorrow's trek; she was just leaving," he replied hastily.

"I leave to go for a walk, and you've already got another woman in here?" Peri's voice dripped with fake annoyance.

Emily's stare flitted between them, her expression shifting from surprise to embarrassment, caught in the act. "Ah, you two are... But you don't share a tent," she stammered, her confidence faltering.

"You try sharing a tent with someone you work with all day. We need some space sometimes," Peri shot back, her tone biting.

"Ah, well," Emily murmured, the façade of confidence slipping as she retreated to the edge of the tent. "I'll be going then. Thanks for your advice, Uneze. I'll make sure I do that trek tomorrow." Her voice trailed off, leaving behind a lingering sense of humiliation masked by a faint smile as she disappeared into the darkness.

Her footsteps in the sand faded into the distance. Uneze and Peri repressed giggles until finally, with a straighter face, Uneze said, "I told you, I predicted that one. Thanks for saving me, though."

"You did see that one coming. I'm glad to be of help," Peri said.

"I like having a female guide; it's definitely got its benefits," Uneze chuckled. "Give it a day or two and it will be your turn."

"Not if everyone thinks we're together," Peri pointed out.

"Emily won't admit that she was here, so maybe she'll be quiet about It," Uneze said.

"I'm not sure if I'm relieved by that or not." Peri laughed as she snuggled into her sleeping bag and let the sounds of the night send her into a deep sleep.

88 - PERI

At the breakfast table, the group settled in, and Peri grabbed a steaming cup of fresh coffee before sliding into the seat next to Emily. Peri's cheerful smile was met with Emily's gaze darting all around her as she played with the brim of her sun hat hanging around her neck on a piece of rope.

"Morning, Emily. I hope you slept well," Peri said, her tone light and teasing.

Emily adjusted her hat for the third time, her cheeks tinged with pink. "Erm, yes. Look, about last night—I'm really sorry," she mumbled, barely audible.

Peri leaned in slightly, her voice soft but laced with a soft undertone. "It's okay. Honestly, it happens on tours more often than you'd think. Consider it our little secret." She pressed a finger to her lips, her smile growing wider.

Emily groaned and buried her face in her hands. "Oh, God. I'm mortified. I'm just one of the many women to embarrass themselves over Uneze, aren't I? I don't even know how I'll face him today."

"He'll have forgotten about it by now, trust me," Peri said reassuringly. "It's all part of the job. He's used to it."

"Are you sure?" Emily asked, peeking at her from between her fingers.

Peri grinned knowingly. "If he hasn't, he's probably flattered. You're a beautiful woman who just wanted a little nighttime tent fun. A man with his rugged good looks and that charming smile? Let's be honest—he's more likely to be grinning about it than anything else."

Emily sighed deeply, the flush on her face refusing to fade. "Even so, I feel like I'll never live it down."

"Of course you will," Peri said with a shrug. "It's easy. Pretend it never happened. That's what he'll do—it's what I always do when it happens to me."

Emily looked at her, wide-eyed. "Wait, does that mean people have tried it on with you?"

Peri raised an eyebrow, gesturing around the table. "Look around. What do you think?"

"Eugh, no way," Emily groaned. "Wait, has anyone actually done that? That's disgusting!" She froze, her face contorting in horror. "Oh no. I'm just like them, aren't I?"

Peri shook her head firmly. "You are nothing like them. Now hold your head high, act like the strong woman I know you are, and get on with your day."

"You mean act like a bitch."

"I mean be yourself," Peri said with a smirk. "Now go on—chin up."

Emily gave a half-hearted laugh. "Thanks, Peri. You're really kind for not making this worse."

"No worries." Peri reached out to pat her shoulder. "And hey—let's never mention this again."

With that, the two women parted ways and took their places at the table. The table was a patchwork of mismatched enamel mugs, tin plates, and thermoses filled with steaming coffee and tea. Loaves of crusty bread sat beside bowls of butter and jam, while a platter of fresh fruit gleamed in the early sunlight, adding a splash of colour to the rustic spread.

The group gathered haphazardly, each person claiming a spot with a mix of sleepy groans and cheerful chatter. Some leaned forward on their elbows, cradling mugs of coffee as though their lives depended on it, while others tore into slices of bread with the ravenous enthusiasm of an outdoor appetite.

Moments later, Michelle entered, her sharp eyes sweeping the room. She stopped mid-step, noticing the suppressed giggles and side glances among the group.

"What's going on?" she asked, her tone suspicious.

"Uh, nothing," Dennis replied, failing to stifle a grin.

Michelle's brow arched. "Dennis, tell me. What did I miss?"

Dennis smirked, leaning back in his chair. "Oh, just your sister's little tent-swapping escapade."

Michelle turned to Emily, her mouth falling open in mock horror. "Ems. What is he talking about?"

Emily's cheeks burned as she tried to compose herself. "Nothing. I was just a bit drunk and got lost last night. I accidentally tried to get into the wrong tent—that's all."

"Yeah, right," Dennis muttered, shaking his head with a cheeky grin. "Next time, try mine. I promise I won't send you away."

Michelle gasped dramatically. "Wait—what did you do? And who sent you away?"

"Uneze is cute, though," Dennis teased. "I mean, come on. It's not like he could see you were batting your eyelashes at him in the dark."

Michelle burst into laughter, clutching her stomach. "You went to Uneze's tent?"

"No, she came to mine," Peri interjected smoothly. "Uneze was there, she got lost, and we sent her back to her own tent. Nothing happened, and it's really not a big deal."

Michelle smirked. "Oh, Peri, don't ruin the fun. This is pure gold. My sister, of all people."

Emily groaned, burying her face in her hands again. "You're impossible. All of you."

"And you're predictable," Michelle said with a grin. "Thanks for trying to cover for her, Peri, but come on—it's Emily. This story is too good."

"Well," Alistair chimed in unexpectedly, his voice carrying across the table, "next time you're drunk and lost, my tent has a spare spot."

"How did you know I went to the wrong tent?" Emily asked, her eyes searching the faces of the group around the table.

"Come on, these are tents, not walls. We all hear everything. Do you think there are any secrets around here?" Johan asked. As he attempted to swat away a persistent fly.

Alistair made a quick sidewards glance in Dave's direction, as he forced a smile and turned his attention to Melanie.

UNEZE – 89

Uneze, his voice bubbling with excitement, explained the day. "Today, we're off to Dune 45, known for its stunning beauty and towering height. Climbing to the top of Dune 45 offers some amazing views of the desert landscape, especially now at sunrise when the colours of the sand shift and change dramatically. So, bring extra batteries; you're in for a treat."

"For those of you eager to climb your way to heat exhaustion, you'll have half an hour to prepare before you leave with Uneze. The lucky few strolling with me will wait for the truck to return. I'll be taking a short nature walk instead," Peri announced.

Across the table, Dave's sheepish grin broke the tension, his eyes sparkling with a mixture of remorse and affection as he turned to Melanie. "Babe, I'm really sorry about last night. I was feeling pretty lousy and, well, you know how I can be." He leant closer, sincerity radiating from him, as the others quietly sipped their drinks, eavesdropping on the moment.

Melanie, taken aback but softening, met his stare. "It's okay. I just need you to believe me—I didn't put anything in your food."

"I know," he replied. "Thanks for understanding." Their lips brushed in a gentle kiss, full of vulnerability and forgiveness. "Stay here; I'll grab your stuff and take care of the tent."

Melanie glanced around the table, her heart racing, the warmth of surprise blooming in her cheeks. She momentarily lost herself in the soft morning light as the group smiled at her, relieved that the tension had been left behind.

With the truck ready, Uneze called Peri over. "Peri, are you going to be okay on your own today?"

"Of course, you've already told me everything I need to know, and the driver is around if I get stuck."

Uneze propped himself against a pole, a teasing smile on his lips. "Great, and Peri, can I just say it was nice having you in my tent last night?"

Peri chuckled, brushing a loose strand of hair behind her ear. "I slept so well, though. I guess the sound of the dunes hypnotized me to sleep," she replied, a lightness in her tone, her cheeks slightly flushed.

Uneze arched an eyebrow, leaning closer. "Or maybe it was just being next to me. If you want to join me again, feel free. And don't worry, I'll be a gentleman."

A spark of intrigue flickered in Peri's eyes. "I may just take you up on that, unless you have any more midnight visits from Emily planned."

Uneze mock-gasped, placing a hand over his heart. "Oh no. I expect Michelle next. Or maybe it's your turn. Want to place a bet on Dennis or Alistair making a midnight visit?"

Peri rolled her eyes, a smirk tugging at her lips. "Dennis maybe, but Alistair is otherwise occupied."

"Explain yourself," Uneze demanded, leaning in like he was about to share a scandalous secret.

"Nothing." Peri's tone was nonchalant, but the smirk on her lips told a different story. "I just saw Alistair and Dave having a quiet moment by the bathroom. Maybe it's nothing, and they both had the same dodgy stomach."

Uneze's expression shifted to one of realization, a grin spreading across his face. "So, it's all making sense. He's not trying to kill her; he's just trying to get her out of the tent so he can sneak out to be with Alistair."

"Really? What about all that talk about Alistair wanting women and hookers?" Peri questioned, feigning skepticism.

Uneze shrugged, a conspiratorial smile dancing in his eyes. "All just for show."

She paused, then added with a knowing glance, "But just now, at breakfast, Dave apologised to Melanie. Maybe we're just seeing things that aren't there."

"As I said, it's all just for show," Uneze teased.

"Stop it. You can't predict everything," Peri retorted, a light laugh escaping her lips.

"Now off you go, and enjoy. I see you have Emily with you too. Behave, or I'll have to get fake jealous again."

"Fake jealous, either you are a very good actress, or there was some real jealousy in there," Uneze teased.

Peri tilted her head, adding, "You wish," before turning to the others.

"Hey, Peri." A cheerful voice echoed across the sandy expanse.

Peri pivoted, her lips curving into a cheeky smile. "Dennis. Morning. I figured you'd be off on that other tour—the one for the 'real men,' you know, the one meant for the weaklings." She raised an eyebrow, mischief dancing in her eyes.

"Come on, don't tease me," Dennis replied, a mock pout tugging at his features, his hands stuffed in the pockets of his cargo shorts. "I just had a tough day yesterday; I don't think my legs can cope with another day like that."

Peri's laughter bubbled up, a melodic sound that cut through the morning stillness. "I just thought you'd want to snap a few selfies at the top of Dune 45. That might just get... what's her name? Eve? To notice your posts."

"Well, I thought it would be more fun to spend some time alone with you," Dennis countered.

Peri shook her head, her voice firm but light. "We won't be alone, Dennis. I'm with Melanie and Anya," she reminded him, gesturing to the two friends already chatting near the bus.

Dennis shrugged, a boyish grin spreading across his face. "I'm sure we can manage a few minutes, right?"

"Dennis, no. I'm your guide, not a possible love interest in your own secret social media show," she replied, her expression shifting to one of mock seriousness that only made him chuckle.

"Ah, right. Not even for a few selfies?" he asked showing disappointment.

"Not even for that. Now go, hop on the bus with Uneze, and have a great day," Peri insisted, her tone lightening again as she turned to glance at the bus, where Uneze stood, laughter lighting up his face as he caught her eye, mouthing, "Told you," before turning back to the group.

As the group split early in the morning after breakfast, the hikers left Anya, Michelle, and Melanie behind. Reaching Dune 45, the group began the arduous climb up its steep slopes, their boots and shoes sinking into the loose, shifting sand with every step. The higher they climbed, the stronger the wind grew, pelting their faces with sharp grains of sand. The desert stretched endlessly in every direction, its raw expanse both awe-inspiring and intimidating.

Descending the dune proved trickier than anticipated. A misstep on the steep incline sent Dave sliding, his rage pulsating around his body.

90 - PERI

Peri swung open the truck's door, her heart racing with excitement as the warm Namibian sun bathed her in golden light. The soft whispers of the wind beckoned her forward, and she felt the fine grains of sand slip between her fingers as she stepped down, the heat rising from the ground beneath her feet. Her group tumbled out behind her, laughter bubbling into the air, their voices mingling with the distant calls of desert birds.

The second day began with a promise of adventure—and danger. The girls joined a guided 4x4 expedition deeper into the desert. The sand grew softer, and the vehicle struggled against the dunes. At one point, the wheels spun uselessly, sinking deeper with each attempt to move forward. The guide's calm movements kept panic at bay as they worked to free the vehicle.

"Really? Do we have to stay here? Is nothing safe?" Melanie complained.

"It's just a bit of sand," Michelle teased.

Later, they ventured toward Hiddenvlei, a more remote and desolate clay pan. The guide pointed out tracks of a brown hyena. As they continued, the wind picked up, and a sudden sandstorm engulfed them in a blinding haze. Visibility dropped to nearly zero, and the guide instructed them to stay put, crouching low to avoid inhaling the fine, abrasive sand. It felt like hours before the storm passed, leaving them disorientated and shaken.

As they climbed off the truck, they waited for people to grab their belongings, and Peri approached Melanie and asked, "So, how are things?"

"It's okay. I did want to do some of that hike today, though, but I can't be near him for too long. I was really surprised that he apologised this morning, though."

"The one thing I know about this tour is that the moods change everywhere we go. We are off to Swakopmund soon, and you've got lots of free time there, so I'm sure you can sort this mess out," Peri said.

"I guess," Melanie said.

"And we are staying in a hotel too, so a bit of privacy. I know it's not easy being the only couple and sleeping in a small tent," Peri said.

"Easy is an understatement. It's lousy, and he sleeps with his camera gear. He actually puts it in his sleeping bag. He doesn't care if I get eaten by a lion or kidnapped, but God forbid anything happens to them," Melanie said.

"Don't be like that. Tomorrow will be fun. You've just got tonight in a tent. If you're hating it so much, why don't you go home and leave him here?" Peri asked.

"No, not until we've done our skydiving trip. That's the highlight of the whole tour," Melanie said.

"Ah, okay," Anya said, clearly baffled and taken aback. "Skydiving? Wow, that'll be fun."

"Yeah, then I think I'll go home," Melanie said, before changing the conversation. "I'm surprised that Emily went on the hike this morning; she doesn't look like the type."

"I don't think she could cope with another day of girl talk," Michelle laughed. "She's making the most of her last day with makeup to search for a new love interest. She used the last of her false eyelash glue this morning, so her world fell apart."

"Ah, how can a girl cope without false eyelashes?" Melanie laughed.

"She isn't totally wrong. This tour would be better with a love interest and a bit of nighttime fun," Michelle suggested. "I think Uneze is cute; maybe I could see if he is interested."

"Isn't anyone interested in poor Dennis, or even Alex? I think there's an interesting man underneath that secretive façade." With a laugh, Peri said, amused that Emily hadn't even told her sister about her nighttime escapades in Uneze's tent. "Come on. You know we've got another group joining us soon; maybe there will be some nice guys on that tour you could meet."

"Oh, fresh meat," Melanie said.

"Wow, Melanie. You are full of surprises," Anya said.

"I was joking; I'm just fine the way I am. I'm married to Dave, and I'm not going to risk being stuck on safari with a jealous prick," Melanie said. "Anyway, he was cool this morning, so I'm taking that win and making the most of it."

"Don't you worry about him. We heard about what happened when he tried to push you over the cliff," Anya said.

"Don't worry; I can look after myself; I've got a trick or two up my sleeve," Melanie said.

91 - PERI

After the sandstorm had passed, Peri helped the driver lay out the stripy picnic blanket, spread out against the backdrop of the endless landscape, a feast of colourful fruits and snacks waiting to be devoured. Sheltered from the sand by a gazebo, they waited for the others to arrive.

Exhausted, the others arrived and threw their bags down. They chatted, exchanged selfies, and dug into the feast. Peri and Uneze began the methodical task of folding blankets and packing picnic remnants into the back of the truck.

Uneze glanced over his shoulder, a mischievous flicker in his eye as he posed the question that had been on his mind. "So, how was it with Melanie?"

"She's fine. Michelle is planning on making a move on you, if that helps. Keep yourself smelling nice tonight for her trip to your tent."

Uneze let out a hearty laugh, his shoulders shaking with genuine amusement. "Ah, so that means you're bunking with me tonight. Is this all just a ruse to keep me all to yourself?"

Peri arched an eyebrow, an exaggerated look of surprise on her face. "You do love yourself, don't you? Although don't forget, I'm expecting Dennis to show up any night now." Her laughter rang out, bright and carefree.

Uneze took a moment, his expression turning thoughtful as he recalled the day's events. "Right, so when we reached the peak today, I handed out snacks and drinks, and then I wandered off to soak in the view and enjoy a little solitude away from them all."

"The best bit of the day," Peri laughed.

"Anyway, that's when Dave and Alistair showed up, sitting together. I had my headphones in, but when they called out to me, I pretended not to hear. They didn't realise I was eavesdropping. I have no doubt at all that they know each other from home, and they were definitely plotting something."

"So, Alistair has a magnetic power to attract men. Did this tour somehow end up on a gay hookup website?" Peri laughed.

"No, just listen. It wasn't that that bothered me. It was Alex; he just stared at Alistair and Dave, taking pictures of them and clearly sending them to someone. I could see it all, and it was a creepy thing to watch."

"Now who is paranoid? Plus, we saw that the other night. Alex doesn't like them, so what? They are both pretty unlikable," Peri said.

"No, it wasn't like that. There was hatred in his eyes," Uneze said. "It's clear Alex doesn't like Alistair one little bit. It was strange to watch."

"Oh god, even more drama. Does this tour seem to get longer and longer by the day?" Peri asked, her tone light despite the undercurrent of concern.

"At least the new group arrives soon," Uneze replied, letting out a sigh. "Do you think Melanie tried to poison Alistair?"

Peri's laughter cut through the air, bright and clear. "You're kidding, right?"

"Not kidding. If I were married to him, I'd want to kill him. Where better to bring him than a safari?" Uneze said.

Peri, enjoying the mystery and scandal, said, "She could have poisoned him anywhere with nuts. Why do it all the way over here?" After a pause, she answered her own question. "To have witnesses."

"You've listened to too many weird podcasts," Uneze chided playfully. "I'm sure Dave will just keep sneaking off; maybe there's a divorce on the horizon once they get back."

92 - PERI

Before dinner, laughter and animated voices filled the air as stories from the day's adventures were told with loud, excited tones. Uneze, with a practised flourish, reached into a wooden crate and began reading aloud the labels of various bottles, his voice playful as he distributed the treasures.

As Uneze rose from his chair, Dennis shot up with an exaggerated stretch, his grin spreading like the dawn breaking over a sleepy town. "Just grabbing a drink," he announced, scooting in beside Peri with a clink of glasses that rang like a soft bell. "So, how was your day?"

"Fine, thanks. But remember what I said: I'm your guide," Peri replied, her tone firm yet fun as she shot him a sidelong glance.

"Can't I sit here?" Dennis feigned innocence, eyebrows raised, but a glimmer of mischief shone in his eyes.

"You can sit anywhere, but don't get any ideas. You have three single girls on tour; try your luck with them," she quipped, a smirk tugging at her lips.

Dennis sighed dramatically, rolling his eyes as he downed the rest of his beer, the bottle clanking against the table as he reached for another. "Ughh, this tour really isn't any fun at all," he lamented.

Just then, Emily entered the room, her shoulders slumped and eyes turned downwards. She approached her sister with hesitant steps, her voice barely a whisper. "Well?"

"Well, what?" Michelle countered, feigning ignorance with a teasing lift of her brow.

"This whole no-makeup thing... I feel naked," Emily admitted, her cheeks flushing with vulnerability.

"Hey, at least you came out in the dark. That's kind of brave," Michelle teased, pointing to her face. "Although you are also kind of scary."

"Michelle, stop it," Emily replied, though a hint of a smile tugged at her lips.

"Sorry, you look great. Like you used to... and so much younger." Michelle insisted, her tone shifting to earnest.

"Really? Do you think men will still look at me like this?" Emily pondered.

"Is that really all you care about? Why not take a break from men? You could just be friends with them without it being complicated. They can be good friends, too," Michelle suggested, her voice sincere.

"Men as friends? What's the point in that?" Emily shot back, shaking her head in disbelief.

"I give up. You're a lost cause," Michelle sighed, exasperation colouring her tone as she threw her hands up in mock surrender.

Glasses clinked and filled, warmth radiating from the spirited exchange. But Alistair sat with an empty glass. He leant toward the nearest bottle and began to pour, his eyes darting around the circle.

"Whoa there," Alex's hand shot out, striking Alistair's wrist, the wine spilling slightly onto the dirt. "What do you think you're doing?"

"Getting some wine. What's it look like?" Alistair shot back, irritation creeping into his tone.

"Grab your own; hands off," Alex snapped, his eyes narrowing.

"Why does it matter to you?" Alistair countered, brow raised defiantly. A silence fell over the group, their eyes flickering between the two men like a tennis match.

"Because you never contribute. You just wait until no one's watching, then you fill your glass to the brim like some kind of thief." Alex's words were sharp, cutting through the twilight air. Alistair scoffed, crossing his arms.

"What am I supposed to do? I'm in the middle of the bush with no wine of my own," Alistair said.

Alex's voice dropped, insistent yet measured. "It's simple. When Uneze tells us he's going to the wine shop, you give him your order like the rest of us."

The group, hushed as Alistair shifted uncomfortably, their glares flitting between the rising tension of the two men.

Michelle, sensing the electric atmosphere, gently offered her glass. "Here, take some of mine. When you get your own, I'll have a glass of yours," she said, her voice soft as a soothing balm.

But Alex was already shaking his head, wagging his finger dismissively at her. "And you think he'll actually buy some? Come on, he's just a cheapskate."

Anya's voice broke through the brewing storm, calm and steady. "Enough, everyone. We have a long safari ahead. Alistair, when Uneze goes to the shop in a day or two, make sure you put your order in."

Michelle lowered her glass to the ground, filled another, and offered it to Alistair with a warm smile. "Cheers," she said, her eyes sparkling with kindness.

Alistair's grip softened as he reached for the glass, his defences lowering. "See? At least someone here is generous. It's just wine, after all."

"If it's just wine, then why not buy your own?" Dennis hissed, his tone laced with venom. "Or maybe you should be drinking from the glass of your lover."

"What?" Alistair's confusion was palpable.

"Don't play innocent. We've all seen you and Dave sneaking off into the night. Why bring your wife here to ruin our safari with your drama?" Dennis's words erupted like a volcano, raw and unforgiving.

Melanie's expression twisted in disbelief, her voice trembling. "What the hell are you talking about?"

"I'm sorry, Melanie," Dennis thrust the accusation forward, "but you're blinded by love. God knows why you'd even love a sleaze like him." He gestured disdainfully at Alistair, who stood frozen, shock etching his features.

Melanie shook her head, her heart pounding in confusion. "Carry on," she whispered, lost in the tumult of emotions.

"Oh, a perfect match—a dick and a sleaze," Alex interrupted, his voice rising, while the rest of the group sat in stunned silence, mouths agape. In a fit of rage, he hurled his wine into Alistair's face, the red liquid splattering against the backdrop of the night, before storming off into the darkness, leaving behind a fractured group and a campfire that flickered uncertainly in the emptiness. Anya and Johan dispersed first, whispering to Melanie to come with them.

93 - MELANIE

Melanie stumbled slightly, her wine glass trembling in her grip, as she followed Michelle deeper into the forest. They found rustic wooden benches, where Melanie sank down, her breath hitching as she fought back tears. "Do you think it's true?" she whispered, her voice barely above the rustling leaves.

Michelle, who had followed the others, shook her head, furrowing her brow. "I've not seen anything weird about them. Alex said we all know what's going on, but I had no idea."

Anya sat nearby, glancing at Johan. He offered a silent nod, and she sighed. "Same here. So, if you guys don't think they're together, then what was all that about?"

Melanie's fingers tightened around her glass as she leant forward, her mouth open with confusion. "I don't know. It's as if Alex has it in for Alistair. It all came up for no reason. I don't get it."

Melanie slumped back, letting out a long breath, her shoulders drooping. "I don't know what to think."

"Don't overthink it, Melanie," Johan chimed in. "I think Alex was drunk or upset about something else and took it out on them."

Melanie's attention drifted towards the darkness. "Where's Dave? He should be here reassuring me, telling me it's not true."

Johan stretched, his silhouette merging with the night as he stepped away. Moments later, he returned with Dennis, hands shoved deep in his pockets.

"Dave and Alistair are still at the fire. They're just slagging off Alex and being idiots."

Melanie wrinkled her nose, her thoughts flowing. "Hmm. So what do I do?"

"You could stay in our tent. I assume you don't want to stay with Dave," Michelle suggested, her voice steady.

"I don't know what I want," Melanie admitted, her tone faltering. "I think I want to see Dave and find out what he has to say about all of this."

"You know where he is. Why not go over there?" Michelle pressed gently.

"No. Angry Dave is someone I need to stay away from," Melanie replied, pouring the last drop of wine into her glass, her mind foggy. "Peri, where are you?" she called out into the night, her words slurring slightly as she drank wine straight from the bottle.

"Shhh," Anya giggled, nudging her shoulder playfully.

Melanie's laughter bubbled up. "Peri is my saviour; she's always got my back." Taking a deep breath, she tried again, this time louder. "Peeerrriiii."

"It's time to get you to sleep. You'll feel better in the morning. We'll snuggle up in our tent. It'll be cosy."

Suddenly, Peri appeared, dressed in a soft pyjama set, her hair tousled, eyes half-open. "What's happened? Why did I hear my name?"

"Sorry, Peri. That was Melanie. She's a bit drunk and needs somewhere to sleep," Johan explained, clearly amused.

"What happened?" Peri asked, concern flickering in her eyes.

"You missed a hell of an after-dinner drinks party. Scandal hit, insults thrown, and voices were raised," Johan said with a smirk.

"Oh god," Peri groaned. "Do I need to know any of it?"

"No, just guy stuff," Johan reassured her.

"Alright, Melanie. Come with me. Mi tent e' tu tent, or something like that."

94 - PERI

With Melanie settled, Peri nestled against Uneze, relishing the comforting warmth radiating from his body. The peaceful stillness of the world outside was suddenly shattered by the sound of giggles, light and teasing, floating through the fabric walls.

Uneze stirred beside her, his eyes blinking awake, curiosity etched across his sleepy features. "What's going on?" he asked, his voice husky with sleep.

A frown formed on Peri's face as she glanced toward the tent entrance. "Melanie is in my tent again. Something must have happened tonight to send her back to us."

Uneze's surprise was written all over his face as he pressed his fingers to his lips. Leaning closer to the edge of the tent, he turned his face to be able to hear better. He mouthed a name: "Dennis."

Peri's hand flew to her mouth, stifling a gasp. "Oh my god," she mouthed back, her mind racing with implications. "What the hell? I wonder if that's why Melanie ended up in your tent."

With a soft grin, Uneze fell back onto the mattress, amusement lighting up his features. "So, that's the scandal we were anticipating—Melanie and Dennis."

Peri chuckled, shaking her head. "Honestly, I was half-expecting him to show up in my tent instead."

"He is in your tent," Uneze countered, a teasing gleam in his eyes. "What if he went looking for you and found her first?"

With laughter bubbling in her chest, Peri smirked. "So, she bounced back quickly—after the brink of death and food poisoning accusations—to another man's arms in a few days. I'm impressed. She's got gumption."

Just then, a cool breeze swept through the tent, causing Peri to snuggle deeper into Uneze's embrace. She nibbled at her lips, the humour of the situation showing in her eyes.

"What's so funny?" Uneze asked, his interest aroused. A lump formed in her throat as she shifted closer, her voice soft and deliberate.

"This whole situation. Us, Melanie, Dennis... Emily. It's all so different from my other tours."

The tent fabric rustled ominously as heavy footsteps approached, the sound growing louder with each heartbeat. Uneze's eyes snapped open, his pulse racing like a drum in his ears.

He exchanged a bewildered glance with Peri, but then came the unmistakable sound—thudding—echoing through the confined space.

Before he could contemplate his next move, Uneze surged forward, pushing aside the flaps of the tent with fierce urgency. His eyes locked onto Dave, whose knuckles were white, fingers wrapped around Melanie's throat, anger radiating from his tense posture.

"What the hell is going on?" Uneze shouted, adrenaline coursing through him as he seized Dave's arm and wrenched it away.

Melanie crumpled to the ground, a choked curse escaping her lips, trembling in the aftermath of the encounter. In that brief chaos, Peri slipped out from behind the tent, her eyes adjusting to the light as she took in the scene. "Let's all take a step back and try to figure out what's going on here," she said, trying to keep her voice steady despite the tension in the air.

Uneze hesitated for a moment, still reeling from the chaos that had just unfolded. Taking a deep breath, he nodded slowly. "Okay," he said quietly. "What is this all about?"

Dave, enraged, let the words fall out. "This slut was in the tent with him. All this pretending to be in love with his ex, and really he's sleeping with my wife."

"And that gives you the right to strangle her?" Uneze asked.

Dave let out a strange cackle as he cracked his knuckles. His fists trembled with anger. "Stay out of this."

"Not when you do it outside my tent. Now, Dennis, what the hell happened?"

Peri stood closer to Dennis and spoke up. "That's my tent, and Dennis was looking for me, right?"

Dennis, feeling cornered and self-conscious, nodded. "Yeah, I was there looking for Peri. Melanie was there, and we were just chatting while

I waited for Peri to get back. I knew she was upset after the campfire fight."

"And Peri, where were you while this idiot was groping my wife?"

"Uneze's tent. Working out the plan for tomorrow," Peri said.

The desperation in Dennis's voice was clear as he spoke unusually quickly: "I thought they would have finished by now, and I saw a light on in the tent. It was dark; I thought it was Peri. I'm sorry. I didn't know Melanie was in the tent, but I wasn't groping her. I was just waiting for Peri."

Dave looked around him, anger burning in his eyes. It looked like he was about to explode. "And you expect me to believe that?"

Uneze stepped forward, cleared his throat, and said, "Yes. I can assure you that these tents are thin. I've been unfortunate enough to hear Peri and Dennis on a few occasions having their nighttime fun."

A few other group members neared to see what the commotion was. Uneze, realizing the situation was spiraling out of control, said, "So, are we all going to forget this and go back to our tents?"

Melanie, sitting on the floor with one hand on her neck and the other on her stomach, tensed with fury before speaking. "Yes, please. Now, Peri has been nice enough to let me stay with her, and you barge in and cause a scene."

"Me? You created this whole mess," Dave said, his temples flaring. "Now, come back to our tent."

"I started this? You are the one who is having an affair with Alistair. Go, have some fun with him. I'm fine just here," Melanie screamed.

"You are my wife, and you will do what I say. Or are you going to try and poison me again?"

Uneze felt his body tense and his face redden with rage. With a sharp intake of breath, he put his hands in the air and shouted, "That's enough. Everyone, go back to your tents and stay there. I think we've had enough tent swapping tonight. Melanie and Peri, get inside. Dennis, go back to your own tent, and Dave, go for a walk, clear your head, and stay away from this area."

Dennis, feeling like he was in hell, kept his eyes cast downwards and stomped back through the long grass. Peri grabbed Melanie by the hand

and took her inside her tent. She placed a finger on her lips in a gesture of silence as they sat on the mattress.

"Dave. Do I need to call security?" Uneze asked, looking at Dave, who hovered outside the tent, unsure what to do or where to go.

Looking deflated and insulted, Dave opened his mouth to say something. Then, with a weak nod, he left, leaving a stream of curses in his wake.

95 - PERI

Within a few moments, Uneze slipped into Peri's tent. He forced himself to smile as he sat down next to Peri and grabbed Melanie's hands. "Are you alright? Let me have a look at your neck."

Melanie rubbed her neck as she fought to find her voice. "I'm fine, honestly."

Peri spoke softly. "Please, come with me to the clinic."

Melanie shook her head and squeezed his hand tightly. "I'm fine. Just please don't leave me alone."

"We won't. We'll all sleep in the same tent," Uneze said.

"And I think it's time for us to think about getting you a flight out of here. It's not safe for you."

"No, he just has a temper, and the guys accused him of sleeping with Alistair. He's proud and homophobic. I'd like to think he came to talk to me and explain the situation. I've never seen him jealous like that before. I'll speak to him, and he'll calm down."

"Calm down? He's violent and impulsive," Peri said.

Uneze looked out of the tent, shone a torch around, and once he was sure no one was around, sat back down. "So, was Dennis there for you, or for Peri?"

"Peri. We were just chatting. I'm sorry. I'm sorry for all of this," Melanie said.

"I'm just disgusted that people now think I'm with Dennis," Peri chuckled. "That's going to confuse things for the next few weeks."

"That's a baffling idea. You and Dennis?" Uneze mused with a smile.

Without warning, Melanie broke into sobs. "What a mess. Dave hates me, and it's all my fault."

"It's not your fault. Violence is never an option; it was obviously about whatever happened at the bonfire," Peri said softly.

Melanie buried her head in her hands as tears poured down her face. Peri blinked back tears for Melanie and the pain she felt.

Peri let her gaze rest for a second before she turned to Melanie, eased her down onto the mattress, and slipped a sleeping bag over her. "Get some sleep."

Uneze tilted his head slightly, a silent invitation for Peri to join him outside. As they stepped away from the dim light of the tent, the night air felt heavy and charged. Peri's heart raced as she caught the intensity in Uneze's eyes—flames of fury flickering behind a mask that was usually calm and reflective.

He released a long, shaky breath, fingers raking through his hair in a gesture that spoke volumes. "This is a tour I'll never forget," he muttered, the words edged with bitter irony that hung between them.

"You can say that again," Peri replied.

Uneze's normally steady demeanor had fractured; anger pulsed just beneath the surface. He paced with a restless energy, muttering words in a language that felt foreign and sharp, showing his pent-up frustration.

After a moment, Uneze paused, his fists clenching and unclenching as if willing his fury to subside. "I think we've hit rock bottom. It can't get much worse than this."

Peri ventured softly, her voice a tentative lifeline. "Don't tempt fate. We have to get rid of Dave," he snapped, the fire in his stare igniting further.

"How? Are you planning on strangling him?" She raised an eyebrow, trying to lighten the mood, though she could sense the gravity of his thoughts.

Uneze's face twisted, a storm brewing, and for a heartbeat, she saw a flash of something primal flicker in his expression. "You have no idea how much I wish I could."

"I was thinking more along the lines of speaking to head office and getting them to kick him off the tour and fly him home. I'll do it first thing in the morning," Peri said.

Uneze nodded, a flicker of unease lingering within him. "Let's get some sleep and hope tomorrow is a better day. I'm just going to check that things are okay back there."

The distant glow of tent lights reassured him that most campers were where they should be—except for one: Dave. Curiosity gnawed at him as he approached Alistair's tent. He could make out two figures within, their silhouettes cast against the canvas.

"They think we're gay. That's good, I guess?" Alistair said.

"Good? Why the hell is that good? I was supposed to be making people think that we are happily married," Dave scoffed.

"Yeah, I guess that plan didn't work out," Alistair laughed. "You were supposed to get Melanie back here, not cause campus chaos."

Uneze leant closer, straining to catch the muffled exchange. Dave's voice cut through the night. "I know. I flipped. Just seeing her flirt made me want to strangle her and forget the consequences," he said, frustrated.

"You do remember why I'm here, don't you?" Alistair pressed, his tone sharp.

"Of course. It's just taking longer than I expected," Dave said, his voice laced with desperation.

"Because you keep letting your rage get in the way. Why can't you just keep your cool? This could have all been over by now—first the ridge, now this," Alistair shot back, frustration evident.

"You have a job to do, and you aren't doing it," Dave's voice snapped. "You aren't letting me do it. I did my part; I put that poisonous little creature in her tent."

Uneze felt the branch beneath him crackle underfoot, and suddenly, the tent fell silent. Panic surged through him as he bolted into the night, the warm air biting at his skin. He slipped back into his own tent, heart pounding.

"Everything good?" Peri asked, her voice a whisper in the darkness.

He pressed a finger to his lips, looked at Melanie, and said, "I'll tell you tomorrow."

"What?" Peri mouthed.

"You don't want to know."

"Oh, for once, I actually agree with you." Peri said with a giggle that she tried to suppress with her hand.

They settled on either side of Melanie, whose quiet sobs broke the stillness.

96 - MELANIE

Melanie awoke to a hazy morning light filtering through the tent, her eyelids heavy with remnants of a restless night. As she sat up, a faint ache pulsed at her neck, and her fingers instinctively sought the spot where her husband's grip had been too firm, leaving a lingering discomfort.

"Are you okay?" Peri asked softly.

"Yeah, whatever that pill was you gave me, it completely knocked me out," Melanie replied, her words tumbling out with a wry smile.

"Magic pills," Peri chuckled, though the laughter felt distant, overshadowed by Melanie's unease. "I use them on long-haul flights."

"Right. I should probably shower. Have you seen Dave yet?" Melanie asked, a hint of tension threading through her voice.

"The camp is quiet. You've got a clear path to the bathroom. Need me to tag along?" Peri offered.

Melanie pondered for a moment, weighing her options. "No, it's okay. I'll take care of it." She shoved a wine bottle into her bag with a determined clink. "I'll whack Dave over the head if he comes anywhere near me."

Uneze watched as Melanie darted toward the shower, her towel clutched tightly, every stride radiating purpose. He turned to Peri, a frown creasing his forehead, and shared what he'd overheard the night before. Peri's mouth fell open in disbelief. "What the hell?" she muttered.

Uneze nodded, his voice low. "I'm not sure what they're talking about, or if whatever it is is still around, but I don't think this is about them wanting alone time or just getting the tent to themselves."

Peri shot a glance at her watch, urgency flickering in her eyes. "I'll email head office now. I'll call them in three hours to request they remove Dave from the tour."

"And Alistair?" Uneze pressed, concern etched into his features.

"Alistair didn't strangle her or try to push her down a ravine," Peri replied firmly. "We can't kick him off just based on a rumour or a feeling."

By breakfast, the usual buzz of excitement had fizzled into a tense cloud; whispers between the group stopped suddenly. Dave and Alistair strolled in separately, frowns plastered on their faces. They exchanged a quick, calculating glance before heading to the buffet.

The clatter of cutlery against plates echoed in the silence as Melanie, Uneze, and Peri entered, all eyes turning toward them like moths to a flame.

"So, who died?" Alistair asked with an amused smile.

In unison, the group turned toward Melanie, who, now sharp and composed, offered a polite, insincere smile. She quickly stuffed a piece of bread into her mouth, grabbed her plate, and vanished from sight. Peri, sensing the shift, followed closely.

"Melanie, are you alright?" she asked gently.

"No. Just looking at Dave makes me feel sick," Melanie confessed.

Peri nodded and said, "I'm calling head office this morning. We're requesting they remove Dave from the tour."

"You can do that?" Melanie's eyes widened, a flicker of hope softening her stance.

"Yes, we can. Just stay away from him today. Hopefully, by tomorrow, we'll have him on a flight back home."

A genuine smile broke across Melanie's face, her tension easing as she nodded. "So, just one more day and then he's gone?"

"Yes, at least I hope so," Peri replied."I've got some things to sort out so just find me if you need me, or even better, scream as loud as you can if Dave bothers you."

Melanie stood at the edge, her fingers anxiously fiddling with the bread, oblivious to the world around her. Her gaze was distant, haunted by dread that clung to her every thought, a silent plea for freedom from the vice grip of fear that Dave had placed around her.

Peri motioned for Anya to join them from the breakfast table and nodded toward Melanie. Peri stepped forward, her voice steady but urgent, breaking the spell of silence that surrounded them. "Listen, girls," she began, glancing at Melanie, "I don't usually get involved in the soap opera on tour, but Melanie needs us. She's trapped in a nightmare, and it's time we band together to lift her up."

"We were at the bonfire and heard about last night," Michelle murmured, her voice barely above a whisper.

"It's more than just that," Peri pressed, her expression fierce. "There's so much more beneath the surface. Help me support her. She's fighting this battle alone, and we can't let that happen."

The group agreed, settling beside Melanie. The sadness in her eyes mirrored the storm within. She had always been the quiet one, but now, with the walls crumbling around her, she shared the turmoil that had haunted her every waking hour. For the first time, a genuine smile broke through her mask, illuminating her face like the sun breaking through clouds after a storm.

Despite the gravity of their conversation, the air crackled with a sense of sisterhood—an unbreakable chain of support. "Come back to breakfast with us," Emily urged, her voice warm. "You're not alone in this. We'll stand by you and make sure he never gets to you again."

"We'll take shifts if we have to," Michelle added, determination in her eyes. "This safari is meant to be enjoyable, and we won't let anything ruin that for you. We'll make sure you come out of this in one piece."

Melanie's expression shifted, revealing a flicker of humour. "Honestly, it would be better if Dave didn't come out of this in one piece. My life would be a whole lot simpler without him."

A brief pause enveloped the group as uncertainty clouded their thoughts. Assuming she was joking, Michelle laughed lightly. "We can use Emily's high heels as a weapon."

"No, I don't need heels," Melanie retorted, a spark igniting within her as she rummaged through her bag. She pulled out a bottle of wine, holding it up like a trophy. "I've got this."

The laughter subsided, replaced by curious intrigue, as Anya asked, "You plan on getting him drunk? He seems to be quite good at doing that all on his own."

Melanie's eyes gleamed with resolve. "No, if he comes near me, I'll protect myself." A plan began to take shape in her mind—a strategy for reclaiming her power. With a nod of gratitude to her friends, she plotted how to confront the nightmare she was living.

"Right, girls, let's get moving. We're off to civilisation today. Emily, you'll be glad to know we're heading towards shops."

"Oh, my credit card is excited," Emily joked, her laughter ringing out.

97 - PERI

By the time the flight arrived in Swakopmund, a German colonial town located on Namibia's famous Skeleton Coast, the group was relieved to drop their bags in real hotel rooms and enjoy the delights of hot water, real beds, and a bit of privacy. The sleek marble floors and elegant chandeliers gave the lobby a luxurious atmosphere, while the plush velvet couches and ornate artwork added a touch of old-world Europe.

Alex grabbed his key and strutted straight up to his room. Dennis, feeling protected by Johan's neutral presence, stayed away from Dave. Alistair, who'd excluded himself from the group completely, kept his head down, scanned the bottles in the bar for the cheapest local liqueur, and nursed it at the bar.

Emily's eyes sparkled with mischief as she jingled a hotel key in the air. "I've booked us a room with three beds for tonight," she said.

Melanie's gaze dropped to the floor as Dave passed; she waited until he'd gone before replying, "Well, I overheard Dave making plans to stay with Alistair tonight, so I'll just stay in my room," she murmured, the softness of her words barely masking the disappointment lurking beneath.

Michelle chimed in, her tone a blend of concern and encouragement. "Unless you're planning on finding a guy tonight, you should really consider staying with us. You wouldn't want Dave barging in like he did last night, would you?"

Melanie stalled for a moment,, her brow furrowing as she weighed her options. "I guess not," she finally conceded, the hint of a smile breaking through her uncertainty.

Just then, Peri glided over, her infectious energy lighting up the space. "Did you manage to get the triple room I requested?" she asked, her enthusiasm contagious.

"Yeah, we're just trying to convince Melanie to join us," Emily replied, her tone hopeful.

"Perfect. Let's plan a girls' evening—dinner and drinks. We should invite Anya too," Peri suggested, her eyes gleaming with excitement.

Melanie's shoulders began to relax, the tension easing as she smiled. "I guess that sounds nice. For the first time in ages, I don't care what Dave thinks."

"Awesome. I'll set it up. I'll even get Uneze to take the guys out for beers," Peri said.

Emily, eager to keep the conversation going, asked, "So, what's the plan for today?"

Melanie hesitated, her smile faltering. "Well, I have to go skydiving with Dave. It's our thing; we've been planning it for ages."

"Aren't you scared to be jumping out of a plane?" Emily asked, raising an eyebrow.

"With him?" Michelle chimed in, a teasing grin on her face.

"No way. It's exhilarating—there's nothing like it up there." Melanie's face lit up, her passion for the thrill momentarily pushing aside her worries.

"Alright, just promise to text us when you're back. I can't wait to ditch these shapeless clothes for some heels and concrete," Emily said, her excitement bubbling over.

"Oh, and your suitcase is finally arriving today," Peri added.

"Finally. We can rummage through it, and I'd love to lend you something different for tonight. Let's make it a real girls' night out," Emily suggested, her enthusiasm contagious.

"Definitely, although I doubt any of you have anything that'll fit me," Melanie replied, a soft lilt in her voice.

"We'll accessorise instead. You'll be my new project," Emily declared, her eyes sparkling with creative ideas.

"Alright, I just have to get this jump out of the way, and then I'll be back," Melanie said.

Her fingers hovered over her phone, a silent battle waged between longing and caution. Julius's number haunted her contact list like a forbidden fruit. The phone felt like a ticking time bomb in her hand, every notification a potential exposure. Blocking him on day one of the tour had felt like carving a wound into her own heart, but it was the only way to safeguard the fragile peace, the precarious balance she desperately tried to maintain while living in such close quarters with a person that couldn't mind their own business.

98 - EMILY

The coastal air of Swakopmund carried the salty tang of the Atlantic as Emily and Anya strolled down the cobblestone streets, lined with pastel-coloured buildings that seemed to sparkle under the midday sun. Tourists ambled past, their arms full of bags bearing logos from boutiques and curio shops.

Emily's eyes darted from window to window, each store offering a new trove of treasures. "This place is amazing," she said, clutching her sleek, metallic credit card like a golden ticket.

"Mmm," Anya replied absently, her hands stuffed into the pockets of her denim jacket. She squinted against the glare of the sun, already regretting agreeing to this little excursion. Shopping wasn't exactly her idea of a good time.

They entered a boutique decorated with seashell wreaths and driftwood sculptures. Inside, the air was cool and perfumed with lavender. Emily's face lit up as she immediately gravitated toward a display of hand-carved wooden animals. She picked up a tiny giraffe, marveling at the intricate detail.

"Isn't this adorable?" she asked, holding it up to Anya, who had already wandered to the back of the store. Anya glanced at the figurine, her expression unreadable.

"Yeah, sure," she said with a shrug. "It's cute."

Emily turned to her, a scarf draped over her arm. "What's wrong with wanting to treat myself?" she asked lightly, though her tone hinted at defensiveness.

Anya sighed. "Nothing. It's just..." She pondered for a moment. "Where are you going to put all this stuff, Emily? It's not like you have a place to keep it."

Emily stiffened, her smile fading. The truth of Anya's words stung. She had no home—not anymore. Her life had been reduced to what she could carry in a single suitcase, and yet here she was, seduced by the allure of pretty things she didn't need and had nowhere to store.

"I'll figure it out," she said, her voice tighter than she intended. "You don't have to stick around if you're bored."

Anya's brow tensed.. "Maybe I will leave you to your shopping, but not until you have some suitable safari clothes. I promised Michelle I'd help you."

"Really, with your taste?" Emily replied. She exhaled sharply, her chest tightening. She felt a pang of guilt but pushed it aside.

By the time she left the shops, the sunlight had softened, and her arms were laden with paper bags full of clothes she hoped she'd never wear again after this safari.

Eventually, she found the café, a cozy spot with wicker chairs and sprawling umbrellas. Anya was there, sipping an iced coffee, her sunglasses perched on her head. She looked up as Emily approached, her expression unreadable.

"Feel better?" Anya asked as Emily set her bags down and slid into the seat across from her.

"I'll let you know," Emily replied, managing a small smile. She flagged down a waiter and ordered a cappuccino, the warm drink a small comfort in the face of her tense emotions.

They sat in silence for a while, the bustle of the café filling the gaps between them. Finally, Anya spoke. "I'm not trying to be a jerk," she said. "I just... I don't get it. Shopping doesn't fix anything, you know?"

Emily stirred her cappuccino, watching the foam move. "I know it doesn't," she said quietly. "But for a little while, it makes me feel like I have something."

Meanwhile, across town, Michelle's eyebrow arched as she surveyed Dennis nursing a drink, his phone clutched in his hand like a lifeline.

The boat bobbed gently on the Atlantic Ocean, the salty breeze ruffling Michelle's hair as she leant over the railing, scanning the water for any sign of dolphins. Swakopmund's coastline stretched in the distance, its dunes shimmering under the morning light.

Dennis stood a few feet away, fiddling with his phone. "Alright, Michelle, let's make her jealous," he said with a mischievous grin, holding up his phone for a selfie.

Michelle rolled her eyes but couldn't hide her amusement. "You're ridiculous, you know that?"

"Eve deserves it," Dennis replied, his tone half-serious.

Michelle sighed but stepped closer. "Fine. But only because I can't wait to see how this backfires. If she hasn't reacted to any of the others we put on already, then why bother with more?"

Dennis held the phone up, angling it to capture the ocean in the background. Michelle flashed a wide smile, throwing up a peace sign. Dennis's grin widened as he clicked the shutter.

"Perfect," he said, inspecting the photo. "You've got the best happy face, by the way."

Michelle laughed, lightly shoving his arm. "Flattery will get you nowhere, Dennis."

"Worth a shot," he replied, his voice teasing.

As Dennis posted the picture on social media, Michelle turned back to the ocean. A sudden ripple caught her eye, followed by the unmistakable curve of a dolphin's dorsal fin slicing through the water.

"There," she exclaimed, pointing.

"Worth a shot," he replied, his voice teasing.

The tour guide, a cheerful Namibian woman named Elina, stepped forward. "Good eye. That's a bottlenose dolphin. Let's see if the pod is nearby."

The boat slowed, and soon more dolphins appeared, leaping gracefully out of the water in synchronized arcs. The small group of passengers erupted in cheers and gasps.

"This is incredible," Michelle murmured, her smile frozen with wonder.

Dennis joined her at the railing, his phone forgotten for the moment. "Yeah," he said softly. "It really is."

Michelle reached for her phone and quickly snapped a selfie with a giggle, nibbling his ear.

"Oh, I liked that. Eve never went anywhere near my ear."

"Dennis. If you ever compare me to her again, I swear I'll stop helping you."

"I'm sorry, it's just that everything makes me think of her."

Michelle shook her head in exasperation. "How the hell can everything make you think of her? You've never been on safari with her, never been to Africa with her, and never been dolphin watching with her. This is your time to shine, and honestly, if I hear Eve's name again, I'll slap you."

Dennis nodded, looking contrite. "Sorry. I'll try."

"Don't try; do. I'll count the slaps and deliver them all at once. It'll be a pain you won't forget."

"Thanks," Dennis said sarcastically.

As they sailed further out into the ocean, Michelle and Dennis scanned the horizon eagerly, hoping for another glimpse of the playful dolphins. Suddenly, a pod appeared, leaping gracefully from the water and swimming alongside the boat.

"Hi, guys," Alex said, appearing out of nowhere.

"Alex, I didn't know you were on this tour," Michelle said.

"I've been watching you two from over there," Alex said. "Thought you might need help with all those photos."

"Oh, well, thanks," Dennis said, handing him his phone.

"What's going on? Didn't know you two had become a thing," Alex said.

"We're not. We're just trying to make Eve jealous," Michelle said.

"Who?" Alex asked.

Michelle let out a roar of laughter. "Alex, what planet are you living on? Eve, Dennis's ex."

"Ah, yeah. All I heard on the first day at introductions was 'blah blah blah,'" Alex said with a grin.

"Alex, what's your story? You keep to yourself a lot," Michelle asked.

"Nothing interesting. I just prefer my own company, and all this drama," Alex said, gesturing to them, "is just more blah, useless time-wasting."

"But it's fun, blah. How else are we supposed to fill six weeks if we don't create some fun?" Michelle grinned.

"Good point. Okay, let's get you those photos," Alex said.

"Your dislike for Alistair is fun, though," Dennis said.

"Ah, even I want a break from the blah every now and then," Alex said with a warm smile, then paused before turning to photograph the dolphins.

Dennis broke the silence. "You know, I'm glad you came today."

Michelle glanced at him, surprised. "I'm glad, too. I wasn't sure at first, but this is nice."

Dennis smirked. "Nice enough to take another selfie?"

She groaned, but the laughter in her eyes betrayed her. "Fine. One more."

This time, they posed with the dolphins in the background, their faces lit up with genuine excitement. Michelle felt a warmth she hadn't expected—not just from the sun, but from Dennis's easy charm and the way he made her laugh.

As the boat began its journey back to shore, Michelle found herself wishing the day would stretch on. She liked his company more than she cared to admit. Maybe it was the shared laughter, or the way he seemed to let his guard down around her, but she felt a flicker of something— something she wasn't ready to name just yet. With an almost flat battery, Dennis rested his phone and asked, "How's your sister coping with all this, and where the hell is she?"

"She's testing Dad's credit card, trying to get some more fitting and sexy safari clothes, and she's booked herself into a beauty salon for the day while waiting for her suitcase to show up."

"Is she okay with the whole cancelled wedding thing?"

"Yeah, she's better than okay. I haven't seen her smile like this in years. It's taken ten years off her. Honestly, she was a bit of a selfish bitch, but now she's softer and more vulnerable," Michelle said. "I'm trying to teach her how to be nice; I think she's getting there. She actually offered to help Melanie look nice and lend her some clothes and makeup for tonight. That's a first."

"I like soft and vulnerable in a woman," Dennis said.

"Oh, no. For your safety, stay away from her. She'll chew you up and spit you out in a second. She likes her men tough, loaded, and charismatic—no, I mean arrogant."

"Just like...," Dennis said.

"Well done for stopping yourself from saying her name." Michelle laughed. "We all have our own type, and there's no forcing things."

"What's your type?" Alex leant back in his chair, brow arched in playful curiosity as he joined the conversation.

"Kind, honest, thoughtful, respectful, hard-working," Michelle replied, her voice laced with a hint of exasperation. She gestured dramatically, her hands slicing through the air as if to cut away the thin veil of hope. "It's just that there aren't any of those left on this planet."

Dennis shifted uncomfortably, his gaze dropping to the table as he sighed. "I don't know. I mean, that's how I see myself, just with an added slice of pathetic right now." He rubbed the back of his neck, tension evident in his shoulders.

Alex let out a laugh, shaking his head. "Slice? More like a bucket full," he teased.

"Am I that bad?" Dennis asked, his voice filled with self-doubt.

"Look, we've all been there," Alex said, his tone softening. "The idea is to make sure you don't get stuck there. Oh, what was that whole Melanie–Peri thing?"

"Ah, that," Dennis groaned, leaning forward, elbows on the table, as he ran a hand through his hair. "I went to Peri's tent to try and hit on her and found Melanie instead."

"You wanted to hit on Peri? Come on, that was just stupid," Alex said, a grin breaking across his face.

"Why?" Dennis shot back, brows knitting in confusion.

"So many reasons," Alex chuckled, counting them off on his fingers. "One, she's our tour guide. Two, she's a woman with a good head on her shoulders, and I'm sure 'pathetic and needy' isn't her thing. And three..." Alex raised a finger to his lips, eyes sparkling with mischief. "I'm pretty sure she's with Uneze."

"Really?" Dennis's eyes blinked in shock as the realization dawned on him. "Yep. I'm a silent observer, but I'm pretty sure they're a thing," Alex said with a knowing nod, the corners of his mouth curling upward.

"Ah, wow. Alright. That makes more sense. I guess it was a stupid rebound thing," Dennis muttered.

"Very stupid. Anyway," Michelle said, her tone lightening, "thanks for today; it's been amazing. And you know what? When you're not waffling on about Eve, you aren't half bad." She smiled genuinely, the sun catching her eyes. "And Alex," she continued, "it's been nice to speak to you too. I know there's a lot of drama going on, but just enjoy it, embrace it, and have some fun."

"No," Alex said firmly, shaking his head. His expression hardened, a flicker of determination sparking in his eyes. "I'm here for two reasons, and once I've sorted those, I'm going home. This isn't the place for me."

98 - PERI

As the last of the group disappeared on their excursions, the air shifted, leaving Peri and Uneze cocooned in a stillness that felt foreign after the whirlwind of activity.

Uneze placed a bottle of water and two tall glasses filled with lemon-infused drinks, their surfaces glistening in the sunlight. He settled into his chair, the leather creaking under his weight, setting a comfortable ambiance that almost felt intimate.

"You handled Melanie brilliantly," he remarked, his tone low and appreciative, eyes glimmering with admiration. "Getting the girls to rally around her was a stroke of genius."

Peri shrugged, a hint of a smile breaking through her usual self-assured demeanour. "At least she's not alone. Head office is sending Dave home tomorrow—they'll call him this morning," she replied, her fingers tracing the condensation on her glass. The small droplets slid down like fleeting moments that shouldn't be wasted.

"At least you're spared the unpleasantness," Uneze said.

Peri twisted a lemon wedge in her drink. "I offered, honestly. I'd love to see the smug look wiped off his face, but they said it was too risky. Lisa, my roommate, who works in head office, offered to do it. She said she's missing the action of guiding."

"When's the call?"

Peri shrugged again, a flicker of unease flashing in her eyes. "Today. They'll let me know after they've spoken to him. I'm dreading seeing his reaction, but... relieved, too."

A silence stretched between them, broken only by the faint hum of the air conditioning. Peri traced the rim of her glass, her eyes distant. "This whole thing is... intense," she murmured finally. "My safari research said mosquitoes were the biggest threat. Now... I think it's this group."

"There's something... off. Let's hope Dave leaving brings things back to normal."

Peri looked sceptical, her focus drifting upward to the clear blue sky. "Is there such a thing as 'normal' here?"

Uneze chuckled, a brittle sound. "Usually. So... your day off? Any plans?"

"No, I'm worried about Melanie... up there with Dave." Her eyes followed a distant speck in the sky. "I'm just going to wait here until she gets back."

"I can't believe she actually went up with him." Uneze's voice dropped to a near whisper. "Maybe it'll bring them closer," he said, then paused, his jaw clenching.

"Or maybe she'll push him out of the plane in a huge plot twist," Peri laughed. "Or... beat him with that bottle she always carries."

"Where are Anya and Johan?" Uneze asked.

"Oh, Anya is shopping with Emily. And Johan? Well, he's lounging by the pool, caught up in conversation with an American girl."

"At least he's keeping his drama out of the group." Uneze chuckled, shaking his head.

"I know, right? I never thought I'd see the day when Emily would actually bond with the girls," Peri said. "She's a completely different person from the stuck-up snob we met on the first day. You should see her and Michelle together—it's a riot. Michelle is practically giving her a crash course in being normal and nice. It's like watching a comedy duo in action."

"So, the whole group is accounted for except for Alistair. Where is he?" Uneze asked.

"I have no idea; he just left at breakfast without saying a word."

98 - MELANIE

As Melanie and Dave geared up for the skydiving trip, she returned his rage-filled stare with a smile. The pilot checked their harnesses and helmets, making sure everything was secure before they boarded the small plane that would take them up to ten thousand feet. Melanie felt adrenaline flood her body as she took her seat on the small, cramped plane. Dave had stayed away from her, messaging on his phone and casting angry, accusative glances in her direction until he finally returned when the instructor insisted that he board and prepare for the flight.

"How dare you?" Dave demanded, his voice marked by uncontrollable rage.

"What?" Melanie asked, her tone steady.

The muscles around his eyes twitched as he spat out his words in rage, "Don't play innocent. You know exactly what I mean. The tour operator just called and told me I'm off the tour. They've booked me a flight back home for tomorrow."

Her voice was steely calm as she replied, "I didn't know. It must have been Peri and Uneze. You did cause a scene the other night, and before that."

"You bitch. You'll pay for this," Dave hissed.

A wave of fear caught in Melanie's heart, paralysing her for a moment at his threat. She knew he loved to see her crawl into herself in fear, so this time she shouted back, "How? You'll divorce me? Good. I can't wait to be rid of you."

"You have no idea what I'm capable of," Dave hollered.

Melanie's face wrinkled, and her frown deepened as she struggled to find a witty reply. Instead, she rolled her shoulders and turned away from him, trying to steady her breathing.

She turned to Alistair, who'd tagged along at the last minute, and forced herself to be polite. Something, in fact everything, about him annoyed her. "You had to bring your lover with you for protection?" Melanie asked, the words slipping from her mouth before she could stop them.

She regretted her words the minute they left her lips. Of all the things she knew about her husband, one thing was for sure: he was not gay.

"Ahh, shut it. I can't even look at you, never mind listen to you," Alistair shot back.

Melanie glanced at him, then turned to look out of the window. She couldn't quite put her finger on it, but something about Alistair rubbed her the wrong way. Maybe it was his constant need for attention or the way he hovered around, always waiting with his hands behind his back for an invitation to dinner or a free glass of wine. Or perhaps it was his knack for one-upping everyone in the room, hovering around like he was listening in on private conversations.

"So, how long have you been diving?" Melanie asked, trying to make conversation.

"Long enough," Alistair replied dismissively.

Finally, the pilot climbed aboard and turned to face them. "Pack your patience and be prepared to wait. Take deep breaths; keep yourself centered and calm. What goes up must dive down." The pilot turned forward, and the engines sputtered to life, slowly lifting them off the ground.

Strapped into the narrow confines of the plane, Melanie shifted uncomfortably in her seat, her earlier enthusiasm evaporating like the clouds outside. The two men in front, enraptured in their own conversation, seemed oblivious to her presence, their laughter intensifying her growing sense of isolation.

She turned her gaze toward the view beyond the window. The bright blue sky stretched infinitely, a stark reminder of the adventure that awaited. As the plane climbed higher, the world below shrank to a patchwork of gold and brown fields, a dizzying sight that sent a thrill racing through her veins.

Nerves twisted in her stomach like a coiled spring, but a spark of exhilaration ignited within her, compelling her to lean back and mentally prepare. She visualised each step—the rush of air, the freedom of falling, the adrenaline surging through her veins.

The pilot's voice broke through her thoughts, a casual inquiry hanging in the air. "So, are you ready for this?"

Dave's response was clipped, his focus solely on the horizon. "I just hope the wind is right and we haven't come up here for nothing," he muttered, eyes fixed ahead, embodying a tense anticipation.

As the plane levelled off at altitude, the pilot's confident voice rang out, "It's a perfect day. Let's get this show on the road."

The words hung in the cabin, charged with excitement, and Melanie felt her heart race in time with the thrum of the engines, a feeling she couldn't ignore any longer. Suddenly, she couldn't wipe the grin off her face. Giddy with excitement, she no longer cared about Alistair or Dave. In that instant, she only cared about the feeling she knew she'd experience as soon as she let her body be taken by the wind. All that energy spent learning, practicing, and studying had paid off.

The doors swung open with a metallic click, and a gust of crisp air rushed in, tousling Melanie's hair and filling her lungs with the scent of freedom and adrenaline. Her heart raced, each beat syncing with the roar of the wind as it whipped past her, beckoning her to leap into the vast expanse below.

Dave grinned, his eyes sparkling with excitement, before launching himself into the open air, arms spread wide like an eagle. The wind whipped fiercely against his face. The usual warmth of their ritual—the playful pinky twist and lingering kiss—was absent, leaving her with a strange chill deep in her bones. She caught Dave's fleeting glance, but it felt more like a shadow than a connection, a flicker of something unspoken hanging in the air. Below him, patchwork fields and tiny houses looked like a patchwork quilt, but there was no time to admire the view. For a split second, gravity forgot its hold, and Dave felt weightless, like a bird soaring through the sky. The rush of air enveloped him, filling him with a sense of freedom.

In an instant, he became a tiny dot against the endless expanse, spiralling and tumbling through the clouds, a trail of exhilaration in his wake.

Melanie longed for the feeling of weightlessness and freedom she knew would come once she was out of the plane. She neared the exit, tightening the straps of her harness and feeling the reassuring weight of the skydiving gear against her body. The cool metal of the altimetre clinked softly as she adjusted it, glancing at the bright red parachute, neatly packed but bursting with potential just a heartbeat away. With every tug of the nylon straps, she could sense the adrenaline surging through her veins, her heart racing in sync with the thrum of the plane's engines.

Melanie tapped her foot against the floor, her eyes flickering between Alistair and the instructor, who stood at the edge of the aircraft, urgency radiating from his posture. The command echoed in her ears, but Alistair lingered by the door, his fingers twitching as if testing the air.

"Go," the instructor insisted, his tone sharp and firm, slicing through the tension thick in the cabin.

Melanie's frustration bubbled beneath the surface. She turned to Alistair and screamed, "Go on, it's your turn."

Alistair's gaze shifted to her, a wild glint in his eyes that sent a shiver down her spine. "No, I think it's your turn," he shot back, his words tumbling out with an edge that hinted at his own unease.

"Really, Alistair? Go. I always like to go last," she replied, struggling to maintain her composure. "It's just a thing we always do."

The instructor's voice rang out again: "One of you needs to go, now."

"Stop being a baby," Alistair snapped, his voice trembling, caught between bravado and the simmering fear that lurked just beneath. The tension coiled tighter, thickening the air around them as Melanie fought to break the standoff.

Melanie's heart thundered in her chest as she clutched the edge of the plane's open door, her knuckles white against the cold metal. The roar of the wind drowned out everything else, and the vast expanse of blue sky stretched endlessly before her, broken only by the patchwork of fields far below. She had dreamed of this moment for weeks, imagining the thrill, the freedom—but now, faced with the reality, she was frozen.

Her breaths came in shallow gasps, each one barely reaching her lungs before the next took its place. "I... I'm not ready," she shouted, her voice cracking. She clung tighter to the doorframe, her body trembling.

Alistair placed a reassuring hand on her shoulder. "The first step's always the hardest," he said, leaning in close. "But you'll thank me when it's over."

She shook her head vehemently. "No, I need a minute. Just—"

But before she could finish her sentence, Alistair's hands were on her back, firm and unyielding. A sharp shove sent her tumbling forward into the void.

The scream tore from her throat, raw and primal, as the wind ripped at her face and body. Her stomach lurched, left behind in the plane as she plummeted downward. For a moment, sheer terror consumed her, the ground rushing up to meet her with terrifying speed. Instinctively, she flailed, arms and legs pinwheeling in a desperate attempt to grab hold of something—anything. But there was nothing but air and the relentless pull of gravity. The wind roared past her ears, muffling every coherent thought and drowning out the sound of her own screams

99 - MELANIE

The videoman, Gabriel, appeared in her peripheral vision like an angel. His calm, controlled presence cut through the chaos, his movements deliberate and practised. He gestured sharply, signaling for her to extend her arms and arch her back.

Her mind raced, but she tried to focus. His gestures were clear, almost urgent, and she mimicked them, though her limbs trembled with the effort to control her rising panic. Slowly, her body steadied, the spin reducing to a manageable sway.

Gabriel floated closer, his eyes locked onto hers behind his goggles, exuding an unshakable calm that she desperately needed. He motioned again, a fluid sequence of pointing, miming, and nodding that she followed like her life depended on it—because it did.

The ground seemed impossibly far yet terrifyingly close. Time warped between seconds and eternity. Gabriel stayed nearby, guiding her with precision until, at last, her parachute deployed with a snap, jerking her upward and slowing her descent.

Relief washed over her, though her breath came in ragged gasps. Gabriel gave her a thumbs-up, his grin wide and reassuring. As she drifted toward the earth, the panic ebbed, replaced by a shaky, surreal sense of triumph.
She had survived the fall—thanks to him, and no thanks to Alistair.

Gabriel moved around her, helping her out of her gear. "What happened up there?" he asked.

Melanie struggled to catch her breath. Ashen, pale, and shaken, she muttered, "He pushed me."

Gabriel's smile faded. "What? Who?"

"Alistair. He pushed me. I wasn't ready to go." Melanie's voice wobbled as she grabbed his arm for support, her mouth as dry as the sand beneath her boots.

Gabriel's expression darkened. "Who's Alistair?"

"The last guy to jump after me."

He studied her face, unsure if she was confused or making an accusation. "He didn't jump. He said he couldn't do it."

Melanie's breath hitched as the words sank in. "What?"

Gabriel repeated slowly, "He said he'd changed his mind and didn't jump."

Her gaze hardened as realisation dawned. "What the hell?"

Gabriel shrugged uneasily. "Yeah, it happens sometimes."

But Melanie wasn't buying it. Her stomach churned as the pieces clicked into place. "So, he stayed up there for one reason: to push me."

100 - MELANIE

Confused and disorientated, Melanie wobbled toward the wooden hut, her mind racing as she tried to make sense of what had just happened.

She spotted Dave and froze.

"Melanie. You made it." Dave called, standing a distance away, offering no effort to approach her.

Melanie's scowl was sharp and accusing. "Why wouldn't I? Because your friend pushed me?"

Dave's face twisted into a frown. "What are you talking about?"

"You know damn well what I'm talking about. Your creepy little friend Alistair pushed me out of that plane when I wasn't ready."

"Don't be ridiculous." Dave's voice bristled with bitterness as he unclasped his helmet and tossed it to the ground. "Why would he do that?"

"Because you couldn't do it yourself. That would've been too obvious. But if someone we barely know did it, it could be passed off as an accident. You tried to kill me."

Dave's jaw tightened, his expression shifting from anger to disgust. "Unbelievable. Just because things don't go your way, you make wild accusations? You know what? When we get home, I want a divorce."

"Good," Melanie shot back, her voice steady despite her trembling hands. "Because after what just happened, I want exactly the same thing. And just so you know, I've already started the paperwork."

Shaking, she turned away and marched toward the hut. She barely registered Alistair as he crossed her path, eyes cast downward.

"Hey," she barked, stomping toward him. "What the hell was that? Why did you push me?"

"I didn't push you," Alistair muttered, avoiding her glare.

"Oh, really? You think I didn't feel it?"

"I gave you a little nudge," he admitted reluctantly. "You were stalling. I just...helped."

Melanie's eyes burned with fury. "A nudge? You call that a nudge? You pushed me."

"I saw you about to chicken out," Alistair said, voice defensive.

"Like you? You didn't jump either. Coward." Her words hit their mark, and Alistair flinched.

"The wind shifted," he said weakly. "They wouldn't let me."

"Liar. I don't want to hear another word from you. Ever."

101 – MELANIE

The pilot sprinted across the tarmac, his eyes scanning her pale, shocked face. "Are you alright?"

"Yeah." Melanie forced a nod, though her voice trembled. "Now that I'm back on solid ground, I'm much better. Thanks."

"What happened up there?" he pressed. "I saw you spinning out of control."

Melanie exhaled shakily. "I wasn't ready to jump. I was pushed."

The pilot's brows creased as he asked, "Pushed?"

"Yes, by my husband's friend. The one who didn't jump."

"Why would he do that?"

Melanie shrugged, her voice tight. "I think my husband is trying to get rid of me."

The pilot's frown deepened. "And you still went up there with him?"

"I know. My friends warned me. But this was my dream." She swallowed hard, her voice cracking. "I didn't think he'd actually..."

The pilot's gaze softened. "Well, we've got cameras on board. If you want, I can get you the footage."

She trembled before nodding and replying, "I'll take it. I need to see it for myself before I decide what to do."

"You sure you're okay?" he asked gently.

Melanie exhaled deeply. "Not really."

"Why don't you wait inside? I'll take you back to your hotel after I finish my post-flight paperwork."

Reluctantly, Melanie nodded and sank into a worn sofa inside the hut. The pilot returned moments later with a steaming cup of coffee, setting it in her trembling hands.

"Thanks," she murmured, the warmth grounding her as her mind spun.

102 - PERI

After a quick wander around the town with Uneze to get a wine supply for the next few days, Peri returned to her spot in the shade on the terrace outside the hotel reception and watched the darkening sky. She listened to Dave as he bragged and raved about his jump to Alistair as they walked past her.

Peri jumped to her feet, stepped forward, and asked, "Where's Melanie?"

"She stomped off in a strop after the jump. She ran off to the pilot like a child asking for a lift home," Dave said.

"Dave, may I talk to you alone?" Peri asked.

Dave nodded to Alistair, and with annoyance on his face, turned to Peri and hissed his question, "Were you the one who got me thrown off the safari?"

Unimpressed by his tone, she tried to reply in a calm manner and explained, "No, it was you. We have to file a daily report to head office on tours like these. Head office read my reports and made their own decision."

"So, I have no choice in the matter?" Dave hissed in rage, his harsh gaze locked onto Peri.

Peri broke the stare, stepping aside as she smiled at Alex, who wandered past. "Well, you have no choice about staying on the tour. You have to leave us. Tomorrow will be your last day. We have arranged a flight for you, but it's your choice if you want to take it or stay in Africa."

"Mmm, so I do have a choice," Dave said, inching closer and prodding his finger on Peri's chest as she stepped back.

"If you don't take the flight that head office has arranged, then you're on your own. They won't offer you another flight."

"Hmm," Dave muttered.

A wave of distrust hit her as a chilling thought took hold. She imagined Dave stalking the tour from a distance, booking the same campsites and hotels, and shadowing them. His overpowering presence had pushed her so far back that she was almost cornered between Dave and a wall.

Peri ducked under his arm and broke away from him. "Think about it all you like, but a car will be here in reception tomorrow morning at 11 a.m." With that, she turned her back to him, checking his movements in the reflection of the mirrored reception desk. Exasperated, Peri turned to the receptionist and let out a long sigh.

"Are you okay?" the receptionist asked.

"I will be happy tomorrow morning when I know I never have to see that man again." She waved to a barman in the distance and called out, "A large gin and tonic, please."

Peri cradled her drink, her gaze fixated on the front door, the ice clinking softly as she shifted her weight.

Uneze burst through the entrance, a confident stride accentuated by a wide grin, as he made a beeline for her table. "Sorry I took so long," he said, shaking his head as he slid into the seat beside her. "I was chatting with Dennis, Michelle, and Alex, who just got back from the dolphin tour."

Peri raised an eyebrow, a smirk playing on her lips. "That's a trio I didn't expect. Anyway, perfect timing—you dodged the Dave showdown."

Uneze grimaced, his brow furrowing slightly. "I'm so sorry. How was it?"

"Not good, but he knows he's leaving."

A glimmer of relief crossed Uneze's eyes. "I'm actually glad I wasn't there. I'm going to play the innocent tonight at boys' night out."

"Probably best. Just shift the blame to head office; that's what I did," she replied, her voice laced with sarcasm.

"Did Melanie make it down alive?" he asked, glancing at the door with mild concern.

Peri's gaze darted back, her unease clear. "That's why I'm staring at the door. She didn't return with Dave and Alistair."

"Oh, wow. Can I join you in the fascinating door-staring game?"

"Sure," she said, gesturing to the empty chair, "but I need another drink first."

As they sipped their drinks, the conversation flowed effortlessly, mapping out their evening plans to keep boys' and girls' nights separate. Suddenly, Peri's heart jumped as she spotted Melanie emerging from a truck. Peri sprang to her feet, rushing over to envelop Melanie in a tight embrace. "Oh, thank god you're back."

"Yeah, me too. I almost didn't make it," Melanie replied.

"What? How?" Peri's eyes widened, concern flooding her features.

"Alistair pushed me out of the plane before I was ready. If it hadn't been for the videographer guiding me down, I'd be nothing but a red stain on the earth right now," Melanie recounted, her fear still filled with lingering adrenaline.

Uneze leant back, his expression shifting to skepticism. "Are you sure?"

"Yep. The pilot agreed and will send me the footage. I asked him to send it to you; is that okay? I don't want Dave getting his hands on it," Melanie confided, her voice a low whisper.

"Mmm, yeah, sure," Peri replied, her mind racing. "You really think he's trying to kill you?" Peri asked.

"After today? I'm pretty sure of it," Melanie affirmed, her gaze steely.

Peri shook her head and said, "Well, Dave is off the tour as of now. Tomorrow morning, he's flying home. So tonight, you're on girls' night with us, and then he'll be gone."

"Great, but he's gone from this safari, not from my life. I'll still have to face him at home, and that's going to be unpleasant, to say the least."

103 - MELANIE

Melanie knocked on the door of the room she would be sharing with her friends and let out a long, deep sigh. She wanted to tell them what had happened, yet the words wouldn't form in her mouth. Emily and Michelle looked so glamorous that she almost backed out of the night out. She didn't need to feel any more frumpy than she already did.

Melanie couldn't remember the last time she'd taken care of her appearance. As she sat in the chair, the expert hands of her new friends worked their magic, transforming her unkempt hair into a sleek and stylish new ponytail. She marvelled at how a simple brushing and some makeup could make her feel like a whole new person.

The reflection staring back at her in the mirror was almost unrecognizable. Gone was the tired, dishevelled woman she had become accustomed to seeing. In her place was a confident and radiant version of herself that she had long forgotten existed. One of her three frumpy dresses had been tacked and shortened at the bottom, the ruffled sleeves shortened, and a large black belt added to emphasise her waistline.

"My god, look at you," Michelle said.

Melanie gasped and giggled as she replied, "I can't believe this is me."

"You've been hiding behind those dresses, but there is a beautiful, curvy, and sexy woman in there," Emily said.

"You girls watch too much Gok Wan, but I like it. Thank you so much."

"Maybe, but look at you. Oh, and we picked these up in town today when you were flying," Emily said, handing out a pair of moccasin-style shoes. "We thought about getting you some heels, but we decided you weren't a heel girl and didn't want you to break your neck."

"Oh my god, thank you so much. These are amazing," Melanie said.

"Well, we decided they'd look good with that dress. So, pop them on. It's showtime," Michelle said.

Along with Anja, the girls strutted down to the meeting point, and the five girls left a bunch of turned heads in their wake as they walked down the bustling town streets.

They entered the restaurant and made their way to their allocated table. Melanie couldn't stop patting her hair and straightening down her dress. She was nervous, her hands fidgeting with the napkin in her lap as she tried to relax. This was her first official outing as a new woman. One tiny change in events, and she would be in a coffin right now. She snapped some selfies, wanting to send them to Julius but scared to open that door. She knew he'd be frustrated, angry even, and to just send him a photo would be impossible to do without the backstory. She placed her phone back in her bag and returned to the conversation.

The waiter came over to take their drink orders, and Melanie fumbled over her words as she tried to decide what to order.

"So, let's raise our glasses to Melanie—her new life, and most importantly, her survival of today's wild escapades," Peri said, her voice ringing with warmth as she lifted her glass high, the clinking sound resonating around the table.

"What happened to Melanie?" Michelle leant forward, eyes wide with curiosity, sensing the shift in the atmosphere.

"Oh no, you didn't tell them?" Peri's face fell, guilt flashing across her features.

"It's not your fault. I was too caught up in the fun to spoil the night with the details of that crappy incident."

Faces tensed, and jaws dropped in unison as Melanie recounted her tale, each horrified revelation pulling them deeper into her narrative.

"No way. I can't believe it," Anya whispered, disbelief etched on her face.

"Yeah, there's been so much happening since we arrived here," Melanie continued, her tone both incredulous and frustrated. "I just can't wrap my head around how Alistair got tangled up in all this."

"Can't we just get him kicked off the tour too?" Anya pressed, her brow scrunched with concern.

"We can try, but it'll depend on the footage and what the police say," Peri replied, her voice steady despite the rising tension.

Melanie paused mid-bite, her fork hovering above her plate. Swallowing hard, she forced a grin, trying to shake off the seriousness. "I don't think I can go to the police. We're leaving in the morning, and we haven't even got the tape yet."

"We can find the next police station. We're still in Namibia; it doesn't matter," Peri said. "At least, that's how I think it works."

"I just want to enjoy tonight. He's been kicked off the tour; he's out of here by eleven tomorrow," Melanie insisted, her voice firmer now.

"We leave at seven, so we won't have to see him again," Peri reassured her.

"Where are they headed tonight?" Anya asked.

"They're off to a little fish and chip place by the jetty, a beer joint."

Anya chimed in, her tone lightening. "Was the pilot cute, at least? You could have some fun while we're here."

Melanie teased, trying to lighten the mood. "He was cute, but no thanks; I don't need that kind of stress with Dave lurking around."

"He'll be gone tomorrow. So, who's left?" Emily grinned, mischief sparking in her eyes.

Anya's expression transformed. "Well, I think we'll all steer clear of Alistair," she stated, shaking her head. "Alex is cute but too broody for me."

"Totally," Michelle agreed.

"Then there's Dennis and Uneze," Anya added.

Michelle feigned surprise. "Wait, I think Anya's forgotten that you and Dennis have a thing."

Peri grimaced, a shudder running through her. "Oh, no way. I do not have a thing with Dennis. I just said that to protect Melanie from Dave's fists."

Anya raised an eyebrow, glancing between Melanie and Peri. "That actually makes sense. I mean, you and Dennis? I just don't see it."

Michelle took a breath and blurted out something she hadn't intended on saying. "Can I just say something surprising? I went dolphin watching with Dennis today, and he's actually really fun."

"Dennis? Pathetic Dennis?" Emily asked.

"Yeah. He wasn't needy and only mentioned Eve once. He was great fun. We took selfies to put online for Eve, but honestly, there was a bit of a connection."

"No way. Michelle, come on, sis. Not Dennis. Look, in a few days we have another group joining us. Hold out for a better selection," Emily laughed.

The girls let out a roar of laughter as they asked for the bill. They walked the short distance to the hotel, and Michelle and Emily invited the girls up for a nightcap.

"Sorry, I have to go and prepare for tomorrow. You girls have fun, though," Peri said.

"It's only eight; it gets dark so early." Emily noted.

They giggled their way down the corridor to their rooms. Melanie stepped inside, left her shoes, grabbed her charger, and moved next door to Emily and Michelle's room. As she entered, they handed her a filled glass of red wine.

Michelle raised her glass and said, "To Melanie, survivor of the week award."

"Don't speak too soon; Dave is still here tonight. Anything can happen," Melanie said.

103 - MELANIE

The girls chatted with ease until, not long after nine, Emily and Melanie sat upright, exchanging intense glares. A faint banging noise from the adjacent room interrupted their conversation, drawing their attention to the source. They strained to listen.

The banging stopped abruptly. Melanie gasped. "That's my room. Who's in there?"

"Come on," Emily replied, her curiosity ignited. "Let's play detectives." She cautiously rested her hand on the doorknob, then pushed the door ajar, allowing the girls to peer into the dimly lit corridor.

A tall figure emerged from Melanie's room, a bag slung over his shoulder. His face was hidden by a hoodie, making it impossible to identify him.

"Who's that?" Melanie whispered.

Emily grabbed Melanie's hand and pulled her back into their room, shutting the door quietly. They stood in silence, listening as the figure's footsteps faded down the hallway. Dragging Emily with her, Melanie cracked the door open as Michelle joined them.

"We need to call security," Emily whispered. She nudged Michelle towards the hotel reception.

Melanie, trembling, said, "I'm going in."

"No, wait for security," Emily insisted. "Stay here. After today, I'm not letting you out of my sight."

Melanie paced the room, peeking through the door. "I can't do this anymore. He's ruining my life."

"Look, he's here," Emily said, flinging the door open and motioning to a uniformed security guard marching down the hallway.

The guard asked, "Ladies, what seems to be the problem?"

"That's my room," Melanie said. "We were next door having a drink when we heard noises. Someone was in there. We saw a man in a hoodie leave."

"Stay here while I check it out," the guard instructed. He entered the room, checking wardrobes, under the bed, and the balcony. Finally, he gestured for them to come in. "Everything seems fine. Are you sure you didn't imagine it?"

"No, we definitely heard noises," Melanie insisted. Her gaze swept the room. "The bed—I didn't use it. Look at the cover; it's ruffled."

The guard inspected the bed, tilting his head. "Yes, it does look disturbed. Maybe they stood here?"

"Why would someone stand on the bed?" Emily asked.

"The fan," the guard said grimly. "Stand back. I'm going to test it."

He switched on the ceiling fan. It wobbled violently, then gave way with a metallic screech. Detached, it crashed onto the bed, scattering feathers from a punctured pillow. The room filled with a loud thud as the fan lay still, its wires swaying ominously.

Melanie jumped in shock, clinging to Emily. Her legs gave way, and she sank to the floor, trembling. The security guard gasped, glancing between the girls.

"What just happened?" Michelle whispered.

Inspecting the fan, the guard muttered about faulty wiring. Melanie, pale and shaken, stammered, "That could've been me."

"Do you think it was Alistair or Dave?" Emily asked.

"One of them," Melanie said firmly. "Go get Peri."

Michelle sprinted down the corridor and banged on Peri's door. Peri, still dressed and holding a pen between her teeth, answered with a questioning glance.

"Come on—it's Melanie. Something's happened," Michelle said.

Peri grabbed her key and followed Michelle. Inside the room, she knelt beside Melanie, wrapping her arms around her quaking shoulders. The other girls shouted out theories, their voices chaotic.

"May I ask what's going on?" Peri finally interjected.

"This wasn't an accident," Emily declared. "It was deliberate."

The guard, joined by another, said, "We'll review the CCTV footage. For now, we'll arrange another room."

"Are you sure this isn't just faulty wiring?" Peri asked.

The guard shook his head. "This fan was tampered with."

Melanie, thoughtful, said, "Dave might've thought I was out. I posted a bar picture earlier, but I delayed it until I got Wi-Fi."

"Can we have security outside our room?" Michelle asked.

"Of course," the guard replied.

Melanie grabbed her belongings and moved next door. The guard inspected the room thoroughly before letting them in. Outside, another guard sat by their door, keeping watch.

Inside, the girls opened another bottle of wine, sitting in silence. Fear loomed over them.

"My God, Melanie," Michelle said. "That's the fourth time something's happened to you. We can't ignore this anymore."

Anger crept into Melanie's voice. "Dave's leaving tomorrow, but Alistair's staying. That's bad."

"I'll email head office," Peri said. "I'll push to get him off the tour, but I can't promise anything."

"You have to. I can't stay if he's here," Melanie said, her voice trembling.

Peri stood. "I'll handle it. Call if you need anything."

The girls barricaded the door with suitcases and sat huddled, dread tightening its grip on them.

105 - PERI

Peri, once out of the door, went first to her room, grabbed her computer, and then let herself into Uneze's room, shaking him awake.

Groggily, Uneze opened his eyes, blinking a few times before focusing on her face. "Oh, it's my lucky night?" he chuckled, flashing a cheeky grin.

"Oh, stop being so in love with yourself. I have to tell you what just happened."

He quickly sat up, fully awake now. Without another word, he jumped out of bed and reached for a pair of shorts. Tugging at his t-shirt, he said, "Oh my god, your hands are trembling." He took her hands, looking her in the eye. "It's okay. Just tell me."

"It looks like the gruesome twosome has struck again," Peri said, launching into an explanation of what had happened.

Uneze let out a stream of curses under his breath as he slipped into his sandals. "What are you doing? Let's go."

"No, we don't need to go. The girls are together, and security is outside the room. I need to send this email requesting we get Alistair off the tour," Peri said.

"Without any proof?"

"So, you're on Alistair's side now? Did you have a nice male-bonding evening or something?" Peri said.

"No, there are no sides. To be honest, I left before dessert arrived. It was weird. The whole thing was awkward. It was like a collision of alter egos and arrogance. Johan left with me too, and Alex didn't bother coming."

"Ah, okay. Sorry, we had a lovely evening. So, we need to ask hotel security if they have video of someone going into the room."

"I'll go and do that. Give me a couple of minutes," Uneze said.

"Thanks. Just check the security guy is still there," Peri said.

Peri pulled her laptop toward her and rested it on her knees. She felt an exhilarating rush as she spotted an email at the top of the list. The title read 'Video from plane,' and it had been sent by the skydiving company.

Peri clicked on the link, her breathing coming fast and hard. "Come on," she muttered to herself. She clicked download and waited for the video file to appear in her inbox, but it wasn't in a readable format.

Frustrated, Peri searched online for a solution, but nothing worked. She furiously typed, "I can't open it; please resend it in a different format."

The door burst open as Uneze shook his head. "We won't be able to see it until tomorrow. The manager has all the backup tapes."

"So, without that or the plane video, we're just stuck with him?" Peri said. "I think we leave earlier than planned, just in case Dave has another plan."

"Right, so we throw a spanner in his plan," Uneze confirmed.

"Can we leave now?" Peri asked.

"No, we can't drive through the night. Alistair and Dave are sharing a room, so we can't change plans without Dave finding out. We are going to have to act like nothing happened. The girls will have to pretend Melanie doesn't even know about the fan. That way, Alistair won't do anything stupid."

"Exactly."

106 - MELANIE

The girls whispered nervously to each other, trying to distract themselves from the fear that threatened to consume them. Melanie's heart raced with every creak of the floorboards or rustle of the wind outside. As the first light of dawn began to fill the room, a sense of relief washed over them. The guard outside still stood watch, his presence a comforting reassurance that they were not alone.

At six, the girls were startled by a knock on the door of the room, and a voice called through it. "It's Peri and Uneze."

Emily opened the door slowly, peeking through and looking behind them. "Hi, sorry. We just need to be careful."

"Of course, that's understandable," Uneze said as he placed the tray on a table in the room. "We've brought you breakfast so you don't need to go down to the breakfast room."

"Are Dave and Alistair there?" Melanie asked.

"No, not yet, but I thought I'd preempt any unexpected drama and bring breakfast to you. I'm a full-service guide," Uneze said with a laugh.

"In another moment, I'd make a pass at you with a comment like that," Michelle said.

"Did you get any sleep?" Peri asked.

Calmed by the male presence, Melanie managed a tiny smile, saying, "No, every time I closed my eyes, I wondered if it would be the last time, so I just stared at the door all night."

"Do you have any news on Alistair? Will he be kicked off the tour?" Emily asked.

"I've sent an email, but it's only 3 am in the UK, so we won't get an answer for a few hours. Today we're stuck with him. We got the video from the plane, but I can't open it. I've asked them to send it in another format, and as soon as the manager gets here, we'll have access to security from last night. But don't worry; we'll keep an eye on you," Peri said.

"Ladies, I know this is hard, but Melanie, I suggest you pretend like nothing happened. We don't want to scare Alistair; if he thinks you suspect him of anything, he may act out and try again."

"With Dave gone, maybe he won't try anything else," Melanie said.

"Maybe, let's hope so. But just in case, please, talk about your wild night out and you crashing with the girls."

"But surely I'd have noticed my bags were there, and I went into the room."

"You could have done it first thing in the morning. It was dark, and you easily could have missed it. He doesn't know that the whole bed collapsed."

"Alright, I'll try," Melanie muttered.

Peri smiled and replied, "After what Alistair did on the plane, you don't even have to pretend to talk to him. Just don't mention what happened. Talk about your great night out, all the fun you had, and leave it at that."

Emily agreed first, then the others. They pulled the table in from the balcony and placed their breakfast on it.

Peri stole a strawberry, popped it in her mouth, and said, "I'll get the porter to bring your bags down now and get them in the truck. See you on board. Remember, act like nothing happened."

107 - DENNIS

The early morning departure took place without any confrontations. Alistair shifted in his seat, his eyes glued to the window, watching the world outside blur into a wash of muted colours. The lingering shock of seeing Melanie still hung in the air, like a thick fog, but he said nothing, choosing instead to focus on the road ahead.

In the front seat, Uneze turned momentarily toward Melanie, their eyes locking in a silent exchange. A subtle nod passed between them—a shared understanding, perhaps relief—that spoke volumes without a single word.

The truck rolled away from the hotel, the tires crunching against the gravel, leaving behind the echoes of conversations unspoken. The girls huddled together, gossiping and laughing. Anya, confused, refrained from asking what was going on and, assuming it was somehow linked to the plane jump situation, joined in. "I can't believe that guy from the pub. He was such fun."

"How many drinks did he buy us?" Melanie asked.

"I can't believe you passed out on my bed," Michelle said. "The first night out of a tent, and I still had to sleep next to my sister to make room for you."

After a few minutes, the chatter faded, leaving a comfortable hush that wrapped around the group like a soft blanket. The only exception was Dennis, who slid into the empty seat beside Michelle with a soft grin, his phone already in hand. They leant closer, their laughter bubbling up as they scrolled through a gallery of selfies, their whispers punctuated by secret giggles that danced in the air like confetti.

Later, during the lunch break, Peri's eyes drifted to Dennis standing at the fringe of the lunch area. His phone, once a constant companion, lay forgotten in his pocket. Instead, he stood still, his gaze fixed on the horizon.

A smile graced his lips, radiating a warmth that spoke volumes, as if he were savouring an unspoken connection with the world around him.

Peri felt a spark of curiosity and approached him, breaking the spell. "So, Dennis, how's the safari going so far? You look happier," she asked, her voice light.

"Yeah, it's been cool," he replied, the smile lingering. "The guys are great, although I'm glad Dave's gone. I didn't want to face his fist again. But when are we going to do the fun stuff? Wine tasting, climbing sand dunes, and watching dolphins isn't really what I had in mind."

Peri looked surprised as she said, "You could have done a tandem skydiving trip."

"I wanted to, but Dave talked me out of it," Dennis shrugged, his brow furrowing at the thought. "When will we be seeing some animal action?"

"Soon," Peri assured him, her eyes sparkling with excitement. "Tomorrow, we'll head to Spitzkoppe, then off to Etosha National Park. We'll camp by a floodlit waterhole, where we sometimes have four-legged night visitors—elephants, giraffes, zebras, and even lions and hyenas. For many, it's the highlight of the tour."

"Finally," Dennis huffed.

Just then, Michelle breezed in, her keen eyes catching the hint of boredom etched on Peri's face. She shot Dennis an animated sideways glance. "Are you talking about Eve, or are you complaining you've not seen the animals yet?"

"Animals," he laughed, a mischievous twinkle in his eye as he slid his fingers down her back, eliciting a surprised giggle from her.

"We've seen lots of animals, Dennis. Just none of the big five yet, but don't worry, they're coming soon," she teased, her smile infectious.

"Good. Finally, something interesting on this tour," he replied, mustering a grin that lit up his entire face.

"Ehherm," Michelle giggled in jest, "Dolphins, attempted murder, scorpions, nighttime cliff jumping—not enough for you?"

"Ah, shut up and take a selfie with me," Dennis urged, his excitement bubbling over.

"Here in a car park? Hardly exciting," she replied, her laughter ringing out. "This isn't going to make for a particularly interesting TikTok feed."

"This isn't for that; this is for me. Come on," he insisted, wrapping his arm around her shoulder and pulling her close. "Kiss, please," he said, his eyes sparkling with mischief.

Michelle's surprise quickly melted into a smile as he pressed a quick kiss to her lips. Pulling away slowly, a grin plastered across his face.

"You didn't even take the photo?" Peri interjected, her eyebrow raised in playful disbelief.

"Nope, that was just me tricking you. I just wanted a kiss," Dennis said, a satisfied smirk on his face.

108 - PERI

After a seemingly never-ending drive, the rugged landscape around Skizokoppe unfolded before them: a desert stretching endlessly, an otherworldly panorama more akin to a barren moonscape than a destination on Earth. Dust flew around the tires of their vehicle, the dry air settling in as Alex sat silently, his fingers gripping the straps of his rucksack, his gaze locked on the window.

The rhythmic hum of the engine was almost hypnotic, lulling the group into deeper slumber. Uneze, grinning widely, called out, "Rise and shine, campers. Time to get your asses off this wobble wagon." With a collective yawn, they stirred awake, arms stretching toward the ceiling of the vehicle like sunflowers reaching for sunlight, their eyes squinting at the strange beauty outside.

Once checked in to their campsite, Uneze gestured toward a nearby bench that overlooked the striking rock formations of the Namib Desert. He handed a glass of wine to Peri, and they settled onto a bench.

Uneze pulled out his device, the screen illuminating his face. "The hotel sent me the link from the security feed. The guy who left Melanie's room kept his head down, but look at his shoes."

Peri squinted at the screen, confusion knitting her brows as she studied the image. "You're going to need to explain yourself," she replied, her tone flat.

Uneze's finger traced the outline of the shoes, zooming in. "See the yellow stripes and laces?"

Her eyes flickered with confusion as she said, "Still means nothing."

Uneze's expression sharpened, a trace of urgency creeping into his voice.

"The day we trekked the dunes, Dave wore those shoes."

"Shit. So, it was Dave, not Alistair?" Peri's voice was barely a whisper, disbelief etched across her face.

Uneze sighed, the importance of the revelation settling in. "Well, with that, we can't ask Alistair to leave."

"And the video from the plane shows Alistair hovering by the edge, but we can't see him pushing Melanie," Peri explained. "So, we've got nothing. Not a shred of evidence."

"Correct," Uneze replied, his voice heavy with resignation. "And we're stuck with Alistair until we finally get something on him."

"Please, let's just hope that nothing else happens. Melanie needs some peace." After a sip of her wine, she continued, "Did you see the way that Alex stared at Alistair for the whole trip?"

"Maybe he was sleeping with his eyes open," Uneze said.

"No, he just stared; I have a feeling that he's going to be our next problem," Peri explained.

"Be positive. The good parts of the safari start soon. People will be way too distracted by scary animals to bother about anything else," Uneze said.

109 - DENNIS

The campsite dinner in Spitzkoppe was at a long table groaning under the weight of food. The space buzzed with a nervous energy that belied the exhaustion etched on every face.

Alex, the instigator, tapped his wine glass, the sharp metallic ping cutting through the low hum of conversation. All eyes turned to him. He raised his glass slightly. "I think this moment deserves a few raised glasses as we approach the elephant in the room."

"Huh," Johan replied as he looked around him, "Where?"

"Dave's gone. And I, for one, am damn glad." A murmur of agreement rippled through the assembled.

Melanie's nod was sharp and agreeable. "I second that."

Alex continued, his voice low but firm, "This... this is a good thing."

As if on cue, Alistair arrived, hovering with his hands around his back. "No drink again, Ali boy?" Alex said.

"Unless someone wants to offer me a glass, then no." Alistair replied.

Heads were lowered, avoiding his eyes. The unspoken refusal hung heavier than the silence itself. Alex abruptly lurched forward with a swift movement, and helped himself to a plate piled high with food. With a quick step, he strode to a lone table further down and sat, his back to the group.

Johan's voice rumbled low. "What's with him and the wine? Or rather, the lack of it?"

Alex shrugged, his eyes fixed on Alistair's retreating figure. "Don't worry. I have a feeling he won't be sticking around much longer."

"Why not?" Johan asked.

Alex simply replied, "Gut feeling." Silence settled, thick and heavy, broken only by the clinking of cutlery. "So, goodbye, Dave. And Melanie, we're glad you're still here."

Melanie's smile widened as she poured herself another glass of wine, genuine but tinged with something more. "Guess I don't need to drink quite so much anymore. It was Dave who made me. He looked... well, with enough wine, and if I squinted really hard, sometimes he looked a bit like Brad Pitt."

Emily's laughter was a bright spark in the dimming light. "Girl, I need whatever you're drinking."

Alex's laugh was unexpected, a full-bodied sound that surprised even himself. "Yeah, maybe if you'd had a few more on your wedding day, that string bean would've looked a little better, and you might have actually gone through with it."

The table erupted in laughter, glasses clinked, and Emily joined in the merriment. "While we're at it," she said, "a toast to Dennis, who hasn't mentioned Eve in, what, at least a week?"

Dennis rested a hand on Michelle's knee, the other raising his glass. "I'm... growing," he said softly.

Michelle added, "And his finger hurts from all those pointless social media posts."

"No reply? No comments?" Alex asked.

"Nothing," Dennis replied. "It's like she's vanished offline."

Johan's voice was laced with skepticism. "Do you even care?"

Dennis's answer was quiet but firm. "Honestly? No. Not anymore. She's part of my past. And it's all thanks to you guys and this trip."

Johan teased, "Oh, look who's getting all sentimental."

Dennis shook his head, a flicker of genuine emotion in his eyes. "No, seriously. For the first time I can remember, I don't feel completely alone.

Even when I was... with, ehm, her, I was alone."

Michelle's touch was gentle as her finger traced his cheek, then she leant in, kissing him softly.

A collective "Wow" rippled around the table, followed by a round of applause.

"Oh, it looks like I missed something fun," Peri said as she joined the crowd waving some papers around. "Sign-up sheets for the next two days. Hiking and trekking to rock arch and rock pool, and san murals. The campsite offers cooking classes, horse riding, trips, painting classes, pottery making, and village visits. It's all here. Just pop a tick by the name; the times are listed too. You know the deal."

Uneze spoke up and said, "They are all done with local guides, so don't get yourselves into any trouble as Peri and I are having a day off."

"Speak for yourself. I'm going horse riding," Peri interjected.

"Is that what the young folks call it?" Dennis said with a cheeky cackle.

Peri shook her head and replied, "Enjoy your free days. You'll find us on or nearby the campsite, or on one of the tours on this list. There's even another cooking course for anyone who wants it."

"Remember to stay away from Melanie's cooking," Emily said in jest.

"Just give me a list of allergies, and I'll make sure to put those ingredients in the dishes, just to make it all a bit more fun," Melanie said with a loud chuckle.

"Whatever you do, just tick the boxes and delegate someone to bring it over to us by the time the sun goes down," Peri said.

110 - PERI

Under the vast, star-studded sky of the Namib Desert, a gentle breeze rustled the tablecloth, carrying the scent of grilled game and spiced vegetables.

Uneze and Peri sat across from each other, laughter mingling with the whispers of the evening. Their plates were filled with dull local cuisine—maize fritters and flavoured rice—each bite a celebration of the region's flavours. They chatted about the upcoming merger of groups, wondering how they'd gel with a group that had already been through so much.

His playful grin mirrored the twinkling constellations above. Peri chuckled, the sound light and carefree. "Well, they have no choice; whoever arrives has two choices: form their own subgroup or join the chaos already underway," Uneze said.

"It'll be fun no matter what," Peri laughed. "How does it normally work with new arrivals?" she asked, her eyes sparkling with curiosity.

"It depends on who they are," Uneze replied, leaning closer, the warmth of their connection palpable. "Couples blend in well; they've got nothing to prove and no need to fit in."

With a quick motion, Peri retrieved her phone, fingers dancing across the screen as she pulled up the latest email with the details of the new arrivals. "Alright, so we have a couple from Australia, a guy from the UK on his own from the states, and two guys in a tent together, also from the UK," she announced, a teasing lilt in her voice.

"So, the couple should be fine, and maybe the three guys can hang out together, or with Dennis and Alex. If Alistair would leave, then it would make it so much easier." Uneze laughed.

"There are three guys, though, that could work well with Emily and even Melanie and Anya." Peri said with a chuckle.

Uneze's smile faded slightly, replaced by a hint of nostalgia. "Anyway, we won't have Melanie joining us in your tent; that's a shame. I liked it when you'd appear and snuggle up to me."

Peri's laughter rang out like a melody. "Hmm, I liked it too. Maybe the new group will bring more damsels in distress that will need my tent."

"Ah, so you aren't James anymore?" Uneze quipped, raising an eyebrow.

"Well, we're getting towards the halfway mark of the tour, and then I'll think about it," Peri replied, her tone light but her gaze lingering on Uneze as their fingers touched.

Just then, a shadow broke the spell. Uneze pulled back, eyes narrowing as a figure approached. "Alistair?" he called out, the warmth of the intimate moment dissipating.

"Um, yes. Look, I'm sorry; it was clear you were having a moment, but I needed to talk to you," Alistair said.

"Shoot?" Uneze beckoned.

"I want off the tour. Everyone hates me, and I don't belong here," Alistair confessed, his shoulders sagging as if the weight of the world rested upon them.

Peri interjected, her voice steady. She knew she should try and talk him out of it but decided against it and said, "You won't get a refund unless you have insurance."

Alistair waved a dismissive hand. "No, that's not the problem. I just wanted to let you know I'm leaving. I don't need a flight; I'm going to spend some time here on my own and do Africa my way. I'm in no rush to go back home."

"Ah, okay. When do you want to leave?" Peri asked.

"In a few days, I want to do a wildlife safari first, then I'll go. Just don't tell the others; I'll pack up early one morning and get a cab out of wherever we are, and they'll never see me again," Alistair said.

"Alright, just let us know when you're planning to leave, okay?" Peri said.

"Yeah, of course," Alistair replied, his eyes darting around, as if the words might summon the others to appear and overhear the conversation.

Uneze shrugged, his expression casual, though the playful shimmer in his eyes betrayed his amusement. "Alright, whatever works for you."

They watched Alistair's figure retreat, his shoulders hunched slightly as he blended into the gathering crowd heading towards the star viewing station.

"He has really bad timing, that guy, doesn't he?" Uneze asked.

"Or maybe it was perfect timing," Peri said.

"So, remind me, how many days until we're halfway through the tour and I don't have to call you James?" Uneze teased.

"I seem to have forgotten. I'll have a recount tomorrow. Goodnight, Uneze, sleep well," Peri said as she wandered in the direction of her tent.

111 – PERI

As the sun rose over Spitzkoppe the group erupted with excitement. Their quiet chatter paled in comparison to the towering granite peaks. Most of them gathered their gear for a rock-climbing adventure.

Uneze sauntered over, a teasing grin plastered across his face. "So, do you fancy a day together?" he asked.

Peri paused, an amused furrow forming between her brows. "Well, I really want to say yes, honestly, but—"

"No buts," Uneze interrupted, waving a dismissive hand. "We could go horse-riding. None of the group are doing that, so we can enjoy it without all the drama."

A laugh escaped Peri's lips, rich with irony. "Me on a horse? That's drama enough. It's not a pretty sight."

Uneze chuckled, his eyes alight with mischief. "I'd still love to see it."

"It sounds great, but not now. Emily's on her own, and I promised I'd do a painting class with her," Peri replied, her tone apologetic yet firm.

"On your day off?" Uneze raised an eyebrow, feigning disbelief.

"It's for two hours. Can you keep yourself busy until then? I promise I'll be all yours for the afternoon," she insisted, a spark of determination evident in her voice. With an amused smirk, she added, "Now, get something special planned that doesn't involve me getting an itchy rash between my thighs and a sore bum."

Emily and Peri set up their easels beneath the sprawling, sun-kissed sky. The desert landscape spread before them; the gentle breeze played with the edges of their canvases. Emily's brush glided effortlessly, swirling reds into the earth tones of the towering cliffs. Beside her, Peri struggled to capture the scene, her strokes thick and sludgy, resembling a rich, melted chocolate bar more than the impressive landscape they had in front of them.

Peri glanced sideways, her brow tense. "How come you didn't go out there today?" she asked, her voice laced with concern.

Emily dipped her brush into a deep ochre, her movements lacking the usual vigour. "More hiking and walking. No thanks. I'm actually not feeling great. Just weak and tired and sick," she replied, her eyes downcast, focusing on the canvas as if it were a lifeline.

Peri's gaze softened. "I've got a medicine kit—do you need anything?"

Emily paused, biting her lip. "I'm worried that it's malaria," she murmured, glancing at the distant hills as though they held the answers. Peri's brow twisted deeper.

"Already? I thought it took longer to make you sick," Peri said, but I'm not a doctor. We can ask the lobby if they can arrange one for you," she replied.

Emily bit her lip, her fingers fidgeting with her finger nails. "No, I'm fine. It's just this weird food. I'm used to something a little more... ehm, classier." Her voice lacked its usual confidence, wavering like a leaf caught in a gust of wind.

Peri's expression softened. "I'm sorry. I've got some stomach pills, but they won't help with whatever else is bothering you," she offered gently.

Emily's face paled, the colour draining as she lowered her voice, hands shaking wide with dread. "Damn. I'm really hoping it's malaria. Because the other option is that I'm pregnant."

"String bean?" Peri's tone was cautious as she asked, wondering if there was already another scandal to handle.

"Yes, unfortunately. Do you have a pregnancy test in that bag?" Emily's question cut through the tension like a knife, her gaze finally locking onto Peri's, revealing the vulnerability she had kept hidden from everyone.

Peri shook her head. "No, but we can definitely get one at the next big town or roadside mall on the way," she reassured her friend, the weight of the situation settling between them.

"Don't tell my sister, alright?" Emily's plea was frantic, her eyes narrowing as if to shield her secret from the world. "I don't need to hear her opinion on this."

"Of course not," Peri promised as she reached out to squeeze Emily's hand. "It's not my news; it's yours."

Later that day, with Emily tucked away for some much-needed rest, Peri climbed into the golf buggy beside Uneze, heading to a secluded spot, dappled sunlight filtering through the leafy canopy above. A long wooden table, filled with an inviting spread of mouthwatering dishes, beckoned them to feast: a spread of artisan cheeses, fresh fruits, and gourmet pastries, alongside a bottle of vintage champagne chilling in a silver ice bucket. Behind them, the towering peaks of Spitzkoppe rose dramatically, cloaked in patches of cloud that glimmered like silver against the deepening blue of the sky.

Nearby, a bouquet of freshly picked wildflowers rested in a small vase, their dazzling colours echoing the wild beauty of their surroundings. The gentle sound of a mountain stream could be heard in the distance, blending harmoniously with the occasional song of birds returning to their nests.

"What is this place?" Peri asked, taking in the serene surroundings.

Uneze's eyes sparkled with mischief. "It's a special place they use for honeymooners."

Peri grinned, her heart fluttering at the thought. "It's our honeymoon, nice. How was our wedding?"

"Amazing. White doves and all that romantic stuff," Uneze replied, his playful tone making her giggle.

"Ah, the true romantic," Peri teased, raising her glass. After just a few bites, they sank into the soft embrace of a double swing chair.

Uneze entwined his fingers with hers, and the world around them faded as he leant in, capturing her lips in a kiss that had been long anticipated. "Worth the wait," Peri murmured, a teasing bite on her lip as she savoured the moment.

But the blissful spell was broken when Uneze's face suddenly twisted in confusion. "What's that? Over there, look." He pointed into the distance, jumped off the swing chair, and reached for the binoculars.

Peri squinted, spotting a flash of yellow against the rugged brown of the Namibian mountains. "What now?" she asked.

"Over there, look. Alistair, in yellow. Who is he fighting with?" Uneze's tone shifted, urgency replacing the earlier lightness.

"I can't work it out, but it's gotta be Alex," Peri replied, her heart racing. Uneze swore under his breath.

"God, Alistair and his goddamn timing again." Uneze chuckled.

"What are they doing on the edge of a cliff? What the hell?" Panic laced Peri's voice.

"Stay here," Uneze commanded, his eyes never leaving the troubling scene as he called for the server. He gestured toward the distant commotion, desperation lacing his words as he ordered him to call a ranger.

"By the time they get there, it'll be too late," Peri said, her voice almost trembling.

"Yeah, I know," Uneze admitted, his jaw clenched. "But it feels better than doing nothing. Let's get all of this packed up, and at least we can drink the wine later."

By the time they, along with the server, placed everything into baskets and rushed back to the campsite, the colourful figure on the mountainside had gone. Uneze scanned the trail, shaking his head. "Let's go to the entrance and wait to see what the hell happened."

Peri scoffed and muttered, "Oh, waiting to see if another one of the group has done something stupid; my favourite new hobby."

Gone was the romantic atmosphere between them. Peri sank into her chair, her fingers drumming nervously against the wooden armrest.

Uneze paced nearby, each step a silent march of tension. The heavy thud of boots echoed through the campsite as Alistair stormed in, his rucksack swinging wildly from his wrist.

A storm brewed behind his eyes, and his scowl directed at Uneze was sharp enough to cut through the thickening silence.

"What was that up there on the cliff?" Uneze asked.

Alistair shrugged, dismissing her concern with a wave of his hand. "It was nothing, just Alex being a total dick." His words were laced with contempt, resonating like a warning bell ringing in Peri's ears.

"Alex?" Uneze echoed, disbelief etched across her face.

"Yeah, Alex. He's got you all fooled." Alistair's posture was rigid, a barbed-wire fence of frustration.

Peri's heart raced, the tension knitting her stomach into a tight knot. "Is Alex alright?" she ventured, her voice barely above a whisper.

"Probably just a bruised ego, but yes." Alistair's bravado was briming with menace as he continued, "He had the smarts to walk away from me before I pushed him off that trail." With a huff, he stormed off, leaving an air heavy with unresolved conflict.

"Ugh, I can't face this right now," Peri muttered, forcing herself back into the chair as if it could halt her anxious thoughts.

Minutes dragged by like hours, and when Alex finally appeared through the gates, he seemed carefree, chatting animatedly with Anya and Johan, laughter spilling from his lips.

Uneze's cautious question pierced the jovial atmosphere. "Guys, everything alright out there?" His eyes darted between them, searching for clues.

"Yeah, it was great. Well worth the blisters and sore legs I'll have tomorrow," Johan chuckled.

Peri shuffled forward. "Can I ask about Alistair? I thought you all left together."

"Alistair has a chip on his shoulder. He flipped on Alex for no reason at all," Johan replied, his voice light, but the flicker in his eyes told another story.

"Alex, are you alright?" Peri's concern bubbled to the surface. "Yeah, it takes a lot more than an idiot like that to rattle me." His grin was defiant, but Peri saw the annoyance lurking just beneath.

"It looked like there was some sort of fight up there," Peri pointed out.

"He wanted a fight, but I just walked off." Alex's tone was casual, yet the tension in his jaw betrayed him.

"What about?" Peri pressed.

"I just made a comment that he didn't appreciate." Alex explained.

"Nothing new there then," Johan added, laughter attempting to break the tension of the moment.

"Great, as long as nothing happened, I'll see you all at dinner," Peri said, her voice steadier than she felt.

Peri and Uneze looked at each other with confused faces. "Just another day on safari," Uneze laughed as he grabbed her elbow and led her inside.

112 - MELANIE

The following day, a small plane carrying a hungover group of tourists descended toward Skeleton Coast. Below, a vast expanse of shimmering white sand unfolded like a soft blanket, twinkling under the brilliant sun. The gentle movement of the ocean waves played a soothing melody, lapping against the shore in a dance that beckoned travellers to explore.

The group trekked along the sandy path, their footsteps leaving temporary imprints on the wind-swept dunes. Skeletons of ancient shipwrecks peeked through the sand, their rusted metal and weathered wood telling tales of long-lost voyages. Laughter echoed as they discovered a bleached whale vertebra half-buried in the sand, its massive size evoking a sense of wonder.

The salty breeze tangled in their hair as the group excitedly piled into the buggies, engines roaring to life with a promise of adventure. As they tore across the golden sand dunes, their laughter could be heard all around, mingling with the crunch of tires on the soft grains. The buggies bounced and swerved, sending plumes of sand spiraling into the air. The thrill of the ride quickened their pulses, each rise and fall of the dunes igniting a sense of freedom.

Once they'd checked in to their unique, boat-shaped tents, Peri approached Melanie, who was laughing and chatting with Anya.

"Are you okay to sleep alone tonight, Melanie?" Peri asked.

"I think so. I mean, Alistair seems to have calmed down," Melanie replied.

"Exactly," Peri said. "I have the footage from the plane and from the hotel. Neither of them shows Alistair was involved. We can't see Alistair pushing you, and it looks like Dave's shoes in the corridor at the hotel. So, I think that now, with Dave gone, you should be safe."

"Really? So it was all in my head?" Melanie asked.

"On those two issues, yes, but the other incidents with Dave, we saw those, and they were real."

"You'll see your tent between mine and Uneze's, so we'll hear if anything happens; however, I hope you can start to enjoy this safari with your new friends."

"Yes, and I can't wait. We're going to have a party tonight in the sunken boat at the campsite. Do you and Uneze want to come?" Melanie asked

"The what?" Peri asked.

"There is an old boat in the sand behind the pool. It's set up for a bar, so we've booked ourselves in," Melanie explained.

"Thanks for the invite, but, you know, parties aren't really for us. We need to be sober enough to look after you," Peri said.

Melanie moved to the edge of a golden sand dune that rolled like waves under the afternoon sun. She sank down onto the cool, grainy surface, tucking her knees to her chest as the laughter of her friends echoed around her. The thrill of others sliding down the slopes filled the air, the excitement palpable, yet she remained untouched by it, lost in the deep darkness of her own mind.

Anya spotted her from the bustling group, the sun catching her hair in a halo as she walked over. With a curious smile, she settled next to Melanie, the warmth of their friendship bridging the quiet gap. "How does freedom taste?" she asked, her voice a gentle breeze that pulled Melanie back to the moment.

Melanie let out a shaky breath, the impact of the past lingering in her voice. "You have no idea. I can't believe he's really gone. Facing him when I get home is overwhelming, but I'll cross that bridge when I come to it." She glanced sidelong at Anya, a spark of mischief returning to her features. "I've already got a divorce lawyer set up."

"Okay, that's huge."

"I know, but you know what else is huge? Michelle and Dennis. How did I miss that? Or was I just really drunk?" Melanie asked.

"Not exactly; you've just been wrapped up in your own stuff," Anya chuckled, rolling her eyes. "Michelle's been helping Dennis make his wife jealous by flooding social media with selfies of them together. It was practically a full-time job for them, but now they're pretty into each other."

"They seem to be having a lot of fun, so who cares?" Melanie asked. "Anything else slip past me?"

"Emily made a move on Johan."

Melanie raised her hands in mock surrender. "What the hell? Sorry, that must have been tough."

Anya shrugged nonchalantly. "Not at all. He's a free man, and honestly, Emily isn't his type. Plus, she's a runaway bride, so it's not the perfect timing."

"Can I ask?" Melanie asked cautiously, "He's so gorgeous. Why isn't he with anyone?"

"He was, with a much younger girl—eighteen. One of his art students, and then it got complicated. Her dad found out and threatened Johan. It got nasty."

"What happened?" Melanie pressed, intrigued.

Anya shrugged her shoulders and tried to explain, "It was all wrong, but he fell for her. When her dad kicked her out, she moved in with us. It started off fine, until she tried to come between us. She'd drop hints, do things that twisted his perception of me. I could see it, but he was blind. I moved in with my brother, and that was it."

"You clearly sorted things out," Melanie confirmed.

"It took a while," Anya admitted, a tentative smile creeping across her face. "For the first time, it felt nice not to be in his shadow. I found myself—started yoga, travelled, got a great job, and even dated."

Melanie leant in, intrigued. "Oh, and?"

Anya let her fingers trace the rim of her water bottle and said, "It was incredible at first, you know? But every time he smiled at me, I found my thoughts drifting to Johan—his laugh, the way his eyes sparkled like sunlight on water. No matter how sweet my boyfriend was, he just couldn't match that magic. So, I ended it."

Melanie raised an eyebrow, curiosity etched on her face. "Did you still talk to Johan during that time?"

"Not a single word," Anya replied, her voice tight. "He vanished from my life as if he'd never existed. Then one night, as I swiped through

Tinder, there he was—his handsome face frozen in a snapshot. It felt like a knife twisting in my gut, those images of him glaring back at me, yet he'd cut me out of the pictures, reminding me that my best friend had erased me from his life without a trace."

"Why was he even on Tinder if he was with that girl?" Melanie frowned, her brow furrowing in confusion.

Anya's fingers curled into fists on the table. "That's what I wondered too, but I didn't have the courage to ask. I snapped screenshots of his profile, each click feeling like a betrayal, and swiped left."

"What does that mean?" Melanie asked, tilting her head.

"It means I'm not interested, but it also means he would see me there or find out soon enough. I spent an entire week in torment, my heart a mess, before I finally gave up," Anya said softly, taking a moment before she continued, "I took a leap and started seeing someone new. But then... everything shattered. My brother died in a car crash."

Melanie gasped, her expression shifting to one of deep sympathy. "Oh no, I'm so sorry."

"At the funeral, it was like the world paused when Johan walked in. He strode straight to me, and when he took my hand, it felt like the universe had realigned. It was like we were the only two people in the room and I forgot about everything that had happened."

"Did you discuss everything?" Melanie pressed.

"About his breakup? Sure, we touched on that. But I couldn't bring myself to tell him how I felt. It felt trivial in the moment. Since then, he's moved back in with me, and well, here we are."

Melanie gazed at her, a soft smile creeping across her lips. "And how does it feel having him around now?"

"Good," Anya said, a serene smile breaking across her face. "Easy. It's like wrapping myself in my favourite sweater after a long day. I feel like myself again."

Melanie's eyes sparkled with mischief. "Sounds to me like you're in love with him."

Anya's laughter rang out, but it held a hint of nervousness. "What? No way. I'm not in love with Johan."

"Really? You constantly compare everyone to him, and it bothers you when Emily shows interest in him. You seem whole again when he's near—sounds like love to me," Melanie said, a knowing spark in her eyes.

Anya paused, her smile firm as Melanie's words settled in. "Was it like that with you and Dave at the beginning?"

"Never," Melanie replied, her gaze shifting to the floor.

"I found love once, though—a great man, a wonderful soul. I miss him every day." Anya's heart ached at Melanie's admission as she looked at the sad expression in her eyes.

"Oh, I'm sorry. That must be hard, being in a loveless marriage and yearning for someone from your past."

"It is what it is," Melanie said softly, her fingers tapping on her phone. "But Johan is here. You need to do something about it."

Anya shook her head and muttered a quiet, "No."

"And one day, if I survive this safari, I'll find my love. I can't wait," Melanie said.

113 - MELANIE

After dinner, Uneze stood, used his little gong, and said, "Okay, so, tomorrow is a long day. We'll be leaving at dawn and heading down to the beach to see the shipwrecks, otters, and go out on a boat. We'll end the day on the lookout for sea lions. It's an ever-changing landscape that sees rolling sand dunes melt into vast salt pans, dry riverbeds, and rocky mountains. Bring suntan lotion or long sleeves. It's one of the most remote and unspoiled places on earth, and tomorrow it's yours to see."

The group let out a collective round of applause as Uneze suggested it was time to make a move towards the tents. Peri and Uneze exchanged a glance, hesitating for a moment, before going to their separate tents for the night.

The following morning, as Uneze stocked the rugged jeep, Melanie's shoulders sagged under an invisible weight, her gaze drifting to the horizon where the sun hung low, radiating long shadows across the dusty ground. The colours of the landscape felt muted to her, like a painting faded from too many sunlit days.

"Is it okay if I don't do the trip today?" Melanie's voice was barely above a whisper, laced with exhaustion. She ran her fingers over the worn cover of her Kindle, the texture offering a fleeting sense of comfort. "I think I need some alone time to think and just shake off all this mess."

Peri stalled for a moment,, then asked, "Are you sure?"

Melanie's nod was slow and deliberate, as if each movement took effort. "Yeah, I've got my Kindle. I'll just enjoy some time on the terrace. I know Dave's gone, but it's a huge deal for me. I'm exhausted, and I want to be away from Alistair."

"Well, if you are sure..." Peri said.

"One hundred percent. It's what I need." Her fingers tightened around the Kindle, a lifeline in her solitude. "What time will you be back?"

"After sunset. I'm sorry, it's a long tour."

"That's fine. Don't worry about me." A soft chuckle escaped Melanie's lips as she attempted to lift the heaviness from the moment. "As long as Dave is gone, then I'm safe. I want some me time, alone. And that pool is so tempting."

"Of course," Peri said.

"Great, well, today, I'm skipping it," Melanie said. "I'll see you later."

Melanie lingered near the edge of the campsite as the last groups of tourists strolled away, their laughter fading into the distance. The vivid greens of fresh grass brushed against her ankles, and the air danced with the sweet perfume of blooming flowers.

Once the chatter of voices faded, she snatched her phone, her fingers trembling slightly as she opened the tracking app to make sure Dave was back home and far from her. A chill of dread washed over her, and with a sharp intake of breath, she tossed the device onto the poolside table, its screen flickering in the sun. After a moment, she snatched it back and checked again to make sure she hadn't made a mistake. "Hell, no," she muttered.

Realising Dave was somewhere in the area, she strolled around the campsite, snapping photos of the scenery. Her gaze flitted to the video cameras, a sly smile creeping onto her lips as she noted their outward focus—none aimed at her.

On her second round, she memorised potential hideouts, shady areas, hidden by trees or buildings that would shield her from the moonlight and the glaring campsite floodlights. She placed two empty wine bottles in a hollowed tree trunk, draping leaves and branches over them with the care of a masterful artist, before doing the same in other spots and retreating to the sun terrace.

"Melanie? I thought you were on Safari today," Alex said.

"Right back at you," Melanie replied. "I couldn't face Alistair."

"Me neither. I'm working, having a computer day. I just came out to watch the sunset. I've been cooped up in that hotel lobby all day."

"I've been by the pool most of the day," Melanie said, pulling back her dress straps to show her bright red skin and tan lines. Raising her glass, she asked, "Do you want to join me?"

"Why the hell not?" he said, clinking his glass with hers.

Her gaze lingered on him, a flicker of curiosity igniting in her eyes, as if she were rediscovering a familiar landscape after a long absence. "How are you enjoying the safari?" she asked, tilting her head slightly, the question more than just a polite inquiry.

"Yeah, it's nice... different from what I expected," Alex replied, his fingers tapping nervously against the table's edge, a faint blush creeping up his cheeks. "I mean, I didn't really look at the itinerary much when I booked it."

"So, you really don't like Alistair, do you?" Melanie asked.

"No, I really don't," he muttered, a shadow crossing his face, as if the mere mention of Alistair darkened the room. "I didn't like Dave either, but at least he's gone."

"Is there a reason? You can't hate Alistair that much just because he never bought wine," she countered, a teasing lilt in her voice, but the undercurrent of seriousness was unmistakable.

Alex's expression hardened, the jovial atmosphere evaporating like the last drops of wine in his glass. "No, it's more than that. He gives me the creeps. I'm just trying to find out more about him than I already do. I've been doing background searches on him to find out what his story is."

"Why? Have you stalked all of us?" Melanie's eyes sparkled with a teasing glimmer.

"No, but Alistair is different." His tone shifted, a steely determination replacing the uncertainty. "Don't worry; I should have more proof soon, and it will all come out in the wash." He sighed, the burden of unsaid words pressing down on him. With a grateful nod, he gestured at his laptop. "Anyway, thanks for this. I'm going to get back to my laptop and finish up."

Melanie watched Alex leave, and she settled into a lounge chair, her eyelids drifting shut. In her mind, she conjured an image of Julius—tall and dashing, with a smile that melted her worries away. She could almost feel the warmth of his embrace, the intoxicating scent of his cologne wrapping around her like a comforting blanket. The memory of their stolen kisses danced on her lips, a bittersweet reminder of love shrouded in secrecy. She pondered unblocking his number, but instead, her fingers scrolled through Instagram, only to find his latest post—a mundane image of his dogs. Frustration bubbled within her, and she set the phone aside, allowing the soft echo of Julius's voice to envelop her, whispering sweet dreams of a life they could share.

The moment of bliss shattered as an unwelcome presence loomed above her. Dave's tanned face twisted in disapproval, his beer belly pushing against his belt as he crossed his arms. "So, this is how you want to spend your holiday? Sipping cocktails and pretending everyone else doesn't exist?"

"What are you doing here?" she snapped, surprise lacing her tone. "You were supposed to be with one of your bimbos in the UK right now."

"Not a chance. I can pay my way and crash wherever I want. You can't just get rid of me," he shot back, a taunting smirk creeping onto his lips. "That was your plan all along, wasn't it? To ditch me and have a nice holiday solo?"

"No, but now that you mention it..." she trailed off, her voice dripping with sarcasm.

"Everyone knows about your little 'nut stunt,' Mel. You think you can hide the truth forever? It'll come out; just wait." Dave growled, yanking her up from her chair by the elbow.

"Let go of me. You're hurting me." She gasped, wrenching her arms free and stomping away, anger fuelling her strides as she searched for anyone who could help her, bolting away from him.

"Where do you think you're going?" he called after her.

"Anywhere but here," she shouted back, fury propelling her toward the sanctuary of her hidden bottles, a whirlwind of desperate rage bubbling within her.

Melanie's pulse thundered in her ears, each beat igniting a fire that coursed through her veins. The echo of his footsteps haunted her, urging her to move quicker. Her fingers brushed against the rough bark of a gnarled tree, where she spotted the shimmer of glass hidden amongst the leaves. With a swift yank, she pulled out the bottle, the glass feeling both foreign and familiar in her grip. Melanie's breath quickened as she turned to face him, her resolve hardening like stone.

Her eyes flared, filled with equal parts fear and rage. With no time to think, she swung the bottle in a wide arc. The thick glass connected with the side of Dave's neck and shoulder with a dull thwack. The force of the impact sent him staggering, his hand instinctively flying up to the spot where pain now pulsed.

He crumpled to the floor in a heap, the air rushing from his lungs in a groan. The world around him spun as he tried to regain his senses, his body sprawled awkwardly on the cold tile. The bottle slipped from Melanie's trembling hand and clattered noisily onto the counter, the sound cutting through the heavy silence that followed.

Melanie stood frozen, her chest heaving, the reality of what she had done dawning on her as Dave lay motionless below her.

114 - MELANIE

Melanie's hands trembled as she stared at his limp form beside her. She pushed herself up, the world around her fading into silence. She looked around, hearing nothing except the rustle of tents and trees all around her.

Melanie stood at the crest of a steep, dusty hill, her silhouette stark against the golden horizon. Her chest heaved with exertion and fury as she gazed down at Dave's limp body sprawled before her, a mixture of anger and cold determination flickering across her face.

With a sudden, calculated motion, Melanie rummaged through his pockets and removed his wallet and personal belongings, shoving them deep in her pocket. She lashed out with her foot, the force sending Dave's body tumbling over the edge. The dry, loose earth gave way beneath him, and he rolled awkwardly, his limbs flailing like a ragdoll. Dust and pebbles cascaded in his wake, creating tiny clouds that caught the sunlight in a grim spectacle.

As he descended, his body collided with jagged rocks and sparse tufts of brittle grass, each impact reverberating through the air with a dull thud. The hill's incline grew sharper, accelerating his descent until, with a final jolt, he disappeared into the shadowy grove of thorny trees at the base. The branches groaned and snapped under his weight, their sharp edges snagging at his clothes as he came to a halt in the underbrush.

Melanie stood motionless for a moment, her gaze fixed on the spot where Dave's body now lay hidden among the trees. The oppressive heat and the distant cry of a scavenging bird were the only witnesses to her act. Finally, she turned away, her expression unreadable, leaving the scene to the unrelenting wilderness of Namibia.

115 - MELANIE

Melanie felt her stomach twist and turn as she clutched the bottle tightly to her chest, the cool glass a stark contrast to the burning heat in her cheeks. She felt the weight what she'd done pressing down on her shoulders, but there was a strange thrill that flickered in her stomach. Her legs trembled, as if they were made of whipped cream, and she stumbled into the bathroom, the scent of soap and disinfectant tickling her nostrils. She sank onto the toilet, her breaths coming in shallow gasps, trying to steady the whirlwind of panic that threatened to engulf her.

The distant sound of laughter and chatter broke through her daze, pulling her back to reality. She leant against the cool tiles, feeling the rough texture scrape against her fingertips as she pushed herself upright. With a heavy exhale, she plastered a smile on her face, though the effort felt like lifting a boulder.

"Alex?" Her voice wavered as surprise filled her words. "Finished your work already?"

Alex leant casually against a tree, his expression brightening with a hint of mischief. "I decided the sunset was too good to miss." He cocked his head, concern flickering in his eyes as he studied her. "Are you alright? You look... I don't know, sick."

A small wave of embarrassment washed over her, and she shook her head slightly. "I'm fine, thanks. Just had a moment when I thought I saw Dave, and it got me all... flustered. Today was our wedding anniversary. I even have this, look. It was to surprise him. It's our wedding invite from all those years ago."

"He's in the UK. You're safe now." Alex stepped closer, his hand resting gently on her shoulder, grounding her in the present.

She inhaled deeply, the warmth of his touch offering brief comfort. "I guess it's still surreal." With a reassuring smile, Alex glanced toward the fading light outside.

"I know. Anyway, see you at dinner in a bit. The others should be back soon."

The flickering shimmer of the campfire drew her in, its warmth beckoning like an old friend. As she approached the group, the lack of voices became even more inviting. She pulled her bottle from her bag, topped up her glass, and sat on one of the empty chairs.

"Are you all alone?" A woman's voice cut through the crackling flames. Melanie tilted her head, feigning casualness.

"Nope. I just didn't feel up to a whole day out in the sun, so I opted to stay here. Oddly enough, I spent most of the day in the sun anyway. But sun and pool is different from sun and sand."

"I couldn't agree more," the woman replied with a sympathetic smile. "We're at the end of our safari, and I'm looking forward to civilisation when we get to Cape Town in a couple of days."

Melanie nodded, her mind briefly drifting to the chaos she had just left behind. "You're going the other way from us. We came from there."

"I'm a bit sick of camping, to be honest. No, I'm sick of my group. They are so boring."

"Ha." Melanie laughed loudly, the sound bubbling up from somewhere deep inside her. "My group is the opposite of boring. It's like everyone has issues one way or another and has come here to figure things out with a bunch of strangers."

Their conversation paused as a man tossed another log onto the fire, the sparks dancing upward like tiny fireflies. Seizing the moment, Melanie's heart thudded in her chest as she discreetly pulled her wedding invite from her pocket. With a swift flick of her wrist, she cast it into the flames, watching as it curled and blackened, a silent declaration of her newfound freedom.

The woman squinted at the flames, her gaze fixated on a charred piece of paper curling at the edges, its bright colours fading to ash. "Was that a passport?" she asked, a hint of curiosity threading through her voice.

Melanie fidgeted with her glass, the cool glass slipping slightly in her grip. "No," she replied, her heart racing. "It was a wedding invitation in the shape of a passport. We're not together anymore." The words tumbled out like marbles rolling down a hill, each one battling to land first.

"Ah, hence the need to be alone today and that strange, sickly look on your face." The woman nodded knowingly, her eyes softening.

"Exactly," Melanie replied, a smile creeping across her face as she lifted her glass, its clink echoing like a toast to unearthing buried emotions. "Let's cheers to moving on, forgetting the past, and to whatever comes next." The woman mirrored her gesture, their glasses meeting with a satisfying chime, the sound blending with the crackling fire—a bittersweet symphony of new beginnings.

"I like the sound of that," Melanie said, and for a moment, the air was thick with hope. "Look, that's my group. I'd best go. Thanks for the company."

"Thanks to you, too. It was nice to meet you. Good luck with whatever comes next."

116 - ALEX

After two days on Skeleton Coast, they finally made it to a beautiful, luxurious campsite in the heart of Etosha National Park, where they were due to stay for three days. As they checked in, they watched other campers sit around their crackling fire, roasting nuts and sharing stories as they watched the sky turn shades of pink and orange. The campfire flickered and danced, casting long shadows across the forest floor below them.

"Tonight we'll view and listen to the sounds of the desert from the viewing terrace of our campsite. Tomorrow, we are going deep into the salt pans in an open vehicle game drive. It's the closest you'll get to the animals you've been dreaming of. We'll be driving across salt pans, and as it rained recently, we may get to see flamingos, too."

"Dinner is at six, then at seven we'll all hit the viewing terrace, and Uneze will explain what you are seeing, or rather hearing," Peri said.

Anya and Melanie laughed together in quiet whispers; the sun warmed their faces, and the sound of their giggles danced through the air. They were first off the bus and grabbed their welcome drinks as they admired the beauty of the lodge. With their tent numbers and a map of the campsite in hand, they watched Emily, her eyes sparkling as she nudged Johan, her laughter mingling with flirty banter as they approached.

Michelle and Dennis seemed lost in whispered conversations and shared glances, their world a bubble of intimacy until they reached the entrance and rejoined the world.

"Bro, come on. The tent waits for no one," Anya called out.

"Same for you, Emily," Michelle said.

Emily rolled her eyes, ran her fingers down Johan's t-shirt, shrugged her shoulders, and reluctantly moved forward.

After a flurry of activity in the cramped bathroom, the sound of water cascading down and the rustle of towels filled the air. Finally, they exited fresh and invigorated, laughter spilling into the evening as they cracked open their bottles of chosen drinks.

Stepping onto the terrace, they were greeted by a breathtaking sight of oranges and purples as the sun hung low on the horizon. The distant silhouettes of safari animals meandered gracefully across the landscape, their movements enhanced by the pulsating sounds of the African wilderness—a chorus of rustling leaves, distant calls, and the soft patter of hooves on earth. Side by side with fellow travellers, they found themselves lost in the moment, eyes wide with wonder as nature performed its evening spectacle.

Alistair perched alone in the dim corner of the bustling terrace, his gaze flitting over the animated group, laughter and chatter hanging around him like an uninvited breeze. He shifted his weight, hands clasped behind his back, every instinct urging him to join, yet he remained suspended in silence, looking at people's bottles and glasses.

"I'm sorry, Alistair. I didn't get your wine order, so I didn't get you any. I'm sure you can get a drink from the bar," Uneze said.

Alistair remained silent, hovering with his hands behind his back, his neck straining as he looked for a full bottle of wine.

"Here, have some of mine," Johan offered, extending a bottle with a casual smile.

Just then, Alex erupted as if from nowhere, his presence slicing through the air like a thunderbolt. "Hell no, get your own drink," he barked, eyes blazing with accusation. "I'm sick of you taking, taking, taking, and never giving back. This isn't how the world works. Wine is expensive over here, and we all paid for it. You should buy your own. If you can afford to come on this safari, then you can afford to buy some goddamn drink, too."

The laughter around them faded, curiosity piquing as the group turned to witness the unfolding drama. Alistair's heart raced, his grip tightening around the glass as he met Alex's fiery gaze. "What's your problem?" he stammered, frustration bubbling within him.

"You. You are my problem. I know who you are. I know what you did." Alex shot back, venom dripping from his words. A hush fell, the strain of

Alex's outburst hanging for everyone to catch. Alex reached into his wallet and flashed a photo of a smiling boy.

"Oh, so exactly what is it that I did?" Alistair questioned.

"You murdered my son and my wife," Alex accused.

Alistair stared for a moment, jaw agape, and asked, "What the hell are you talking about?"

Alex reached for his phone and pulled out a picture of his son. "This is my son." He turned to the group and said, "My son was beaten to death by this man." He turned in a slow circle, making sure every single person in the group saw the face of the boy. "He was left in a pool of blood. He was eighteen years old; he was about to go to uni. He had his life ahead of him, and this thug here murdered him in cold blood."

Gasps rippled through the crowd, and Alistair's breath quickened, the space closing in as he struggled to comprehend the storm gathering around him. "I don't even know him," he protested, voice trembling.

"Liar," Alex protested. Alex gripped Alistair's arm.

Alistair jerked away, desperation igniting his defiance. "Get your hands off me."

"So, you're denying it?" Alex screamed.

Alistair scoffed, shook his head, and replied, "If I've not been arrested for it, then I guess you have no proof."

"Oh, I have proof. My private investigator has found it. You are a dead man, Alistair. As soon as you set foot back on UK soil, you will be locked away for life."

Alistair was silent for a moment; he threw the glass to the ground and turned away. "You have no idea what you're talking about."

The confrontation spiralled, accusations flying like darts as the truth twisted and curled between them. Uneze and Peri stood still, arms crossed, their presence a silent plea for resolution as the tension crackled in   the   air.
Alex's voice sliced through the tranquil ambiance, eyebrows arched skeptically. "So, you didn't take money from Dave to come here and kill his wife?"

Alistair shot back, his eyes narrowing, "Hell no. Of course not." His fists clenched, fingers digging into the worn fabric of his shorts, betraying his unease.

Alex, his tone dripping with sarcasm, screamed, "A loser like you—broke enough to hustle for cash, a paid bully—somehow pulls off an expensive safari? You can't even buy a bottle of wine to drown your sorrows in." He crossed his arms, a smug grin plastered on his face, revelling in his accusation.

Alistair shrugged, a defiant glimmer in his eye. "I just like to get things for free. Especially booze. Is that a crime?" His half-smile belied the tension, a challenge lingering in the air between them.

Peri, her patience waning, rolled her eyes as she interjected. "Enough, guys. As entertaining as this little drama is, I think everyone else wants to enjoy the sunset in peace."

Dennis chimed in, eyes sparkling with mischief, "Oh, no, this is much more interesting."

Uneze stepped forward, his expression serious, cutting through the squabble, urging them to step away from the gathering shadows and the sinking sun. "Guys, take it over there, out of view and out of sight, please."

Alex's voice trembled with raw emotion, his fists clenched at his sides. "They don't know who they're dealing with," he muttered, shaking his head as if trying to dispel the nightmare playing in his mind. "They need to know that camping with them is..."

As Alex turned away, Alistair snatched Dennis's drink from the table and gulped it down in one swift motion, the liquid burning his throat yet somehow grounding him.

"What the hell is all this about?" Uneze's voice cut through the murmur of uncertainty.

"You heard me," Alex shot back, fury igniting his words.

"Come on," Alistair laughed nervously, "He's talking nonsense. I've never even met his wife."

The denial hung heavy in the air, but Alex's piercing gaze only intensified. "So, you admit you've met my son?" He pressed, his eyes narrowing into slits.

"No. I don't know what you're on about." Alistair's voice cracked, desperation creeping in.

"Keep him here," Alex ordered, sprinting towards his tent, the crunch of grass underfoot echoing his urgency.

"Alistair, while he's gone, you need to tell us what's happening," Uneze urged, his brow puckered with concern.

"I... I don't know," Alistair stammered, rubbing his forehead in frustration, as if erasing the confusion that clung to him.

"Come on, man, for your sake. Alex is accusing you of some serious stuff." Uneze's voice grew louder, pushing Alistair to the edge, nearer to some sort of confession.

With a heavy sigh, Alistair stalled for a moment,, his mind racing. "He's got the wrong man, honestly. I don't know what game he's playing." The words slipped out, a feeble attempt to deflect the growing tension.

Alex's footsteps thundered back, an envelope clutched tightly in his hand. He thrust it towards Alistair, the fury in his eyes unmistakable. "Here, this is all the proof I need."

Alistair's heart sank as his eyes scanned the contents, confusion painting his features. "This is just a police report about a dead boy. There's nothing in here that says I did it."

"Keep reading, fool. It's all in there," Alex snapped, the desperation in his voice rising like smoke.

Alistair stepped away, seeking better light, the world around him fading as he focused on the papers. Sweat formed on his brow, his breath quickening with each line he read. "This says nothing at all."

"What? Can't you read? It's all in there." Alex shouted, his voice a thunderclap in the silence.

"I can't see my name or my face." Alistair waved the folder, frustration bubbling over. "Now, if you're done, I'd like to enjoy my glass of wine."

With that, he stormed back toward the group, eyes fixed on Johan's bottle as if it were his lifeline. But in a move that left everyone breathless, Alistair hurled the folder into the campfire. Flames danced hungrily, devouring the evidence as Alex lunged forward, horror etched across his face. "No. What the hell did you do?"

"I put an end to this freaky, wild story in your head. You're crazy." Alistair shot back, triumph lighting his features, but Alex was relentless.

"How did you get your head so far up your own ass?" Alex screamed, fury and determination mingling in his voice, as the flames crackled mockingly behind him, consuming the remnants of his once solid proof. "I can get copies by tomorrow. You aren't getting away with this so easily."

117 - UNEZE

"Right, that's it," Uneze called out, firm and resolute as he stood with arms crossed, his jaw clenched. The flicker of the campfire cast stark shadows across his face, accentuating the tension rippling through the group.

"Alex, Alistair. Calm down," Peri intervened, her tone soothing yet edged with urgency. The crackling flames mirrored the simmering emotions between the two friends, who were still bristling from their earlier confrontation.

"Right, we're doing some tent swapping," Uneze announced, his eyes darting between them like a hawk assessing its prey. "Alistair, you're in the tent to my right. Alex, you're on my left. If I hear even a blade of grass moving during the night, you're both off this tour. I'll have camp security keeping watch right outside all night."

Alistair's indignation erupted like a geyser. "Why me? I did nothing wrong. He's the freak." He pointed an accusing finger at Alex, whose face was flushed from anger.

Alex raised his hands defensively, but Uneze was already closing the distance, gripping his shoulder firmly. "Enough. To your tents, both of you."

Later, as Peri balanced plates of food and carefully made her way to the tents, she delivered the selection of grilled meats and vegetables.

Uneze sat cross-legged, his gaze locked on the dimly lit fabric walls that separated the two boys. The air was thick with tension, and he nodded to the security guard, signalling for vigilance. "Stay here; I'll be back in five minutes," he instructed.

"So, what are we going to do?" Peri asked, concern threading through her words as she placed a plate in front of Uneze.

"Alistair already said he was leaving, so we'll make that happen tomorrow. Maybe Alex was just drunk," he shrugged, though the uncertainty in his eyes contradicted his casual demeanour.

"He didn't look it," Peri replied, crossing her arms as she studied Uneze's expression.

"Well, why did he flip over a glass of wine? Alistair seemed believable to me." Uneze said.

"Then why did he burn that file?" Peri shot back, her voice rising slightly in frustration.

"I have no idea," Uneze admitted, his gaze drifting towards the flickering lights of the camp.

"Ask your friend in head office to get in touch with the police and do a background check on Alistair. Maybe if we have proof, we can get him off the tour tomorrow," Uneze suggested.

"I'll talk to him first thing in the morning; he'll have calmed down then," Peri said.

Uneze sighed, the burden of responsibility heavy on his shoulders. "I guess we're on babysitting duty for two days then. How are all the others?"

"Drunk and amused," she replied, a hint of a smile breaking through her concern. "They think the whole thing is hilarious."

"Thankfully, that's something at least," he said.

Peri grabbed a potato from the plate and said, "No one likes Alistair. What Alex said just confirmed their theory that Alistair and Dave were in on a plan together. Melanie is pretty shocked, but the girls are with her. She'll have a hangover from hell tomorrow."

"Good. So, as far as they're concerned, we're good. It was just a man fight?" Uneze asked with scepticism in his tone.

"Yep," Peri replied with softness rekindling in her voice. "I'm going back to them. I'll come back here once they're all settled in for the night. I'll stay with you if that's okay—double the ears."

Peri strolled back to the group, a bright smile lighting up her face as laughter bubbled from her lips. "I'd like to say the party's over, but clearly, it's not," she chirped, her voice dancing with amusement.

"What happened down there?" Melanie asked.

"Nothing much," Peri replied, motioning toward Dennis with an amused grin. "We moved your stuff from your tent to the end tent, Alex's spot, and Alex's tent is flanking Uneze's and mine. There's a security guard keeping an eye on everything tonight."

"Emily, hands off the security guard; he's got a job to do," Michelle teased, her laughter ringing through the air.

"Your side of the tent is empty, at least. I'm guessing you'll be with Dennis?" Emily shot back, her voice tinged with irritation.

"So, how is everyone feeling about that showdown?" Peri asked.

"It was fun," Dennis laughed, a twinkle of adventure in his eyes, "but I've got more fun things to do." He tugged on Michelle's hand, leading her away toward his tent.

"Melanie?" Peri asked her tone shifting slightly. Melanie squeezed Anya's hand tightly, her gaze serious as she replied, "I need to speak to Alex and find out what he meant about Dave paying Alistair to kill me."

"I hear you but do it in the morning. Both of them are too angry to make any sense right now. To be honest, I don't think Alistair will dare step out of that tent until morning," Peri reassured, her tone firm yet gentle.

Peri slipped into Uneze's tent, the fabric rustling softly around her. She fluffed the pillow beside him, his scent wrapping around her like a warm blanket. As she nestled under the thin bedsheet, her arms instinctively wrapped around his strong arms, and she placed a tender kiss on Uneze's cheek. "Goodnight," she whispered, her heart fluttering.

"Mmmmm, welcome back," he murmured, turning slightly toward her, a sleepy smile creeping onto his face. "Who are you? James or Peri?" he teased, an amused twinkle in his eyes.

"Is it important?" She replied coyly, her body inching closer as her fingers lightly traced his chest, their breaths mingling in the intimate space.

"Not really," he said, closing the distance between them, finally pressing his lips against hers. Time seemed to stand still as they savoured the moment, a longing fulfilled, until their playful movements accidentally illuminated the tent, sending a burst of light spilling into the cosy darkness.

"Oops." Peri giggled, pulling back, their laughter echoing softly against the tent walls.

"That was probably a bad idea," she said, her cheeks flushed.

"It definitely wasn't," Uneze shot back, a grin playing on his lips.

"We are in the middle of a row of tents, with a security guard outside," she whispered, a note of concern creeping into her voice.

"If we do this, tomorrow morning everyone will have heard everything." Peri laughed.

"I can be quiet," he teased, his eyes sparkling with mischief.

"Oh, sweetie. I can't," Peri replied, placing a soft finger on his lips, silencing him.

"Alright, I'll be patient, again," Uneze said, flicking the light switch off, plunging them back into soft darkness.

"Goodnight," Peri whispered, turning away from him, a smile lingering on her lips as the night wrapped around them like a secret.

118 - ALISTAIR

At breakfast, Alistair sat hunched over his plate at the far end of the table, fork scraping against porcelain with a discordant clatter, his brow etched with a deep scowl. His eyes, dark and stormy, flickered up only to cast accusatory glances at Alex, who breezed in as though the previous night's confrontation had never happened.

Anya's voice broke the silence as she invited Alex to join her and Melanie. "Are you okay, Alex?" she asked.

"Yeah, I'm sorry I did that in front of everyone. I planned to do it in private." Alex's response was calm, yet the quick flicker of rage in Alistair's direction in his gaze betrayed him.

Anya chuckled lightly, though her laughter felt forced. "Well, with everything else that's happened in the last couple of days, it's been too quiet. We needed a bit of scandal."

"I didn't want scandal, I just wanted the truth," Alex replied sharply, his jaw tightening as he looked over at Alistair, who was now pushing his food around the plate, refusing to meet anyone's eyes.

"And you didn't get it," Anya probed, her brow arching as she studied Alex's face.

"Nope. But he knows I'm on to him. That's better than nothing. He knows he isn't going to get away with it." Alex's voice was steady, but the tension in his shoulders suggested otherwise.

"Are you going to be okay on the trip with him today?" Anya asked, concern etched on her face.

"Sure, I'll just ignore him. After last night, he's going to want to be the centre of attention and defend himself from my accusations. That will frustrate him more than anything else." Alex's smirk hinted at a simmering confidence.

"Or maybe he'll carry on sulking all day," Anya replied as Peri joined the group, followed by the scent of fresh beauty products.

"Peri, did you have a good night's sleep?" Anya asked, her voice laced with playful teasing.

"No, not really. I was too busy wondering about all of you guys."

Anya and Melanie exchanged knowing glances, laughter bubbling up between them. "Yes, that's the reason you didn't sleep well," Melanie quipped, her eyes sparkling with mischief.

Peri felt the heat rise to her cheeks as Anya added, "You do know that tent walls are very thin, James?"

Peri's mouth fell open in shock, and she plopped onto the bench, pressing her fingers to her lips in a desperate plea for silence. "Shhh, please," she whispered, wide-eyed and mortified.

"It's our little secret, but honestly, all this James talk has been driving me crazy. Just do him already—get it out of your system," Melanie said.

"Promise me you won't say anything to anyone," Peri insisted, her voice barely above a whisper.

"We promise. It's the least I can do for all those times you've lent me your tent," Melanie replied, a smirk still plastered on her face. "And now I see why you were always so keen to do it."

Peri buried her face in her hands, laughter mixing with embarrassment as Uneze strolled up behind her and greeted the group.

119 - PERI

With a flurry of excitement, the group fumbled to grab their day sacks, zippers clinking as they zipped up pockets filled with snacks and cameras.

They clambered into the game viewer as Peri pulled Emily aside and asked, "Are you going to be okay today?"

Emily forced a smile, but her eyes betrayed her turmoil. "Yeah, I'll be fine. It's the distraction I need to keep my mind off this mess," she replied, glancing away towards her sister. "I don't know what I'm going to do if I have a mini string bean. I can't do this on my own, and after what I did to him, he won't take me back. Do I look like someone who could be a single mum?"

Peri studied her, a spark of amusement lighting in her eyes. "I think you've changed since you joined us. You've made friends, you've lightened up, you've, well, grown up a lot."

Emily crossed her arms, her brow furrowing deeper. "Alright, but I'm still not going to be able to do this."

"Don't be so hard on yourself," Peri urged gently, a smile pulling at her lips. "Did you ever think you'd camp in a tent with no electricity, no private facilities, and face the world in shorts and t-shirts?"

Emily let out a loud, snort like laugh. "Well, no, of course not."

"Well, if your worst fear comes true," Peri said, her tone steady and warm, "then I think you'll embrace it like a pro. You've already proved that you are much stronger than you think you are."

With a sudden rush of emotion, Emily stepped forward, pulling Peri into a tight embrace. "You're right," she said, her voice muffled against Peri's shoulder. "If I survive this safari, then I can survive everything."

120 - PERI

Duma, perched confidently on a metal chair bolted to the front of the truck, seemed almost carved out of the rugged landscape himself. His skin gleamed under the relentless African sun, the lines on his face telling stories of a lifetime spent in the wild.

Alex dropped heavily onto the seat next to Emily, their shoulders jarring together. She was already murmuring, her words tumbling over themselves in anticipation of the adventure that lay ahead.

Beside Duma, a rifle rested within arm's reach, a silent guardian. With the ease of a maestro commanding an orchestra, he swung a long poker stick, pointing toward the horizon. "Over there." he called into the crackling microphone, his voice charged with energy. "Zebra—hundreds of them—and just beyond, springbok grazing... but they're not alone. See the lioness watching them?"

The truck travelled through the ochre-coloured national park, kicking up clouds of dust that hung in the air like smoke.

Duma's running commentary was as vivid as the land itself. "We've got lions and elephants in abundance, but keep an eye out for the leopard. It's shy, a phantom among the dense vegetation. And then there's the black rhino—a relic from another age."

"Do you think we'll get close enough to see them properly?" Dennis asked.

"Close enough, if luck's on our side," Duma answered. "Patience, my friend. The waterholes will be teeming after last night's storm."

"And can we touch them?" Dennis added with a grin.

Michelle snorted. "Sure, if you want to lose an arm—or your life."

Laughter rippled through the truck as Dennis muttered something about selfies. But their humour was short-lived as a towering giraffe materialised from the trees. Cameras clicked in a frenzy, capturing its every movement. The giraffe seemed almost mythical, its tall frame bending and swaying as it nibbled the treetop canopy.

Ahead, a coalition of lions sprawled across a sun-warmed rock. Cubs tumbled over one another, swiping at their siblings. The truck slowed, the passengers' chatter hushed to whispers.

"Can we get any closer?" Alistair asked with a note of urgency in his words.

Duma shot him a pointed look. "Trust me; this is as close as you want to get."

Alistair wasn't satisfied. His hands braced against the edge of the vehicle as he shoved himself through the pop-up roof.

Duma, seated nearby, barked a warning in Swahili, but Alistair paid no attention. Dennis passed him a selfie stick, egging him on.

"Idiots," Michelle hissed, grabbing at Dennis's arm to keep him from joining the spectacle.

Alistair stretched the selfie stick to its limit, leaning dangerously far. Just then, the truck rolled forward, and he was forced to retreat under Duma's glare.

The vehicle edged away, stirring the tall grass, and that's when it happened. A lion stepped into view, its movements liquid and precise. The passengers froze.

Peri darted a glance at Uneze, her expression a mixture of questioning and forced calm. She managed a shaky smile, but when a lion's rough tongue brushed her arm through the open window, her composure shattered.

She yanked her arm inside, shifting closer to Uneze. "Is this normal?" she demanded, her voice cracking.

"Of course," Uneze replied dryly, though his gaze flicked warily to the circling predator. "We're on safari, after all."

The lion's eyes fixed on the truck. A roar split the air—raw, thunderous, and terrifying. The truck felt like a fragile bubble amidst the predator's charge. The group huddled together, some gripping seats, others each other. Fear crackled through the air like a wildfire.

Duma's voice sliced through the tension. "Stay calm. Do not move!"

The lion stopped abruptly, muscles taut, a storm of fury contained in its imposing frame. It stared them down for an eternal moment before turning away, disappearing into the bush as silently as it had appeared.

The group exhaled collectively.

Dennis and Alistair seemed fuelled by a reckless need to outdo one another. With cameras poised, they recorded every movement of the retreat. Adrenaline sharpened their focus, the beast's raw power etched into their frames like a scene stolen from a fevered dream—or a nightmare made real.

Uneze, catching their foolish intent, barked a warning. "Sit down. Don't you dare pop those dim heads out of the roof." His voice cut through the loud chatter, but their cameras remained locked on the unfolding spectacle.

The tension in the truck cracked, giving way to whispered prayers and nervous laughter. Relief poured out in shaky exhalations, though unease lingered like the echo of a predator's growl.

"They're not following," Duma muttered, his voice steady but clipped. His knuckles remained bone-white on the wheel, betraying the fragility of his calm.

"That was... unreal," Alex murmured, his voice breaking the fragile quiet.

"Right?" Peri said, her tone tinged with awe.

Alex leaned forward slightly, his expression softening. "My late wife loved lions. She always dreamt of seeing them in the wild. That's why I'm here—to take her on this journey, even if it's only in spirit." His voice cracked slightly at the end, but he straightened, his hands gripping the edge of the seat. "Mission accomplished."

Peri's face softened, her words tender. "I'm happy for you, Alex. That's beautiful."

Emily reached over and stroked his arm. "It's more than beautiful. It's romantic," she said softly.

Alex nodded, retreating into his seat, his smile unguarded and full of meaning. For the first time in the trip, the lines on his face seemed lighter, as though he had laid a piece of his burden to rest.

121 - PERI

The day stretched on. Elephants ambled with slow thuds, giraffes stretched for leaves atop the highest canopies, zebras merged into hypnotic stripes, and lions prowled with regal indifference. The truck hummed with energy, though fatigue began to weigh on the passengers.

Just as their enthusiasm waned, the vehicle rolled to a halt. Ahead, a herd of elephants loomed, a living barricade of immense, grey titans. Trunks swayed and flapped, their massive bodies asserting a silent command: wait. As the group watched, more elephants emerged from the grass, encircling the truck like shadowy phantoms. The first, biggest elephant's ears flared, its tusks gleaming like ivory blades. It stared at the truck with an intensity that made the air feel suffocating.

"Oh, shit," Emily whispered, gripping Johan's hand tightly, her knuckles white.

Anya's response was brittle, more for her own reassurance than anyone else's. "It's fine. The ranger knows what he's doing."

The beasts moved with purpose, their movements.

Duma's voice rang out, calm but commanding. "Stay calm. They're alert. Loud noises will aggravate them."

Alistair raised his camera. "Smile for the camera," he taunted, aiming at a lioness sniffing curiously in his direction.

"I don't feel good about this," Michelle muttered, her eyes darting between the advancing beast and its companions blocking the path. "They look like they want to squash us flat and serve us for dinner."

A hush fell, the quiet so dense it seemed to absorb the sound of breath. Duma's voice cut through the tension. "Stay calm. Don't move. These are wild animals; we're intruders in their world."

Alistair ignored the warning. With a grin that bordered on maniacal, he slipped through the skylight and perched precariously on the roof. His selfie stick extended like a challenge to the giant.

The elephant froze, its trunk curling inward before snapping toward the truck. The sound came next—a trumpeting blast so powerful it rattled their bones. It wasn't just a warning; it was a declaration of dominance.

The trunk lashed out, swiping Alistair's selfie stick from his hands. The stick spiralled through the air, clattering to the ground as gasps erupted from the group.

"Alistair." Uneze's voice cracked with rage and terror, but it was swallowed by the elephant's next step, a thunderous declaration of its supremacy.

"I need to get my phone," Alistair called as he tried to move into a lying position to be able to slide nearer to his device. He lurched forward, trying to reach for the ground, failing with each wide movement of his arms.

The massive ears flared again, each flap like a war banner unfurled. Its tusks the perfect blend of beauty and destruction. The passengers huddled together, wide-eyed and frozen, as the elephant loomed closer, a force of nature that no human could hope to defy.

The truck lurched suddenly. A brutal shove from the elephant sent it reeling. Tires spun uselessly, kicking up plumes of dust. Inside, panic erupted.

"Move. Move." Uneze shouted, his voice commanding, trying to cut through the panic.

Duma's grip on the wheel faltered. "I can't go anywhere with that idiot on top of the truck." he snapped, his voice tight with rising panic.

Above, Alistair was transfixed by the unfolding scene. After grabbing the phone that Dennis had slid through, He adjusted it, aiming for the perfect shot. "Just… one more angle," he muttered, his tone eerily detached.

And then, it happened.

The ground beneath them seemed to vanish. The truck tilted violently, the world shifting sideways. Tires scraped against loose dirt, and then came the crash—deafening, bone-shaking. Something massive slammed into the vehicle with terrifying force.

Metal screeched and groaned as the truck rocked again, teetering on the edge of collapse. The elephant's next shove sealed their fate. The truck flipped.

Time fractured into surreal fragments. Bodies tumbled like leaves in a storm, screams mingling with the grinding of metal and the shatter of glass.

The world spun with it—bodies tumbled; screams mingled with the grinding metal. Time seemed to warp, the seconds drawn out in a brutal, disorienting rush. And then—silence.

The world, upside down, settled into a strange stillness.

The air was thick with dust. The truck was no longer a vehicle but a crumpled shell. It was a moment frozen in time, each heartbeat louder than the last as those trapped tried to make sense of the chaos, their minds reeling.

What happens next?

Grab a copy of the next book: Murmurs of the Wild.

ABOUT THE AUTHOR

Gwen Courtman, originally from Manchester, UK, has called Italy home for most of her adult life. She moved to Italy following her heart, and today, she divides her time between the serene Italian lakes and the African island of Zanzibar. It is here, gazing out over the emerald waters of the Indian Ocean, that Gwen becomes fully immersed in the captivating lives of her fictional characters, breathing life into their stories.

When she's not writing, Gwen leads a busy life as a wedding planner and photographer in Italy. She also travels the globe, gathering inspiration for her next book.

Books in this series:

Whispers of the Wild.

Murmurs of the Wild.

Secrets of the Wild.

Treasures of the Wild.

Also by Gwen Courtman: The *Raw Mistakes* Series: *Raw Mistakes, Better Mistakes, Secret Mistakes, Inevitable Mistakes, Final Mistakes.*

Stay up-to-date with new releases, behind-the-scenes glimpses, stories, Q&A, and videos from the locations that inspired her books.

Visit her blog at: **www.gwencourtmanauthor.com**

Printed by Amazon Italia Logistica S.r.l.
Torrazza Piemonte (TO), Italy

72535279R00219